MARIA PLACIDO

"GOD, YOU'RE LOVELY," HE SAID HOARSELY.

"I had no idea you'd be so perfect." He kissed her deeply, passionately, then buried his face in the curve of her neck as he ran his hands over her satiny skin.

Clare returned his kisses with equal intensity, savoring each moment, drawing out each pleasure. She unbuttoned his shirt and let her hands stroke the smoothness of his chest. His muscles were taut beneath her fingers, and as she removed the shirt, she brushed her breasts against his skin. With awe, she ran her palms across the hard perfection of his body. It was nothing at all like Elliot's. Ryan's lean belly was ridged with muscles, and there was no sign of surplus weight around his narrow waist. She liked it immensely. Clare bent her head and left a trail of butterfly kisses across his chest.

Again she raised her mouth to meet his and marveled at the excitement of his tongue tracing fire between her lips. She'd never been kissed like this before, and she hungrily kissed him again.

Dear Reader:

We trust you will enjoy this Richard Gallen romance. We plan to bring you more of the best in both contemporary and historical romantic fiction with four exciting new titles each month.

We'd like your help.

We value your suggestions and opinions. They will help us to publish the kind of romances you want to read. Please send us your comments, or just let us know which Richard Gallen romances you have especially enjoyed. Write to the address below. We're looking forward to hearing from you!

Happy reading!

Richard Gallen Books
330 Steelcase Road East,
Markham, Ontario L3R 2M1

Opal Fires

LYNDA TRENT

PUBLISHED BY RICHARD GALLEN BOOKS
Distributed by POCKET BOOKS

Distributed in Canada by PaperJacks Ltd., a Licensee
of the trademarks of Simon & Schuster, a division of
Gulf+Western Corporation.

This novel is a work of fiction. Names, characters, places and incidents are either the product of the author's imagination or are used fictitiously, and any resemblance to actual persons, living or dead, events or locales is entirely coincidental.

 A RICHARD GALLEN BOOKS *Original* publication

Distributed by
POCKET BOOKS, a Simon & Schuster division of
GULF & WESTERN CORPORATION
1230 Avenue of the Americas, New York, N.Y. 10020
In Canada distributed by PaperJacks Ltd.,
330 Steelcase Road, Markham, Ontario.

ISBN: 0-671-43936-7

First Pocket Books printing February, 1982

10 9 8 7 6 5 4 3 2 1

RICHARD GALLEN and colophon are trademarks
of Simon & Schuster and Richard Gallen & Co., Inc.

Printed in Canada

To Star
for the world she opened
and a unicorn named Perseverance

Opal Fires

Chapter One

Clare Marshall shifted uncomfortably under the pounding rays of the hot East Texas sun. She was aware of the preacher's monotonous, droning voice, the pungent smell of the chocolate-brown earth, and of the other people who stood knotted around her. Somewhere nearby someone had been mowing grass, and the warm smell of wild onions hung in the air. From the house beyond the cemetery came the faint shouts of children playing and the yaps of a dog.

Clare shifted her weight to the other foot. In unison, several pairs of pitying eyes swung toward her with somber expressions. She ignored them.

"Earth to earth, ashes to ashes, dust to dust," the perspiring preacher mournfully intoned. "The Lord giveth and the Lord taketh away. Blessed be the name of the Lord."

Across the grave, a tall blonde, with an elegantly coiled chignon, touched a lacy handkerchief to her eyes and sighed dolorously, as if the weight of the world rested on her shoulders. Clare gazed silently at the woman, then let her attention return to the coffin.

An angular, dark-haired woman briefly put her arm around

Clare's shoulders, then resumed a position of studied gravity. Clare glanced sideways at her best friend, Marla Gentry. She knew the tears in Marla's eyes were those of sympathy rather than grief. Clare was careful to let no expression alter her own features.

". . . And bless, O, Lord, this your handmaiden," the preacher implored, gesturing with his Bible toward Clare. "Guide her and keep her, so soon bereaved, so young a widow." He rolled his eyes heavenward and clasped the Bible to his chest.

The new widow gazed steadfastly at the charcoal-gray coffin, its silver handles glinting brightly in the merciless sun. Soon it would be lowered into the waiting grave, and her thoughts were on her husband, who lay within.

"Damn you, Elliot Marshall," she cried beneath her breath. "Damn you to hell! If you weren't already dead, I think I'd be tempted to kill you myself." Realizing the impropriety of her thoughts, she carefully soothed all emotion from her features.

Only the night before, she had learned that Elliot had not only spent all their savings to feed his gambling addiction, but he had mortgaged her parents' old homeplace as well. Although Clare had no intention of ever living on the farm, she still considered it as her inheritance, her roots. Elliot knew how she felt and he had mortgaged it anyway, and without her consent!

Clare blinked against the glare of the sun and tried to ignore the headache forming behind her eyes. A weak breeze ruffled her shoulder-length, dark brown hair and she absentmindedly pushed it back in place. Her smoky gray eyes were cloudy with rebellious thoughts as she looked across the heat-shimmering ground. Resolutely, she squared her slender shoulders.

The sun glanced off the hood ornament of the black hearse, and Clare wondered wryly how she would pay for the funeral. Or the preacher, for that matter. The man from the bank who had told her about the impending foreclosure had been quite definite about the state of her savings balance. There was virtually nothing.

She stared accusingly at the dignified and stately coffin. It had been selected before she learned she had no money. Although she knew very little about the mortuary business,

Clare was certain they would have held a dim view of her asking to exchange Elliot's coffin for a cheaper one after he had been in possession of it for a day and a half.

Hysterical laughter began to rise in her throat. Even from his grave, Elliot had succeeded in outwitting her! As she choked back her hysteria, the sound resembled a sob.

Where had the love gone? She had loved him once . . . surely she had! Again she thought of him as he had been in college—charming, debonair and incredibly wealthy; a man capable of turning the head of a poor farm girl who was barely making her way through school on an art scholarship. Even if he hadn't given up drinking and gambling as he had promised, still he hadn't been really bad. She flushed. That wasn't entirely true.

Again she looked across the carnation-bedecked coffin at Regina Wharton, the tall blonde. Had Elliot and Regina been having an affair? she pondered unemotionally. How odd that she didn't care. Clare wondered if she was losing her mind. She should be feeling at least some sorrow, rather than this grinding anger. Certainly she should feel jealousy or even remorse that Elliot had made love with a woman that Clare must see several times a week whether she liked her or not. But Clare felt only numbness toward Regina.

Clare stared stonily at the red and white flowers as the mourners sang "Rock of Ages." She sighed and closed her eyes against the sun's glare. The headache was worse and her back was beginning to ache from her rigid posture.

How am I going to make it? she demanded silently of the coffin.

She opened her eyes and realized with embarrassment that the preacher thought she was overcome with grief. But he didn't know Elliot. Not the real Elliot, at any rate. The Elliot who dutifully sang in the church choir on Sunday had no connection with the man Clare had been married to for four years.

Compassionately, the preacher cut short his prayer and stepped to her side.

"We got to bear up, Miz Marshall," he murmured solicitously. "I'll let you bid him goodbye, then I'll see you home." The aging man's eyes were full of genuine concern, and she felt guilty at her improper thoughts.

Clare stepped nearer the coffin, her face deliberately

3

expressionless. The mound of dirt beside the hole, hidden by a green cloth, provided a backdrop against the charcoal metal and vivid flowers. Beyond it, waves of heat shimmered among the white tombstones. A mockingbird called dismally in the distance.

The young widow regarded the receptacle of the earthly remains of her husband. I'm going to make it, you rotten son-of-a-bitch! she thought. I'm going to make a good life for myself. You just see if I don't!

Feeling on the verge of hysteria again, she stepped quickly away, flanked by the preacher and other mourners, and left Elliot to the ministrations of the gravediggers.

The large red brick house commanded the top of the wooded knoll like a castle. Two immense porches, one below and one above, swept around three sides of the house in a snowy expanse of heavy white wood. The many-paned windows barricaded the hot air from the airconditioned shadows within. On either side of the immense double door of hand-carved oak, twin panes of crystal cut glass towered up to meet the fan-shaped window above. Sunlight streaming through the large pine and oak trees was broken apart in the crystal prisms of the window, and fell in a splash of rainbow colors on the terrazzo floor of the entryway.

Clare sat on one of the cushioned seats in the bay window of the morning room and watched cars drive up the winding private lane. She had come here to steel herself to greet the mourners following the funeral. Already the parking area was filled, and the latecomers were beginning to block the curved front drive.

She shifted uneasily and leaned against the wall, letting the gauzy white curtain drop back in place. She couldn't possibly admit to her strange lack of emotion, yet she was far too honest to pretend a grief she didn't feel. Still, the strange numbness persisted. Why didn't she feel grief, she wondered, or at least loneliness? Even her earlier anger had subsided, and she felt hollow. Clare looked about her as if searching for an answer in the comfortable familiarity of her favorite room.

The furniture was rattan, covered with billowy cushions of navy, emerald and white cotton. Tall palms and numerous hanging baskets of overflowing folage made an atmosphere of jungle lushness, offset by the starkly severe lines of a chrome and glass étagère. Several vases of zinnias and roses adorned side tables and the breakfast nook—partially because of the funeral, but more because Clare loved flowers and color and had them about her as often as possible.

In contrast to the room, her dress was an uncompromising slash of black that made her skin pale by comparison and her gray eyes even darker than usual.

As she again absently peered across the expanse of well-manicured lawn, a midnight-blue Cadillac caught her attention as it rolled to a stop perilously close to a row of her favorite camilla bushes. A small muscle tightened in Clare's jaw as she watched Regina Wharton being helped out of her car by her husband, Howard. She carried a small, covered dish at arm's length, taking care not to soil her white linen suit or her image.

The women had disliked each other since that day, four years before, when Elliot had introduced his bride to his circle of friends. Although Clare had been raised on a farm between the two small towns of Kilgore and Gladewater in East Texas, she had gone to grade school in Gladewater and had not, until college, met Elliot nor any of his Kilgore friends. The clannish isolationism of this area, coupled with the fact that the schools were in separate sports districts, had precluded even a chance meeting. As a teenager, Clare had been chafed by what she considered narrowmindedness. Now she viewed the social separateness as heaven-sent, knowing what Regina would say if she learned her wealthy childhood sweetheart had married the daughter of a dirt farmer. It was a cinch that Elliot had never mentioned his wife's background.

"Clare?" a voice called out from the doorway. "Are you all right?"

"Yes. Come in, Marla." Clare managed a smile that quickly faded.

"Why are you in here all by yourself? Are you sure you're all right?" Marla Gentry came over and sat beside Clare on the window seat.

"Regina and Howard just drove up," Clare said, as if this answered Marla's question. "Do you think she and Elliot were really having an affair?" Her voice was as calm as if she were commenting on the weather.

"Clare! You shouldn't be thinking about that!"

Again Clare smiled faintly. "I think so, too."

5

Marla frowned but didn't pursue the subject. Regina had often bragged about her liaison with Elliot in Clare's absence.

Clare looked back outside. "I was also thinking how very different my life has been since I married Elliot. And wondering what it will be like from now on." She looked at her friend and her eyes were dark and brooding. "I can't go back to what I came from, Marla. I just can't!" She turned her gaze back to the windows and said softly, "You don't know what it was like. Being teased because my clothes were faded and my shoes were worn out. I never had a new pair of shoes until I was in high school. Even then, the money I earned mainly went toward Papa's medical bills."

"It must have been very difficult for you," Marla said gently. She had rarely heard her friend talk about her impoverished childhood.

"My parents were good to me, but there just wasn't any money. After Papa lost his arm in the cotton gin accident, he couldn't get work and his health wasn't ever very good again. I guess he never really healed up properly. Mama did her best, but we never had any extra money for nice things." She turned her haunted eyes back to Marla. "I remember one Christmas when we had nothing to eat but cornbread and dried red beans. I swore then that I wouldn't live all my life like that. Mama couldn't have been more than thirty-five or so, but she looked so tired! Not even forty and she was already an old woman!" Clare shoved a tear away with the palm of her hand and drew a ragged breath. "I'm sorry, Marla. I shouldn't be going on like this, but you're the only one I can talk to. No one else has any idea about my background. They don't even know who I am. But, Marla," she said with gritty determination, "I won't go back to living like that! Not ever!"

"Now, Clare, there now," Marla said gently. "It seems worse now than it will later. Of course you're upset over losing Elliot."

Clare frowned. "He mortgaged my farm."

"What?" Marla drew back in astonishment. "When? *All* of it?"

"Yes. All of it. He took out a loan months ago and never paid one cent on it. I just found out about it yesterday. And I don't have the money to give it back."

"Yesterday! That's terrible! Who on earth would hit you with news like that just before your husband's funeral?" she demanded.

"The honorable Neal Thorndyke, our illustrious bank president, sent word." Clare picked up a small pillow and absently straightened its row of ecru fringe.

"What are you going to do?"

"That's why I just told you. I don't know."

"How long do you have before they . . . do something?"

"Foreclose, you mean?" Clare probed at the word, as if to test her pain level. "I don't know. I have to go in and talk to him Friday." Her eyes suddenly flashed angrily. "How could Elliot do this to me! He knew what that land means to me!"

"I know you're fond of it," Marla said with the logic of a town dweller, "but there doesn't seem to be much you can do. No matter what you owe, if you can't raise it in three days—"

"I'm more than just fond of it," Clare interrupted defensively. "It's as if it's a part of me. I know every inch of that land. I learned to swim in the creek. My parents built that house and lived in it until they died. It's not just land. It's the only place where I was truly loved." Clare eased somewhat, but her gray eyes were intense. "Marla, swear to me you'll not tell a soul about this. I'll figure my way out of this, somehow."

Marla got up and tried to smile encouragingly. "You have my promise. We'll think of something." She cocked her head slightly and said, "Wait a minute. You said he mortgaged the farm without your knowledge? This is a community property state. He couldn't do that without your signature. Did you sign anything?"

"I don't know. If I did, I didn't realize what it was. Thorndyke's message indicated that he thinks it's all legal and proper. The last papers I signed at the bank were the ones on Elliot's airplane." Clare's eyes narrowed slightly as she thought back. "And that was just five or six months ago."

"Sounds like you may have an out, after all," Marla offered. "You just tell the bank it was all a mistake. But right now you have to go greet your guests."

"The man from the bank didn't think it was a mistake." Clare grimaced, then a smile lit just the corners of her well-shaped mouth. "What would I do without you?" She stood, smoothed her skirt and followed Marla out of the sanctuary.

As they neared the living room, a subdued murmur enveloped them as people touched Clare reassuringly and mumbled condolences. The preacher managed to look not only miserable over Elliot's untimely death, but piously confident, as well, of Elliot's certain arrival in heaven. Clare wondered how the preacher could possibly convey two such opposing emotions, as she nodded appreciation of his offer to pray for her. He said something about "bands of angels" and "joys not of this world" that Clare only half heard.

Regina was making her way toward Clare.

"Hello, Regina. Howard."

Howard made an embarrassed motion of wiping his fingers on his greasy napkin before engulfing her hand in his. "So sorry, Clare. So very sorry." His wife nodded coolly in agreement, but Clare noticed with guilty satisfaction that Regina's eyes were as red as if she had shed real tears.

"Thank you, Howard. It was so sudden. The doctor assured me that Elliot died at once."

Regina shuddered in spite of herself. "Such a terrible way to die. He was so proud of learning to fly. And the Cessna 150's are supposed to be so safe. I suppose we'll never know what happened."

At once Clare recalled the day—was it only two days ago?—that she had gone out to surprise Elliot at the airstrip. As she watched him approach in his landing pattern, he had suddenly nosed up again, high into the sky. The plane had made a long, graceful loop, its engine purring in perfect order. Then Elliot had flown straight into the ground.

Clare's hands still bore cuts from where she had gripped the chain-link fence in those panic-filled moments as she watched the huge ball of flames beneath the black, black smoke.

Elliot's death had not been accidental, but she alone knew it. She wondered numbly if the insurance company would be able to discover that her husband's death was, in fact, suicide. Not that she wanted to defraud anyone, but the money would be a godsend. It would be enough to put her back on her feet. Unless, of course, Elliot had cashed in the policy without telling her. It seemed unlikely that a man so desperate for money would continue to pay for life insurance. Clare pushed the thought from her mind.

"No, I don't suppose we'll ever know what happened," she said levelly. "Are you finding everything, Howard? I see Betty's put out some fruitcake and poundcake on the side table." Clare nodded to where her maid was working efficiently. "Go help yourself." She moved away to speak to the other guests, but not before she overheard Regina's comment that Clare must have ice in her veins to be so composed. Clare forced herself not to acknowledge the barb.

Marla came to her carrying a plate of food. "Here's some more chicken. Where should I put it?"

"Take it out to the kitchen. The table's too full to hold another plate."

"Why do people always bring fried chicken and poundcake?" Marla wondered. "Even when I was a little girl, people did that."

"Tradition, I suppose." Clare's expression saddened at the recollection of the only other funerals she had attended—her mother's and her father's. Before she could shake off the emotion, first one, then another tear coursed down the soft curve of her cheek and came to rest at the corner of her sensuous lips, which were tightly drawn in an effort to maintain control. In Clare's twenty-five years, she had seen more sadness than most people twice her age. It had been only two tears, but she carefully turned away from her guests and discreetly extracted a small lace handkerchief from her pocket and dabbed away the evidence from her luminous gray eyes.

"Clare? Is everything okay?" Marla asked.

"Sure. Everything is fine," Clare answered with a broad smile.

Clare caught the disapproving stare of two old ladies with blue-gray hair and quickly smoothed the smile from her face. She had no wish to be accused of insensitivity again.

What's wrong with me? she wondered. My husband is barely in the ground and I'm worried about hurting my reputation by smiling! But no matter how hard she tried, she couldn't summon up a bit of sadness over Elliot . . . only frustrated anger at being left alone and penniless.

And worry. The deep-seated, gnawing worry that she

hadn't known for four years. The kind of worry her mother had shown when there were more bills than money and her disabled father was unable to work. The kind of worry that Clare had thought she was safe from forever.

The cut-velvet couches were never empty of people; crystal ashtrays filled and were emptied by Betty and filled again. The food on the huge rosewood table dwindled, then was gone, and the crowd overflowed in solemn decorum into the broad entryway and paneled den.

Now and then, one of the men, forgetting the circumstance that brought them together, would laugh aloud, then choke with embarrassment at his breach of manners. Everywhere she looked, Clare saw studiedly solemn faces and somber manners that befitted the occasion.

Somehow she managed to live through the afternoon.

By the time the preacher excused himself, dusk was falling. As if on cue, all the other mourners followed him. Once again the older women clutched Clare to their bosoms and the younger women squeezed her hands one last time. The men mumbled self-conscious condolences once more. All assured her that it was both a shame and the Lord's will, then left.

Clare followed the last couple to the door and leaned against the white wood frame. In the deep shadow of the porch, the evening breeze was cool, and she could hear the cicadas calling for rain.

The inky latticework of the oil derrick on her front lawn, silhouetted against the rosy sky, looked like a prehistoric monster in the gloom; its pump was long since stilled. Elliot's father had made his money in the Great Oil Boom of the early 1930's. Even when the wells went dry, he let them remain like relics of the past. They had supplied his fortune and he had built his mansion in their shadows. In time, most of the derricks had been removed. This one remained as a monument to the fortune gained, and now lost, by two generations of Marshalls.

Clare stepped back into the house and firmly closed the heavy door. The maid was moving busily around the room, straightening the furniture, cleaning ashtrays and removing the last vestiges of food and drink.

"Don't worry about that tonight," Clare said. "I'll take the plates and glasses into the kitchen, and tomorrow we can air out the tobacco smoke. I know you need to get home."

"Won't take me but a minute. I can't leave wet glasses to circle up a good table." Betty firmly pursed her lips as she wiped a ring of water from the marble-topped end table. Betty had worked for Marshalls all her adult life, as had her mother before her. Her proprietary kinship to the house was obvious, and she looked after it as if it were her own.

"Thanks, Betty. What would I ever do without you?" Clare stacked three saucers and wiped the crumbs onto the top one. "You'd think grown people would know not to make such a mess, wouldn't you?"

Betty snorted. "Some folks can't be taught nothing." She fished a crust of bread out of the folds of an armchair. "Not nothing at all."

Clare glanced nervously at the dark-skinned older woman. In view of her new financial straits, she should do her own housekeeping, but she wasn't sure how to fire someone who had been a part of the household for so long. "Betty, I need to talk to you," she said uncertainly.

"Ain't got time now," Betty said gruffly as she shoved a chair back in a practiced move that stopped it two inches short of hitting the wall. "I got to go cook Eldon's supper."

Clare frowned. Eldon, Betty's husband, was the gardener. Gardeners were also luxuries, but Clare knew she wouldn't be able to take care of three acres of landscaped lawn and the house as well.

"Besides, I got to talk to you first," Betty continued without looking at Clare. "Me and Eldon, we're getting old. Slowing down. I told him the other day, I said, 'Eldon, we can't do all we used to.' He allowed as how I was right. I told him we sure was lucky to have us a place to live yonder over the garage. He said that was true. Fact is, Miss Clare, we don't need all that salary you been paying us. We up and die, who's that money gonna go to? Don't make no sense." She shook the folds of the pale blue curtains back into the correct line and found the coffee cup that was almost hidden behind them. "Me and Eldon can get by fine on a whole lot less a month." Finally, she met Clare's eyes.

Clare stared at her, then blushed. Without meeting her eyes, she said, "I gather you know about my . . . problems?"

"Of course I do," Betty answered gruffly as she flicked ashes off a marble-topped table and into an ashtray.

"How . . . did you . . . ?" Clare stammered unable to ask

the question. Surely her financial straits weren't common knowledge already!

"Lordy, child, I raised Mr. Elliot! I knowed that boy before he was out of diapers. When I noticed things commencing to go missing, I asked him about it, and he allowed as how he was in need of money. He knowed he couldn't never keep nothing from me. Came right out and said he owed it to some gambling man, though he didn't never speak his name. He made me promise I wouldn't tell nobody. Said he'd get ever' thing straightened out himself. Wouldn't be no need to bother you or tell no one nothing about it."

Clare turned away to hide her embarrassment, her cheeks aflame. "I'm so ashamed, Betty."

"Miss Clare, it ain't nothing for you to be ashamed about. It was Mr. Elliot's fault. Don't nobody else know. I kept my word to him. It's nobody else's business what goes on in this house. Never was. Never will be. You'll get back on your feet after a bit, young as you are. You'll see."

Clare was touched by the honest concern on Betty's wrinkled face. "I understand. Let's keep things as they are for now. Maybe none of us will have to get by on less. I've decided to let Lily go, though. With just myself to cook for, it seems silly to keep her on."

Betty nodded. "Sounds good to me. She always was a hard one to get along with." She gave a last swipe with her cloth over the French provincial mantelpiece. "I'll be getting on now, before Eldon tries to cook for himself and burns the garage down."

"All right. And, Betty . . . thanks."

Clare realized she shouldn't be surprised or concerned that Betty and Eldon were aware of the sad state of the Marshall finances. After all, they had watched Elliot grow from the cradle up, and had known him as well or better than she had. She was confident her secret was safe with them.

Left alone in the house, Clare carried the saucers she still held into the kitchen. Most of her friends would have insisted that Betty stay until the house was clean. But Clare had a need to do something useful; something to make her life seem real again.

She tied a towel around her small waist, as she had seen her mother do, and ran water into the sink. By the time she finished washing the dishes and had placed the last dried cup into the china cabinet, it seemed like her world was easing back into place.

As she climbed the stairs to her bedroom, a healthy tiredness was settling on her. For a moment, she paused outside Elliot's room. They had not even shared a bedroom for over a year. Somehow that seemed to be the saddest thought she had had all day. It had been even longer than that since Elliot had touched her.

Tears glistened in her eyes and trembled on the fringe of her long eyelashes. At last, she gave way to her pent-up emotions, and sobbed as if her heart would burst.

Chapter Two

In New Orleans, several hundred miles away, a tall man walked through the cloying scent of magnolia blossoms to meet his girlfriend. Doré Armound wasn't his steady girl—nor anyone else's—but earlier on this balmy evening, the musky scent of flowers from his small courtyard had brought her to his mind. Then, when she had called him on the telephone, almost as if she were in tune with his thoughts, he'd agreed to meet her.

Ryan Hastings paused in the yellow glow of a street light, his physique casting a long shadow. The handsome man's powerful broad shoulders tapered to a narrow waist, and the hard muscles of his chest could be seen beneath the fabric of his open-collared shirt. The high cheekbones, straight nose and firm-set jaw of his well-tanned face bespoke his strength and determination, while the laugh wrinkles at the corners of his hazel eyes revealed his innate tenderness. His thick, golden-brown hair, the shade of sun-ripened wheat, had been tousled by the warm night breeze, giving him a boyish appearance.

Yet Ryan Hastings, at thirty-five, was almost legendary in

the Louisiana oil fields. Straight out of high school he had gone to work for the small but expanding Huntly Oil Company as a roughneck in the Louisiana fields. He'd alternated his college semesters at LSU with long, grueling hours on the rigs. Not long after graduating, he'd become Huntly's head geologist. His track record had been excellent and most of his innovative ideas had been well-received, and highly profitable for Huntly Oil. However, recently Ryan had run into stiff opposition with his theory that oil was yet to be discovered in the old, nearly depleted, East Texas oil field near Kilgore. Huntly's chief engineer, one of Ryan's staunchest supporters, had cautioned him to back off before anyone noticed he had his head full of drilling mud. But Ryan had studied the history of the field, and its known geology of faults and salt domes near the surface, and what little he could find out about the two new "routine" exploration wells being quietly and deeply drilled by a subsidiary of Exxon.

Ryan was certain that just below twenty thousand feet lay a huge reserve of oil, even larger than the giant discovery in the Woodbine sand in the 1930's.

This morning, he'd decided the time was right. The most recent Middle East crisis had the oil industry stirred up again, and the "Old Man" had appeared to be in a receptive mood. But Ryan wasn't even allowed to finish his presentation. The company president hastened to explain that the deep well Ryan proposed was much too risky and, with money being so tight, it would be a mistake for Huntly to get in too quickly. Ryan was allowed one concession, however. He was told not to stop his study on the idea and was authorized to go to East Texas and lease a little land if it felt right.

The ultra-conservative stand Huntly had taken had left Ryan cold. By the end of the work day, he'd begun to toy with the idea of wildcatting the well himself. The prospect of drilling his own well had always fascinated him, but he had to be realistic. Getting investors would be the problem, he reasoned. Even though he'd inherited a great deal of money and was well-paid professionally, he hardly had a spare million to test his theory. So Ryan temporarily shelved the idea of going out on his own.

All in all, his day had not been easy. As he walked along the deserted street, his thoughts returned to Doré. It had been almost two months since he'd last seen her, and his step quickened a little. At least he had no illusions about the reception she'd give him. Doré had a singleminded interest in physical pleasure . . . which Ryan had never found cause to dispute. He smiled ruefully. In fact, there were a lot of rumors about Doré and her social life.

Ryan stepped off the sidewalk and slipped into the dusky bushes that shielded their usual rendezvous. This was a typical ploy of hers. Though her father liked Ryan, she preferred the cloak-and-dagger thrill of clandestine meetings.

As he'd suspected, she wasn't in the small clearing. It was all part of her game. With a somewhat irritated sigh, Ryan sat on a moonlight-silvered log and leaned back against a tree. As on the most recent occasions, he began to question why he was there. Certainly Doré was no intellectual giant. He found their rare conversations awkward and dull. It certainly wasn't the melodrama she wrapped about her—he found that tedious in the extreme. Her devious ways of playing him against his friends in return for sexual favors was infuriating. Even her alluring body and the love tricks she had so efficiently perfected were quickly losing their appeal. Ryan glanced at his watch. Perhaps she wasn't coming at all. With a feeling of growing annoyance, he rose to leave.

At that instant, Doré rushed into the clearing and ran into the circle of his arms.

"Were you there all along?" Ryan asked suspiciously. "You aren't even out of breath."

Doré ignored the question, burying her head against his muscular chest so that the heady scent of her perfume was unavoidable. She raised her chin to look up at him. Her night-black eyes, which he had once found so enticing, appeared concerned. "I was so afraid you wouldn't come. I had a hard time slipping out of the house. Papa almost saw me."

Ryan moved her body back from his, gently but firmly. "Doré, I've been thinking. I don't think we should—"

"Ryan, I'm pregnant."

For a moment, the words made no sense to him. "What?" he finally asked.

"I said I'm pregnant."

Ryan stared down at her in confusion. "Why are you telling me this?"

"Why, because you're the father, of course." She gazed up at him with artful innocence.

Ryan looked blankly at her as if her words held no meaning. "I can't be. We haven't been together since . . ." he thought a minute, then concluded, "late May."

"It was June," she purred, "and I'm certain."

"No, I was in the field all during June, working on the offshore Colter rig."

Her black eyes flashed with anger and she stomped her foot like a spoiled child. "All right then, it was May. Anyway, I'm pregnant, and you have to marry me. Soon!"

Marry! Ryan looked at her as if she'd lost her mind. "Look, if I were the father, I'd marry you, but I was out of town in June. Was it Harry? Or Bill? Tell me who it really is, and I'll go talk to him for you."

"May, June—so I made a mistake! You aren't getting off that easy! This baby is yours, Ryan Hastings! And you've got to do the right thing by me!" Hysteria was creeping into her voice, and her pretty face looked crumpled.

Marry Doré? The most blatantly promiscuous woman he had ever met? Ryan frowned. Could she possibly be telling him the truth for once? "Look, I don't think—"

"Think!" she interrupted furiously. "You sure didn't do much thinking all those times you went to bed with me! Did you?" Her voice had risen to a shriek and her already pale skin was chalk-white against her black hair.

Ryan frowned but made no reply. She was right. He'd never thought of a baby when he'd been busy with her sensuous body.

"Oh!" she wailed, sensing victory. "How can you be so heartless! I . . . I thought you would be glad! I thought you *loved* me!"

"Now, wait a minute," Ryan objected. "We never once talked about love and you know it!"

"But I *thought* you did!" She wheeled away from him and ran across the clearing. At the edge of the bushes, she stopped. "You'd better marry me, Ryan Hastings, or I'll . . . I'll tell everybody you raped me!"

"Doré!" He stared at her, dumbfounded.

"I will!" she screamed. "And they'll all believe me, too!"

"Damn it, you know it was never like that at all! I want you to calm down. Give me time to figure out how to help you!"

"Time! I haven't *got* time! Soon everyone will know!" She turned and dove into the inky bushes.

He listened as her footsteps died away on the path to her house. "A *baby!*" He said the word as if it were as foreign to him as was the thought. Doré had assured him that she was on the pill and he had naturally assumed that there was no threat of pregnancy. Slowly, he picked his way through the bushes and back toward the street. The twigs caught at his clothing like so many witches' fingers, and a drift of Spanish moss settled across his face like a cobweb. He yanked savagely at the moss and ground it underfoot. How could he have fathered a baby when he was on an offshore rig at the time?

"That baby could belong to anyone" he commented to the night. With Doré's track record, he seriously doubted if she herself knew who the father was . . . if she was indeed pregnant. With her penchant for lies, he wasn't even convinced of that. Still, if it was true, he pitied her situation.

Ryan was deep in thought all the way home. He let himself into the courtyard he shared with several other tenants and with the overflow of the Blue Crystal Lounge. The club was quiet for a change, but still he could hear the muted notes of a trumpet playing the blues.

Gas lamps threw a muted yellow light on the flagstone patio, and the droplets of water in the fountain glistened like diamonds. Ryan walked across and climbed the outside stairs to his apartment above.

He unlocked the door and automatically flipped on the light switch as he went to the bar and made himself a drink.

Sinking down onto his couch, he leaned his head back and stared at the ceiling. Dully, he wondered if the real father of Doré's baby had turned her down, and how many of her other lovers she had confronted before tonight. Maybe he was, indeed, the father. If she was wrong about it being June, then it wasn't impossible.

He tried to envision Doré in the role of motherhood, but the prospect was simply too unlikely. She flitted through life on a cloud of irresponsibility that had been intoxicating in a lover, but would create mayhem in the life of a child. She could spend hours deciding what dress to wear to a party, then at the last minute decide not to go at all. When he'd first met Doré, this mercurial quality, coupled with her eager

18

sensuality and dark beauty, had been irresistible. But Ryan knew she'd never be able to adjust to the demands of raising a child. He doubted she would even try. No, the baby would soon become the responsibility of her aging father—a man who had not been young when Doré herself was born. Ryan let out a long sigh. She couldn't possibly keep the child; it would be too wrong to the innocent baby.

A loud knock on his door startled him. "Doré?" he said as he opened it and she stormed into the room.

"Of course it's me! Who else were you expecting? I drove over to give you one more chance. Are you going to marry me, or do I have to tell daddy you raped me?"

"Calm down. Calm down," he tried to soothe her. "I think I have a solution to this."

"So do I! *Marry* me!"

"Doré, you can put the baby up for adoption. There are a lot of couples who desperately want a child who could give it a good home."

"What? You want me to sell my baby? *Our* baby!"

"Don't be ridiculous," he said angrily. "I'm not talking about selling your baby. I said put it up for adoption." It infuriated him when someone twisted his words. He tried to calm himself. Doré was always high-strung, and now she looked almost wild.

"I can't do that! I can't just give my baby to strangers!"

"Well, you certainly can't keep it. You don't have a job, and your father can't be expected to raise another child at his age. Be reasonable!"

"Reasonable! You'd throw our baby away like a bundle of trash!" Her eyes were glassy and she paced the room frantically.

" Stop staying that! I don't think you even know who the father is."

Doré had a trapped look on her face, like a cornered animal, but she didn't reply.

"Furthermore, why didn't you tell me you stopped taking the pill? Surely you must have realized that this could happen. And besides, you've told me over and over that you never wanted to have children!"

"You don't have any right to accuse me like that. You don't own me!"

"If it's a question of money or your pride, I'll pay for you to go away until it's over. You can get an apartment and send the bills to me. Then, afterward, you can come home and nobody will know."

"You can't expect me to agree to that!"

"Doré! You can't keep it!"

"Abortion! You think I would agree to an *abortion?*" A thin line of foam flecked her contorted lips. "You want me to agree to having some backstreet butcher cut me up?"

"I never suggested such a thing!" Ryan stared. The thought had never crossed his mind.

"Well, that's what you meant! *Abortion!*" She spat the word out as if it were dirty. "I can't have an abortion! I'm Catholic!"

"Will you quiet down before you make yourself sick? I don't want you to have an abortion."

"Oh, yes, you do! You don't care if somebody cuts me to pieces! Damn you, Ryan Hastings, I'll *die* before I agree to such a disgusting thing!" She ran to the door and threw it open so that it hit the wall and left an indentation of the knob in the plaster. "You're not going to get off the hook that easily. Do you hear me? I'll *die* first!" She ran through the open door and out into the night.

"Doré! Wait!" Ryan saw her pause and look back at him, then she turned and raced across the courtyard.

"Damn!" he muttered as he chased after her. He couldn't let her go away so upset.

She was pulling away from the curb when he reached the street. Quickly, he fumbled his car keys from his pocket and headed to the garage.

Within a few blocks, he had pulled alongside her car, and he wondered if she had planned that he would. This was just the sort of melodrama that Doré loved. But he felt she needed help.

With a scowl, he motioned for her to pull over.

She tossed her head angrily and her car shot forward. They passed the city limit signs on Interstate 10 in a blur of speed. Now Ryan was following her in earnest. Doré was a skillful driver ordinarily, but in her present state of hysteria, she was driving like a madwoman.

The lake appeared on his right like a silver mirror in the moonlight. On the other side of the road, black trees loomed into his view, then whipped behind him as he tried to overtake Doré.

Ryan knew the curve was coming up. So did Doré. She had lived in New Orleans all her life, and knew the road as well as she knew her name. And she didn't slow down.

Her car left the road. For a moment, it seemed to fly through the air in slow motion. Then it crashed into a large cypress tree, twisted to one side and plunged into the lake like a grotesquely crippled bird.

"Doré!"

Ryan ground his car to a screeching stop and threw himself out the door. Ripples were still widening across the lake's surface and air bubbles were ballooning up out of the dark water.

"Doré!" he cried out again as he kicked off his shoes.

Ryan plunged into the lake and fought his way down. Beneath the surface, the water was pitch-black, and he could see nothing. Lungs aching, he surfaced, gulped at the air and dove under again.

For a moment, he thought he touched the car's slick surface, but then it shifted and he couldn't find it again. He was beginning to see bright flashes before his eyes and his head reeled from lack of oxygen.

He broke the surface to gasp for air. Headlights from the nearby highway shone on him, and he cried out for help. Without waiting to see if anyone was coming to his aid, he dove again.

Somewhere he'd heard that submerged cars would hold an air pocket. It was possible that Doré was still able to breathe. At any rate, he couldn't stop looking for her.

He was vaguely aware of other people in the water with him, and of diving again and again. Then large hands were hauling him toward the store, and even though he fought, they dragged him out of the lake.

"Take it easy, mister," the policeman said.

"I can't! She's in there! Her car went in!" Ryan gulped air into his burning lungs and tried to crawl back into the water.

"I've already radioed in for a team of rescue divers. They should be here in a few minutes," the officer said as he tried to reassure Ryan. The policeman had been patrolling Interstate 10 in the opposite lane as the speeding cars swept by, and was on the scene in minutes. But it was almost half an hour before another pair of blue and red emergency lights joined the others, pulsating like the heartbeat of horror itself, the cry of the siren beginning to wane.

Ryan saw two men, dressed in wet suits and wearing lights on their heads, jump out of the back of a police van. Pointing at the water, he yelled, "She's in there! In a car. Hurry!"

As the divers shrugged on their oxygen tanks and slid beneath the oily water, Ryan gave the policeman Doré's name and address, as well as his own.

When the divers finally surfaced, they were alone.

"It's no use," one of them said as he came to Ryan. "We found her, but she's gone."

"What? She can't be! There would have been air pockets. She can't be gone!" he couldn't bring himself to say "dead."

"I'm sorry, sir. She must have died when she hit that tree." He nodded toward the deep gash on the cypress by the road. "She never knew what hit her. I can tell you she died quickly and didn't drown."

"You must have made a mistake!"

"No, sir. There's no way I made a mistake. I'm sorry."

Despite the policeman's insistence that there was nothing else he could do, Ryan stayed until the tow truck pulled up the mangled wreckage of the car. After one nauseous glance, he saw why the diver had been so sure that Doré had died on impact.

In a state of shock, Ryan at last went home.

The light was still on and his drink sat on the coffee table, though the ice had long since melted. Slowly, he sank down on the couch and stared at the doorway where Doré had stood seemingly moments before.

When dawn turned the sky to pewter, then rose, Ryan stood up and made his way to the bedroom. Although he wasn't scheduled to leave for Kilgore until Monday, he knew he had to get away for a while. Away from New Orleans and his apartment and everything that reminded him of Doré.

When he left town, he took a longer route than was necessary. One that didn't take him within sight of the lake and the scarred cypress tree.

22

Chapter Three

Clare slipped into her burgundy linen skirt and straightened the collar of her ruffled white silk blouse. Her appointment with the bank president was for one o'clock, and she had no intention of being late or looking as if she needed more time on the loan. Very early in her marriage, she had learned from observing Elliot that it was easier to get money if you looked and acted as though you didn't need it.

She ran a brush through her thick brown hair and tied it at the nape of her neck with a narrow ribbon. Needing very little makeup, Clare smudged just a hint of smoky gray eye shadow on her lids and touched her black eyelashes with mascara. She carefully applied a rosy lip gloss to her full and sensuous lips, then surveyed herself in the mirror. Her eyes looked too large and dark in her pale face from lack of sleep, but that would have to do. Resolutely, she took her clutch bag from the dresser and hurried out of her room.

Eldon was cutting the lawn, and the aroma of the fresh-mown grass followed her into her Mercedes. This was a scent that she usually found very pleasing, but today she was far too worried to enjoy it. If the meeting didn't go well, she'd lose her property.

The tree-lined drive wound past the old oil derrick in the front yard and down the hill to the curving street. Although Clare had neighbors, their homes were blocked from view by the dense foliage surrounding the Marshall home. Most of the other houses sat on three acres and were clearly visible from the road. For the most part, they were square, severe-looking structures of World War II vintage, and were made of a hodge-podge of various colored bricks that lacked the clean, classic lines of her own red brick house with its elegant white columns and pristine woodwork. Clare gripped the steering wheel firmly and vowed that no matter what happened, she wouldn't give up the home she had grown to love. Besides, she had nowhere else to go, she reminded herself. This gave her an even greater determination to succeed. Efficiently, she turned onto the broad street and drove the few blocks into downtown.

The Farmers' Bank and Trust, Kilgore's only financial institution, was housed in the largest building in town, and its lines were classic. The designer of the building, in the late twenties or early thirties, had probably drawn his plans with marble in mind, or perhaps granite. However, the contractors, being rather independent in their thinking and probably very close to their pocketbooks, had erected it with native bricks of a dirty yellow hue. At a later date, someone had erected tall granite columns on either side of the glass door, but they only supported a small lintel that was placed too high to either shade the door from the sun or to shelter it from the rain. The columns had always looked quite strange growing out of the narrow sidewalk, and to Clare it seemed as if they had been left there en route to a more likely destination, then forgotten.

The building to the left of the bank was of a wooden-frame construction, with faded paint. Once the home of the Ben Franklin Five and Dime, it had been vacant for several years and seemed to be clutching the ugly but solid bank for moral support. At present, its only purpose in the life of this little town of thirteen thousand was to serve as a billboard, its length painted with a cracked and peeling ad for Coca-Cola. Clare wondered why the city council allowed it to remain. For years, no one had even tried to rent it, and its very structure looked unsafe. On the right side of the bank was the office of Nelson, Clawson and Wade, attorneys at law, which squatted on its cement steps as if it were too proud to associate with the derelict building, but was humbled by the massive bank. None of the buildings in town showed any sort of bond, architecturally speaking. Across the street was Lenoir's Fashions, a clothing store that appeared to have been built out of blue tile and concrete blocks. A "help wanted" sign shared the display with Gloria Vanderbilt jeans and a mid-sixties style prom dress.

Clare bit her lower lip. She hadn't had a job since her marriage. As a teenager, she had done the usual babysitting and had spent a hot and unhappy stint in an unairconditioned dry cleaner's in nearby Gladewater just before she left for college. While pursuing her education, she'd supplemented her art scholarship by washing cars and walking dogs in her spare time. None of these skills could possibly help her meet the debts she now faced. Even if she was qualified to sell clothing, would she be able to keep the position if she got it? Elliot had destroyed much of her self-esteem through his constant assurances that she was only fit for ornamenting a room. She knew this wasn't true, but she was terrified of failing. "No," she said aloud. "I won't try that yet."

She stepped out of the cool car and into the broiling heat. The temperature gauge on the drugstore down the street read 101. Clare knew the gauge had always read four degrees low.

Inside the bank was cool, like a cave. The high, old-fashioned ceilings were ornately carved, and the smell of tobacco smoke and old money that always accompanied such buildings pervaded. The bank's only concession to modern times were airconditioning and up-to-date office equipment. The tellers still worked behind ornate wire grills, the secretaries' desks were made of heavy oak and the walls were decorated with a huge fresco of unwieldy oxen and pioneers.

Clare's heels clicked loudly on the polished maroon and white mosaic floor. The bank was one of the few places she had ever seen that made her feel inadequate and childish.

She approached a teller's window and said, more loudly that she had expected, "I have an appointment with Mr. Thorndyke. Is he in?"

The teller, a gray-haired woman who somewhat resembled a chicken, looked up and over the rims of her glasses. "Certainly. His office is through that door over there."

Clare felt the woman's eyes follow her, but she refused to

look back. Bracing her shoulders, she knocked firmly on the door that bore the brass plate reading "Neal R. Thorndyke, President."

"Come in," a brusque voice instructed.

Feeling childishly afraid, Clare entered the banker's office. Her footsteps were cushioned by a plush beige carpet. Sunlight filtered through transparently white sheer curtains between drapes of a dark gold fabric. The desk was huge and Danish modern, with a slab of smooth black slate for its top. Behind it sat Neal Thorndyke.

He rose on seeing the beautiful young woman. "Hello, Mrs. Marshall. So sorry about your husband. Such a pity. Have a seat, will you?"

Clare sat on one of the brown leather chairs opposite the desk. "Thank you."

Thorndyke was a large man on the far side of forty, but he still retained an echo of the physique that put him through school on a football scholarship. Even though he maintained a rigorous jogging schedule, his fondness for beer was apparent around his waistline.

"I've come to discuss the mortgage my husband took out on my land. You see, there must have been some sort of mistake," Clare said with more composure than she felt. "The property is mine, and I never agreed to use it as collateral."

The banker cleared his throat and shuffled some papers on his desk in his most intimidating manner. Beautiful women fascinated him, but business was his god. He opened a folder and pulled out a legal document, then pushed it across the desk for her inspection. "I beg to differ with you, Mrs. Marshall, but this is your signature, here at the bottom just below your husband's." She looked quite composed, but one could never tell about new widows, he thought as he studied Clare's face. Sometimes they went all to pieces at the worst possible moment. "And as you can see on the account ledger, it has been quite a while and no payments were ever made."

Clare blanched. It was clearly her signature on the page. But when . . . ? "Mr. Thorndyke, this wasn't my idea. I mean . . . I didn't know anything about this until I got the bank notice last Monday," Clare tried to explain. She racked her brain for some clue as to how this could have happened. It must have occurred when Elliot bought that plane. Damn him!

"Whether it was your idea or not, Mrs. Marshall, you did sign the mortgage. This is a community property state, you know, and I assure you that this is legally binding on you."

I'll never be able to prove that I didn't study those papers carefully enough, she reasoned with herself before answering. "Nevertheless, *I* had no knowledge of it. Surely, realizing that, you can extend your payment period or give me some extra time to catch up," she argued resignedly. "Exactly how much do I owe you?"

"It's a rather large amount, Mrs. Marshall," he said slowly. God, she's beautiful, he was thinking. He had seen her from a distance for years, but he hadn't been aware of the magnetism of her dark eyes. With mounting desire, he noticed that she was perfectly proportioned, with high, firm breasts, a slender waist and rounded hips. Her soft, sensuous lips looked more prone to smiles than to frowns, and they were slightly parted, giving her a breathless look as if she were about to speak. Her eyes were the deep gray of a stormy sky, with no pretense of being blue, and were set like jewels in her lightly tanned skin.

He cleared his throat and proceeded cautiously. "As I said, Mr. Marshall mortgaged the land for a rather large sum. I've examined your bank records and, well, I see nothing to do but foreclose."

Clare steadied herself and refused to drop her eyes. "How much, Mr. Thorndyke?"

"The thirty-year note is for a hundred sixty-five thousand dollars, but—"

"What!" she interrupted with a gasp.

"But only nine thousand is currently due." He watched the tiny pulse race in her slender throat. "That's for the six back payments and interest to date.

"That seems rather high. Have you doublechecked your figures?" Clare was stalling for time. How could even Elliot have gambled away all that money? The room seemed to dip and swirl around her.

"Our figures are quite accurate," Thorndyke replied. "Unfortunately, so is the accounting of your checking and savings account. This is, of course, confidential, but you must have known about it for quite some time."

"No," Clare said hoarsely, "I didn't. As you know, Mr. Thorndyke, I—"

"Please," he smiled generously. "Call me Neal. I knew your husband quite well. We were on a first-name basis. Besides, I'm not that much older than you," he joked with a low chuckle.

Clare glanced over at him. In his youth, Neal Thorndyke had probably been a fine-looking man. Now his sandy hair was thin and graying, and his green eyes had an odd, calculating look about them, as if he never said what he was thinking. His skin was tanned, but it had the slack look that comes from too many years and too much alcohol. Trying to be polite, she ignored the older man's ridiculous reference to the similarity in their ages.

"Elliot had a very large life insurance policy, as you probably know. I haven't notified the office yet, but I'm certain it will pay off what I owe." There was a strong possibility the policy might never be paid, but she needed to stall for time until she could think of some way to come up with the money.

"No, no, I checked into that. Elliot had taken too many chances in that airplane of his. The insurance company sent him a notice several months ago that he wouldn't be covered any longer while flying." Thorndyke shrugged philosophically.

"Mr. Thorndyke—"

"Neal," he interrupted, smiling.

"Neal," she conceded hesitantly. "I can get the money for you, but it will take me a little while. I . . . I have other assets I can cash in." She hoped he wouldn't ask her what they were, because she had no idea.

"Well . . ." he drew the word out on a long sigh. "Naturally we don't like foreclosures. Nobody does. The bank's stockholders are just a bunch of people like you and me." He bent his head and pursed his lips as if he were pondering carefully. "Tell you what, Clare," he said, sliding quickly over the familiarity, "I'll take it on myself to give you, oh, let's say a week. I'll stick my neck out for you. Because I believe you can do it." He nodded decisively.

Clare was startled at the use of her first name, but didn't rebuff him. He smiled reassuringly at her as he reached out and patted her hand. He left his hand covering hers as if he were unaware that he hadn't withdrawn it.

"I don't suppose it would look right if you went out to supper with me so soon after Elliot's death," he said as his eyes rested lewdly on the curve of her full breasts, "even for the purpose of discussing your terms of payment. Perhaps I could drive out to your place tonight with the necessary papers." Slowly, he stroked her wrist with his thumb as his palm grew hot and moist.

Stunned, Clare stared at him. Her hand felt slick from his touch, as if she had accidentally touched something slimy from under a rock, and she jerked her hand free. This, coupled with the expression in his voice when he had used her name and the odd suggestion of an after-hours meeting could mean only one thing.

"Mr. Thorndyke! I don't think—"

"Now, Clare," he soothed. "Don't thank me. I want to do all I can to help you." His green eyes met hers and there was no humor in them. "After all, if it wasn't for me, how would you keep your property?"

For a moment, the silence was deafening, then Clare stood up and replied coolly, "I appreciate your offer to help. As you say, whom else can I turn to?" She moved quickly away and opened the door before he could touch her again. "But there's no need to come out tonight. I . . . I have company coming over and I'll be in town tomorrow, anyway. I can tell you then how much I will be able to pay each month." She flashed him her most dazzling smile and stepped gracefully into the bank lobby. "It's been *interesting* doing business with you . . . Neal."

Clare restrained herself from running across the lobby and out of the front door, but felt a wave of relief wash over her as she slid into her car. Nine thousand dollars! And on top of that, the banker's thinly veiled proposal! Had she misunderstood? What else could he possibly have meant?

She put her key in the ignition and listened to the powerful engine purr to life. How ironical, she thought, to be driving a Mercedez-Benz and wearing a Christian Dior blouse and have not one red cent in the bank. If she hadn't been so miserable, she might have laughed.

Clare ran into her house and up the broad staircase to Elliot's room. For a second, she hesitated at the sight of his clothes and personal belongings, lying about as if he might still use them.

On several occasions in the past week, she'd considered getting rid of his things, but somehow it had all seemed to be too much trouble, too fresh a hurt, too difficult a decision. Now she jerked out one drawer after another in a frantic search for money he hadn't had enough time to spend, or a deposit slip from some other bank. Anything.

"Surely he left something!" she reasoned desperately.

But she knew he hadn't. She'd seen the plane deliberately crash. Elliot wouldn't have done such a thing unless he was positive there was no way out of his problems.

She lay back on his bed and tried to think. He'd driven his new Datsun 280 ZX to the airport that fateful day, but his creditors had repossessed it from the parking lot before she'd thought to go get it. That didn't matter, though. He probably owed more on it than it was worth.

Most of his rings and neck chains were gone, but she found a neat stack of pawn tickets. How strange, she mused, that I never even noticed he had stopped wearing jewelry. The last few months of their marriage, they'd avoided each other as much as possible. It had been during this time that Clare realized that Elliot was having an affair with Regina . . . and taking few pains to hide it.

Systematically, Clare searched the house for something she could sell quickly. Something no one would notice was gone. Unfortunately, Elliot had had the same idea, and she found nothing.

Clare ended her search in the den. Of all the rooms in the house, she liked this one the least because it bore Elliot's stamp everywhere. Golden pine block paneling lined the walls, and animal trophies from past hunting expeditions hung everywhere. Clare hated them. She'd always believed it was wrong to kill animals needlessly; Elliot had taken a perverse pleasure in collecting trophies after she'd objected.

Angrily, she began taking the heads off the walls. She'd

have Eldon dispose of them however he thought best. In the meantime, she piled them in a heap beside the door.

Another wall held a glass gun case. Elliot's collection! She pressed her fingertips against the cool glass. Of course! He had acquired the guns for years, buying and trading them with an avid interest that she'd found chilling. At one time, she recalled, he'd had eight or nine handguns, but only four remained. It appeared as though Elliot had overlooked them, or more likely, couldn't bring himself to part with them all even in his desperate need. Clare, however, had no such awe of the weapons. They were all collector's items and must be worth a considerable sum!

But whom should she call? Clare racked her brain to come up with the name of the collector Elliot had always preferred dealing with.

Quickly, she sat down at his desk. The file drawer was locked, but she wasted no time searching for the key. With the aid of a long, stiletto-shaped letter opener which was lying beside his desk calendar, she soon had the lock open.

Here were the papers she needed. Fingers flying, she sorted through Elliot's records and receipts. Attached to a recent bill of sale was the business card of his local contact.

As exactly as she could, Clare figured from the descriptions he had marked in some books and letters which guns were still in the cabinet and what price they would fetch. Finally, she arrived at what she felt was reasonably close to their correct value and dialed the number on the card.

"Hello? Burleson speaking," a gruff voice sounded over the phone.

"Hello. My name is Clare Marshall. We haven't met, but my late husband dealt with you in regard to his gun collection." Only a week had passed since the funeral, and it still seemed very awkward to refer to Elliot in this way. She forced herself to continue. "I have no desire to keep the collection and I thought perhaps you'd be interested in it."

"Yeah, I would. Hey, I was real sorry to hear about Elliot going like that. God, that must have been awful."

"Yes, well, I doubt he ever felt any pain, Mr. Burleson. I understand he died on impact. But about the guns, are you interested? If not, I have some other names to contact." She was bluffing, but she doubted the man could tell.

"Oh, yeah. Elliot had some real fine pieces. How about me coming over and taking a look at them this afternoon?"

"Of course. Would it be convenient for you to come by early?" Mustn't sound too anxious, she cautioned herself.

"Sure. I can kick loose from here at about twelve-thirty and be at your house by one o'clock. Okay?"

"That will be fine. I'll see you then." With a grimace, she hung up the receiver. Elliot's friend was clearly the sort that she avoided as often as possible.

At precisely one o'clock, the doorbell chimed, and Betty showed Mr. Burleson into the den.

"Burleson, ma'am. Chet Burleson." He engulfed her hand in a painful handshake. "God, that was just awful about old Elliot."

Clare glanced at him. "Yes, yes, it was. The gun collection is over here. I've unlocked the cabinet so you can see them better."

Like a boy in a candy store, Burleson moved over to the case, removed a palm-sized derringer and whistled. "Just look at that. Ain't she a beauty?" Recalling he was the buyer and not the seller, he cleared his throat. "Of course, most of these are just a drag on the market. You know what I mean?"

Clare hid her amusement. "Oh, yes, I know exactly what you mean. Which ones are you interested in?"

Burleson picked up one gun after another, examined them for wear, then replaced them almost reverently on the green felt pad Clare had laid on top of the desk. "I might be able to place these here," he said, motioning vaguely. "Maybe that little derringer, too." He pushed the Smith and Wesson .38 apart from the others and shrugged. "That one has some bad scratches on the handle. I can't use it at all. Maybe you ought to keep it for your own protection. You know, seeing as you're alone now and all."

Clare glanced at him suspiciously, but his concentration was entirely on the array of guns. "Maybe you're right. I hadn't thought of that."

"Yep, that's a good idea, what with you being alone," he repeated. "That's a real pretty one for a lady. That's real pearl and silver in that inlaid handle, you know. Too scratched for a show, though. Here, let me show you how to load it. See? You just stick the bullets in there. Got it?"

Clare, who had helped her father load his guns most of her life, forced a smile to her lips. "Yes. I understand."

He turned back to the display case. "Yeah, I know women are all scared of guns. I ain't surprised you want to get rid of them. I reckon we can work out a deal."

"That's nice. What would you estimate they're worth?"

Burleson's lips moved silently as he added up totals in his head. "You being Elliot's widow and all, I guess I could give you four thousand."

Clare fought down her anger. Even *she* knew they were worth more than that! "I'm afraid that won't be good enough. According to the receipts, they're worth at least five thousand."

"Oh, no, ma'am. I don't know where you come up with those numbers, but nobody wouldn't give that for these three here."

"Elliot did. I have the papers right here."

"But what you aren't figuring is the depreciation and all. I imagine it's real hard for you to understand, but these guns won't bring as much now as they did then."

Clare's voice was noticeably cooler when she replied, "I have no trouble understanding finances, Mr. Burleson. These guns are all collector's items. Their price has gone up, not down." She made a move to shut the case. "I guess you aren't really interested in them, after all."

"Now, hold on a minute. Let me look at them again. Yeah, I guess I could go four thousand, five hundred."

"Five thousand, Mr. Burleson."

"Forty-seven hundred and that's just because I know you're a widow woman."

Clare's eyes narrowed. "Five thousand and I'll throw in Elliot's game trophies to boot."

Burleson's eyes flickered over the animal heads by the door. "Done."

Clare helped him wrap the guns in cloth to prevent scratches, and held the door open for him as he carried out the trophies before she could change her mind.

"Now, you can call the bank on this check if you want to. Won't hurt my feelings none," he said as she took his check for five thousand dollars. "Like I said, that was awful about Elliot. That's an awful way to go."

"Yes, I doubt that anyone truly enjoys dying in a plane crash, Mr. Burleson," she said between clenched teeth.

"Yeah. Well, take care of yourself."

She refrained from slamming the door as he left, but smiled triumphantly to herself. Now she wouldn't have to haul out those hideous heads.

However, she still had to raise nearly half the amount she owed the bank, then figure out where she would get the money for the monthly payment on the loan. Time was running out.

Restlessly, she went to the morning room. She dropped down on the couch and ran her fingers through her hair. There was nothing else she could sell on such short notice.

On the wall behind her hung a painting she'd done. It was a spring scene on her parents' farm—the swimming hole and the huge dogwood in full bloom, mirrored on the water's reddish surface.

"I could teach art!" she exclaimed.

Elliot had never let her show her paintings, much less sell them. He had firmly maintained that the Marshall women did not work. Yet she felt her paintings must be worth something.

She grabbed a sheet of paper and a pencil from the drawer of the side table and began to figure feverishly. Based on what she had paid for lessons some years before, and estimating two two-hour lessons per week, Clare decided she could make the land payments and eke out enough to get by for a while with just nine students. Surely she could find nine students, somewhere! Especially with the college right there in town. This didn't solve the immediate problem of the back payments she owed, but it gave Clare a boost to know she was doing something positive instead of just worrying. Before her courage could waver, she dialed Marla's number.

Marla lived two doors down, in a yellowish house that she referred to as Kilgore's answer to Stonehenge. She was at Clare's back door in five minutes.

"What's up?" Marla asked as she lowered her angular body into a chair. She had been repotting plants and still wore a blue chambray blouse knotted at her waist and tight, faded cut-off jeans that exposed a great deal of her deeply bronzed legs.

"I talked to Neal Thorndyke and it's even worse than I

thought," Clare started hesitantly. Even though she and Marla were closer than most sisters, Clare found it hard to talk about her desperate financial plight. "The land is legally mortgaged, and I don't have any money in either the checking account or the savings account."

"But what about your signature? It can't be binding on you unless you signed."

"I don't know yet how Elliot did it, but it's my signature on the loan. I'd never be able to prove that I was tricked into signing that paper. The notary public that witnessed the signatures works for the bank, too."

Marla whistled softly. "Looks like you're stuck. And Elliot took it all? Without telling you? That's really rough!"

Clare gazed out of the back window toward the lagoon-shaped pool. "Thorndyke said I owe nine thousand dollars in back payments, immediately."

This time, Marla didn't answer. No words were adequate.

"I sold Elliot's gun collection and even managed to unload all those hideous trophy heads, but I'm still four thousand short."

"Listen, Clare, I can loan you the money. I can do it without telling Tom. It'll be okay. You can pay me back whenever you can."

"No. I hate being in debt. You know how I feel about that."

"You'll be paying us back. It's not a gift. For goodness sake, what are friends for?"

Clare smiled. "I appreciate it, Marla. I really do. But I have to stand on my own two feet."

"Won't Neal give you more time? Maybe I could have Tom talk to him. They play golf together almost every Sunday."

"No. Thanks, but I have to handle this myself. I know it must sound as though I'm ungrateful, but it's about time I learned to solve my own problems." She recalled Thorndyke's proposition. If she would allow herself to become his mistress, he'd delay the paperwork until she could raise the money. But the thought of having to prostitute herself made her feel sick.

She turned back to Marla. "Anyway, assuming I can raise the mortgage money, I've been trying to think of ways to earn a living."

"You could always go to work in one of the dress stores. With your taste and reputation for style, they might even hire you on as a fashion consultant," Marla suggested.

"I just couldn't, Marla. Regina and all her friends would be coming in and looking down their noses at me. You know how sarcastic she is toward me already. That would be just what she'd like." Clare realized it sounded like false pride speaking, but it really wasn't. Regina would take any advantage that came along and Clare had to do her best to minimize that. Besides, since Marla had always had money, she had no true conception of what it was like to be on the other side of the fence. Those memories were still vivid in Clare's mind.

"Well," Marla suggested uncertainly. "you could probably get a job as a receptionist, or maybe a switchboard operator."

"What I have in mind is teaching art. I have it all down on paper. See?" She knelt beside her friend's chair and pointed out the figures she had jotted down earlier. "If I can get nine students for lessons twice a week, I can get by."

Marla read the list carefully. "You know, I think you have something here."

"I'd have two separate groups. Maybe one group with four in the early afternoon and the other with five at night. That way, I could reach the women whose children are in school, and the ones who work. Look!" She stood up and crossed the room to the back door that led to the glassed-in portico. "I could teach out there. It's airconditioned and the oil paint wouldn't hurt the Mexican quarry tiles. It overlooks the pool as well as the willow trees and the rose garden, so its inspirational." Her eyes were bright with excitement.

"You're right! It's perfect! And not only that, think how many people would like to say they come to the Marshall mansion to paint. This could become a status symbol!"

"I never thought of that! And by teaching on the patio, the students can come to the class without coming through the house."

"Good idea. It's amazing how much paint can be tracked across a carpet after an art lesson. You never realize you've stepped in it until you see the trail behind you." She grimaced. "Not to mention the invasion of your privacy. You are, after all, giving lessons, not holding open house." Marla had painted on an amateur level for years, and had taken lessons from many of the local artists. "Besides, if you teach, say, in an inside room, like the den, your entire house will reek of turpentine. Now, where can you get students?" She frowned over the puzzle, then brightened. "I know. If you don't mind doing a few free classes, you could volunteer to teach at some of the women's groups. You know, give them just a taste and tell them you're starting classes?"

"That's a good idea. I can put ads in the papers, too—in Kilgore and all the surrounding towns. And, advertise on the bulletin boards in art stores." Clare's pencil flew across the paper as she made notes. "For supplies, the students will need a medium-sized canvas, say fourteen by eighteen, or eighteen by twenty-four. Also, two small sable brushes and two large bristle ones. A paper palette and a palette knife. Oil medium, turpentine and rags to clean their brushes on. Now for the paint."

"If you teach the under-painting method, you'll only need black, browns and white. That means less initial outlay. They won't need color until it's time to glaze the painting."

"True. It's also easier to teach a person to mix paints if you don't have to consider the neutralizing effects. I think I'll start off with that technique. If I have enough people who want to learn direct painting, I'll make a separate list of colors for them."

"Don't forget pencils to sketch out the picture and fixative to set the lead on the canvas. And, a smock to cover their clothes. Lord, I must have ruined a dozen blouses just by forgetting to cover myself up."

"I wish I had done all this sooner," Clare said as she moved to a chair beside the couch. "I feel as if I'm in charge now, for the first time in a long time."

"Elliot would have had a fit if you'd told him you wanted to teach on the portico," Marla snorted. She had never liked Clare's husband.

"I know, I did suggest it once. You know, Marla, all my life I've relied on someone else to take care of me and tell me what to do. I depended on everyone but myself. Now I'm standing up alone, and it feels good!"

Marla grinned at her friend. "Sure, kid, I understand what you mean. I've been lucky that Tom never tries to put me under his thumb."

Clare laughed. "I can't even imagine you being submissive. In college, you were a rabble-rouser if there ever was one."

"The rabble needed rousing. By the way, do you have a Coke? I feel like I'm turning to dust."

"Sure. Help yourself." Clare nodded toward the kitchen. "Bring me one, too." She was wondering how many garden stakes Eldon would have to do without in order for her to make easels.

Marla came back with a frosty can in each hand. "Here you go. No need to get glasses dirty."

"I want to sell my own paintings, too. I thought I'd load some into the car and go to the different galleries around here and see if I can get them out in front of the public." Clare smiled her thanks as she took the cold can from Marla, took a sip and placed it on the table beside her chair.

"Good idea. I know several art dealers in Dallas and Houston. Of course, that doesn't mean you can automatically get anything hung there, but at least it will get you in the door. It never hurts to have contacts in the art business."

Clare smiled at her. "Do you get the feeling that if I knew what I was doing, I'd be afraid to do it?"

"Sure. Any minute now, I expect Mickey Rooney to pop out and say, 'I just *know* we can save the Widow Benson's farm!' But it still sounds like a great idea. You're good. Why not put all that talent to work?"

"Still, this doesn't do a thing about saving the land from foreclosure. I can keep my house and lifestyle, but I want the farm, too."

"Have you thought of anything else you can sell? Maybe some silver or those china pieces you had Betty pack up and put in the attic."

She shook her head. "I've already thought of that, but Elliot thought of it first. He sold them. I also thought of selling the Mercedes, but I couldn't get enough for it and I'd still have to buy another car."

Marla nodded. "That car would look impressive pulling up to art shows, too. Don't sell your image down the tube. If you're going for the real money, you have to look the part. The artists that look like rejects from a hippie colony end up selling their pictures by the side of the road."

"I'm going to make it, Marla," Clare said seriously. "I really am. And I'm going to find a way to keep the farm as well. You know, Elliot's a lucky man."

"In what way?"

"In that I can't get my hands on him."

Marla lifted her Coke in a salute.

Chapter Four

The desk top was littered with pieces of paper as Clare sat in the den laboriously trying to condense her words for an ad in the paper. The day had been tiring. She and Eldon had managed to complete only two easels before supper. Afterward, a long, hot bath had relaxed her enough to attempt writing the advertisement.

The desk lamp cast a pale light on the pine walls, making them glow like warm honey. She had hung some of her paintings and had brought in a large potted palm to soften one corner. In the gun cabinet, she draped a small tapestry she'd found in the attic and filled the shelves with woodcarvings and ceramic pieces she'd collected over the years. The one remaining gun had been placed in a drawer in the living room, as this was a more central location. Now the room felt more feminine, more her own.

Clare pushed back the sleeve of her pink velour robe as if that would make her think more precisely. It was difficult keeping what she had to say short and at the same time making the lessons sound enticing.

In the entryway, the doorbell chimed melodiously.

"Who could that be at this time of night?" she grumbled.

Betty had already left the house. "Maybe if I don't answer, whoever it is will go away." She turned back to the paper.

The bell sounded again.

Her visitor could see the light from the den, she realized, and must have known she was home. Clare frowned as the bell rang once more, this time more urgently. Could something have happened to one of the neighbors?

Reluctantly, she got up and stepped into the entryway. She could see a man's bulk through the side window.

"Tom?" she called out. "Is that you?"

The man straighted at the sound of her voice and called out a muffled reply.

"What? I didn't understand you," Clare said as she unlocked the door. "Is Marla . . . ?" Her voice dwindled away as she swung the door open to reveal not Tom Gentry, but Neal Thorndyke, on her front porch.

Her mouth dropped open and she became very aware that she wore only a wraparound robe over her gossamer nightgown. And that she was totally alone in the house.

"Mr. Thorndyke!" she exclaimed as he maneuvered past her and into the hall. "What . . . Why . . . ?"

"Neal, my dear, Neal. You keep forgetting. What am I doing here? Well, I happened to be driving by and thought I'd drop in." His flat green eyes moved down from her tumbled hair, still damp from her bath, to where the curve of her breast was revealed as her robe gaped away from her body.

Clare blushed and pulled her robe more securely around her. "I don't see why you're here . . . Neal. My note isn't due until tomorrow." Did he know she hadn't been able to raise the money? Apprehension made the blood pound in her temples. Her lips parted slightly as they always did when she was disconcerted.

"Come, come now. We don't need to stand on formalities, do we? It's so hard to get anything done at the bank. Phones are always ringing, people always coming in with messages." He laughed jovially. "I don't mind telling you, it's a rat race at times." He had crossed the entry and was going into the living room.

Clare had no choice but to follow him. He flipped on a light switch as naturally as if he owned the house, and sat down on the couch.

"You don't mind if I sit down, do you?"

Uneasily, Clare shook her head. When he'd passed by her, she'd smelled scotch on his breath and had noticed his somewhat unsteady gait.

"Can I get you a cup of coffee?" she asked reluctantly. More than anything else she wanted to get rid of him, but if he really was here on business, she could hardly imply he had ulterior motives.

"Coffee? No, no. I wouldn't care for any. Say, you wouldn't have a drop of scotch around, now would you?"

"No," she quickly lied.

He shrugged his massive shoulders. "That's all right. I had a nip before I left home." He laughed again and loosened his tie as if from the heat. "This weather has been rough, hasn't it? I can't recall a hotter summer. You don't mind if I loosen my tie, do you?" he asked as he unbuttoned the collar button of his shirt.

"It's bound to rain soon," Clare said absently as she tried to comprehend the man's actions. She felt so very alone. No one could hear her if she screamed. As tactfully as she could, she said, "Since I live on a dead-end street, we don't have many people 'driving by.' What exactly did you want to talk to me about, Mr. Thorndyke?"

"Neal."

"I prefer to call you Mr. Thorndyke," she said nervously. "Why are you here?"

He gave her his peculiarly blank gaze. "As you know, the bank note is due tomorrow." He picked up a marble gazelle from the end table and rubbed it possessively between his fingers. "Have you been able to raise the money?"

Clare paled but lifted her chin defiantly. "Not yet, but I still have until the bank closes tomorrow."

Neal Thorndyke shook his large head sadly, as if he had expected just such an answer. "That's what I was afraid of. I see it so often. Our economic system is so unfair. So terribly unfair." He looked around the room as if he expected soon to own it.

"I haven't given up yet," Clare protested, fighting back her tears. "I'll find a way. You'll see." Fatigue, both physical and emotional, had weakened Clare, but her determination was steadfast.

The large man heaved himself off the couch and placed the gazelle back on the table. He came to stand by her in the center of the room. "I'm sure we can work something out," he said softly, as if someone might overhear him. "There're ways around these things." He raised his hamlike hand and placed it on her slender shoulder.

Clare's heart beat like a frightened bird in a trap. She wanted to flinch and pull away, but forced herself to show no fear. She had no way to raise the money, and the land was so very important to her. Maybe this was the only way. It would be so simple, really. All she had to do was not protest.

Encouraged by her silence, Thorndyke moved his thumb off the robe and onto the velvety skin of her neck. When she remained stock still, he stroked downward, pushing the cloth from her skin. It fell back, exposing the curve of her full breasts beneath the sheer fabric of her nightgown. Lifting his other hand, he pushed the robe from her shoulders. It slipped off her arms and over her clenched fists to fall at her feet. In his excitement, Thorndyke failed to notice that Clare was not merely compliant, but was rigid with fear.

His eyes narrowed cruelly as he contemplated what he wanted to do with her body. "As you probably know, Clare, I've been more or less alone since my wife left me. A man gets lonely." He had hoped she'd be less docile, but her youth and beauty would more than make up for that. Besides, he had ways of bringing the fight out in a woman; he'd have her clawing and fighting against him before the night was over. He planned to have the proud Clare Marshall begging for pity before dawn. The thought pleased him. Slowly, savoring the moment, he grasped the shoulder straps of her gown and began to pull them down to expose her fully rounded breasts.

Clare fought the nausea that was building inside her. Be still! she commanded her body. It'll be over soon! But it had been so long since anyone had touched or even looked at her naked body, and to have to resort to this degradation almost choked her. His fetid breath and faint, but noticeable, body odor repulsed her, and she trembled at the touch of his hands, which were too soft.

As he grabbed her breast and began to knead it roughly, she felt outrage begin to spread through her, galvanizing her into action.

He pulled her to him and sank his mouth to the cool curve of her throat. She moaned in protest as his teeth nipped her sharply. "No!" she hissed through clenched teeth. His fingers cruelly pinched her tender nipple and his hot breath gasped raggedly below her ear. *"No!"*

She would not prostitute herself, not even for her beloved land. Clare shoved him as hard as she could. Caught off guard, Thorndyke stumbled and fell onto the couch.

"Get out of my house!" she cried, grabbing the .38 revolver out of the table drawer. "Get out of here! Now!" Hysteria had replaced shock. Tears streamed down her face as the barrel of the gun waggled dangerously.

"Now, Clare! Mrs. Marshall!" Thorndyke protested quickly, instantly sober. "Don't get excited!"

"Go away!" she cried. "Get out!"

Thorndyke leaped from the couch and crossed the room in one stride. At the front door, he hesitated and pointed his finger at her. "You'd better come up with that money, or else! Don't think you can wheedle any more time out of me!" He blanched as she aimed the revolver at his chest. As he jumped out into the night, he called back, "Tomorrow! You'd better have the money tomorrow!"

Clare heard him run across the porch and down the steps. Tires squealed, and she knew he had gone. Only then did she run across the entryway and slam the door shut, throwing the bolt into place. Weakly, she leaned against the safety of the barricade.

The full import of what she'd almost done beat upon her, causing her to sink onto the cold tiles, trying to cover her nakedness with crossed arms as sobs tore through her body.

"Men!" she muttered to herself. The early morning light streamed through the window as she angrily threw Elliot's golf sweater into a box on top of his dress shirts. "You can't trust any of them!" She glared at a smudge on one of his handkerchiefs. She'd never worn lipstick that color in her life.

Marla was organizing a neighborhood garage sale for the next day. The proceeds were to be donated to the Gregg Home for the Aged, and for Clare it was as good a way as any to get rid of Elliot's clothes. She tossed his winter coat in with the rest and threw in a double handful of ties. When that box was full, she started filling another one. One of his drawers contained several packs of cards and a tray of poker chips. She dumped them into the carton without a pause.

I should have known better, she thought bitterly. He was a

woman-chaser and a heavy drinker in college. I should have realized he wouldn't change. After all those long-winded promises to straighten up. I was supposed to be his salvation! The only change he made was to add gambling to his vices as well! She knotted together the laces in his shoes and tossed them into the box.

And then there was that trouble last night! I wish I had at least shot at him! How could I have ever even considered letting him use me like that?

She dropped to her knees and fished around under Elliot's bed with his tennis racket until she nudged out both his bedroom slippers. They went in with the rest.

"Might as well keep the tennis racket," she said. "I may lose something under my bed one day." She tossed it onto the mattress. She was examining the strangely shaped metal object which had also come from beneath his bed. "Now, what on earth is that? Oh, well, if I can't identify it, I'm not likely to ever need it." It followed the slippers.

Below her, Clare heard the doorbell ring and she froze. She wasn't expecting anyone. Could it be Thorndyke again?

Cautiously, she got to her feet. Betty had gone to the market and she could hear Eldon running the electric edger in the backyard. Damn! She was alone again!

Hesitantly, Clare went to the top of the stairs and looked down as the bell rang again. Whoever it was was standing directly in front of the door, and she couldn't see him through the narrow glass side panels.

She went back to her bedroom and got the revolver from the top of her bedside table. After the problem with Neal, she had felt more secure having it close at hand while she slept. When she opened the front door, she was surprised to see a tall stranger. He was equally startled to see the pistol she held at her side.

"Do you plan to shoot me with that thing, or do I get a chance to leave quietly?" he asked. His voice was deep and strong and it stirred her oddly. Dark gold hair, tousled boyishly by the wind, contrasted with his tanned skin, and his sensuous lips were tilted in a smile. But his hazel-green eyes watched her warily.

Clare looked puzzled, then realized she still had the gun. Blushing slightly, she laid it on the hall table just inside the doorway. "I'm sorry. I thought you were someone else."

"I'm glad I'm not him. My name is Ryan Hastings. I'm with Huntly Oil out of New Orleans, and I'd like to talk to your husband about some property. This *is* Elliot Marshall's home isn't it?"

"Yes," she said, realizing she was staring. "I'm Clare Marshall." Never in her life had she seen so handsome a man. That strange something within her stirred again.

"Is Mr. Marshall in?"

"No," she said in a dazed manner. "He's dead." The slow, rhythmic cadence of the man's voice had a hypnotizing effect on her.

Ryan blinked and bent his head to one side. "I beg your pardon?"

Clare blushed hotly. "I'm sorry. You've caught me quite by surprise." Of all the dumb things to say! she groaned inwardly.

Was he from the bank? Clare wondered. Had the land been put up for sale already? Impossible! Caution crept into her voice. "What I mean to say is that my husband is dead. What can I do for you?"

Ryan gazed down at the beautiful woman. She was certainly not what he had expected. Awkwardly, he realized some reply was necessary. "I'm sorry about your husband. The land office didn't tell me."

She bobbed her head in acceptance and waited quietly for him to continue.

"I represent Huntly Oil," he said confidently. "We're interested in your land and would like to drill on it." His tone of voice indicated that he fully expected her to jump at the opportunity.

"It isn't for sale," Clare said between colorless lips. "I think you'd better leave." They are all alike, she thought, even the handsome ones.

He smiled down at her, his teeth startlingly white in his bronzed face. "You misunderstand. I don't want to *buy* your land. Just lease it." Ryan found himself looking deep into her smoky eyes. They seemed to have no end to their depths. What could be so threatening to this incredibly beautiful woman that she'd have to answer her door with a gun?

"My company feels there is the possibility of oil on land between here and Gladewater. I've been authorized to offer you a lease," he explained again.

"Oil?" she asked. "All the oil around here is gone. You're about fifty years too late, Mr. Hastings." She'd recovered her composure and spoke coolly to cover her earlier confusion.

"This is a different field we're looking for. Could I come in and talk to you about it?"

Clare hesitated, then stepped outside to join him. After the incident with Neal Thorndyke, she wasn't about to let a stranger into her house, no matter how charming he appeared to be.

"Why don't we sit on the side porch?" she suggested. "There's a breeze today." She glanced at him curiously as she led him down the wide, relatively cool veranda. His very presence was acting like a magnet to her senses. She was acutely aware of the muscular leanness of his lithe body and how his broad shoulders strained against the pale blue cloth of his dress shirt.

As they rounded the corner, she motioned for him to sit down in one of the chairs. Ryan thought it looked like a sculpture made of white plastic plumbing pipe covered with nylon mesh, but he sat down anyway. It was surprisingly comfortable.

"I've been to the courthouse in Longview," he explained, "and they gave me your name as the owner of the land I'm interested in. I had no idea your husband had died. I'm sorry."

She briefly nodded her head again and leaned gracefully back into the chair cushions.

"I also went to the two deep well sites that are being drilled near here. One is just south of Laneville and the other is between here and Tyler. By my calculations, both of them are too far south. I think the oil is here. Under Kilgore."

"So do a lot of other people. Land is leased around here regularly, but nobody ever hits oil."

"That's because they aren't going deep enough." He leaned forward eagerly. "Think of it as if the oil deposit is shaped like a figure eight, with the top part near the surface. The top of the eight has been pumped dry, but the bottom of the eight is still full of oil. There are fissures and very deep caverns all throughout this part of Texas, but this is the only spot where one of the caverns is directly below the oil-bearing sands. For millions of years, the oil formed near the surface and drained into the caverns."

Clare watched him intently as he spoke, almost mesmerized by his irresistible masculinity. The firm set of his jaw indicated a determination that was evidenced by the fervor of his words. His robust virility was not to be denied. Clare was having considerable difficulty keeping her mind on oil, and cautioned herself that this was business. "What terms did you have in mind, Mr. Hastings?" Clare offered, not sure what his last words had been.

"I was thinking of fifty dollars an acre for your entire thousand acres, and a one-eighth royalty on a five-year lease, with annual payments. Just sign these papers and I'll be on my way." Confidently, he pulled a standard lease form out of a leather folder. He had taken the liberty ahead of time to fill in all the blanks with the terms he was offering.

Clare's thoughts of her dire financial straits snapped back her attention. She was astute enough to realize a better deal could be made. She smiled sweetly. "I was thinking more in terms of a hundred and fifty an acre for *three* years . . . with a three-sixteenth royalty."

"How's that?" Ryan queried, his hand halfway to the pen in his pocket.

"If you're so sure the oil is there, your offer will be matched by any of the major companies."

"I can't authorize that much for a thousand acres!"

"Good. I only want to lease five hundred acres. That'll give you almost a full block and plenty to drill on."

"I'd prefer to lease all the land, but fifty an acre is the best I can do. If we strike oil, that means you could have wells on the entire amount."

Clare laughed. "Mr. Hastings, we both know that if you strike oil, I won't have any trouble finding somebody to drill on the rest of it . . . and at a better price." She looked as collected and utterly feminine as if she were at a tea party. She hoped she hadn't pushed him too far. His original offer of ten thousand dollars a year for five years was certainly more than enough to get the mortgage note up to date. But, the more she could get, the easier it'd be to get back on her feet financially.

"A hundred and fifty is out of the question." Ryan began to gather up his papers again. Often a bluff like this helped in stubborn cases. It had to work; he needed this lease. His theory was right and he had to prove it, not just to himself, but to Huntly Oil as well.

Clare hadn't been married to a gambler for four years without learning a few tricks. She shrugged elegantly and looked slightly bored. "Very well, Mr. Hastings. I'm willing to meet you halfway. I'll take a hundred dollars an acre for five hundred acres, with the three-sixteenths royalty. The duration of the lease can stay as you first said."

Ryan studied her closely. Never had he met a woman who was so intriguing. It was not only her obvious intelligence, though he admired this in a woman, or even her physical appearance that had so captivated him, but rather some mysterious quality she seemed to exude. He moved restlessly and tried to keep his mind on business.

"Of course, if you're not interested. . . ." she bluffed in turn, hoping it wasn't a mistake.

She smiled and appeared at ease; yet, as Ryan gazed into her eyes, he saw something totally different. This was a look he had seen more than once—a desperate need for money.

"All right," he agreed. "The head office won't be happy, but it's a deal." He was rewarded by a look of momentary, but intense, relief on her face. She never took her gaze from his pen as he changed the figures on the contract and made out a draft of ten thousand dollars for the first year's lease. When he handed Clare the pen, she signed her name with determined strokes, but her hand shook slightly as she took the draft. As her fingers brushed his, he felt a sharp rush of excitement and was very aware of her nearness. The warm breeze in her hair brought him her sweet aroma and he held himself cautiously in check.

Careful, he thought, remember Doré. You don't need to get involved with another woman. Yet he found himself trying to think of some reason to prolong the interview.

Clare studied the draft for a moment. "Mr. Hastings, this is a collection draft, not a check," she said, trying to cover the anxiety she felt.

"Yes, it is. It's our customary twenty-day collection draft. You just deposit that in your bank and it'll be sent to our bank and—"

"That won't do. I mean . . . I'd rather have a cashier's check. I don't like doing business with collection drafts. Why should your company have the lease for twenty days before I get any money?" she asked defensively.

Ryan heard the words of a shrewd business woman, but the glint of desperation had shone again in the depths of her gray eyes. Without being consciously aware of why he did it, he agreed to arrange for a cashier's check to be deposited to her bank account before the end of the day.

When he stood up to indicate the end of the discussion, Ryan felt a twinge of regret. He wanted to get to know her better. "Can I buy you lunch to celebrate your entry into the oil business?" he asked as he smiled down at her.

Clare faltered as if there were nothing she wanted more to do. "No. I'd . . . I'd love to, but I have a great deal more to do today. And I have a very important meeting this afternoon." She held out her hand. "I have enjoyed doing business with you, Mr. Hastings."

Ryan took her hand in his. The bones felt so fragile beneath the smooth skin. An oddly protective feeling swept over him. "It's been a pleasure, Mrs. Marshall. I hope we meet again." Before the unusual emotion could stop him, he strode purposefully down the walk that curved to accommodate the sprawling base of the antiquated oil derrick.

Clare leaned against one of the large white columns that supported the upper veranda and watched him walk with catlike grace to his car, fold his tall frame inside and drive out of sight around the bend in her woods-lined drive. Her hand still tingled from his electrifying touch, and her heart beat fast as if she had been running.

"Clare Marshall, you're a fool," she whispered.

Chapter Five

Ryan Hastings had kept his promise, so Clare smiled triumphantly as she stepped away from the teller's window. The bank lobby no longer seemed so vast and frightening. Without hesitation, she walked purposefully across the lobby, knocked on Neal Thorndyke's oak door and entered at the growled summons.

He glared warily at her over his steepled fingertips, making no move to rise when she entered. At last taking his elbows off his desk, Thorndyke said, "At least you're prompt. I've already drawn up the papers deeding your farm to the bank. Our lawyer has looked them over and everything is in order. Now, if you'll sign here, you can be on your way and I can get back to business." He pushed the papers and pen across the desk.

"Not so fast *Mr*. Thorndyke!"

To her surprise, as her hand dipped into her purse, he jumped and his skin became waxy. He must think I've reconsidered shooting·him, she thought with amusement, though she kept her expression solemn. Thorndyke swallowed hard and began easing himself away from the desk.

Getting all the mileage she could out of the spontaneous deception, Clare paused a moment longer, then withdrew the roll of green bills from her purse.

"Count it, please," she said. "You'll find it to be the complete nine thousand dollars I owed. Exactly." With the remainder of the lease money now safely deposited in her account, plus the art lesson income, Clare felt she'd be able to meet the monthly payments. It would be tight, but she was prepared to do without quite a bit in order to keep Thorndyke from having the satisfaction of foreclosing. Best of all, she had done it without having to compromise herself with him.

Silently, Thorndyke eased back to his desk, his breathing still somewhat rapid. He quickly counted the bills and hastily shoved them into a drawer. Clare was glad she had cashed the check rather than having it transferred to the bank. Thorndyke's discomfort was worth the extra effort.

"Well," he said reluctantly, "it looks as if it's all in order. You realize, of course, you must meet *every* due date, and on time. I won't allow even a single payment to lapse again."

"The lapse wasn't my fault to begin with," she stated firmly. "It was Elliot's. I don't intend to lose *my* land. I want a receipt, please."

"See that you aren't even a day late in paying from here on. I won't stand for it," the banker blustered, seeming confident now that he wouldn't be shot. He scrawled out the receipt. "After the way you led me on last night, I'd like nothing better than to turn you out, lock, stock and barrel."

Clare's eyes narrowed dangerously. "I led *you* on? You're quite lucky not to be in jail today for attempted rape," she countered as she leaned on his desk, forcing him to draw back involuntarily. "As for turning me out of my house, you can't. You see, I've spent quite a bit of time in the library lately. According to Texas law, you can't take my house. It's homesteaded."

Thorndyke rose behind his desk, his face purple with rage. "Maybe I can't take the house, but I can . . . and will . . . take every goddamn acre you own!"

Clare smiled coolly. "Not unless I miss a payment. And I never intend to do that. Good day, Mr. Thorndyke. I'll deliver the monthly payment to you in cash, personally, at the first of each month."

With a swish of her yellow pleated skirt, Clare was gone, leaving Neal gripping the edge of his desk and glaring after her.

Clare felt the buoyancy of success as she crossed the lobby. She had every intention of doing exactly as she'd said she would. By the time the mortgage was paid off, Neal would be sick of the very sight of her. Revenge was sweet, she decided. An afternoon in the castlelike gray stone library seemed to be a good idea. She wanted to learn as much as possible about the oil business.

She hurried out the door, skipped down the steps and ran headlong into a tall man. Papers flew about them like confetti as he caught her to keep her from falling.

"Oh!" she gasped, seeing Ryan Hastings' hazel eyes so close to her own and feeling the steel muscles of his arms protectively around her. "I . . . I should have been watching where I was going."

Ryan grinned in glad recognition. "So should I. I was on my way to the law office next door and wasn't paying any attention."

Suddenly aware of her position in his arms and the strange sense of excitement she felt, Clare blushed and moved away. To cover her confusion, she bent to help him pick up the scattered papers. Neither of them spoke.

As they both reached for the last page, their hands brushed together and, again, their eyes met. For a moment, time seemed suspended.

"Have dinner with me," Ryan said softly.

"Yes."

Ryan looked down at the papers in his hand as if surprised to see them. "I have to take care of this first. I'll pick you up at eight."

Clare could only nod.

As she washed her hair, Clare wondered why on earth she had agreed to go out with Ryan Hastings. Not only was he a total stranger, but she had no intention of becoming interested in another man. She had had enough of marriage. On another level, too, she still thought of herself as Elliot's wife, and felt guilty going on a date.

"Why do I get myself into these things?" she asked herself

as she blew her hair dry. It flowed in a soft umber cloud away from her heart-shaped face and fell into a natural style as it dried.

"Maybe when he gets here, I should tell him I've changed my mind about going out with him. After all, it hasn't been that long since Elliot died. Surely he'll understand."

While she put on her makeup, she pondered just how she would tactfully and graciously explain to Ryan Hastings that she really couldn't see him tonight. As she brushed her teeth, she decided that no matter what he said, she'd stand firm. Slipping into her gold Quiana knit dress with the flowing lines and deeply plunging neckline, she congratulated herself on her strength of character.

She put on pearl earrings and fastened the clasp of a thin gold chain with three matching pearls about her neck, then went downstairs.

"Betty?" she called out as she poked her head into the living room. "I've decided not to keep that dinner date, after all. Do you know if there's any sandwich meat left in the refrigerator?"

Betty eyed her speculatively. "You sure have fixed yourself up nice just to eat a piece of bologna and bread."

Clare reddened. "I just haven't changed yet, that's all."

"Nope. There's not a thing to eat in this whole house. You'd best go out with him."

"Good try, but I know you went grocery shopping this morning."

The doorbell made her jump.

"Will you answer that, Betty? I really don't want to have to explain. Just tell him I had to leave suddenly and you don't know when I'll be back." Her eyes pleaded with the older woman and she clasped her hands nervously.

"All right," Betty agreed after a pause, and went to the entryway.

Clare heard Betty open the front door.

"Come right on in. Miss Clare's in the living room waiting for you."

Clare groaned.

"Miss Clare?" Betty said as she ushered Ryan into the room. "Mr. Hastings is here." She wore the stubborn expression of a mother bird determined to teach her young to fly.

"Hello," he said as he smiled down at her. "You look beautiful." He looked even more handsome in his well-cut dark suit with a maroon and white tie, causing a disquieting rush of excitement in Clare.

"Thank you." She tried to catch Betty's eyes, but the maid seemed to be engrossed in the pattern of the wallpaper. "We won't be out late, Betty."

"Okay, Miss Clare. That don't matter to me. I'll be finished in the kitchen and gone in an hour. You go have a good time."

"Thanks," Clare said grimly.

Ryan took her arm to guide her down the front steps, and in spite of her decision to remain aloof, Clare felt her elbow tingle from the touch of his fingers. As Ryan held open the door of his black Trans-Am, Clare slid into the luxurious interior. She watched him as he came around to get in behind the wheel.

"You really do look beautiful," he said as they drove away. "I'm glad you said you would go out with me tonight."

Clare smiled hesitantly. Years had passed since she'd dated and carried on a semi-flirtatious conversation. She wasn't sure she still knew how. Unbidden memories of Elliot and their courtship came to mind. Never again, she told herself. What should have been a fairy-tale marriage had become a nightmare within a matter of months. From now on, I'll let my head rule my heart instead of the other way around, she reminded herself. "Where are we going?"

"Anywhere you'd like. I've heard of a place on Lake Cherokee that sounds good. Does that suit you?"

She looked at him in surprise. Although she'd never been there, she knew the place he meant. It was noted for its romantic and elegant ambiance.

"Nathan's?" she asked. Perhaps he had meant somewhere else.

"That's it. I asked the lawyer this afternoon where he'd take a pretty lady out for dinner, and that's the one he suggested."

"Mr. Hastings," she said in embarrassment, "I don't think . . ."

"Please call me Ryan. I like that a lot better." He put his large hand over hers and smiled at her.

Clare took a deep breath and continued, "I don't think we should go there. First of all, as he might not have mentioned, it's terribly expensive."

"That's no problem. What else?"

How could she explain that Nathan's was a place for lovers? It lay at the end of a long, unpopulated road overlooking the lake in the most romantic way possible. Uneasily, she recalled conversations with other single women who had assured her that men expected—and often demanded—sexual favors after even a casual date. Suddenly, she realized she knew nothing at all about Ryan Hastings. Only the night before, a man she'd known for several years—if only slightly—had tried to rape her. Why did she think she could trust Ryan?

Glancing over, Ryan saw her pale face and frightened eyes. "Hey, what's wrong?" He eased the car to a stop on the lane just behind the black, wrought-iron gates that guarded her driveway from the street. He turned to face her. "Did I say something to upset you?"

"No, no. Of course not."

"Then what's wrong? A minute ago, you were so happy, and now you're almost shaking."

Clare forced a smile to her lips. "There's something I need to tell you about myself. My husband has only been dead two weeks."

Ryan covered her hand with his in a comforting, friendly gesture. "I'm sorry. I had no idea. Then this is the first time you've been out on a date?"

She nodded silently.

Smiling tenderly, Ryan cupped her chin in his hand and gently made her face him. "Now I understand quite a bit. You're also worried about *where* Nathan's is located."

Again Clare nodded. Her eyes melted into his and she fought against the warm wave of emotion that he stirred within her. "I've never really dated anyone except my husband. We went steady all through college and were married for four years. I've forgotten how to date, if I ever knew. Before you came, I told my maid to tell you I wasn't home. I was that afraid of going out. Not just with you," she added quickly, "but with anybody."

"I understand," he said softly. "And Nathan's is reported

to be emphatically romantic." He gently pulled her chin back when she tried to look away in embarrassment. "You can trust me. Only an animal would force his attentions on a woman. I'm nothing like that. Something tells me you've had some pretty bad experiences with men. I want you to let me prove to you that we aren't all bad." He smiled tenderly into her searching eyes. "Okay? If you start feeling uneasy about anything, say the word and I'll bring you straight home."

Clare studied his face for any sign of duplicity, then smiled. "There's nothing I'd like better than to go to Nathan's with you."

The drive through the rolling hills and tall pines and oaks was beautiful. The stifling heat had abated to a warm breeze, heavy with the scent of the pines. The shadows were lengthening like long fingers across the meadows and the road, as the sky mellowed in preparation for a brilliant sunset. In the distance, Clare watched a line of cows in a pasture, one followed the other, on their way to the feed lot. But most of all, she was aware of Ryan.

Ryan Hastings was not only handsome; she soon learned his sense of humor exactly matched her own. Not only was he obviously very intelligent and well-traveled, but he had a natural aura of wealth about him. Earlier, she had noticed a subtleness, a confident way of moving and speaking that she found intriguing after Elliot's flamboyantly extravagant style. Soon she had forgotten her earlier fears and was laughing with him.

Nathan's was situated along the curve of the lake, as if it were a jewel held in the palm of a lover's hand. Already the lights were gleaming in the dusk and were mirrored in the silken water. The sky had turned a rose that deepened into purple and lemon-yellow, and pink clouds streaked the low horizon. The sun itself was a fiery red ball suspended in the silhouetted treetops.

Clare walked along the wooden bridge that led from the parking lot to the ornately carved teakwood doors. She wanted to remember this night, to impress it in her memory forever, because she knew that Ryan would soon leave Kilgore and go out of her life. She breathed the air deeply. Even the cool breeze off the lake seemed to be rose-colored and sweetly scented. Along the shoreline, lightning bugs glowed, then disappeared to glow again in another place. An owl hooted in the woods, but it sounded melodious rather than mournful to Clare.

Ryan watched her walk a little ahead of him as he tried to understand the odd emotion he was feeling. Her hair waved softly to below her shoulders, and he longed to touch it. In the dim light, her eyes were mysterious and compelling. The colors of the setting sun played across her face in a way that made his heart catch in his throat. The sound of her low voice and the graceful movement of her body stirred him in a way he'd never known before.

They were seated at a table beside tall green plants where they could watch the moon rise over the glassy water. A small candle burned between them, sending flickering lights over their faces.

The supper was expertly served. As the main course dishes were being removed, Clare realized that she hadn't really tasted the meal at all. Delicious as it must have been, it could never have been as pleasurable as merely being with Ryan. Clare found herself smiling into his hazel eyes, wondering what it would be like to run her fingers through his thick hair. She noticed that Ryan's eyes followed her every movement, and she found herself smiling at the realization. Suddenly they both became aware that several minutes had passed in which neither had spoken, but only studied the other's face. To cover their mutual embarrassment, they began talking at the same time.

"How long have you been in the oil business?" she said when he motioned for her to go first.

"In a way, the answer is always. My father was also a geologist, and I grew up in the oil fields. I never considered being anything but a geologist; though I spent a few years working as a roughneck. Someday, though, I may wildcat a well of my own. One of my earliest memories is of following dad around on a rig platform. My mother was always afraid I'd get hurt or fall into the slush pit, or a dozen other things, but I never did. This business gets in your blood. It's not uncommon to find several generations in oil, in one form or another." He saw no reason to mention that the field his father worked in belonged entirely to his grandfather. "What about you? When you aren't horsetrading oil leases, what do you do?" He was rewarded by seeing amusement sparkle in the depths of her clear gray eyes.

Clare laughed. "I'm an artist." The words sounded strange to her, but he didn't question them.

"Yeah? You're the first artist I've ever met. Where do you exhibit? Maybe I'm familiar with your work."

Only if you've been inside my house, she thought. Aloud she answered, "I'm not that well-known yet. Actually, I'm just now really becoming established."

"I'd like to see some of your work. Are you showing in any galleries in New Orleans? That's where I live."

"No, not yet. I'm considering branching out in that direction, though. Could you recommend two or three good galleries there?" Clare was amazed at how proficiently the half-truths fell out of her mouth. This was a facet of her personality she'd never seen before.

"I'm not very in touch with the art world," he confessed. "I'm afraid I can't help you there." As she talked about her work, he saw her changeable eyes darken and grow mysterious and shadowed.

"That's all right. I can ask my contacts in Dallas for names."

"Did you know you have the loveliest eyes I've ever seen?" he said abruptly.

"Why, thank you," she stammered, taken completely off balance. Was he making a play for her?

"How would you like some hot apple strudel? I hear this place is famous for it."

Clare nodded, again thrown off stride.

Ryan kept her laughing for the rest of the meal with stories from his childhood and college days.

"What were you like as a child?" he asked later as they recrossed the boardwalk to the parking lot. He put his arm comfortably around her waist as they walked to the car.

Clare's smile wavered and she touched the chain at her neck as if for reassurance. "Studious. I was no fun at all."

"I find that hard to believe. You must be a late bloomer." He held open the door of the car, which had probably cost more than her parents' entire house. Clare got in as if she'd been born to luxury.

The ride home was as pleasant as the whole evening had

been, and when Ryan reached across and covered her hand with his, Clare felt only a moment's apprehension. His hand was warm and protecting and she found she rather liked the feeling it gave her, so she didn't pull away.

Against the ebony sky, the trees and bushes were blue-gray smudges. Here and there, Clare could see golden squares of light from farmhouse windows. A small glow against the dark sky showed the location of Kilgore.

All too soon they reached the huge iron gates that always stood open to her drive. The house was skillfully hidden from view by huge azalea bushes beneath the enormous old oak trees. The curve of the drive was lined with tall gardenia bushes that reached well above the top of a car.

"Looks as if your maid left the lights on for you," he commented as he parked at the foot of the wide front steps.

"Yes, Betty wanted me to get out tonight—she's afraid I stay home too much—but she didn't want you to think I'm totally alone. The lights are her way of showing a middle ground."

Ryan gazed at her. "And what about you? Are you still afraid of me?"

"No." Clare smiled, shaking her head.

She began to pull her hand away from his, but when he gently tightened his hold, she stopped and tried to decide whether to stay or go.

"I'm not ready for the evening to end. Are you?"

"No," she said softly. "I'm not."

"At the same time, I don't want to appear to be pushing you by asking if I could come in. So, instead, would you like to go somewhere for a drink?"

Clare tilted her head in puzzlement. "Now?"

"I know I said I'd get you home early, and I did. I'm asking you for a second date. Now. Tonight."

"All right," she laughed. "Why not?"

At Clare's suggestion, they went to a small lounge with a large name—Conjunction Junction—that was too expensive for the college crowd and too camp for the older crowd. The tiny tables circled a postage-stamp-sized dance floor. Along the walls and hanging from the ceiling was an array of memorabilia. A gaudy Mardi Gras mask hung beside an old washboard; a plow, spray-painted metallic gold, served as a rack for various plumed hats; a tawdry plaster parrot balanced on its swing beside a mangy bear's head that stuck out of a sequined ball gown.

"Can you believe this place?" Clare shouted above the rock and roll music of the fifties.

"How did they ever find all this junk?" he laughed, fingering a gumball machine turned into a telephone stand.

"Talent. Sheer talent. And a lot of nerve."

Across the dance floor, a neon jukebox flashed, and Little Richard yelled out a lyric about a girl named Sally.

Ryan studied Clare. This was the last sort of place he would have expected her to like. Yet she fit in here as well as she had in the contained opulence of Nathan's. Her eyes sparkled as her foot tapped to the hypnotic music. Ryan was intrigued.

The sultry strains of "Greenfields" threaded their way through the bizarre room. "Would you like to dance?" he asked.

Clare only hesitated a second. She loved to dance and Elliot had never taken her. "Yes."

She followed Ryan's lead to the dance floor and settled easily in his arms, as though she had always belonged there. As he pulled her close, she noticed that her head barely reached his chin. The spicy scent of his aftershave wafted gently to her nostrils and she sighed. Ryan was an excellent dancer, and she felt as light as a feather in his strong arms. Beneath her hand, she could feel his hard shoulder muscles, and when he pulled her closer, she lay her head against his neck. She could feel his breath stirring her hair, and her heart beat faster. After the music ended, he released her, but only reluctantly, and led her back to their table.

As they sipped the gin and tonics Ryan had ordered, they gazed around the room.

"Look over there," he said, "beyond the bicycle for two and the old Mobile flying horse sign. It's a stuffed shirt. A *real* stuffed shirt!"

Clare laughed. "Over on that other wall is a map of the moon and someone has inked in the locations of all the McDonald's drive-ins."

"Would you like to dance again?" he asked. A love song was starting to play, and several couples were wandering toward the floor.

"Yes." She wanted very much to feel his arms around her again.

They moved very slowly in time with the music, and his lips gently traveled along the edge of her hairline. Instead of being frightened, she felt an excitement building. Then he stopped, but continued to hold her lovingly close.

"Let's go," he said huskily, knowing she felt as he did.

Clare was quiet as they got into the car. Inside she was wrestling with what she knew she wanted to do and what she knew she ought to do.

"Do you want me to take you home now?" he asked.

Clare took a deep breath to steady her voice. "No."

Ryan put his arm around her and drove to the Community Inn where he was staying. Clare was silent most of the way. It was as though she had blocked any thoughts about their destination. When Ryan parked out front of the hotel, she trembled with nervous excitement. If she were going to back out, this was the time to do it.

"Clare, are you sure?" he asked, as if he were reading her thoughts. "I want you. I'm fascinated by you. But I don't want you to feel this is what I had in mind all evening, because it isn't."

"I know. That's one reason I feel it's all right."

"The same promise holds," he reminded her as he stroked her hair back from her face. "If you feel frightened at any time, I'll take you home."

She nodded.

The hotel was a rambling, two-story building with private doors that opened onto a grassy courtyard and palm terrace. Clare felt a momentary hesitation when she realized she could possibly be seen by someone she knew, but she put the small worry aside. After all, she was no longer a married woman, and more than anything else, she wanted to be with Ryan and feel his strong arms around her. And, somehow, being at an impersonal hotel, rather than in the home she had shared with Elliot, made it all right.

They walked hand in hand to his room. He turned on a small lamp and she looked about. It was almost a suite rather than a mere bedroom. At one end was a dark blue couch and two armchairs grouped around a coffee table on which a jumble of charts and papers were strewn. At the other end of the room was a large bed with a blue and white bedspread. The maid had already turned it down for the night.

Ryan put his arms around Clare and pulled her close. She

let herself lean against him and felt the rough texture of his suit jacket beneath her cheek. For a long time, he held her, securely, tenderly. Then he cupped her chin in his hand and tilted her head up to meet his lips. Clare reached up to touch his hair. It was softer than she had expected, and even thicker. She entwined her fingers in the tawny strands and again lifted her face to meet his.

Ryan felt confused at the emotions she triggered in him. He had wanted to kiss her since he'd met her that afternoon, but hadn't really expected she'd let him. Now she stood in his arms, in his hotel room, and he felt an intense longing, not only of sexual desire, but also of protection and caring. Of love. But how could that be? He had only just met her! With wonder, he cradled her head on his chest and breathed in the clean aroma of her hair. He felt shaken to the core by emotions he had never felt before. Had she been any other woman, he would have had her in bed by now with no hesitation, no questions asked. Ryan tightened his arms about her and felt her move even closer. "I meant what I said about taking you home if you want to go."

For a long time, Clare was silent. Then she lifted her head to look steadily into his eyes. "That won't be necessary, Ryan."

As he bent his head to kiss her, she wondered at the gentle expression in his eyes. She had no way of knowing that her own eyes held the same softness. As his lips touched hers, she felt an urgent warmth spread through her; and as his large hand tenderly cupped her breast, the warmth kindled into flame. With growing desire, she ran her hands across the firm muscles of his back.

Ryan placed kisses of fire along her cheek, her ear and down her neck, then nuzzled in the hollow of her throat. She sighed with pleasure.

Slowly, he unzipped her dress, savoring each inch of creamy skin he revealed. He slipped it from her shoulders and let it fall loosely about her waist, then to the floor.

As his eyes swept over her loveliness, his heart pounded. Almost reverently, he touched the full swell of her breasts and gently rolled the rosy nipples between his fingertips until they were erect and sensitive.

He gently knotted his hands in the abundant silkiness of her hair and pulled her to him.

"God, you're lovely," he said hoarsely. "I had no idea you'd be so perfect." He kissed her deeply, passionately, then buried his face in the curve of her neck as he ran his hands over her satiny skin.

Clare returned his kisses with equal intensity, savoring each moment, drawing out each pleasure. She unbuttoned his shirt and let her hands stroke the smoothness of his chest. His muscles were taut beneath her fingers, and as she removed the shirt, she brushed her breasts against his skin. With awe, she ran her palms across the hard perfection of his body. It was nothing at all like Elliot's. Ryan's lean belly was ridged with muscles, and there was no sign of surplus weight around his narrow waist. She liked it immensely. Clare bent her head and left a trail of butterfly kisses across his chest.

Again she raised her mouth to meet his and marveled at the excitement of his tongue tracing fire between her lips. She'd never been kissed like this before, and she hungrily kissed him again.

With a low laugh, Ryan smoothed her hair back from her face. "Clare," he whispered as if her name were a caress. "Clare." He held her closely, as though he couldn't bear to let her go for even a minute. Then his fingers slipped beneath the waistband of her brief silky panties, gently easing them over her hips.

Clare struggled with his belt, but soon he, too, stood nude, letting Clare roam her eyes over him. With a smile of delight, she stroked his erect maleness and felt it grow even harder in her fingers.

Without a word, Ryan bent down and lifted her in his arms as easily as he would have a child, and carried her to the bed. He laid her down and lowered himself to lie beside her.

"Ryan," she whispered, running her fingers along the firm line of his jaw. "Ryan, I'm so glad I met you."

His head lowered to her breasts and his hot tongue flicked across first one nipple, then the other. His hands were gentle on her body, but they were rousing her to undreamed of delight.

As his fingers slid seductively between her legs and urged them to part so he could fondle her further, she moaned. She wanted him inside her, quenching the fires he had lit. But still he waited, teasing her to yet greater passion.

"I want you," she whispered as his hands smoothed over

her body. "I want you." She had never said those words before, nor thought them, but now they came easily to her lips.

"And you will have me, love," he reassured her, as he again felt the soft wetness of her most secret recesses. "We have all night." He kissed her, teaching her to accept his searching tongue and to do the same to him.

When at last he knelt between her thighs and entered her, she cried out with desire. It was as though she were in a whirlwind, spiraling upward, ever higher. She wrapped her legs around his hips, forcing him even deeper inside her as he held her tightly in his arms, kissing her.

Clare thrust against him, giving herself to him totally. Suddenly, it was as though something deep inside her exploded, and she cried out in ecstasy as wave after wave of pleasure swept through her. A languorous warmth gentled her, only to be fanned again into a flame before she could question what had happened. This time, the newly found rapture came faster, easier, almost painfully in the intenseness of its passion. Clare clung to Ryan and buried her face in the curve of his shoulder.

As the bubble inside her rose and burst into ecstasy, Ryan gave a low moan and held her tightly as his own climax was reached. For a while, they seemed to float in each other's arms in a glow of love. Clare felt a great peace, a oneness that seemed to transcend all barriers, merging her soul with his. When she opened her eyes, she saw that he lay watching her, an expression of love on his face. She smiled and lay her hand on his cheek as he smoothed her tumbled hair from her face. Her body still trembled, and she snuggled closer in his arms.

"I never felt anything like that," she said at last, as he held her tenderly.

"Never?"

"No. I had no idea it could be so wonderful."

He kissed her forehead and stroked her silken shoulder. "You should have. A woman like you should be loved, not used. And often."

Clare smiled contentedly and kissed his neck where the pulse beat so quickly and steadily. She had been so fulfilled. With a sigh, she settled more comfortably in the circle of his arms and let sleep drift over her as he gently stroked her hair.

Drowsily, Ryan sensed her breathing slow and deepen and

knew that she slept. With a smile, he kissed the top of her head and wondered again at the odd emotion she had aroused in him. As he, too, drifted into sleep, he put a name to this new feeling. He had fallen in love.

Opening her eyes, Clare was confused at her surroundings. The window was in the wrong place and the bed wasn't familiar. Then she stretched out her hand and felt Ryan's warm body beside her and it all came back to her. Clare felt the memory of the previous night's loving begin to warm and excite her. All she had to do was touch Ryan again, cuddle up to him, wake him. All the magic could be hers again. In the early morning light beyond the curtained window, a car horn honked and brakes squealed. The everyday sounds woke Clare to reality.

Suddenly, she was very aware that she lay naked under the sheet, as did Ryan. She had slept the night with a man she had not even met twenty-four hours before! Hot shame flooded over her. What on earth had possessed her?

Slowly, ever so slowly, Clare slipped out of bed, taking care that there was no sudden movement that might wake Ryan. Quietly, she moved about the room gathering up her clothes from where they lay on the floor in careless abandon along with his. She dressed as quickly as possible, but when she found only one shoe, she panicked. For a moment, all she could think of was what people would say if she hobbled across the parking lot missing a shoe, or worse yet, if she were barefoot. She drew in a deep breath to quell the anxiety. Then she discovered the missing shoe beneath the bed. As she bent to retrieve it, she lost her balance and bumped the bed frame. Ryan moved in his sleep and put out his arm as if to pull her near. Clare froze. When she was sure that he slept on, she moved carefully away from the bed.

Hastily, she grabbed her purse from the top of the dresser and hurried to the door, hoping that Ryan would sleep soundly a few minutes longer. She let herself out and stood motionless in the cool air. Clare Marshall—sneaking out of a stranger's hotel room at dawn! She clenched her teeth.

At an outside phone booth, she called a cab; and, as the sky became more pale than dark, she entered the front door of her house. On tiptoe, she went through it, switching off the unnecessary lights. Had Betty or Eldon noticed they were on

66

all night? Clare went upstairs and ran water for a bath. Now that she was safely at home, she could think more clearly.

The night had been a revealing one. Not only had she discovered that her emotions were only dormant and not dead, but she had let someone love her for the first time in years and she had thoroughly enjoyed every minute of it. As she poured her favorite pink bath oil into the hot water, Clare recalled the way Ryan had touched her and kissed her and taught her to respond. There had been nothing dirty or shameful about it, as she had always been told. Only two people, together, expressing love.

Expressing love? Is that what it had been? Clare thoughtfully turned off the water and took a fluffy washcloth and towel from the linen cabinet. She had never believed in love at first sight, and certainly was not the sort to hop from one bed to another without a qualm. Yet something had happened last night, something she was afraid to name.

Feeling like a conspirator, Clare went into her room and rumpled the bed before she got into the tub. Her new-found emotions were too fragile to expose to Betty's motherly questions, whether expressed verbally or merely through a look, and she wanted to keep her secret to herself.

By midmorning, Clare had stretched several small to medium canvases and was deep in thought. Maybe New Orleans might be more than an ordinary outlet for her. Every year, hundreds, if not thousands, of tourists flocked there, most of them wanting to take home something of the grand city's old-world charm. These were generally people who wanted a painting but could not afford tremendous prices. They usually bought a sketch or water color from a street artist and went away happy.

Seeing no reason why she couldn't create good yet inexpensive paintings, Clare armed herself with a book of photographs of New Orleans and began to sketch several views of the French Quarter, using a weak wash on the canvas. Although she was soon engrossed in her work, Clare found her thoughts drifting back to Ryan again and again. Had he ever paused under that archway, strolled by that fountain? In several pictures, she found herself sketching in a tall man with broad shoulders and a narrow waist. She scrubbed him out of a Mardi Gras parade, only to find him reappearing in an outdoor café scene. Every detail of their conversation stood out in her mind. Each of his movements and his voice inflections were as much a part of her memory as if she had known him for years.

Slowly, Clare put down her brushes. Did every woman feel this way after having made love with a man? Was she merely being ridiculous because she had gone for so long without any physical contact? She longed to confide in Marla, but some part of her rebelled prudishly at just the thought of discussing Ryan, even with her best friend.

"Well, it's over. If he calls me back, I'll be very cool and refuse to see him," she said to herself. "New morality or not, I'm not going to jump in bed with just anyone." Feeling somewhat reassured, she started painting again.

Working on three canvases at once, she began building a scene. A parade with tall, papier-maché masks and brilliant streamers, a rain-misty courtyard with a fountain and a tall wooden sculpture and small tables beneath a red and white striped awning in front of a building with ornate black grillwork. With difficulty, she kept Ryan's form out of all the paintings but one, and left him in that out of desperation.

"After all," she said under her breath as she cleaned her brushes in turpentine, "why should I be upset? He probably thought nothing of it." Yet she knew it wasn't true and that she'd be more disturbed if it were. "Blast!" she muttered, and threw her paint rag onto a chair.

That afternoon she did several watercolors of New Orleans and blocked out three more. The oils were drying nicely and would be ready for more paint by the next day. As she washed in a pale sky, she wondered what it would be like to walk down that street with Ryan. It was a famous location and he was sure to be familiar with it. He had said he lived above one of the tiny, enclosed courtyards. It was possible that she'd painted the very building he lived in.

Unable to fight herself any longer, Clare went to the telephone. When she found the number of the hotel and heard the desk clerk's voice, she felt panicky.

"Room 209, please," she said in a businesslike voice. Surely there was nothing wrong in explaining her sudden disappearance, she reasoned.

"I'm sorry, there's no one occupying that room." The clerk sounded bored, as if he were more than tired of his job.

"There must be. Will you look again? I'm looking for Mr. Ryan Hastings."

"Mr. Hastings *was* in that room, but he checked out this morning."

"Oh!" Clare felt foolish but she had to ask. "Did he leave a forwarding address or say when he'd be back?"

The clerk sighed irritably. "No. No one ever leaves a forwarding address or tells us about plans."

Clare's fingers were numb. She was suddenly aware that she was very lonely.

Chapter Six

The Antoine Thompson Art Gallery was located on one of Tyler's busiest streets about halfway between downtown and the only shopping mall. Clare drove by it twice before she discovered that the entrance to its parking lot was around the corner, almost behind the building. As her Mercedes crunched to a stop on the gravel lot, she carefully examined herself in her rearview mirror. Clare had pulled her dark hair back into a chignon—a style that made her look more businesslike and confident. Her simple black suit was well-cut and obviously expensive, as was the white silk blouse she wore beneath it. The three strands of shimmering gold chains offset the severity, while also lending the perfect accent of elegance to her attire. But Clare was so nervous she smeared her lip gloss and had to reapply it. Was her clothing too straight-laced? she wondered. Did she look more like an accountant than an artist? The butterflies in her stomach fluttered wildly as she got out of the car.

As she entered the store, a tiny brass bell jingled. Clare jumped in spite of herself, when a small, thin man came forward. He had a plastic smile and a tiny mustache that looked as if it had been applied that morning. His hair was slick, black and receding, and made his yellowish skin look even more sallow. When he stood directly in front of Clare, he smiled with his lips pursed. "Good day. May I help you?"

"Yes. I'm looking for Mr. Thompson. Is he in?"

"I'm Mr. Thompson. I'd be glad to be of service to you." He rocked from heel to toe as if he were unable to stand still for more than a moment.

Clare extended her hand, and he shook it using his fingers and thumb but not his palm. "I'm Clare Marshall. I'm looking for an outlet for some of my paintings and I thought perhaps you'd be interested. I have a formal still life and two landscapes in my car. Would you like me to bring them in?"

"Marshall. Marshall," he puckered his brow and became distinctly cooler now that he realized he was not addressing a customer. "Your name isn't familiar at all. What are your credentials?"

"I have a degree in art from Sam Houston State, where I attended college on an art scholarship. Presently, I'm teaching in Kilgore." Her first class would be that afternoon so she felt this was honest enough.

"Teaching? At the college?"

"No, privately."

He looked at her as if she were a not too interesting insect specimen. "I see. What other credentials do you have? What shows have you placed in? What other galleries are you hanging in? How many private exhibitions have you held, and where?"

Clare felt her courage ebbing. "None as yet. Perhaps if I bring in some of my work to show you? I have three canvases in my car."

"I think not, Ms. Marshall," he said, smiling thinly, and only with his lips. "I don't believe you are quite ready for the Antoine Thompson Gallery."

"But you haven't even seen my paintings!" Clare protested. "Everybody has to start somewhere!"

"Perhaps. But not here. Good day, Ms. Marshall," he said as he indicated the door.

Clare had no choice but to leave. She refrained from slamming the door with its tinkling bell as she left.

The next gallery was located in a small shopping center,

sandwiched in between a shoe store and a craft shop. This time, Clare took her paintings inside with her.

"Hello. What can I do for you today?" a plump woman with rosy cheeks asked.

"Are you the owner of the gallery?" Clare asked uncertainly. The woman looked as if she would be more at home in a kitchen baking brownies.

"Yep. I'm Bessie Chaimbridge. What have you got there?"

"I'm Clare Marshall. I'd like to sell some of my work and I thought perhaps Tyler would be a good place to start." Wrong, Clare cringed at her words. All wrong.

"Sure! The more the merrier, I always say." Bessie waved her round arm vaguely. "Just put them up on that wall over there. Wherever there's room. I charge fifteen percent and I'll call you when they sell. Price 'em low so we can keep a good turnover. Better to sell two at thirty dollars than one at forty-five, I always say. She turned and was waddling away. "Just write your name and phone number in that notebook on the desk back there." She chuckled. "I'm so bad at names I'd forget my own if somebody didn't remind me now and again. I have to get back to my glue now. Just make yourself at home."

"Glue?" Clare asked uncertainly.

"I'm gluing sequins on a Christmas tree skirt for my craft shop next door. Come in sometime. I'll give you a discount." With a wave, she bustled through a narrow doorway.

Clare groaned but wrote her name on the school tablet. There weren't many spaces available on the wall, but Clare added her three paintings to the collection and tried not to notice that the oil next to hers looked more than a little dusty. Stepping back, she surveyed the effect. Next to the pink and blue clowns and various still lifes of apples, her pictures looked very professional. She cut a blank recipe card from the desk into thirds, wrote seventy-five dollars on each, and slipped them into the corners of the frames. Better to sell one at seventy-five than to sell two at thirty, she decided.

As she drove the short distance toward home, Clare recalled that Ryan had told her one of the two deep wells being drilled in the area was located just off the Tyler Highway. Clare slowed somewhat and searched the treetops for the derrick. Soon she saw it towering above the tops of the trees. She turned off the highway and onto the newly constructed red dirt road that led back through the tall pines. The road, deeply rutted from much use and rain, was now bone-dry and as hard as concrete. Despite her car's excellent suspension, Clare felt jostled by the time she reached the clearing. As the settling dust changed the pristine whiteness of her car to rose, Clare got out.

The clearing was a hive of activity. Roughnecks were going from the geologist's long silver trailer to the rig, calling unintelligible directions to each other as they walked. On the platform at the base of the rig, two men were tightening pipe lengths together with a large chain and a tool that resembled a giant wrench, while another man worked a series of long levers that controlled the machinery. At precisely the same moment as the two stepped back, the engine growled as the chain twisted the upper pipe into the one already in the hole. Some ninety feet above them on the narrow monkey board, a man pulled another section of pipe from the rack and waited for the pulley to return to the top so that he could attach the new section. The precise coordination of the crew went beyond mere teamwork. Clare found great pleasure in watching the men. But this type of activity was an accustomed sight to Clare, who had grown up near oil fields. What was unusual was the size of the rig. This silver-gray derrick stretched to a height of one hundred seventy-five feet, much taller than any she had seen before. The most impressive thought was that the hole they were drilling would be not hundreds of feet deep, but almost four miles in depth. Clare watched a few moments more, until a man wearing a yellow hard hat and carrying a roll of charts climbed down from the platform and walked toward the trailer. Clare hurried across the rutted ground to intercept him.

"Wait! Could I talk to you a minute?"

The man stopped and looked at her.

Taking this to be a sign of agreement, she said, "I'm Clare Marshall. I own some land northeast of here that has been leased for a deep well. Could you tell me something about them?"

He looked at her silently for a long time. "Yep," he finally admitted. "They's just like any other well, but deeper."

Clare waited for him to continue, but the man was quiet. "Well, are the chances good of hitting oil that deep and around here?"

"Yep." He spit a brown stream of chewing tobacco juice at a clump of bitterweed.

"Are you the geologist?" she asked uncertainly.

"Yep."

Clare prompted, "And you really think there's oil still in this area?"

"Yep. If my company didn't, they'd be damn fools to sink a million dollars on a well." The dialogue seemed to tire him and he chewed his tobacco cud more slowly.

Clare sighed. It was clear that she would learn nothing from this man. "Thank you. I'm sorry I interrupted your work."

"Any time." He nodded his head and briefly tugged on his metal hat brim.

Clare got back into her car and sat for a few minutes watching the drilling. Soon this would be happening on her own land. As she backed up to turn around, Clare thought, This must be the way for me to go. An oil well, a really good producer, would eliminate all my problems. I'd have no trouble paying off the mortgage with even one good well. She made a mental note to call Huntly Oil to ask when they intended to start work.

Clare was able to get home, change clothes and eat a salad for lunch before her students were due to arrive for their first class. She had hurried to be through, and consequently had more than enough time to prepare.

She readjusted an easel for the fourth time, and again ran over her mental notes. She wondered if she could really make it as an artist. Although she was new to the professional end of the business, she had no rosy illusions that it would be easy to break into the art world. On the contrary. For the hundredth time in the last two weeks, she wished she had pursued her higher education in a more practical field, or certainly a more profitable one. But then, maybe they'll find oil, she mused. She pushed her wishful thinking aside for the reality of the moment.

The first student, a square-built, middle-aged woman, arrived in a flourish of smocks, paint rags, a folding canvas stool, a collapsible easel and a hugh fishing-tackle box smudged with all colors of oil paints. "Hello!" she greeted as loudly as if Clare were standing on the far side of a large field.

"Hello. I'm Clare Marshall. I see you've come prepared. Just pick out a spot and set up." Clare motioned toward the portico. "As you can see, you're the first to arrive."

"I'm Hildy Barnett," the woman announced, "and I believe in being early." She laughed and nudged Clare. "I'll probably be the last to leave, too. I believe in getting my money's worth."

"That's nice. You sound very eager to learn."

"Shoot. I was taking art classes before you were born, I'll bet. I just love to paint. It's my hobby. Why don't I take this place here?" Hildy unloaded her paraphernalia with a crash and, as she hummed off key, began to dig out her paints.

"I beg your pardon," a soft voice said behind Clare. "Is this where I come for art classes?"

Clare turned to the newcomer. She was a tall, angular woman in her early twenties, who slumped deprecatingly. Her limp hair was flaxen-colored and her small, close-set eyes were pale blue. The rest of her face seemed to be hiding behind her rather prominent nose. When she had spoken, she had avoided making eye-contact with Clare, and appeared ready to run at any moment.

"Yes, come in," Clare said cheerfully. "I'm Clare Marshall. Just put your things anywhere."

"I'm Sarah May Beinhard." She shifted her material, all of which still bore price tags. "I . . . I don't know where I should be."

"Why not right here?" Clare suggested, patting a chair's back. "Is this all right?"

"Anywhere," Sarah May whispered as she eased herself onto the edge of the chair.

Hildy was humming more loudly and mumbling words to some unrecognizable song; Sarah May glanced at her nervously; Clare wondered if she had indeed taken on more than she could handle. Later, an older woman named Lorena, who moved like a tiny gray bird, and her teenage daughter, Delia, who had a perpetual sniff and looked as though she might be a fullback in her spare time, joined them.

Clare began her class with the simple instruction to sketch onto the canvas one of the prepared still-life subjects at either end of the room. She launched into a detailed dissertation on the values of the underpainting method, in which the entire oil painting is done in black and white or brown and white and glazed later with the desired colors.

Hildy disregarded Clare's instructions as being "new-fangled nonsense," though she said it cheerfully, and sketched off a likeness of the lagoon-shaped pool and the willows beyond the window. Lorena turned out to be Hildy's best friend. They hummed and chatted, and Lorena occasionally even worked on the canvas she had brought. Clare noticed that every time she spoke to any of her students, Sarah May would stop work, lay down her brush and wait patiently for her to finish. Delia had holed up at the farthest end of the room and had erected a barricade of paint box, easel and sketch pads between herself and the others.

By the time the two-hour lesson was over, Clare had learned more than she cared to about Hildy's friends and family, had encouraged Lorena until she felt as if she were nagging and had "helped" Sarah May to the extent of doing most of the work for her. Delia had glared at her canvas and answered in grunts whenever she was spoken to. As they were putting their paintings on the drying racks, Clare was astonished to see Delia's carefully guarded picture. The girl showed real promise. Clare tried to compliment her, but Delia only snorted and stalked away.

When the last student, Hildy, was finally bustled away, Clare poured herself a tall glass of iced tea and sank thankfully down into the softness of her couch. Tentatively, she sipped the cooling liquid and tried to relax her tense muscles.

She was exhausted from trying to draw out the talent from such an incongruous potpourri of students, and she closed her eyes tiredly. But she smiled.

Chapter Seven

Clare walked past the pair of large and improbable stone lions that guarded Marla's front steps and into the cool shade of the porch, which stretched across the right two thirds of the front of the house. The semi-enclosed porch was bordered by a waist-high wall of rough-textured yellow brick. The area between the three brick columns, which rose from the top of the wall to support the roof, was arched so that from a distance the house appeared fronted with two gaping mouths. The heavy shade and concrete floor kept the porch perpetually cool.

"Clare! I'm so glad you could come," Marla exclaimed, as if it were a rare treat to find her best friend on her doorstep. "Come in. Everyone is in the living room. I love your dress. Where did you get it?"

Clare's dress was a white silk shirtwaist with navy piping and a gathered skirt that flowed softly around her silken legs. It wasn't new, but it had a simple style that was classically fashionable. Clare smiled. "This? Oh, Marla, you must have seen it before."

"No, I'm sure I would've remembered."

"I love your hair. Are you going to someone new?"

"Yes. It's not cut too short, is it?"

"No, it's perfect."

Moments later, Clare was following Marla into the living room.

The Thursday Garden Club was in fact a misnomer. In the first place, Thursdays had proved inconvenient for many of the women, so it now met on Wednesday. In the second place, the gardening exchanges consisted solely of each admiring the other's yards and perhaps, on rare occasion, a debate as to whether pansies or vinca would look better against a rock wall or a tree. The actual physical work was done by hired gardeners and most of the club members didn't care, or even wonder, about the value of the various fertilizers or mulches. But to belong to the Thursday Garden Club of Kilgore was an honor not afforded to everyone. Only Kilgore's elite was admitted, and more than one social aspirant longed to join its ranks.

Clare sat down on an ice-blue satin wing chair and took an hors d'oeuvre from the offered tray. There was no need to tell the maid that she preferred cream and sugar in her coffee; the maid had long since memorized all the ladies' preferences. At times, Clare toyed with the idea of learning to drink her coffee black, just to see what ripples it would cause.

"Why, hello, Clare," a husky voice said just as she took a bite of the gooey tidbit.

Clare glanced up and tried to swallow gracefully. "Hello, Regina."

Regina had been an established member of the garden club long before Clare had been invited to join, and was the only sour note in the gathering as far as Clare was concerned. None of the others seemed to care much for Regina, either—she had no close women friends—but no one would dream of having a social gathering without her. She was a caustic woman who had managed to attach herself to the group by aggression and monetary prestige. Regina was the sole heir of the only family in Kilgore who was wealthy before the Great Oil Boom. Whatever Regina wanted, Regina got; one way or another.

The animosity between Clare and Regina had begun with Elliot's introduction of his new bride to his former girlfriend. Regina's jealousy was clearly obvious in the way she had off-handedly dismissed Clare as insignificant, and possessively alluded to her former intimacy with Elliot. Clare had hoped that Regina's attitude would soften with time, but the hope was vain.

"I see you're already out of mourning," Regina commented. "So sensible, really." She sipped coffee from the thin porcelain cup.

"No one wears black forever anymore. That went out with Queen Victoria," Clare said.

Regina raised her pale, thinly arched eyebrows. "I've always liked that dress. It's so logical of you to buy fashions that last." Before Clare could retort, Regina moved away to speak to another woman.

Putting aside her empty cup, Clare went to the large, plate-glass window and gazed out at Marla's backyard. It was large and well-landscaped, and Marla looked after it with impeccable taste. Long double rows of huge sycamore trees dappled the St. Augustine grass with shade, tall hedges of azaleas and gardenias formed backdrops for the roses. Everywhere there were roses. From the tiny, old-fashioned Seven Sisters that formed an archway over a stone bench, to Mirandys and Tropicanas that bloomed profusely beside the gravel walk. Somehow Marla had magically harmonized what might have been a gargantuan jumble of plants into a symphony of color. Clare realized that Marla was probably the only one in the club who was seriously interested in gardening.

Behind her, Clare could hear the usual polite glissando of conversation, now rising, now falling, but always within an acceptable range. She realized she should make an effort to join in, but she had no interest in Katie Hamner's vegetable soup recipe nor the scholastic progress of Dyna Carrington's twins. In fact, Clare had considered not coming at all. She only had because they were to meet at Marla's. This was time Clare badly needed to finish up her tourist paintings. Marla thought Clare was out of her mind to waste her efforts turning out twenty-five-dollar paintings when she was capable of three-hundred-dollar ones. Clare wondered if Marla might be right. There was so much she didn't know!

"I was just chatting with Mabel and she said you've started teaching art! Surely she must be mistaken," Regina said, interrupting Clare's thoughts.

"No, she was absolutely correct," Clare replied. "I'm also

exhibiting some of my paintings here and there," she added vaguely.

"Goodness! Whatever would Elliot have said? A Marshall working?"

"Exhibiting oil paintings is hardly manual labor, Regina, and I enjoy it. It's really no different from Marla's garage sale or your class in flower arrangement."

"How can you say that? My class was only a six-week affair and the proceeds went to charity."

"And my art classes alleviate my boredom." Clare shrugged. "Perhaps I'll donate the money to charity, too. Surely you're not suggesting that I'm doing it for the money?"

Regina looked shocked and placed her long, thin hand on the diamond pendant at her neck. "Why, I never meant to suggest that! I only wondered why you'd tie yourself down like that. Dear me, you can hardly have a moment to call your own, with students traipsing through at all hours of the day and night."

Clare relaxed and smiled. "It's not quite that bleak. All my classes are on Tuesdays and Thursdays, for two hours twice a day. The rest of the time, I can do as I please."

Regina shrugged. Already the subject was tedious to her, as she saw no way of turning it to herself. "It's certainly nothing I would care to do. I'd be bored silly in two weeks."

"It's quite interesting, really. Although Elliot and I had our own interests, the house does seem too quiet at times now that he's gone. I suppose it's always like that when a woman loses a husband." Clare smiled innocently, but took pleasure in the flash of jealousy she saw in Regina's cold blue eyes. So she *had* been having an affair with Elliot!

Marla, as president, called the meeting to order. For the next half hour, they listened to Dyna Carrington's discourse on the comparative value of larkspur versus gladioli. The tedium was ended by a unanimous vote for adjournment.

The other women left, but Clare stayed to help Marla finish off the pot of coffee. They eagerly retreated from the rigid formality of the blue and crystal living room to the den, the true heart of Marla's house. Here, all was wood, tweed and soft leathers. The walls were lined with readable books, the furniture was comfortable rather than classic and the colors were warm and inviting. Clare kicked off her high heels and curled up in an oversized armchair. "I can't stay long. I have some canvases that need help."

Marla glanced at her sideways. "You aren't still on that weirdo scheme to paint color-by-the-number pictures, are you?"

"They aren't *that* bad, for goodness sake. And they may bring in some extra money."

"Or they may ruin your reputation as an artist! Clare, what if someone connects you with them?"

"I hardly think all the leading art critics in America make a habit of studying tourist shops to discover what 'real' artist is moonlighting."

"I guess not. But at least you could change your signature."

"You're getting paranoid," Clare observed conversationally. "Seen any art spies following me lately? They'll be the ones with paintbrushes dribbling from their pockets."

"Have you gone out with anyone interesting lately?" Marla asked to change the subject. "You'll be glad to know that nobody has started linking your name with anyone yet."

"There's no reason why they should," Clare answered. "I'm not dating."

"Not at all? Why not? You're certainly well-liked."

Clare shrugged. "A few men asked me, but I just wasn't interested. I guess the right one hasn't called." She thought of a certain tall man with a southern slowness in his drawl and lips that lit unquenchable fires in her. "Maybe I'll go to the country club dance next month and meet my Prince Charming there. I hear Dyna Carrington's sponsoring it. Are you and Tom going?"

Marla nodded. "That reminds me. I heard Dyna say that the landman from Huntly Oil is back in town. He's interested in leasing some of her property to finish out the drilling block."

"Oh?" Clare carefully put her coffee cup onto the end table and tried to look nonchalant.

"Maybe this means they plan to start drilling soon. Have you heard anything?"

"No. Where did Dyna say he's staying? Maybe I could call and ask him," Clare said with as even a tone as she could muster. She had told Marla nothing about the night she had spent with Ryan, nor was she ready to now, but restraining the excitement she felt at the mention of him was almost impossible.

"She said she called him at the Trail's End, but from what else she said, I gather he's spending most of his time at the Cowboy Lounge."

Clare frowned. The Trail's End Motel was a seedy row of buildings linked by a mottled green composition roof at the edge of town, where it was said the weary truck driver could seek solace and avail himself of a little entertainment to relieve his boredom. The Cowboy Lounge was little more than a rundown beer joint. Why would Ryan pick those places?

"I think I'll give him a call tonight to find out when Huntly Oil plans to drill," Clare said offhandedly. "Well, it's been fun, but I've got to run. Picasso didn't get where he is by sitting around all day, and neither will I."

Marla saw her to the door. "If anyone ever asks me if you painted those tourist pictures, I'll lie."

"I knew I could count on you," Clare said with a grin. "See you tomorrow."

Ryan was in town and he hadn't called! Clare remembered every moment of the last two days that she had been away from the telephone. Of course! That was it. He'd called and she'd been gone. Often Betty forgot to write down who had called, or absentmindedly put the notes in a place where they showed up days later.

Clare smiled happily as she got into her car. Why bother with a phone call when she already knew where to find him?

The Cowboy Lounge was a long, dark cedar building at the edge of town on the old Longview highway, not far from the Trail's End Motel. Four red wagon wheels chained to a rustic hitching post adorned the entrance, while a green and red covered wagon perched on the roof. A nasal, melancholy tune blared out at the parking lot from speakers hidden beneath the eaves. A nostalgic wave briefly washed over her as she recalled her high school days and the twang of the jukebox sounds that had reverberated across the Dairy Queen parking lot.

Clare had always liked country-western music—a fact Elliot would have teased her about unmercifully had he known—but this was pure backwoods and unmistakably amateurish. Her face distorted at the cacophony.

Resolutely, she shouldered open the screen door and the wooden one behind it. Inside, the music was muffled by the whir of the giant fan set in the upper wall on one end of the room. The floor was slippery with sawdust and the tables were cheap, round wooden ones with bentwood legs. Only a few of the chairs matched. Elaborate beer advertisement signs hawking Budweiser, Pearl and Lone Star were the only adornment these walls had ever seen. Clare went uncertainly to the bar and asked the bartender if Ryan Hastings were there.

"What?" he bellowed above the noise of the fan and the whine of the music.

"Hastings!" she yelled back. "Ryan Hastings! The man from Huntly Oil!"

"Huntly! Yeah!" the bartender blasted. "That's him over yonder!" He nodded his head toward the rear corner.

Clare threaded her way back. The room was so dim she hadn't noticed the man when she entered. But as she drew nearer, she realized this man wasn't Ryan.

He was in his sixties, gray-haired and sickly looking, with dark liver spots on his hands and cheeks. "Yeah?" he said, looking at her out of his rheumy blue eyes. "You looking for me?"

"No," Clare said in confusion. "I'm looking for Ryan Hastings, the landman from Huntly Oil."

"Yep. Huntly Oil. That's me." He shoved the other chair out with his foot. "Have a seat."

Mercifully, the music was not as loud on this end of the room, but Clare wondered if she had heard correctly. *"You're* the landman? Where's Mr. Hastings?"

"He ain't no landman, he's our head geologist. He come out here and leased a bit of land, but he didn't get enough for a block. I'm trying to tie up the rest of it." He noisily sucked some beer from the can into his mouth and wiped his chin on the back of his hand. "I ain't interested in your land, though, unless it borders on the Marshall acres."

"My land *is* the Marshall land," Clare said haughtily, trying to ignore the grime and unidentifiable stains on the table.

"Decided to lease some more of it? I ain't going to give you the price Mr. Hastings did. I can tell you that right off."

"No. I haven't decided to lease more land. I want to know when you plan to start the well."

He looked away and grinned as if she had said something funny. "How should I know?"

"Well, *you're* the landman! You work for Huntly Oil!"

"Yeah, but I ain't Mr. Huntly. The Old Man don't go around telling me things like that."

"I understand. But it's important to me to get a well started as soon as possible."

He glanced derisively at her expensive clothes and snorted. "Look, lady, Huntly Oil is a small company. We can't afford to throw away a million dollars on one well like Exxon or Gulf can."

"Then why did you lease it?"

"There's two deep wells going in south of here. If they strike oil, maybe we'll drill then."

"But that could take months! Even years!"

He shrugged. "That's the breaks of the game. These ain't the old wildcat days, when anybody with a rig could get rich on oil. Today it takes money. A lot of it. And somebody who knows what's what."

The door slammed open and three young men came in. Clad in faded, tight jeans and cotton shirts, they tossed their feather-trimmed stetsons onto the bar and slouched on the stools as if they were run by a common mind. The noise level rose sharply. Clare glanced at them nervously.

"Thank you for the information," she said as she edged away from the table and toward the door.

He nodded and raised the beer can to his lips.

Clare walked to the door amid catcalls and lewd suggestions from the three young psuedo-cowboys, but no one tried to stop her. When she got outside, she walked as quickly as possible to her car. Never had she noticed that air smelled so fresh. As she drove home she marveled at the disappointment of not having seen Ryan. But the conversation had planted the seed of an idea in her mind. The gamble was great—much more daring than she had ever considered before—but if it paid off, she'd never have to worry about money again.

Chapter Eight

Clare loaded all her paintings into her Mercedes, taking care to cushion each with a layer of quilting. There were half a dozen oils of large dimensions and free-flowing designs of the sort galleries would consider. The other fifteen were smaller canvases in ready-made frames supplied by a local craft supply house. These were well done, but the subject matter was more marketable than artful, the themes obvious rather than illusory. The more dignified paintings were signed "C. Marshall," the others simply "Clare."

Since Clare had never gone on a trip alone, the drive to New Orleans was a bit of an adventure for her. She left long before sunup, and by the time it was light enough to see, the tall East Texas pines had given way to oak and sweet gum forests. The further southeast Clare went across Louisiana, the more magnolias she noticed. Somewhere beyond Alexandria but before Baton Rouge, she first saw the cypress trees with their bony knees jutting out of the water. Then appeared the telltale sign of the Deep South—Spanish moss, dripping in great gray beards from the hardwood trees.

Clare found a motel on the outskirts of the city, still in sight of Lake Pontchartrain. The Seven Fountains was not the

Fontainebleau, to be sure, but it appeared clean, safe and, above all, inexpensive. Feeling awkward, she went into the lobby and asked for a room. The rates were even better than she had hoped, and soon she had paid for the night in advance, and had her key.

The room was on the ground floor in the corner behind the swimming pool. The pool had been drained for repairs, but that didn't matter since the view of it from Clare's room was totally obstructed by a prickly shrub that had gone berserk in its growth pattern. Inside Clare found the room spacious and clean. The bedspread was neatly but obviously mended, the bathroom sink was chipped, the glasses were disposable plastic and the television looked as if it might or might not work.

It was all Clare needed.

Carefully, she bathed, put on new makeup and dressed. She topped her red slacks with a gaily printed silk blouse and a red vest that matched the slacks. Her heels were white with tiny straps, and her handbag had been bought especially to carry with them. A sliver of gold chain gleamed at her neck and another at her right wrist. She placed tiny gold earrings in her ears before twisting her heavy, chestnut-colored hair into a chignon across the nape of her neck. Clare looked in the mirror and smiled. She looked elegant enough to impress any gallery owner, yet flamboyant enough to be unmistakable as an artist.

The bath had refreshed her somewhat, and little of the stiff achiness from the long drive remained. Knowing that it was getting late, she tore the page from the phone book that listed the New Orleans art galleries.

The first two Clare tried promptly turned her away. With the third, she adopted a different attitude.

"Hello," she said frostily to the woman who identified herself as the owner. "I'm Clare Marshall. As you may have read, I have decided to increase my area of shows to include New Orleans. Naturally, I have heard," she glanced at the name on the shop's window, "that the Newman Gallery is the best in the city. I also understand you charge a twenty percent commission, is that correct?" Clare looked directly and confidently into the woman's eyes.

"Well, yes, but. . . ."

"Very well. You do have someone here who will help me

unload my paintings, don't you?" Clare gazed around the room as if she were choosing her wall space.

"Certainly, but I don't believe . . . that is, your name isn't entirely familiar to me."

Clare looked at her incredulously. "No? How can that be? Have you been to the Dallas Fine Arts Museum recently? Or to the Rice Museum in Houston during the first week of March this past spring?"

"No," the woman admitted.

Clare smiled brilliantly. "That's it, of course. I imagine you're kept quite busy here. I've heard nothing but the most glowing reports of your establishment. And from what I see, it's all true," she said magnanimously.

The woman beamed at the compliment. "Thank you, Miss Marshall." She turned to a silver bell on her desk and tapped it. "My assistant will be right out. Would you care for coffee?" She gestured to an alcove where a coffee urn sat.

"No, thank you, I find it inhibits my creative flow."

A young man emerged from the back room and Clare went with him to her car.

"Careful now," she said, keeping the tourist pictures covered beneath the quilt. "Only these top three go in. Everything else is on its way to a show in Birmingham." She smiled conspiratorily at the gallery owner, who had joined them. "I suppose it's an eccentricity on my part, but I always insist on carrying out my canvases myself. One never knows how they will arrive otherwise."

"True," the woman murmured. "So true."

Clare helped the woman hang the canvases to their best possible advantage, then smiled in a businesslike way. "It's so good to deal with a connoisseur like yourself. I expect these canvases will bring, oh, say, five hundred? I really can't let them go for under four-fifty, you know. Here is my address and the unlisted phone number of my studio. I can be reached there most of the time. Do let me know when you need some more paintings."

"Of course. I'll stay in close touch."

As Clare got back into the Mercedes, she grinned triumphantly. "So *that's* how Regina does it!" she chortled.

At the next gallery, she introduced herself, then admitted that, even though she was being exhibited in the Newman Gallery, she felt the need to expand in the area. The gallery owner, who could not mask his eagerness to share an artist with his rival, jumped at the chance to hang her pictures. Clare's expensive clothes and car, as well as her imperial manner, did much to convince him that he could hardly afford to let her get away.

After driving randomly through several nice neighborhoods, Clare found a park and pulled up under the shade of one of the massive oaks. She moved the small styrofoam ice chest and the sack of groceries from the trunk to the seat beside her and began to eat the cheese and crackers she had brought from home. As she leaned her head back on the seat and sipped her Coke, she watched some squirrels frolicking in the tree above her head. Her victories had renewed her energy, and she felt surprisingly rested. It felt good to be on a winning streak.

She peered into the sack. There was a can of tuna fish, some bread and a can opener. "Not a fancy supper," she told herself, "but filling and cheap." There was also a jar of instant coffee for her breakfast and a container of honey to put on the remaining bread. She would be home the next day in time for a late dinner.

"I've heard all artists start off starving in a garret," she comforted herself. "I'm lucky my garret is attached to a twenty-room mansion." But she found the tuna was tasteless in her mouth. She didn't want to spend the rest of her life scrimping and scraping just to get by. The memories of the want and need of her childhood swept over her, leaving the pain of those days weighing heavily on her sensibilities. There was no guarantee she'd make it as an artist—most who tried didn't—and she certainly couldn't survive very well on the yearly lease money. It was only a short lease, anyway.

Her new idea surfaced again, and again she found herself struggling with mixed emotions. The risk would be very high; she could lose everything. But she could secure her future and rid herself of the gripping fear that she might be forced to return to the poverty she'd known most of her life. But, first things first, she reminded herself as she rose to leave.

She found the Vieux Carré almost by accident, and instantly felt as if she had been hurtled back a hundred years in time. The streets were little more than narrow alleys sandwiched between two and three-story buildings of elaborately ornate designs. Black wrought iron, which seemed too heavy for the ancient buildings to support, formed fantastic columns, balcony railings and window grillwork. White painted iron that must have been equally heavy interlocked like massive lace, one story to the next. Loud blues music blared out of one of the corner saloons. The photographs of the establishment's nude dancers were prominently displayed on both sides of the entrance.

And everywhere there were people.

Clare had trouble driving down the narrow street because of all the people who crossed and recrossed the street in front of her and eddied behind the car in her wake. At last, she finally found a parking space—at the side of a small park. In the center of the beautifully landscaped green, and above the yellow flowering candelabras, a dark equestrian statue of General Jackson reared proudly. Across the street at the far side, the enormous edifice of a Catholic church loomed in gothic splendor.

Clare removed the pins and shook her hair loose onto her shoulders. Ignoring the curious stares of passersby, she slipped off her vest, pulled out her shirt tail and kicked off her heels. As she pushed her feet into low-heeled sandals, Clare tissued off her lip gloss. She unfastened her gold jewelry and put it into the zipper pocket of her purse. Then she took out a pair of exotic earrings, three bangle bracelets and a neck chain on which hung a Pisces zodiac pendant. She dropped her white leather purse into a woven shoulder bag. With as many of her paintings as she could carry, Clare went into the art shop that seemed to be the most crowded.

"Hi," she said cheerfully, and in a voice calculated to catch the attention of the nearest tourist. "I'm Clare. I'd like to show you some of my work, if you're the owner of this place."

The young man grinned at her from behind the counter. "Hi. I'm Doug. I'm not the owner, but I'm the manager." He noticed the tourists beginning to peer surreptitiously at her pictures. "What have you got there?"

He agreed to hang all eight when he saw a blousy woman dickering with her husband to possess one. Clare bargained with the manager until he agreed on a fifteen percent commission on the pictures, which ranged in price from twenty to thirty dollars, and a monthly statement, and then shook hands with him.

"Here's my name and address," she said, writing it on a

piece of paper. "I'd be much obliged to you if you let me know when you're almost sold out so I can get more to you."

"Sure enough, Clare," he said jovially, as if he'd known her half his life.

The next shop was not so receptive, nor was the next, but by four o'clock Clare had placed all her paintings before the public and had returned to her car, tired but happy.

For a few minutes, Clare allowed herself the luxury of merely sitting still, her eyes closed, her head tilted back on the glove-leather upholstery. Then she began to coil her hair back into a bun as she stepped back into her high heels.

Chapter Nine

At the nearest pay phone, Clare dialed the number of Huntly Oil Company and, with a flutter of nerves, asked for Ryan Hastings.

"Mr. Hastings has gone for the day," the secretary replied. "May I leave a message for him to call you on Monday?"

"No," Clare said, trying to hide the disappointment in her voice. "I won't be in town that long. It's very important for me to reach him. I have business to discuss with him. Do you have another number I might call?"

"Yes," the woman said in surprisingly fast response. "His home telephone is 555-8966. But he's probably not there. You might check the Blue Crystal Lounge in the Quarter."

"Oh. Perhaps you misunderstood me. I'm looking for *Ryan* Hastings," Clare said dubiously. The Blue Crystal Lounge sounded too much like the hangout of the Huntly landman she had encountered in Kilgore.

"Yes, ma'am, that's right. His father has retired, and Ryan is—I mean, Mr. Ryan Hastings is the only Hastings in the company." Her voice had faltered with the breach in formality and Clare could hear another line ringing in the background.

"Thank you. You've been very helpful."

Both Ryan and his father had worked for the same oil company? Interesting, Clare thought, as she dialed his home number.

After the fifteenth ring, she hung up. Obviously, the secretary knew a good bit about Ryan. She even had his home number on the tip of her tongue. Clare vanquished the blush of jealousy and sent it back to wherever it had come from, almost without conscious thought. She did, however, retain a vaguely uneasy feeling. Clare thumbed through the Yellow Pages looking under lounges, bars and finally taverns, before she found the Blue Crystal. But she decided not to call. The idea of having him paged in a bar seemed wrong. It might look too much as though she was on a manhunt. Instead, she jotted down the lounge's address.

The Blue Crystal sat in the middle of the eight hundred block of Royale. Clare walked by it twice before she saw its small, weather-beaten sign. Carefully avoiding a sleeping wino who lay propped against the wall, Clare pushed open the faded turquoise door and stepped hesitantly into the dim interior.

Somewhere in the dark recesses someone was playing the blues on a trumpet, but from the babble of the crowd she assumed nobody was listening. She squinted through the haze of tobacco smoke and tried to get her eyes to adjust to the dimness after the sunlight outside.

To her left, she saw a bar backed by a mirror, glasses and a large variety of liquor bottles. All around the room were tables and chairs, some of them occupied by rather rough-looking men. On a small stage in the back corner, an old black man made his trumpet wail to the tune of his soul. He looked as if he'd grown old in that same spot, playing that same tune. Mingled in with the smell of alcohol and cigarettes was the odor of greasy hamburgers.

Clare was uncomfortably aware of the fact that she was the only woman in the place.

"Well, now," a burly man rumbled as he staggered toward her. *"Une petit bessé, bébé?"* He screwed his mouth into a hideous pucker.

"What . . . did you say?" Clare asked as she took one step back.

"Just a little kiss, 'ey?" he repeated as he grabbed her arm and thrust his sweaty, smelly face into hers.

"Let go of me!" she snapped, twisting around but not loose. Clare thrust the point of her elbow as hard as she could beneath his ribcage. With a whoosh of air, the surprised man let go and doubled over. Mistaking this move for an attack, Clare clenched her fist and hit him in the nose with all her strength. The man fell to the floor and, with an outraged bellow, leaped to his feet, hands ready to grasp her. But to her amazement, he cowered and backed away. Mumbling obscenities in an odd mixture of ungrammatical Cajun French and English, he turned and left the bar, holding a dirty handkerchief to his bloodied nose.

"It seems rather useless to offer you any assistance," an amused voice said just behind her. "But I'm not sure you can take on the entire bar singlehandedly."

Clare whirled around, expecting another attacker, her purse poised as a weapon, but found herself staring up into the laughing eyes that had haunted her dreams for weeks.

"Ryan," she said more softly than she had intended.

"Clare?" he asked incredulously. "What in the world are you doing here?" He realized suddenly they were the center of attention in the bar. "Come out to the courtyard where we can talk." Protectively, he guided her across the dusky room.

Clare's heart pounded as he tried to slip his arm about her waist. She forced herself to walk briskly ahead of him. She had far too much at stake to be swept off her feet. "I called your office and your secretary told me I could find you here. I hope you don't mind."

"Not at all. I'm glad you came. I often come down here in the evening for a hamburger rather than cook for myself."

Clare glanced doubtfully at the dingy bar as she stepped out into the sunshine, which was softly filtered through a chinaberry tree. "Oh. You eat here?"

He laughed. "It's not all that bad. And it's handy. I live just up those stairs over there."

"Oh."

A balmy breeze rustled through the dark green umbrella of leaves above her and she heard the music of the small white fountain. The sultry scent of flowers unfamiliar to her hung heavily in the air.

"This courtyard is amazing," she said to cover the excitement she felt whenever he looked at her. "One would never know it's here from the street. I can't even hear the traffic."

"The walls are very thick," he said. "I've missed you."

Clare's eyes met his and she felt herself melting into their green-gold depths. "I tried to call you the next day, but you were gone. I wanted to try to explain why I left the way I did."

"Why did you?"

"I had never . . . That is, Elliot . . . " She drew a deep breath and plunged on. "I had never made love before with anyone other than my husband, and not even with him for a long, long time. I woke up and was afraid you'd think badly of me, so I slipped out."

"Out of sight, out of mind?" he suggested.

"Yes, something like that. But I felt bad about it later, and I tried to call and explain. By then you had checked out."

He nodded and sat down next to her on a bench beside the fountain. "It didn't exactly work that way. I didn't stop thinking about you. When I woke up and found you were gone, I worried at first, then decided you'd had second thoughts about me. That's why I didn't phone before I left town."

Clare relaxed somewhat. "I feel so silly. You must think I'm really dumb not to know how to do that casually."

"No, I find it very refreshing." His eyes caressed her face as he took her hand and held it firmly. "Did you come all the way to New Orleans to explain this, or do you have other reasons for being here?"

Clare smiled. "I'm here for two reasons. This afternoon I had to take care of some business with some art galleries that are showing a few of my oils. My other reason is to offer you a proposition."

Ryan lifted his eyebrows and grinned.

She hurried on. "Huntly Oil is taking too long to start operations. I want to get a well underway on my unleased land. Therefore, I've decided that I want to invest two hundred fifty thousand dollars of my own money, and I want you to wildcat it for me—for a percentage of the well." Clare's voice was strained.

Ryan studied her in surprise. "Are you serious?"

"Of course," she answered abruptly. "I'll need two or three days to liquidate some assets, but I assume that will be no problem for you." She had calculated that it would take that long to get a second mortgage on the Marshall house and borrow the rest, with the mineral rights for the farm as collateral. Under no circumstances did she intend to tell Ryan how hard up she was for money. She could never explain the gnawing fear of poverty she felt. No one would understand, and the embarrassment of trying to explain would make it all worse. Besides, as the principle backer, she had to appear very secure financially to coax him into the deal. He just had to agree; everything had to work. Her stomach churned violently.

Ryan whistled softly and got to his feet. Two hundred fifty thousand would go a long way toward getting a well started. And he could realize his dream twofold. Not only could he prove his theory right, but could wildcat the well himself. Yet the way Clare's personality seemed to change the minute she started talking business concerned him. She sounded so cold and overbearing. He gazed into the rippling water of the fountain as he thought.

He recalled the house Clare lived in. It was a mansion, really. But as the heir of several generations of wealthy ancestors, he could easily read people's finances—Clare's money was new money. Despite her aristocratic bearing, her family had clearly not been accustomed to wealth for long. Was it possible that she was one of those grasping people he saw occasionally who never had enough wealth to satisfy them? He hoped not.

"Huntly will drill eventually," he said. "What's your hurry?" A flicker of what—fear?—lit her gray eyes, then disappeared.

"I just don't want to wait. If oil is there, I want it to be produced. As soon as possible. Besides, you and I both know that they may never even start to drill. Most oil leases are never even touched by the company."

Ryan tried to read her expression but failed. She looked perfectly composed now, but he couldn't ignore the brief moment of desperation he had seen. It had been the same when she had signed the oil lease.

"Do you have the money?" he asked bluntly.

"Not on me," she replied with a startled expression. "As I said, it will take me a couple of days to have it in hand. But I assure you, I'll have no trouble producing it."

Ryan stroked his chin and sighed. She sounded quite certain, and he had no reason to disbelieve her. She probably played with a quarter of million dollars the way other people did with a hundred. He'd seen that type before, unfortunately.

"An oil well isn't a toy," he said dryly. "There may not be anything at all down there."

"I realize that. I know it's a gamble, but I want to do it."

"You don't even know if I know what I'm talking about."

She lifted her chin and smiled confidently. "You're Huntly Oil's head geologist. You must know what you're doing."

He glanced at her questioningly. "I didn't tell you that. But it's true."

"Why did you tell me you were a landman?" Clare asked, as the smile faded from her lips.

"It's not how it seems. I had a reason, and a good one. You see, Huntly Oil is in direct competition with the company drilling the two deep wells near you, and I didn't want them to know that Huntly's head geologist was snooping around leasing land."

"Then your company must believe strongly that there's oil to be had, or they wouldn't be so secretive," Clare said hopefully.

"I never said my company was behind me fully. It's my theory that there's oil under your property. But my view is in the minority. Are you still convinced you want to drill?"

"Yes," Clare said simply, as she watched Ryan with renewed confidence.

"Okay. Do you have any other investors in mind? That's not nearly enough money for the whole well. It's enough for a good bit of the equipment and to get the well spudded in, but we'll need much more."

"No, I thought perhaps you might know of someone." She smiled disarmingly. "I've never drilled a well before."

"You're asking a lot. You're risking a great deal of money on the chance that my findings will be correct, or even that I'm in a position to know what I'm talking about."

Clare felt a keen disappointment. "Then you won't do it? I have to find someone else?"

Ryan scowled. "I didn't say that. No, I'll do it. I just want you to realize it's not a sure thing."

Momentary panic chilled Clare, but she pushed it aside. "I know what I'm doing, Ryan. I have confidence in you." She stood up and held out her hand. "Then we have a deal?"

He hesitated only a minute. Her brief panic had not gone by him unnoticed. "Yes," he said slowly, taking her hand, "we have a deal."

Clare relaxed imperceptibly. "Good. I know you'll be able to find oil. Do you have anyone in mind for the other backers?"

"I know a couple of people that might be interested," he said thoughtfully. "If you'll be in town for a few days, we can talk to them together."

"Yes, I can stay over. I don't have any commitments until Tuesday afternoon." She felt a moment of relief that her art classes met Tuesday and Thursday, rather than earlier in the week.

"Great," he grinned. "Now let's go out and celebrate. It won't take me but a few minutes to change, and I'll buy you the biggest steak in town."

She was willing to put aside her planned supper of a tuna sandwich. "I'd love it. I'd like to freshen up, too. Why don't I meet you someplace?"

"Better than that, why don't I come by and pick you up. Where are you staying?"

"What?"

"Your hotel. Don't you have a room yet?"

"Oh, of course. I'm at the Fontainebleau," she said, naming the first prestigious hotel she thought of. "But I don't want you to go to all that trouble. I can meet you."

"Nonsense. I know my way around town, and the Fontainebleau isn't that far from here. I'll pick you up at," he glanced at his watch, "say, eight o'clock? No arguments now, or you'll have to settle for a hamburger from the Blue Crystal."

"You know how to get around my objections, all right," she said with a grimace. "I'll meet you in the lobby at eight."

Clare drove as quickly as possible to the Seven Fountains. All the way across town, she worried as to whether or not she could get away with her deception, yet knew she had to try. Ryan would never understand why the wealthy Clare Marshall might choose to stay in such a place. And if he thought she *had* to stay there, he'd certainly back out of their business agreement.

She bathed as fast as possible and brushed her hair until it gleamed, then fastened it back neatly. Fortunately, she had brought clothes suitable for going out, as she had hoped Ryan would suggest that. With one eye on her travel clock, Clare put in a call to Betty to tell her she wouldn't be home the next day.

After a brief hesitation, Clare decided to leave behind the jacket of her cherry-red dress. With it, the dress was far more proper and would be perfect for a business dinner with the prospective backers; without the jacket, the low cowl neckline, which dipped daringly in front and plunged provocatively in the back almost to her waist, could be seen. The dress was a marvel of engineering design that looked as if it were made of gossamer dreams but fit her body perfectly. The full skirt gathered at her small waist and flowed about her knees in a lightweight fabric that swirled with her movements. She slipped on red evening sandals that matched the dress perfectly. Fastening her gold chains at her neck and wrist, she was ready to go.

She put on lipstick at the first stop light and perfume at the next. The clock on the bank sign read seven forty-five, and since Clare never wore a wristwatch, this was her first indication of how close she had cut the time.

Whipping into the Fontainebleau parking lot, Clare jumped out of her car and ran to the lobby's side door. It was ten minutes after eight.

Breathlessly, she hurried around a potted palm in time to intercept Ryan, who was on his way to the desk, presumably to ask for her room number.

"I'm sorry I'm late, she said, trying to breathe normally. "Have you been here long?"

"No, not long. You look a little flushed. Did I rush you?"

"No, no. Not at all. I'm just excited over having reached our agreement. Are you ready to go?" The desk clerk was watching her suspiciously and Clare wanted no questions to be asked.

"Yes, I'm parked out back."

Ryan escorted her to the lot, where he opened the door of

his Trans-Am for her to get in. Fortunately, her Mercedes wasn't parked nearby.

"I thought the French Quarter was the other way," Clare said, as Ryan turned his car in the opposite direction.

"It is. I want to take you to a very special place for dinner. Then, if you want to, we can go to the Quarter and hear some jazz."

Ryan turned down St. Charles Avenue and stopped in front of the crimson-covered walkway of the Pontchartrain Hotel. A doorman instantly appeared to help Clare onto the sidewalk, then whisked away the car. Inside the front door, she caught her breath in awe. The entrance was lined with white marble columns, topiary trees and an ornately gilded mirror. Oriental rugs silenced their footsteps, and above their heads the vaulted ceiling was brilliantly illumined by crystal chandeliers.

Ryan grinned at her apparent awe. "Do you like it?"

"It's fabulous!" she exclaimed. "I never expected to come here." She was quickly reevaluating Ryan's financial situation. No matter how well Huntly Oil geologists were paid, this must be well beyond his income. Yet he fit easily into it. Much more so than she did.

At the door of the Caribbean Room, they were met by the maître d'hotel, who escorted them to a table set with elegant china and candles in hurricane glasses. She sat on the striped satin upholstered chair and looked around. A gold medallion design in the red carpet gave warmth to the dark wood in the room, and the huge mirrors which hung between groupings of fine prints on the tan leather walls added additional dimension to the spacious surroundings. Discreet lighting created an ambiance, romantic in the extreme.

Clare blushed to see that Ryan was regarding her with amusement, and she tried to look nonchalant. "Do you come here often?"

"No. Only when I particularly want to impress someone."

"It's quite nice," she said in her best Regina-like tone.

He laughed aloud. "I'm glad you approve."

"I didn't mean to sound so snobbish. We don't have anything even close to this in Kilgore and, frankly, I'm intimidated." As Clare spoke, she watched Ryan gaze deeply into her soul. There was a puzzled expression in his hazel eyes.

"Since this is a time of honesty, I have to admit I've been here exactly one other time—when my father retired from Huntly Oil."

Clare relaxed and sipped her water. "I feel better now. Maybe we can be awed together."

The service was impeccable and the food was delicious. By the time they'd finished their cherries jubilee, Clare decided to behave naturally, and both she and Ryan were thoroughly enjoying themselves.

"Tell me," Clare prompted as they were leaving, "was your father as impres sed as I was?"

"Not entirely. He had been here before—often, in fact. My mother's father lived here several years before I was born, and they came to visit him at least once a week."

"Here? Your grandfather lived *here?*" Her jaw had dropped open and she shut it hastily. "Did he work for Huntly Oil, too?"

"Not exactly. He owned it."

Before Clare's mask of gentility could settle back in place, Ryan drove her to the Quarter. Leaving the car in his own garage, they walked the few blocks to a corner bar where strains of heart-rending music were being coaxed from a battered trumpet and a clarinet. The smoke was so thick that Clare felt closed in and almost blinded, but the music was a siren's song which seemed to draw them through the crowd to a small table. The waiter, a rather effeminate young man with masses of curly blond hair, took their orders for drinks and faded away into the throng.

A singer wearing a slinky gold lamé evening gown stepped up onto the small stage to join the musicians, and began belting out the lyrics of a haunting jazz number.

"Are you having a good time?" Ryan asked under the music as he took her hand.

"Yes, I'm so glad I'm here with you."

He smiled and lifted her palm to his lips, never taking his eyes from hers. "I'm glad, too."

His kiss made her tingle, and she nervously pulled her hand away. "I like the singer. She's very good."

"*He's* very good," Ryan corrected.

"What?" Clare said incredulously.

"His name is Billy Chandell. He lives across the street from

100

me, in that apartment house with the green balcony." He was watching her with amusement.

"You're kidding!"

"Not at all. Billy's a female impersonator. One of the best. He also plays a mean game of tennis. I'll introduce you one of these days."

Astounded, Clare gazed at length at the lovely singer, and wondered if Ryan was joking. When Billy's act was finished, "she" glanced at Ryan and waved, bowed again and then made a graceful exit to appreciative applause.

As the musicians picked up the beat for the next entertainer, Ryan said, "Are you ready to go somewhere else? Billy is their best act."

Clare nodded.

As they walked down the side street, the music became fainter and fainter until, at last, it melted into the balmy night air. Several rough-looking men, all too reminiscent of the one who had accosted her earlier, passed them. Clare was thankful for Ryan's muscular body by her side. She put her hand trustingly in his and matched her stride to his own.

On the patio at Pat O'Brian's, Clare and Ryan each had a hurricane in one of the famed glasses. The foliage about them was lush and abundant, the candlelight warm and caressing. And the music from the piano bar inside was soft and melodious. Ryan held her hands firmly, but lovingly, on the tabletop, while he watched her every movement.

"I was afraid I'd never see you again," he said.

"I never left town," she replied, trying to calm her racing emotions. "All you had to do was look for me."

"Believe it or not, I did intend to do just that. I had planned to take a few days off in a couple of weeks to come to Kilgore and find you."

Clare didn't answer, but her hand trembled.

"Ever since I left that day, I've regretted not calling you. I could hardly believe my eyes when you came into the Blue Crystal this afternoon."

"It was important for me to find you," she murmured. "I needed someone to drill a well for me."

"And that's the only reason?" he asked in disappointment.

"No," she replied softly, "That's the reason I could admit. Actually, I wanted to be with you again."

He smiled. "And here you are. Tell me, Clare, is there anyone in Kilgore waiting for you? A man, I mean?"

"No. No one is waiting for me." For some reason, she had turned down all offers of dates. Nobody but Ryan interested her.

"Good." He lifted her hand to his lips. "Did you know that in the candlelight your skin is golden and your hair and eyes are black as jet? And did you also know that you blush beautifully?"

"That's something I'm trying to outgrow."

"I hope you don't. I find it intriguing. But then, I find all of you intriguing."

Clare blushed even more. "Ryan, I really don't go tumbling into bed like that. I don't know what I was thinking of."

"I do," he said, stroking her hand.

"Ryan," she said hesitantly, "I'm not going to go to bed with you tonight."

"Why not?" he asked in surprise.

"Because I don't want to feel that our business deal was based on that."

"Are you always so blatantly honest?"

"Usually. It's a great failing of mine."

Ryan sighed. "All right. Whatever you say. But I want you to know I didn't have your body in mind when I agreed to wildcat your oil well. I'm a better business man than that. And we aren't talking business now."

"No, Ryan," she said firmly.

"All right, how about some coffee and doughnuts to top off the evening instead?" he said with one of his lightning swift subject changes. "By the way, you'll notice I'm giving up reluctantly, but with respect." He grinned at her until she smiled back.

"The coffee sounds great, but I'm not sure about doughnuts after all that dinner and two drinks."

"By the time we get there, you'll change your mind. There's something about this place that makes your very soul whine for doughnuts. You'll see."

The doughnut shop was all Ryan promised, and more. Afterward, they walked for a short while, enjoying the warm summer breeze, before Ryan took her back to her hotel. As Ryan escorted her into the lobby of the Fontainebleau, Clare laughed. "I'm stuffed! That last cup of coffee was too much."

"That's all those doughnuts you packed away," he teased. "See? Didn't I tell you? You can't eat just one."

"That sounds like a commercial for an antacid. Don't remind me. I may never have room to eat again."

"You have to. I'm taking you out for breakfast tomorrow morning. You can run a few laps around the pool in the meantime."

She groaned. "You're kidding. Right?"

"Nope. What time do you get up? I'll be over to pick you up."

She studied his face carefully. "Do you really want to see me tomorrow?"

"Of course. I'm trying to sweep you off your feet." Seriously, he added, "I don't want to lose you again." Before she could stop him, he brushed her lips lightly with his. "May I take you to your room?" he asked gently.

"No," she whispered. "Not tonight."

He punched the button on the elevator for her. "I'll pick you up at nine in the morning. Is that too early?"

"No, that's fine." Then, realizing what she was saying, she stammered, "I mean, I'll come to your place at nine. Really, I'd prefer it that way."

He shrugged. "All right. Park in the space beside my car. Do you remember the street? Good. Come into the courtyard through the gate beside the garage, and go up the stairs I showed you."

The elevator door rolled open and Clare stepped inside. Beyond the desk, the clerk was starting to frown.

"Goodnight, Ryan," she said quickly as the doors shut.

Clare punched the button to the second floor. When it arrived, she got out, stood in the foyer until the elevator went away, then pressed the down button.

Ignoring the desk clerk, Clare crossed the lobby and went out into the parking lot. Ryan's car was gone. As she drove back to the Seven Fountains Motel, Clare hummed a tune.

Chapter Ten

Breakfast was at Brennan's. As Clare ate eggs Benedict in the elegant surroundings, she reminded herself not to be over-whelmed. Much of her infatuation with Elliot, she now realized, had been based on her fascination for the places he took her. Against her will, she was enchanted by both Brennan's and the Pontchartrain the evening before.

Don't be a fool, she scolded herself. You let Elliot wine you, dine you and sweep you off your feet, and it was a disaster. You thought you loved Elliot, too, remember? Stay as far away as possible from rich men.

Resolutely, she tried to view Ryan platonically. But this appeared to be an impossible task. She found herself memo-rizing the sound of his voice, the way the sunlight from the window made his hair golden, the shape of his hands and the curve of his lips.

Ryan spent the rest of the day showing her New Orleans. From the moss-encrusted old mansions to the above-ground cemetery, he presented it all to her with a better itinerary than a tour guide. At last, exhausted, they lay on a blanket in a park, watching squirrels play in the trees above their heads. Ryan rolled over onto his side in order to see her better.

"You can't see the squirrels like that," Clare pointed out.

"I'd much rather see you," he said, tickling her nose with a blade of grass. "I can see squirrels any day."

"Once you get to Kilgore, you can see me any day, too. I'll become as commonplace to you as they have," she teased.

"I doubt that. You fascinate me. Just when I think I have you all figured out, I see a facet of you that seems to be at odds with all the rest."

"Oh?" she asked warily.

"For instance. You look equally at home at Brennan's and here on a blanket with sandwich crumbs all around you. Not once have you said anything about the wind messing up your hair. I think you even enjoyed riding around with the car window down."

"I did. There's a feeling of fall in the air today and I love autumn."

"I'd have figured you to be a spring person."

"That's true, too. Spring and fall are the best. Summer is too hot and winter is too wet. I'm a sissy."

"Yeah, I remember you did whine a lot about that walking tour."

"I did not. That was you."

"Oh, yeah. Well, I knew it was one of us." He tossed the grass away and took her hand. "Clare, stay with me tonight."

She looked over at him. He wore a white pullover shirt that tapered to his narrow waist and jeans that molded the hard columns of his long legs. With the sunlight dappling his face and the breeze ruffling through his hair, he looked irresistibly virile and commanding. "Just like that?"

"Why not? I want to be with you tonight, all night. If I had waited until later to tell you, you might have impulsively rejected the idea and had no time to reconsider. I don't want you to think I'm trying to take advantage of you. I think that's why you felt so guilty before. I know you don't hop from bed to bed. That's obvious. But I want to be with you. All night. And that's why I'm asking you now."

"I want to, Ryan. I really do. But. . . ."

"No buts. If you want to be with me and I want to be with you, there's nothing to stop us."

Clare found his logic faultless, almost irresistible. "When you put it that way, I have to agree. But, on the other hand—"

He leaned over and silenced her with a long kiss. When he lifted his head and she tried to speak, he kissed her again.

Clare was achingly aware of his long, lean body stretched out beside hers, of his muscular arms that held her so gently, yet so masterfully. With a small moan, she slipped her arms around his neck and kissed him again, savoring the taste of his lips and the fresh, clean scent of his skin.

"Is the answer yes?" he asked at last. "Or should I keep kissing you?"

"The answer is yes. Keep kissing me."

With a low chuckle, he complied. Clare felt a warm glow rapidly spreading through her.

"I hate to break this up," she said, after a few minutes, "but if we keep this up, a crowd is going to gather. So I'm going to go back to the hotel and gather up my things and change for dinner. What time are we supposed to meet the potential investors you called?"

"Eight o'clock," he said, nibbling at her neck. "At the Fontainebleau dining room. We can get your suitcase then."

"I'll bring it when I drive my car over. There's no need to wait until tonight." She kissed him again. "I'll race you to the car." Before he had time to react, she jumped up and ran away.

Back at his apartment, Ryan watched as Clare drove away. Then he opened the massive iron gate, not even hearing the familiar squeak of its hinges. As he stepped from the street into the vaulted cave of the entranceway, the shade enclosed him with coolness. The handmade bricks of the tunnel were covered with lichen of various hues and velvety green moss.

He strode into the lemon sunshine of the courtyard. Flat paving stones restricted the tangled riot of late flowers, shrubs and vines that grappled together at all four walls. He passed by the small fountain without even noticing its tinkling music and climbed the steep flight of steps that scaled the outside of the building to his apartment on the second floor. On the small balcony, he paused, inserted his key in the old keyhole and pushed open the door. Inside, thanks to the thick masonry walls, the room was cool, much like the entrance tunnel.

What was it about Clare that so confused him, he wondered. Something wasn't making sense, but he couldn't quite decide what it was.

As Ryan shaved, being careful not to nick himself, he ran water into the ancient, four-legged bathtub. Then he removed his clothes and, with one practiced kick, shoved them into the dirty clothes bin and slammed the door on them. Catching his breath against the steam, Ryan slid into the hot water of the deep tub until he lay reclining against the back, his knees jutting out of the water.

Slowly, he soaped himself, ducking his head under the faucet to rinse his hair. He leaned back against the tub and rested his elbows on the curved rim. Last night when he had taken Clare to her hotel, he had felt something didn't add up. Of course, it had been odd that she was so insistent about him not seeing her to her room, but that might have been because she didn't want him to come in. After her having left so abruptly after their first night together, he had no intention of doing anything which might cause her to feel cornered, but she had no way of knowing that. Still, there was something else. He closed his eyes and furrowed his brow. When she met him in the lobby, she had been breathless, as if she had run downstairs. Then, later, when he had put her on the elevator—

His eyes flew open. *That's* what was wrong! To the best of his knowledge, there were no bedrooms on the second floor. And he had watched the elevator indicator stop on two. Those were all conference rooms and staff offices!

Thoughtfully, Ryan pulled the stopper out of the tub with his toe and stood up to towel dry while the water gurgled down the drain. He rubbed his hair with the towel until it was almost dry, then tossed the towel onto the edge of the tub. As he blew his hair dry, he tried to decipher the puzzle. Why would Clare say she was staying there if she wasn't? It didn't make any sense.

Neither did the fact that Clare appeared to be two very different people. At some times, she was very *nouveau riche*, snobbish and pseudo-sophisticated, as when she had proposed drilling the well. This part of her seemed to have an insatiable greed for money, and Ryan found it most unattractive.

At other times, however, Clare was clearly awed by *his* wealth, but seemed to be going to extremes to avoid it. There was certainly no indication that she had aspirations to marry him for his money. She actually appeared to be running from it. Part of Clare was happy eating sandwiches on a blanket in the park and strolling hand in hand down a magnolia-lined street. This Clare was easy to talk to and a pleasure to be with.

Ryan was more than a little afraid he was falling in love with this aspect of Clare. If only he could understand the grasping side, he thought, it would all be so easy.

That night, as Ryan escorted her past the unsmiling desk clerk to the Fontainebleau dining room, he asked, "Which floor did you stay on?"

"Why, the second," she said in surprise. "Why do you ask?"

"I just wondered. How was your room?"

"Very nice. I had a view of the pool." Clare noticed a tiny muscle clench in his jaw, but she saw no reason to worry. After all, she had checked out of the Seven Fountains and her suitcases were in Ryan's apartment.

The dinner meeting went well. The two men were enthusiastic about partially backing the well, especially when Ryan told them he was investing some of his own capital in the venture. Both of them were familiar with Ryan's reputation as a geologist, and even though Ryan's theory was untested and the risk was high, his good name was enough for them. One of them gave Ryan the name of a business acquaintance in Houston who thrived on high risk investments.

After the men left, Ryan and Clare celebrated their victory by staying to dance for a while. The music was mellow and dreamy, and they moved as though they'd been dancing together for years. At last, Ryan suggested they go home.

He drove through New Orleans' busy streets, which were even more thronged with people by night than by day. Clare luxuriated in the new sense of being protected by someone rather than always having to take care of herself. She glanced across at Ryan's profile as they neared a street light, and she smiled contentedly. One thing was clear—she felt closer to Ryan than she had ever felt to anyone. It was too frightening to label, but she could easily admit that she had come to like him a great deal and that she could trust him wholeheartedly. It was very comforting to know. When he parked in his garage and came around to open her door, she sighed happily.

As they walked arm in arm across the courtyard, they were

serenaded by the muffled strains from the Blue Crystal. The moonlight which filtered through the thick leaves of the chinaberry tree turned the paving stones a silvery blue. Side by side, they climbed the worn stone steps that clung to the outside of the old brick building.

While Ryan made them each a drink, Clare made herself comfortable in the living room. She discovered that the tan couch with puffy, overstuffed cushions, which looked so cozy, was indeed incredibly comfortable. The room was softly lighted by a contemporary chrome lamp which arched on a long rod over the couch. The coffee table was made of polished oak and smoked glass; the thick, luxurious plush carpet was rust-bronze. Several large potted plants gave the room character, as did the free-standing fireplace in the far corner. All of it was distinctively warm and masculine, yet more tastefully decorated than most men could take credit for.

"I love your apartment," she said when Ryan handed her a drink.

"Thanks. I was lucky to get it. Everybody wants to live in the Quarter these days. The waiting list for one of these is as long as my arm." He switched on soft music and sat down beside her on the couch. "You look especially beautiful tonight," he said, kissing her behind the ear.

"It's important for you to realize I didn't try to close the business deal by going to bed with you," Clare reminded him as the tingle from his touch coursed through her.

"I'll remember it always," he agreed amiably as he kissed her temple and her cheek, then her lips.

"And I don't fall into bed with every stranger I meet."

"I'm not all that strange." He ran a trail of fiery caresses down her slender neck and nuzzled in the hollow of her throat.

"And I didn't leave the hotel just to have a place to stay."

"You talk too much," he said as he efficiently silenced her again with his lips.

Clare felt all her reservations vanish like mist before the sun, and she returned his kisses eagerly. Ryan removed her jacket and ran his hands over the smoothness of her bare back. "I like this dress," he whispered in her ear. He found the zipper and released it.

Clare ran her hands across the broad expanse of his chest

109

and loosened and removed his tie, then began to unbutton his shirt. His skin was firm and deeply tanned, and when she kissed his neck, she could feel his quickening pulse beneath her lips. She flicked his skin with the tip of her tongue and felt his arms tighten around her.

Slowly, Ryan pulled the dress from her shoulders and gazed down at her full breasts. Already the nipples were erect and straining in his hand. Rubbing a rosy tip between his thumb and forefinger, Ryan heard Clare sigh with pleasure. Bending his head, Ryan kissed the full curve of her breasts and ran his tongue along their soft contours. Pulling Clare to her feet, Ryan finished undressing her and let her clothes whisper down to the floor. Then he allowed her to remove his clothing. After a long, soul-searching kiss, he led her into the bedroom.

Clare lay on the bed and pulled Ryan down beside her. Her heart was pounding so loudly she thought he must surely hear it.

"You're lovely in the moonlight," he said. "It makes your skin silvery. Your hair is as black as the night sky." He put his hand on the flowing curve of her hip and drew her to him.

"I like to hear your compliments," she said. "And I like to look at you and touch you. Your skin is as smooth as satin, but beneath it your muscles are so hard. You're like a thoroughbred racehorse. All sleek and muscular." As she talked, she ran her hand over his back and along the hard ridges of his ribs.

Ryan kissed her long and deep, his tongue coaxing hers, teaching hers. The sweetness of her mouth was like wine, and he went back to her lips again and again. Then he bent his head to her breasts and sent flames coursing through her veins.

With a moan of pleasure, Clare ran her fingers through his thick hair and pulled him to her. His large hands caressed her, teasing her to passionate responses. When she trembled at his slightest touch, he rolled over onto her and entered her warm recesses.

Clare gasped as her body accepted his, and arched her back to bring him even closer. Then he began to move with her and she felt the white-hot fire build.

He spoke to her softly, encouragingly, and the fires roared. With a few sensuous movements, he brought her to a peak of brilliantly flashing lights that were all within her. When she was able to relax into a golden glow, he again aroused her, sending her to even greater heights and prolonging her ecstasy as much as possible. The next time, as he urged her up to the dizzying heights, he climbed with her, and together they reached the indescribable pleasure.

Clare lay quietly and contentedly in his arms, not asleep but not entirely awake. Her body still seemed to float in the remembered passion of his embrace, and she could not have moved with an effort.

"You're wonderful," she murmured sleepily. "I feel like all my bones have turned to jelly."

He laughed softly and kissed her tumbled hair. "So do I. Are you happy?"

"Yes, oh, yes," she said, snuggling deeper into the security of his arm. "Are you?"

"Yes." He stroked her hair until he felt her breathing deepen and slow. Then he lay still with his cheek against her forehead.

You would be so easy to love, he thought as he drifted into sleep. So very easy.

Clare stirred in the morning light and awoke to find Ryan asleep beside her. His tawny hair was rumpled from their lovemaking, and his features were at peace. He looked boyishly innocent, not at all like the passionate lover who had so excited her the night before. Even so a thrill ran through Clare's body. She had remembered that making love with Ryan was really good, but this time had been ever so much more enjoyable.

Making love. The words hung in her mind and would not be displaced. Love. Slowly, almost reluctantly, she examined her feelings. Could it be that she was falling in love with Ryan? The warm rush of happiness she felt as she looked at him almost obscured the seed of fear.

She *couldn't* love him! She hardly even *knew* him! Clare had no intention of ever marrying again, and especially not a wealthy man. Elliot had all too often accused her of marrying him for his money. She was determined never to put herself in that position again. She moved uneasily, and instantly Ryan was awake.

"Good morning." He smiled drowsily and arched his arm

back around her. Sleepily, he drew her close and kissed her in the warm hollow under her chin.

Clare felt the newborn love claiming her as he nuzzled in her hair. She kissed him on his forehead, his cheek, his ear.

With a soft laugh, Ryan rolled over onto his back, pulling her easily on top of him. The dark curtain of her hair made a twilight around their faces as their lips met.

This time when they made love, he came into her more quickly, and skillfully brought her to one shattering climax after another. She moaned with the exquisite sensation and moved her body to meet his in a rhythm of ecstasy. When they were again still and satisfied, she cradled her head on his shoulder and wondered at the newly aroused wanton streak she had discovered in herself.

"Ryan?" she said quietly as her fingers caressed his chest. "I don't know what's come over me. I mean . . . well. . . ."

He looked at her tenderly and kissed her. "You look so concerned. It's okay. Really it is."

"I mean it," Clare said, as if he had disputed her words.

"I believe you."

She looked crestfallen and perversely asked, "Why? Was I that bad?"

He laughed out loud and hugged her. "You were—and are—magnificent! In bed, you have no equal."

She regarded him narrowly. "No? You're sure I didn't disappoint you?"

He rolled on top of her so that she lay pinned beneath him, her hair spread like a crown around her head. "How could I be disappointed in someone so perfect?" All the laughter was gone from his voice, and only tenderness remained. "You make me feel whole, complete. I want to hug you until you break in two and protect you, all at the same time. I feel something for you that I've never felt before."

Clare put her finger to his lips to stop the words she feared would follow. It was too soon for her to believe he loved her; too soon for her to believe she loved him.

Understanding her reluctance, Ryan smiled. She was a paradox; loving, yet afraid to love. In time, he could calm her fears.

"You've shown me the difference between making love and merely committing sex. Thank you," she said.

"It really was my pleasure," he grinned. "Now, are you

going to lie around here all day, or are you going to help me cook us some breakfast?"

"I'm going to lie around all day."

"Wrong answer!" He tickled her until she squirmed, giggling under his hands.

"Stop!" she shrieked between peals of laughter. Grabbing a pillow, she swung it at him with all her strength. It caught Ryan behind the ear and he tumbled off her as she pummeled him again and again. Following her advantage, Clare sat across his lean stomach, her pillow raised to strike again. "Give up!" she demanded as laughter danced in her eyes.

"You win, you win," he conceded. "But only because I haven't had my coffee yet."

"Excuses, excuses," she replied smugly as she rolled over onto the bed beside him.

He raised up onto one elbow and kissed her lightly. "I'll go start some breakfast. That way I can appear gallant by letting you have the bathroom first."

"Clever ploy," she grinned.

"What can I say?" he responded innocently. "You played right into my hands."

Clare slipped on her robe and went into the bathroom to brush her hair. "Hey," she called out, "did you know you have a duck on your ceiling in here?"

"A duck? Where?"

"Up there, above the tub. See?"

Ryan stared at the water-stain as he buttoned his shirt. "That's no duck," he teased. "Must be a crawdad or something. That's a tail, not a bill."

"Suit yourself. But I heard it quack."

"I know. I was just testing you." Whistling happily, he went across the living room and into the kitchen.

A perfunctory knock sounded at the front door. Almost at once, a key grated in the lock. Before he could reach it, the door swung open and a lovely young woman entered the apartment.

"Well, hello there, Ryan," she greeted him in a loud voice. "It's been a long time since I found you home."

He groaned inwardly. Of all the days for his maid to show up on time, this was undoubtedly the worst. "Hi, Yvonne. I've been gone a lot lately."

"I'll say! We sure been missing you around here!" The

young Cajun woman sidled closer with a provocative swing of her hips. Although she had long ago realized she'd never lure her employer into bed, her flirtations had become almost a game between them.

Hearing voices, Clare came out of the bathroom. Was Ryan talking to someone? Quickly, she tossed her robe onto the bed and slipped on her jeans. As she was buttoning her blouse, the telephone began ringing. Clare hesitated, then answered it.

"Hello? Is Ryan there?" a sultry voice asked on the other end.

Clare frowned. "Yes. Just a minute." On the bedside table was a photograph she hadn't noticed the night before. It was of a dark-eyed beauty and was signed, "To my Ryan with love, Doré." Clare felt a tightening in her throat. Laying the receiver on the rumpled sheets, she went into the living room in time to see Yvonne reach out and swat Ryan playfully on his buttocks.

Yvonne's giggle died as she followed Ryan's stunned expression to where Clare stood stock still in the doorway.

"Clare, this is—"

"When you are finished here, there's another one on the phone," Clare said frostily, not allowing him to explain. She turned and would have run outside, but Ryan was too fast for her.

"Clare, I want you to meet my housekeeper, Yvonne." He caught Clare's wrist and pulled her back into the room. "She takes care of the apartment and waters the plants for me when I'm out of town."

A burning flush crept across Clare's face. Yvonne, too, looked uncomfortable. "Look, I'll come back later. I didn't know you were even in town. Okay?" Hurriedly, she gathered up her mop, broom and cleaning bucket that she had left by the door.

"That's fine, Yvonne. Come back in about two hours. We'll be out of your way by then." Ryan spoke calmly, but he kept a firm grip on Clare's wrist.

When Yvonne backed out and shut the door behind her, Ryan went to the bedroom, dragging Clare behind him.

"Turn me loose!"

"No. If I do, you'll run away." He sat on the bed, drawing her down beside him, and picked up the telephone receiver.

"Hello!" he snapped. After a pause he said, "Yes, Mrs. Harlow. The rent check is in the mail. I'll be going out of town for a few days next week. Keep an eye on things around here, okay? Yeah, I will. You take care, too. 'Bye." He dropped the receiver into the cradle.

"That was my landlady. She's sixty years old and happily married. Any questions?"

Clare shook her head. "No. I feel like a fool."

Ryan took her in his arms and held her. "It's all right, baby. I just wanted you to see there's no one else. If I turn you loose now, are you going to run away?"

"No." But as he hugged her, Clare stared at the photograph of Doré. Who was this woman who could call Ryan, "hers?" Certainly she was no housekeeper or landlady. Clare hadn't the nerve to ask. Don't trust him, her reason instructed. Remember Elliot and Regina.

The following day, they flew to Houston to secure the remaining backing for the well. Clare bit her lip at the price of the airplane ticket—a sum she would once have considered nominal—but without the well, she'd be counting pennies forever. Her car would be safe in Ryan's garage and her return home would merely be delayed another day or two. She still had time to return to Kilgore before her next art class met.

Ryan rented a car at Intercontinental Airport and drove south to the city. Only when he turned into the parking lot of the Warwick Hotel did it occur to Clare that without her own transportation, she couldn't work the ruse she'd used at the Fontainebleau. Ryan hadn't suggested that she stay in his room, and she was well aware that she could not afford to rent one of her own. Would he think it strange if she suggested that they share a room? Would he think it even stranger if they didn't? Clare wished she had had more experience to draw on.

"Is this all right with you?" Ryan asked, noticing the tight line of her lips.

"Of course," she lied.

"I always stay at the Warwick when I'm in town. It's almost like a second home to me."

"You grandfather lived here, too. Right?" she said weakly.

"Nope. My grandmother. They didn't get along very well."

"Oh. I've never been here before, either. It would seem that I've done comparatively little traveling, wouldn't it?"

"Not really. That's only two hotels out of the entire world, as far as I know, that you haven't stayed in. And I've never stayed at the Fontainebleau. That makes us almost even." He watched closely for her reaction, but the doorman was already opening her door.

Wondering what she could do to get herself out of an increasingly embarrassing situation, Clare took a deep breath and got out of the car.

The spacious foyer was decorated in cream, blue and salmon tones. Two enormous crystal chandeliers in the center sparkled above the handwoven ivory rug, which was bordered with a raised design in blue and rust. Seating was provided by a great curving couch and two Louis XV or XVI style chairs. Small shops with wares ranging from expensive jewelry to Persian rugs lined both sides, and a two-hundred-fifty-year-old Aubusson tapestry covered the rear wall. The flooring was rose aurora Portuguese marble. Yet the atmosphere was warm and welcoming.

"Good afternoon, Mr. Hastings," the manager said as they approached the desk. "It's good to see you again." The small blond man spoke with a slightly foreign accent that made Clare feel as if she had been instantly transported to the Continent.

"Hello, Mr. Stagin," Ryan said with a smile. "I hope you have a room available overlooking Main."

"For you, of course." He produced a key and a bellman appeared as if by magic.

Clare hung back and tried to be invisible. At any moment the manager would ask for her room preference. However, aside from a courteous smile, he appeared not to be aware of her. She began to relax somewhat and hoped Ryan would merely assume she wanted to share his.

"Hello, Charlie," Ryan greeted the bellman as he took Clare's arm and—to her relief—moved toward the elevator. "How are things going?"

"Fine, Mr. Hastings. Just fine." The stocky black man maneuvered the luggage dolly onto the elevator and pushed the button for the seventh floor. "It's been a long time since you've been to stay with us." Charlie's attitude was one of respect and not servility.

"Yeah, I've been keeping pretty busy."

The doors glided open and they stepped out onto the thick French blue carpet and turned to the left. Charlie and Ryan discussed the possibility of the Oilers going to the Superbowl that year as they walked down the long hall; Clare was too impressed with her surroundings to even listen to the conversation. More and more, she was realizing the vast difference between old money and new. Ryan stayed in hotels with charm and elegance and discussed football with bellmen who knew him on sight; Elliot would have been offended at such "familiarity" and would have opted for the chrome and glass sparkle of the Hyatt-Regency.

Charlie opened the door to their room, glanced around to see that all was in order, and gave Ryan the key before putting the luggage in the closet. Clare went out on the curved private balcony to gaze down at the view seven stories below. Although she was looking down at a large residential section, several shopping centers and Rice University, all that was visible were the rolling green tops of interlocking live oak trees. Not one roof could be seen, and only a few buildings could be glimpsed in the very far distance. From an aesthetic viewpoint, the Warwick could as easily have been located far out in the country, rather than here on South Main in the middle of the city. Looking to the extreme right, Clare could see a magnificent view of Houston's skyline in the distance.

"It's beautiful," she exclaimed as Ryan came out to join her. "I've heard this view described as being similar to Paris, but I never dreamed it would be so . . . serene."

"According to Bob Hope, it's very similar," he said, watching her closely. How had so wealthy a person remained so secluded all her life? "I gather you and your husband never went there?" he said casually. "To Paris, I mean."

"No. We rarely went anywhere. We were only married four years, and most of that time we hardly even spoke." Her cloudy eyes held pain at the memory. She had known more love in two days with Ryan than she ever had with her husband. I won't fall in love with him, she reminded herself. I *won't!*

"That must have been very difficult," he said gently. "He wasn't nearly good enough for you."

"You never met him."

"No, but I know you. A man who'd mistreat a woman like you is a fool." He put his arms around her.

Clare lay her cheek against his broad chest. On the street far below them, traffic passed in a frantic scurrying to reach unknown destinations.

"Do you suppose any of them see us up here?" she mused, raising her head to kiss his chin.

"Would you mind?"

"No. I hope they do. I find myself wanting to call out to them, 'There *is* life after death!' Or at least after Elliot's. I've never enjoyed myself so much."

"It's just beginning," Ryan assured her.

Cautiously, Clare drew away from him. What had he meant by that?

"Tonight we'll meet our other partners in the Hunt Room for dinner. At least I hope they'll become our partners. After that, I plan to bring you back up here and ravage your body."

"Sounds good," she laughed. "Who could resist such an elegantly phrased proposition?"

"And to keep up your strength, I'm now going to take you to lunch."

Lunch was served downstairs in an open area surrounded by huge potted plants and almost life-sized black marble statues. Over-head a somewhat smaller replica of the great chandelier in the lobby hung in dazzling splendor. Clare noticed that a small brass plaque under one of the hand-carved antique wall panels read, "France, 1857." The food was served by a pretty woman who, like most of the other waitresses, spoke with a French accent.

"I suppose you know I'm becoming completely spoiled by all this. Betty may never forgive you."

Ryan grinned. "My grandmother came here to visit a lady she knew and never left. They used to sit on the porch—it was where the ballroom is now and overlooked the Mecum Fountains and the park—and they'd rock and gossip for hours on end. I remember, when I was a boy, we would sit out there in the twilight, sipping iced tea and watching the couples go out dressed to the teeth. She knew all the other residents, and most of the regular guests. It was quite an education to hear them talk to each other. Many of them were among Houston's founding families."

"That must have been fascinating for you."

"At the time, I took it for granted. It wasn't nearly as interesting as riding the ponies in the park. What about your childhood? I've never heard you mention it."

"I had a horse," she said cautiously, recalling the family plow horse and part-time saddle pony. "I rode quite often, in fact. Of course, in East Texas we rode western, not English, but I enjoyed it."

Ryan looked puzzled. Whenever he asked her anything about herself, she became cool and withdrawn. Almost stilted.

"Do you have any brothers or sisters?" he asked to see her reaction.

"No. I was an only child. My parents died several years back. Except for an aunt in Abilene, whom I haven't seen since I was in high school, I have no one." Clare shifted uneasily in her chair.

Ryan grinned to lift her tension. "You mean I can kidnap you, and nobody will dash to your rescue?"

"Nor would anyone answer your ransom note," she replied solemnly.

"Drat! Foiled again." He shook his head dismally, then cheered. "Oh, well, let's go to the Fine Arts Museum instead. It's right across the street. You can explain the paintings to me."

"Do you always change subjects right in the middle of a breath?" she teased. "I never know what you're going to say from one minute to the next."

"Sure," he grinned. "It keeps you alert and on your toes. This way I know you're paying attention."

After Ryan paid the bill, they strolled past the front desk and down the cream-colored corridor to the monogrammed side door. He held her hand as they waited for a break in the traffic to allow them to cross the street. When they reached the other side, they walked slowly in the shade of the column of live oak trees and gazed at the tortured shape of a free-form sculpture in brownish-hued metal near the entrance to the museum.

"I'll bet you can't guess what that is," Ryan said as they paused to view the sculpture from another angle.

"You're right. I haven't the faintest idea."

"Neither do I. I was just trying to trick you into guessing." He put his arm around her shoulders. "Let's go inside."

In the museum's main room, enormous canvases, some brilliantly colored, some black and white, some of muddy hues, hung in frozen solemnity. Few of these contemporary paintings depicted recognizable objects, and then only in fragments or in odd or unlikely orientations. A large open box of stainless-steel sat alone on the floor, its interior pulsating with a red-orange glow. Clare and Ryan were very drawn to the box, much more so than the canvases, because of the sense of vertigo they experienced on looking down into its fiery emptiness.

"All art isn't necessarily meant to be a serious statement," Clare told him as they moved along to a metal sculpture that could only be described as a twisted spoon. "Some of it's intended only to display a pleasing shape or texture. Then there are others which I think are a tongue-in-cheek experiment by the artist."

"Some of these *must* be." Ryan was staring at an enormous white canvas with a small red dot in the upper corner. "Who would ever want some of this stuff in his house?"

"It's not meant for houses. Only museums," Clare explained. "And you're too close. Oils should be viewed from a distance. Not with your nose pressed against them."

The next room held paintings by such masters as Monet, Rembrandt and Degas, and were of comfortably recognizable subjects.

"This is more like it," Ryan said.

"Just between you and me, I like this better, too," Clare confided, "but don't tell anyone. As an artist, I'm supposed to prefer abstracts."

The back room was filled with Egyptian artifacts. Clare and Ryan took turns challenging each other to guess the use of the strange objects, then consulted the identifying cards to see if they were right. They seldom were.

They strolled back into the vestibule and looked around. "Well, I guess that's it," Clare said as she circled a green copper giant, clad only in a fig leaf. "Ready to leave?"

"Sure. Let's go to the zoo."

Ignoring the hostile stare of the dark-suited museum guard, they left the rarified atmosphere and headed out across Hermann Park.

"I always feel so sorry for the animals," Clare said as they watched the dull-witted pacing of a magnificent Bengal tiger. "When I was a little girl, I wanted to buy all the zoos and free the animals.

"I wish I had known you when you were a child."

"You wouldn't have cared for me then," she said with certainty.

"I disagree. As fascinating as I find you now, you must have been intriguing then. What schools did you attend?"

"You ask more questions than anyone I have ever met," Clare said testily.

"Sorry. Let's go to the aviary."

Ryan watched her face as they stood on the enclosed wooden bridge while brilliantly colored birds flew over their heads. In so many ways, Clare seemed to be new to life. She was as excited as a child as she discovered new species of birds hiding in the thick foliage. This same excitement had been apparent when he had shown her New Orleans. She was different from the other women he had known, in so many ways. Yet her background must be very similar to his own.

"I'm looking forward to wildcatting your well," he said, holding her hand as they walked into the dimness of the birdhouse and out again into the sunshine. "I'll be able to get started on it right after the first of the year."

Clare stopped dead still. "Not until then? Why wait so long?"

"I have some things to finish up first, and I'll need to find an apartment to rent for a few months. Not to mention the crew that I need to hire and get moved up there."

"I'm sorry, but that won't do," Clare said stubbornly. "I want to start much sooner."

Ryan frowned. "I'm not sure that I can. These things take time."

"I can find you a place to live. You can hire whoever is immediately available. I want the well started as quickly as possible."

"Clare, be reasonable. The oil has been there a long, long time. It'll wait for us."

"But I can't wait."

"Can't? What do you mean?"

Clare wished she could bite back the word. "I mean I don't

want to wait. Please, Ryan. It's so very important to me."
Her eyes begged him to do as she asked.

He sighed. "I guess I could try to hurry things into action,
but what's the rush?"

"Please. Don't ask so many questions. Just do as I ask."

Slowly, he started walking again, and she fell into step
beside him. There it was again. The grasping, greedy side of
her that was so at odds with the woman she seemed to be. But
her eyes looked . . . desperate.

"All right. I'll try to start next month. Mind you, I said *try*.
I'm not making any promises."

The strain in her expression eased somewhat. "Good! Let's
get some cotton candy." She was relieved to change the
subject.

The European manor house atmosphere of the Hunt Room
was a perfect setting for Ryan's and Clare's dinner guests.
The room was dimly but cozily lit by wall sconces and a
chandelier made of hunting bugles. In the back corner was a
French Renaissance marble fireplace topped with a crested
hood. Underfoot was a luxurious red Brussels carpeting. The
unabashed grandeur about them made them all feel pampered and prosperous, as Ryan had intended that it should.
Over escargots bourguignon and tournedos béarnaise, Ryan
convinced the three men and two women that they should
join the syndicate to supply the remaining money for the
project. By the time they finished their strawberries Roma-
noff, they were not only willing but eager to be involved.

"You're marvelous," Clare said as they waited for the
elevator. "You had them ready to drill tomorrow."

"I believe in it, or I wouldn't have asked them to do it.
They knew that and they know the risk. But the clincher is the
fact that I'm investing a considerable amount of my own
money. No smart business man would have considered it
otherwise." The indicator for the second floor lighted with his
touch.

"We're on the seventh," she protested. "You pressed the
wrong button."

"I want to show you something."

The elevator doors opened and in front of them Clare saw
the pool. They walked hand in hand beside it. Beneath the

canopy to one side, two couples drank martinis while they talked. A svelte blond, wearing a bikini and carrying her towel, stepped into one of the saunas.

Ryan led Clare beyond the pool to the far end of the upper patio. On the street below, three huge lit fountains spewed their liquid gold high into the air, creating a wonderland. To the left, a bronze statue of General Sam Houston sat astride a permanently prancing horse and pointed the way to the park. A high stone wall, covered with creeper vines, suggested a concealed residence beyond the fountains, but, as from their balcony, no houses could be seen.

"It's truly beautiful," Clare gasped in awe. "Such a magnificent sight. And this is the perfect vantage point!"

Ryan smiled, put his arm around her and kissed her lightly as she leaned against him. "I wanted you to see it for the first time when the lights were on. It's pretty by day, but after dark it's magic."

"Magic fountains grant wishes," Clare said as she looked up into the green depths of his eyes.

"Yes, and mine is going to come true," he said confidently. Slowly, he lowered his head and kissed her, first gently, then with more feeling. With reluctance, he released her and looked down at her with a thoughtful expression. "Come on. Let's go to our room."

"What did you wish?" she asked as they walked back by the pool.

"If I tell you, it may not happen. I'll show you instead . . . as soon as we get to our room." He pushed the button for the seventh floor and put his arms around Clare. Tenderly, he kissed her, skillfully coaxing her to respond. Just at that moment, the elevator doors opened and Clare was all too aware of the disapproving glare of the well-fed ladies who were awaiting the elevator. Blushing furiously, she avoided their eyes and hurried down the hallway with Ryan, who was amused at her discomfort.

"Don't you suppose that those women have seen couples kissing before? Actually, I think they enjoyed it but won't admit it," he observed sagely.

In their room, a cold split of champagne and two wine glasses awaited them.

"To celebrate the beginning of our well," Ryan explained.

"But how . . . ?"

"I asked the waiter to have it sent up when I saw our money was secured. It'll have to wait, though. I have something else in mind first. Remember my wish at the fountains?" He took her masterfully in his arms and kissed her passionately.

Clare felt the blood pound in her temples as his hands roamed over her body. He removed her clothing easily and stroked her breasts, the curve of her hips and her back as his tongue explored her mouth. Her skin tingled against the roughness of his suit and Clare moaned in delicious anticipation. He lifted her easily and carried her to the bed.

The maid had turned down the covers and left an after-dinner wafer on each pillow. Ryan brushed them aside impatiently as he lowered her head to the soft pillow. Again he kissed her ravenously, creating a tense excitement within her. Almost savagely, he pulled off his clothes and lay beside her, his mouth burning hers as his fingers deftly fondled her breasts and then ran lower to tantalize her most secret recesses.

Too impatient to prolong the moment, Clare pulled him onto her and felt him slide deep inside her. With a gasp of pleasure, she felt the aching throb in her loins begin to build immediately. Moving her hips against his, she let the golden bubble of passion burst and grow again. Relentlessly, she urged him to a shuddering release to match her own.

Ryan lay still in her arms, too satisfied to move. Drowsily, they dozed lightly, waking from time to time to kiss tenderly and stroke each other gently.

"Who ravaged who?" he asked at last.

"Whom," she corrected sleepily. "I think it was mutual."

He shifted to one side and drew her head onto his shoulder. As she snuggled against him, he kissed her fragrant hair and stroked her smooth skin.

"That feels so good," she murmured. "Your champagne is probably getting warm, though."

"That doesn't matter. This is much more important." He held her protectively against him.

"Clare, I love you," he said softly when she slept. "Someday you're going to love me, too. That was the wish I made." He knew she didn't hear him, but a faint smile softened her already delicate features as she cuddled closer. He resolved somehow to win her trust enough for her to let him be a permanent part of her world. Whatever it was she was hiding—and he was positive she was hiding something—he was certain it would make no difference to him. He knew now that what he felt for her was love and he welcomed it.

"I love you," he whispered again, in a voice filled with wonder.

Chapter Eleven

Regina Wharton sat at her vanity, turning her head first one way, then another, to study the effects of her new hairstyle. She had spent all day in the beauty shop having her hair frosted in three subtle shades of blonde. The result was the look of a mane bleached by the sun. She shook her head experimentally and the newly formed waves bounced pleasingly. She smiled. It had been worth the exorbitant price the hairdresser had asked.

"Regina? Are you home?" her husband called from the entryway as he slammed the door behind him.

She groaned and a frown wrinkled her forehead. Were those new creases at the corners of her eyes? she wondered. Hastily, she smoothed her skin.

"Regina?"

"Of course I'm here," she snapped. "Where else would I be? And don't track mud onto my clean carpet. You know it's been raining outside."

Shamefaced, Howard looked over his shoulder at the row of smudges on the ivory carpet. There would be hell to pay . . . again. Even though the dirt would be cleaned by the maid and not by his wife, he knew there would be an unpleasant scene. He backtracked and left his shoes at the door.

Regina lit a long black cigarette and let the smoke curl out of her nostrils. She had almost perfected the art of French inhaling and was eager to try it out on an appreciative observer—one more interesting than Howard. She considered this to be the epitome of sensuality. The smoke wafted from her red lips to her nostrils. Perfect, she thought.

"Regina?" Howard asked from the doorway of her bedroom.

She glared at him and turned back to her mirror. "What?" Catching his reflection in the glass, she turned around. "Why in God's name are you standing there in your stocking feet?"

Self-consciously, Howard looked down at his offending members. "I, uh, left my shoes at the door so I wouldn't track mud in. It was a hard rain," he finished lamely.

"Well, you look ridiculous. Go put on your slippers." She stroked bright blue eyeshadow onto her half-closed lids.

"Are you going out?" he asked.

"Yes. I have plans for the evening." She stood up and moved into the middle of her mauve and ivory bedroom, her silvery satin robe clinging to every curve of her body. Pretending to have forgotten her husband was there, Regina loosened the tie belt and slipped the robe from her shoulders. She tossed it onto the expensive satin bedspread, which wasn't as new as she would have preferred. She stood naked before him.

Regina kept her body under a tight rein. She dieted and exercised rigorously in an effort to shed her encroaching years. The result was a too slim, rather muscular body, with more angles than curves. To Regina, it was beautiful.

To Howard, who hadn't been allowed within six feet of her bed for months, it was overwhelmingly desirable. He stood gaping at her, the burning sensation deep within him growing steadily.

Regina turned arrogantly, as if she had just realized he was still there. "Well?" she asked coldly.

Howard swallowed and ran his tongue around his lips. "I . . . I just wondered if you were . . . going out."

"Well, now you know." Regina dismissed him with a toss of her head.

"Will you be late?" Howard persisted, watching hungrily as she stepped into a pair of silk panties and hooked her bra.

"Probably."

He took a deep breath and plunged on. "Where are you going?"

Regina turned and glared stonily at him. "I don't have to account to you for my every move. I'm going out. That's all. Out." She pulled her slip carefully down over her head so as not to muss her hair or makeup.

"I know. It's just that, well, you *are* my wife and—"

"Will you quit badgering me?" Regina exploded. "Just go away and leave me in peace!" She stormed toward him, ready to shove him from her room had he not retreated, and slammed the door in his face.

Several minutes later, when she came out into the hall, the door to his bedroom was closed, and she saw no reason to bother saying goodby. Although the weather wasn't cold enough for her to need a heavy wrap, she pulled her coat from the hall closet and shrugged into it. It was a dress-length silver mink, the color that made her hair appear to be pale gold. She had fallen in love with it when she'd seen it in the showroom of Neiman's. She preferred shopping in Dallas, as did everyone with any taste at all in her opinion. Eventually, she supposed, Howard would finish paying for the coat. As his wife, she saw no reason to use her own money to clothe herself. After all, he had agreed to the premarital contract that kept their monies separate.

She saw the trace of muddy footprints on the carpet and frowned. How could she ever hope to have a nice home with such a clod for a husband? When she'd agreed to marry him, she'd had no idea he'd continue to be such a bore. He was either too stubborn or too stupid to change, and she was heartily tired of the project.

Again the thought she had toyed with for months crept into her mind. Why not divorce him and be rid of him? Thoughtfully, she stepped out into the night.

The parking lot of the Rio Palm Isle was filled as usual, and she could hear strains of dance music. She hoped she wasn't early.

Inside stale smoke filled the air. Regina could see the

dancers only vaguely through the darkened haze. With a practiced shrug of her narrow shoulders, she slipped out of her mink. Her dress was a shimmering pink confection with a jabot ruffling down the front. A narrow belt molded the dress to her waist and accentuated the slight curve of her boyish hips. She wove through the maze of cocktail tables until she saw the person she had come to meet. With a regal air—that of a queen who is determined to mix with the peasants though she is dying of boredom—she edged toward him through the other people.

"Hello," she said in her sultriest voice. "Have you been waiting long?"

Neal Thorndyke looked up from his drink and smiled at Regina admiringly. "Not too long. But I never mind waiting for you. My goodness, you do look lovely tonight. Is the dress new?"

Regina shrugged desultorily. "Yes. I found it in a boutique in Longview. I thought it would be rather amusing." It had cost more than Howard's automobile dealership had brought in that month.

She lowered herself gracefully into the chair Neal held for her and surveyed the bar as she took a cigarette out of her gold case. "There's quite a crowd tonight."

"Yes, the band is good. Would you like to dance?"

"No, not now." She knew from experience that Neal Thorndyke was a terrible dancer and made even the most accomplished partner appear to be awkward. "Perhaps later." She let the smoke slide from her lips to be inhaled through her nose. Neal looked as captivated as she had hoped he would.

"Did you have trouble getting out tonight?" Neal asked.

"Trouble, from Howard? Of course not. What could he do?"

"He could get pretty angry if he knew about us. Maybe we should be more circumspect."

Regina laughed. "Surely you're not worried about Howard! He's too big a fool to notice us, even if we were flaunting ourselves under his very nose. And too cowardly to do anything about it if he did suspect anything." She crushed out her cigarette in the ashtray.

Neal smirked, but then appeared thoughtful. "I just don't want to cause you any trouble."

"Are you getting tired of me?" she teased confidently as she rubbed her foot against his ankle.

"You know better than that."

She smiled and let their knees touch beneath the table. "Why don't we go some place where it's quieter? Like *your* place." She leaned forward and gazed at him seductively.

Neal grinned in anticipation. Regina might look like an ice queen, but he well knew she was almost insatiable in bed. "Let's go." He tossed some money on the table to pay for their drinks.

Trailing her coat over her shoulder and Neal behind her, Regina threaded her way to the door. Neither of them noticed the portly man who watched them from the shadows beyond the bar.

Hours later, Regina let herself into her dark house as she hummed a tune under her breath. Her hair was even more tangled from Neal's lovemaking than it had been from the beautician's fingers, and her original lipstick had been left on his sheets. As she was crossing the living room, the lights suddenly snapped on. She whirled around to see Howard sitting in a chair and holding a glass of bourbon while he stared at her.

"My God, what are you trying to do? Scare me to death?" she said huffily, trying to hide her panic.

He surveyed her pallid skin, which looked loose and worn from lovemaking, and the faint smudges of mascara beneath her eyes. Still he sat without speaking.

Regina tried to calm herself. After all, it was only Howard. "I didn't expect you to wait up for me. I happened to run into an old friend from college and—"

"I already know where you've been," Howard interrupted. His voice sounded dead, totally unlike the thunder that showed in his small eyes.

Regina swallowed. "I have no idea what you've heard, but—"

"No more lies!" he interrupted again. "I told you I *know* where you've been. And who he is!" Howard trembled with agitation. "I've overlooked your flirtations. Your sly innuendoes. But, by God, I'm not overlooking this!" His voice echoed in the stillness of the house.

Regina lifted her chin haughtily. "I want a divorce."

"You've got it! I'll file tomorrow!"

"I also want you out of my house!"

Howard gestured toward three suitcases she hadn't noticed, and heaved his large body out of the chair. "I've been packed for hours. Damn it, Regina, if you had to make a fool of me, did you have to pick one of my friends?" Without waiting for her answer, he picked up his luggage and left, slamming the door behind him.

"Good morning, Mr. Thorndyke," Clare said across the expanse of the banker's slate-topped desk.

"What do you want? Your payment isn't due for another . . ." he glanced at his desk calendar, "week. And, incidentally, there is no need to deliver it to me personally each time. One of my tellers can handle that."

"I know," she said with a maddening smile. "But this way, you know for a fact that I've paid. There can be no possible mistake. However, I'm not here for that today. I have a business proposition for you."

"Oh? What might that be?" He glanced down at the papers in front of him, pointedly ignoring her.

Clare made no sign that she was upset by his rudeness. "I want to drill an oil well."

Neal looked up sharply. "What's that?"

"As you may know, Huntly Oil has leased a portion of my land for a deep well. I want to drill one on the other part."

"You don't just get up one day and decide to strike oil," Thorndyke said derisively. "You don't know what you're talking about."

"Other people do."

"You can't afford it," he pointed out bluntly.

"That's why I'm here. I want to get a loan for two hundred and fifty thousand dollars. As collateral I'll put up the equity in my house and the surface and mineral rights to my land, as well as the Huntly Oil lease."

Neal carefully laid down his pen and leaned back in his chair. "It takes a lot more money than that for a well."

"I know. I've already secured the backing I need." Clare spoke confidently and tried to keep her hands from trembling. "Ryan Hastings, who is a geologist for Huntly, will wildcat it."

Thorndyke began to consider her words carefully. "I've

heard of him." He wondered if she was foolish enough to be as calm as she looked. If she was bluffing, she was a better gambler than her late husband had been—a fact Thorndyke knew from the many poker games where Elliot had lost heavily to him. "Why have you come to me? Our relationship is not what one would call congenial."

Clare's eyes met his unflinchingly. "We don't have *any* relationship, Mr. Thorndyke. But you already know my financial situation. No one else does. If I go to another bank, word may spread that I need money. Naturally, I don't want that to be common knowledge. The payoff from this oil well will put me back on my feet financially."

Making a steeple of his fingertips, Neal Thorndyke studied her. There were two deep exploration wells being drilled in the area, neither of which appeared even close to being promising. Even though the pool of oil in the Woodbine sand below Kilgore had become virtually depleted, several companies had drilled deeper wells, as deep as fourteen thousand feet, with no success. He smiled. "I'd be glad to loan you the money. After all, my bank is here to aid the community. I'll have the papers drawn up immediately. Of course, I'll need the title to your house and property, along with a copy of the lease with Huntly Oil."

Clare nodded, wondering why she felt no surge of relief. Had she overstepped?

"I'll make you the loan for a period of nine months—that's the length of time customary for this sort of business venture —and give it to you at the prime rate of interest."

"All right. I have some errands to run. I'll come by later and sign the papers."

As she got up to leave, Thorndyke said with a smug vindictiveness, "I've always liked that land. It would make a good housing development. If, of course, the well is dry."

Clare looked for a long time into his eyes, then left without answering.

Regina lay beside her kidney-shaped pool, soaking up the last warm days of sun. Soon fall would arrive, and her tan would have to wait until another year. Unless she went away for the winter. But that would put her out of circulation for months, and after a divorce the conservative town matrons might be resentful of her when she returned. Also, it would mean leaving Neal unattended. Someone might move in on her territory during her absence.

She shooed away a pestering fly and readjusted the scarf that protected her hair from the sun. If she married Neal, would she be harnessed to the town as she had been with Howard? But, if she didn't marry Neal, would she find another husband? Kilgore's selection of eligible males was small, but she knew that her family and her wealth gave her an advantage here. In a larger town, the women she'd be competing with would be richer and probably younger. Regina was all too aware that the next month would bring her another birthday.

And then there was this nonsense with Howard. He wanted to split their property fifty-fifty, and she had no intention of agreeing to such a ridiculous demand. To make it even more ludicrous, he'd suggested the day before last that they should go to a marriage counselor and try to patch up their marriage. She had laughed and hung up on him. It would be just like Howard to drag his feet, she thought. If he figured he could get her to agree to his terms or to let him come back to her, he'd string out the legalities forever.

Resolutely, Regina got up and patted the moisture from her lotion-greased skin. She had no intention of dancing to Howard's tune, not when Mexican divorces were so easily obtained. As she went inside to call the airline, she planned the "coming out" party she'd give on her return.

Chapter Twelve

Clare leaned on the rough wooden fence that had long since weathered to a silvery gray and watched the men working in what had once been her father's cow lot. They were slowly but efficiently erecting the oil derrick as if the huge steel beams were pieces of a giant child's construction kit. Already the wooden platform with its massive supporting timbers was in place and gleaming palely in the sunlight. On a flatbed truck nearby, she saw the red and yellow machinery that would be installed beneath the platform. Quite a few changes had taken place in the old cow lot since her visit to the bank a month earlier. It no longer looked like the same place.

Ryan was busy consulting his head driller, Joe Talmidge, about some technical installations, and had not yet acknowledged Clare's presence. She supposed Ryan was angry because she had avoided him for the entire week he had been in town. But she was finding herself becoming far too emotionally involved with him, and she had hoped that refusing to see him would help her regain her objectivity. It hadn't.

Joe Talmidge was not a large man, but he was thick with muscles. He was probably well into his forties or even older, but he looked as tough as granite. Although he was tanned to a leathery brown on his hands, neck and lower face, his hard hat's brim had left a clean line above which his forehead was pale white. Clare had noticed this when she met him half an hour earlier, and it had reminded her of her father—he had had just such a tan from the straw hat he wore. Clare guessed that Joe, like her father, would never dream of going outside bareheaded or shirtless.

That was the real distinction between a new hand and one with experience. The skeletal crew Joe had brought with him from Louisiana all wore metal hats and longsleeved shirts; the college boys Joe had hired locally wore their hats only when necessary and had left their shirts in their cars. Already their skin was reddening in the sun and they looked far hotter and more tired than the older men whose sweat-dampened clothing provided them with a natural cooling.

Clare turned away from the activity and looked at the farm buildings. Directly behind her was an ancient barn, with remnants of rusted equipment beneath its lean-to shed. There, sunlight filtered in streams through the unrepaired roof and lit the dimness so she could see. The square opening of the doors on each end of the barn made it more like a tunnel than a cave. Memories compelled her to go inside.

She saw her father's battered wagon and the row of dusty cubicles where her mother's hens had laid their eggs. The straw inside the cubicles was moldy now, and from the tufts of fur she saw, Clare concluded that the nests' new tenants were barn mice. On the other side of the shadowy barn were three enclosed stalls, each with a feed trough and hay bin with access to the loft above. A water bucket still stood in the corner of one stall, but its bottom had long since rusted out. Pushing aside an age-stiffened harness covered with cobwebs, Clare left the barn and walked across the yard to the house.

Her childhood home consisted of two small buildings joined by an open-ended, covered porch in the style known as a dog-run house. All the walls had windows to catch the slightest breeze; and the porch, which formed a breezeway by design, provided a cool haven even on the hottest summer days. Clare and her doll had lived out many adventures on the back corner of the porch, where a huge chinaberry tree made a brilliant yellow canopy.

She pushed the cracked china doorknob and stepped into the side that had been the living room and kitchen. A chipped, porcelain-topped table, now spotted with rust marks, sat against the far wall beside the free-standing sink of galvanized tin. A Mexican lantern hung like a scrap of rusted lace on the wall. Beside the door, an old rocker, worn and aged to the color of soft earth, waited in the gray shadows for someone who would never return. Clare touched the slatted back lovingly and recalled the woman who had last used it, and the marvelous world of fairy tales that had been told in tune to its now-silenced creaking.

This was Clare's heritage. Not the sweeping azalea-lined curve of the Marshall mansion's drive, nor the glassed-in portico overlooking a pool designed to look like a lagoon, but this. A tin-roofed house that was hot in the summer, cold in the winter and very, very damp in the rain. That icy finger of fear touched her again.

"I love you, Mama," Clare whispered. "And you, too, Papa, but I'm not coming back to this. Not ever! I just can't!" Feeling hot tears sting her eyes, Clare left the room, carefully closing the hand-hewn door behind her.

She went down the back steps, which were made of large, reddish-black rocks from the salt lick down by the creek, and leaned against the smooth trunk of the chinaberry tree.

"I thought you had gone."

Startled, Clare jumped and saw Ryan beside her. "I didn't hear you come up," she said.

"I was afraid you'd leave before I could talk to you."

"Is something wrong?" she asked anxiously.

"No. Everything is going fine. We'll start drilling soon. Joe Talmidge and his wife have found an apartment in Glade-water and I'm having two mobile homes delivered here tomorrow."

"Mobile homes?"

"One for my geology charts and equipment, one to use as a bunkhouse for the crew that will stay on site. A couple of the men are putting up the explosives shed back there in the woods. It won't be much to look at, but it has to be strong. We're using odds and ends left over from the drilling plat-form." He gazed up at the leafy umbrella above them where yellow leaves laced the blue sky. "Why are you avoiding me?"

"I don't know what you're talking about," Clare said obstinately. "I've just been busy."

"Every day and every night for a week? You must be the belle of the ball." Jealousy stabbed Ryan cruelly.

"Don't be silly. I've been starting a group of night students and setting up exhibition dates for some of my paintings."

"I haven't seen you in over a month. That's plenty of time for a man to move into your life."

"Well, one hasn't. Kilgore isn't exactly a hotbed of bachelors and, besides, I'm not looking for one."

"Good." He smiled and put one arm on each side of her against the sloping tree trunk. "Now that I've finally caught up with you, will you have dinner with me?"

"I have a lot to do, Ryan," she protested as her heart pounded at his nearness. He was so close she could see the golden flecks in his eyes. "I really shouldn't."

"How about lunch? Right now."

Clare tried to think of some excuse, but she obviously wasn't busy at the moment. Again she recalled the photograph of Doré she had seen beside Ryan's bed. He has a girlfriend waiting for him, she chided herself. Don't get involved with someone you can't have. But he was too close for her to be firm, and she heard herself saying, "I'd love to have lunch with you."

"Good. Let's have a picnic. There won't be many more days of warm weather."

Clare smiled. "I know just the place."

They went to the general store on the highway and bought cheese, smoked salami, crackers, plastic glasses and wine. Back at the farmhouse, Ryan took a quilt from the trunk of his car and looked at her expectantly.

"This way," she said.

She led him past the barn and weed-infested cow lot to the woods beyond. A small bridge, green and furry with moss, crossed a stream that ran sluggishly after the parching summer. Beneath the trees, the air was cool and moist with a promise of fall. Overhead, the oaks, maples and sweetgums interlaced their gypsy-bright leaves like a towering dome.

"Here?" Ryan asked hopefully.

"No, not yet," Clare said with a smile.

She went up the path that sloped into the woods and away from the stream, Ryan following. An occasional cedar or holly made a splash of dark green against the vivid golds and reds of the fall trees, and even the waist-high bushes were colored in rust, red and oranges. Clare continued briskly, as sure of herself as if there were sign posts to guide the way. As they topped a ridge, the woods changed abruptly.

More slowly, almost reverently, they walked toward the stand of evergreens where the trees soared above their heads. The pine trees stood regal and proud, their glossy needles glistening in the sun as if they were slivers of emeralds. Their silver-bronze trunks were as large as the pillars of some ancient pagan temple, and every bit as straight. Beneath them, a thick carpet of gold pine needles stretched out as if the spot were a carefully tended park. A cathedral hush lay under the soft sighing of the wind in the treetops above.

"Here," Clare said. "This is the place I wanted to show you."

Ryan moved slowly into the stillness of the pines and looked far up into their branches. His footsteps were cushioned by the needles below and made no sound at all.

"It's magnificent," he breathed.

Clare nodded. "It's one of my favorite and most secret places. I used to pretend the elves came here and cleared away all the brush and brambles, and that if I were quiet enough, I might see one."

"Did you?" he smiled.

"Not yet."

He laughed, then looked puzzled. "How did you happen to come all the way out here by yourself? We must be ten miles from town."

"It's not that far," she said uneasily. "Let's eat. I'm starved."

Ryan spread the quilt on the ground and they sat cross-legged on it to eat. As Clare sliced the cheese and salami, Ryan tasted the wine.

"Good," he proclaimed. "Just the right touch of plastic from the glass." He put a slice of meat and cheese on a cracker and held it to her lips.

She took a bite and sighed contentedly. "This is perfect. I'm so glad you suggested it."

He popped the remaining bite into his mouth and constructed another tower of food on a cracker.

"I've missed you this past month. Have you really been all that busy?"

Clare kept her eyes on her glass of wine. "Of course. I've missed you, too." The last part was true. She fed him a slice of cheese between two slices of salami.

Ryan caught her hand and waited until she raised her eyes to his. "Clare, you're special to me. What we shared that weekend wasn't just a casual fling. At least it wasn't for me."

What about the girl in the photograph? Clare's mind demanded. "It wasn't casual for me, either," she said stiffly. "More wine?"

He shook his head. "Will you go out with me tomorrow?"

"No."

"Why not?" he asked sharply.

"Because it *wasn't* a casual fling," she said softly. "I don't want any commitments. At least not right now."

He pulled her closer. "Would that really be so bad?" He kissed her gently. "All men aren't like Elliot."

"At one time, Elliot assured me he wasn't 'like Elliot,' too. But he was. I know now that I should never have married him, but at the time it seemed right. Later, he made it quite clear that our marriage vows were intended primarily for me. He never let it hamper him in any way."

"And because of that you're determined not to trust any man ever again?" Ryan was kissing her cheeks, her eyebrows, her nose.

Clare tried to speak normally. "I think I have good reason to feel that way."

"I don't." He pulled the ribbon from her hair and let the dark waves fall about her shoulders. "Am I anything at all like Elliot?"

"No," she whispered, tilting her head so he could caress her throat under her chin.

"I rest my case." He pulled her to him and kissed her hungrily.

Gently, he laid her back on the quilt. Beneath them, the pine needles made a soft and fragrant cushion. Above their heads, the wind whispered a haunting song in the dark boughs. Ryan leaned over and Clare raised her head to meet his lips.

"Do you think I'm terribly wanton?" she murmured half-jokingly.

"No. I think you're wonderfully wanton," he grinned.

"Oh!" She struggled against him, laughing, but he held her easily until she slipped her arms around his neck. "I give up. Uncle."

He laughed. "You give up easy."

She smiled smugly. "My Mama didn't raise a fool."

Gradually, the teasing fading from his face, Ryan kissed her tenderly, lovingly, coaxing her to meet his growing desire. His tongue explored her lips and the even rows of her white teeth as his large hands stroked her back and slid over the curve of her hip.

With a low moan, Clare moved her body against his and tasted the sweetness of his mouth. Eagerly, she ran her fingers across the hard muscles of his back and pulled him even closer. Ryan tangled his fingers in her thick hair and kissed her until the trees seemed to spin above them and even the ground felt unsteady.

Slowly, tantalizingly, he unbuttoned the top of her blouse and kissed the creamy skin. When Clare felt she could bear the suspense no longer, he leisurely loosened the next button.

She had no intention of maintaining such control, and quickly removed his shirt. He laughed at her impatience but prevented her from helping him in his slow, ever so slow, undressing of her. By the time he finally removed her blouse, Clare was writhing against him in eager anticipation. He lowered his head and flicked his tongue over her nipples. Teasingly, he took the rosy circles into his mouth, and felt her increasing response to his hot urging.

Ryan raised his head and kissed her lips as his hand gently massaged the softness of her stomach. Then he loosened the waist of her jeans and let his fingers caress her hip beneath the heavy denim. Clare trembled at his touch, but still he would not hurry as he eased the pants down her thighs. Lowering his head again to her breast, he kissed the firm, rounded flesh, then ran his tongue across her ribs to the hollow of her waist. As he nuzzled in the warmth there, he stroked her long, slender thighs and ran his hand over the silkiness of her panties before removing them, too.

Clare lay naked before him, her skin cooled and teased by the gentle breeze, the quilt framing her on the bed of golden needles. Ryan raised up on one arm and gazed down at her. Slowly, he touched her breast, massaging, pinching, teasing, as he watched her reaction. Ever so slowly, he caressed the plane of her quivering stomach and made his way to the dark mound of hair below.

Unable to contain herself, Clare pulled him down to her, fumbling with the buckle of his belt and the fastening of his jeans in her eagerness. His skin felt hot against hers, and as smooth as satin. The masses of hard muscles beneath her fingers excited her even more, and she pressed her body demandingly against his. Even as he came into her, her soul rose in a golden explosion of delight and immediately began building to another pinnacle of ecstasy.

Still Ryan held himself in check, giving her pleasure, playing her body as he would a finely tuned musical instrument. Only when he saw she was nearing satisfaction did he release the hold he had on himself, and together they cried out as the shuddering passion swept them up in its whirlwind.

They lay, still entwined, and floating in remembered rapture. Gradually, the earth and its scents and sounds became real to Clare, and she became aware of the cool breeze on her sun-warmed bare skin and the spicy aroma of the woods. She snuggled her head more comfortably on Ryan's broad shoulder and ran her hand over the hardness of his ribs.

Ryan smiled sleepily as he felt her fingers caress him and wished he could tell her of the love that ached within him. But he knew instinctively that to say that word would send her fleeing from him. Why, he couldn't even guess. Virtually all the women he'd ever known wanted love, and usually marriage, above all else. Clare was an enigma.

"You're beautiful," he murmured happily. "In the sunlight, your skin is silvery, and your hair is tumbled about most provocatively."

"How do you know?" she queried. "Your eyes are closed."

He smiled broadly. "That doesn't stop me from seeing you. I can see you even when you aren't anywhere around. I can see the way your hair flows in the breeze and the way your eyes crinkle at the corners when you laugh and the way you frown just a little when you're concentrating on something. I can see you, all right."

"Ryan, why are you so good to me?" she asked tentatively.

"I've given you every reason to avoid me, and still you're here. Why?"

He turned his head and regarded her solemnly. "Do you really want to know?"

"No," she whispered. "Not yet."

High above them, a mockingbird launched into song, and the great pines sighed in agreement.

Chapter Thirteen

"Hi, Clare," Marla said as she walked into the portico.

"Hello, Marla. I was just straightening up after my art class," Clare said, gingerly lifting a wet canvas and sliding it onto a shelf of the drying rack.

"I know. I saw them leave. How are they coming along?"

"Delia is doing great. So well, in fact, that I know I can't take credit for it. If her attitude would change, she could go far, but she's still as surly as a bear. This is Lorena's effort. See for yourself."

The painting was meticulous. Each line stood out in bold relief on the small vase of miniature flowers that huddled in the exact center of too much canvas. The colors were so bright and vibrant that they could only have come straight from the tube.

"I thought I could loosen her up if I let her paint in color like her friend, Hildy, but it seems to be a hopeless task. She doesn't paint—she draws in color! I tried one entire lesson to get her to see that her composition was too small. I even sketched it off for her. She just smiled sweetly, thanked me, and the next time I looked she had put it back exactly as it was. She says she likes it that way. As you can tell, she also prefers raw colors."

Marla laughed, then gasped as she caught sight of a garish puddle of color on canvas. "What in the world is that?"

"Hildy's abstract interpretation of flowers," Clare said dismally. "You might like the canvas of the other student, Sarah May. I've done almost the entire painting for her. I haven't figured out quite how she does it, but she's going to own a Clare Marshall original before the class is over.

Marla shook her head. "There's one in every class, I guess. How are your pictures in the galleries doing?"

Clare laughed. "That little Mom and Pop type place in Tyler sold both my pictures last week. She was giving away recipes with each painting sold. I didn't get as much for them as I was asking, but she wants four more. It seems she's running a special on Christmas tree skirts next month, and is pushing paintings as gifts. The galleries in New Orleans haven't contacted me, so I assume there haven't been any sales."

"What about Houston or Dallas? There must be a market there."

"Probably. I have some canvases ready, but I haven't had time to go out of town to place them. Maybe next week, though, I can drive down to Houston. The art classes are keeping food on the table and the electricity on, but there's not much left over for a long drive."

"How is the oil well coming along?" Marla asked. She had been appalled when Clare told her what she had done, but Marla was too good a friend to harp on what she felt was a foolish gamble.

"They've spudded it in and drilling has started. Now it's a matter of waiting to see. My geologist says it looks good." Clare had not mentioned that she was falling in love with the geologist. "Maybe you'll meet him sometime," she said casually. "He's quite nice. His name is Ryan Hastings."

Marla smiled vaguely. She had seen geologists before. Most were old and pauchy and smelled like the rigs they worked. "Would you like to come over for supper tonight? Beatrice is whipping up her famous soufflé."

"Thanks, but not tonight. I have a date."

"Oh?" Marla perked with sudden interest. "Anyone I know?"

"No," Clare smiled. "You haven't met him."

"Mmm. So you aren't going to become a recluse after all. Is it serious?"

"Oh, for goodness sake, Marla," Care blushed. "It's only a *date*, not an elopement!"

"Still, it's a start," Marla noted as she put away the last easel for Clare. "Have fun. I have to get home now. The church circle meeting is at my house tomorrow, and I want to make some sort of centerpiece for the table."

Marla left. She formed a plan as she cut across the back corner of Clare's yard that connected with her own. Now that Clare was starting to go out, she knew just the man Clare needed to meet. And best of all, he was in the art business. Marla quickened her steps.

Clare leaned back on Ryan's sofa and sipped her Amaretto. They had had supper at Nathan's on Lake Cherokee and had seen a movie afterward. All the way home, they'd laughed at the outrageously funny plot, and Clare still smiled when she recalled the leading lady's predicaments.

Ryan sat down beside her. "The only thing this apartment lacks is a fireplace," he observed. "I appreciate you finding the place for me."

"I probably could've come up with one that had a fireplace, but it would have delayed your moving to Kilgore for me to have looked longer. Besides, whenever you feel your pyromania becoming uncontrollable, you can come over and light a fire in mine."

"I still don't see what the rush was all about. These things take time, you know."

Clare frowned slightly. "I didn't want it to drag out. I want you to find the oil as soon as possible."

"I don't want to waste time, either. After all, the crew gets paid by the hour, not by the well. But you've lived in the oil field long enough to know it's more than a week's work to bring in a well, especially one this deep. You *have* lived here for a while, I suppose?"

"Yes, but that's neither here nor there," she responded evasively. "The point is, how soon can you do it?"

He shrugged. "There's no way of knowing for sure yet. We should know something more in a few months. I can't—"

"A few months!" she gasped. "That's too long. I told you

in New Orleans that I wanted the well brought in quickly!" Clare glared, the mellow mood entirely gone. "You can be so stubborn at times!"

"Me!" he exploded. *"You're* the one that's being unreasonable. What is this about you and money? Isn't it enough for you to be the richest woman in town? Are you going for the state title as well? How about trying for the richest woman in the Western hemisphere? How about the world?"

"Take me home," Clare hissed from between white lips. Her skin was pasty with anger and all her muscles felt rigid.

Wordlessly, Ryan walked her to the car and drove her home. At the front steps, he braked sharply but made no effort to get out and open her door. Angrily, Clare fumbled with the door handle, but he put out his hand and restrained her.

"Clare, look. I'm sorry. I didn't mean to say those things."

"Did you mean them?" she demanded stonily.

For a while, he was silent. At last, he replied, 'Whenever the subject of that well comes up, you're . . . obsessive. I can't understand it. It's as if you're dependent on it for your entire livelihood. Of course, that's ridiculous," he said, motioning at the grandeur of her house and grounds. "And it's almost as bad when I ask you anything about your past. Can't you explain it to me?"

"No. If you've figured out I don't want to discuss my previous life, why do you continue to plague me with questions?" Clare's protective mask of ice was locked firmly in place.

Ryan sighed and made a helpless gesture. "All right. I give up. I'm sorry. I don't want to fight with you."

Clare studied his face in the pale moonlight. "I don't want to fight, either. But I also don't want to play Twenty Questions!" she cautioned quickly.

"Will you come back to my apartment and finish your drink?"

"No. I'm really pretty tired. Maybe I'd better just go inside."

Reluctantly, Ryan got out and came around to open her door. "Will I see you tomorrow?" he asked as they slowly climbed the steps.

She nodded. "Let go on another picnic. There's a place down the road that looks out over a small valley. We'll have to climb a fence but the land belongs to a friend of mine. Marla won't care if we picnic there." She glanced at the still, starry sky. "Tomorrow may be the last chance of the year. I feel something in the air."

"I don't feel anything different," Ryan said. "If anything, it's gotten warmer."

Clare nodded. "I know. Well, I'll see you tomorrow at noon."

Ryan contented himself with a long kiss, then left with hopes of further patching up their quarrel the next day.

Clare and Ryan drove up the gentle incline to the north of Kilgore. "Here we are," she said confidently parking the car on a shallow dirt turnout. "I've got the wine and the quilt. You carry that basket. Betty cooked fried chicken especially for this picnic, and if we know what's good for us, we'll eat it all."

Ryan lifted the basket out of the backseat and raised his eyebrows. "This weighs a ton! We're going to be here a week!"

Clare laughed. "Betty likes you. She's told me a dozen times that her cooking led Eldon down the path of matrimony. Maybe she's after you, too!"

"If this tastes half as good as it smells, I may just give Eldon a run for his money."

Clare was waiting for him at the fence, lifting the top strand of barbed wire while she pushed the middle strand down with her foot. "Climb through, then hold it for me," she instructed.

Although he wondered where a rich woman had learned the art of crossing barbed wire fences, Ryan made no comment.

The view from the top of the hill was magnificent. A long hay meadow offered an unobstructed view of the wide sweep of land to the valley below. In the far distance, Gladewater could be glimpsed among the trees; a sliver of highway threaded in and out of the woods below them.

Clare spread the quilt and glanced at the clear blue sky. "It sure is stuffy today. There isn't a breeze blowing at all."

Ryan shrugged. "At least we won't have to worry about rain."

As they ate, they watched the tiny cars in the distance, now and then disappearing behind a particularly colorful group of sweetgum or persimmon. With the meal consumed, they lay back on the quilt.

"I'm too full to move," Ryan groaned.

"Maybe that's what Betty had in mind," Clare suggested, her eyes closed.

In the far distance, the brilliant sky was darkening just above the tops of the farthest trees. In the woods behind them, the birds fluttered nervously and searched for sheltered limbs.

"I'm so full I'm going to have to lay here until I die," Ryan complained.

"Bitch, bitch, bitch," Clare observed amiably.

The rim of dark sky was wider now, and looked bruised and angry.

Ryan brushed away a thin trickle of sweat from his brow. "What did you do Thanksgiving?"

Without opening her eyes, Clare replied, "I ate with Marla and Tom. What did you do?"

"I went out with some friends. My family is all gone now. I wanted to get up here to see you, but I was trying to hire the crew."

"Will you be here for Christmas?"

"Sure. Everything I'm interested in is here in Kilgore."

Clare had the feeling he was looking at her, but she didn't open her eyes. "I'm not accustomed to asking for dates, but will you have Christmas dinner with me? I don't have any family, either, and I don't want to be alone."

"Is that the only reason?" he asked softly.

"No, I want to be with you." She opened her eyes to kiss him, but looked beyond his head and froze.

The sky was a dark, flat navy blue from almost above their heads to the far horizon, where it was nearly black. Below, the trees were gradually, steadily, almost miraculously turning to silver.

At her indrawn breath, Ryan turned and started. "What—"

"A blue norther. And a really bad one." Clare jumped up and began stuffing the remnants of their meal into the picnic basket. "We have to get off the hill. Fast."

Puzzled, Ryan shook the leaves from the blanket and folded it. "Are you afraid you'll get wet?"

Clare shook her head. "Look at the trees. That's an ice storm."

By the time they reached the fence, the blue-black sky was directly overhead and the temperature had dropped thirty degrees. As they got into the car, the first pellets of ice were stinging their skin and both were shivering. Clare had no objections when Ryan got in behind the wheel, and by the time he started the engine and turned around, the wind was gusting wildly.

As the trees whipped in the gale, eddies of brilliantly colored leaves raced through the air. The highway was already dangerously slick.

When they reached town, a film of ice sheathed every mailbox, fence and tree in sight. Ryan was amazed at the suddenness of the onslaught; Clare was stoical.

"It's the worst one I've ever seen," she said. "But this hot, still weather should have given me a clue. I've seen enough blue northers not to be surprised."

I've heard of them," Ryan admitted, "but I never realized how fast they happen."

She nodded. "The farmers will lose some cattle tonight, I'm afraid. I've never seen it so bad."

Ryan went by his apartment to get a heavy coat, then took Clare home. She wanted to take him back to the oil rig, but he refused to let her risk driving in the storm. Instead, he called one of the roughnecks on the afternoon shift to come by and pick him up at her house.

"You stay inside where it's warm," he instructed her when the man drove up out front and honked. "I don't want to worry about you driving and sliding off into a ditch. Okay?"

"Okay," she agreed passively. "And remember. You're coming here for Christmas dinner. Don't forget."

He kissed her lightly. "I won't. I'll call you tonight."

Clare closed the front door behind him and leaned against it with a smile. She could learn to like having someone take care of her.

The insistent ring of the telephone dragged Clare from her painting. Clutching her palette and an array of brushes in one hand, she lifted the receiver as she tossed her hair back from one ear with an impatient jerk of her head.

"Hello?"

"Hello. Is this the Clare Marshall residence?"

"Yes." It was probably only a pesky salesman and she was already forming her negative reply to whatever he was selling.

"My name is Cliff Anderson. I own the Anderson Gallery in Dallas. Perhaps you've heard of it?"

She hadn't. "Yes, of course, Mr. Anderson."

"I'm in town for the day and I hoped I might be able to see some of your work. I realize this is terribly short notice, but I hope it won't inconvenience you too much."

Calming her voice, Clare replied, "No, of course not. I'd be delighted to show you what I have on hand." She glanced around her studio. Like most artists, she rarely cleaned her workroom, and for the past few weeks it had been doubling as a storage space and a winter nursery for her plants. "When can you come by?"

"Oh, say, in an hour? Would that be suitable?"

"Yes," she lied. "That'll be fine." She gave him directions to her house and hung up.

"Betty!" she yelled. "Can you drop whatever you're doing and straighten up in here? Don't worry about the oils and canvases, but can you collect all the paint rags and put them out back to air?" She looked frantically at the masses of potted plants that had been brought indoors due to the freezing weather. "And I'll help you find somewhere else for most of these plants. A gallery owner from Dallas is coming to see my art, and this room looks more like a greenhouse than a studio."

As she talked, Clare tried to straighten a pile of sketch books she had stacked in one corner in lieu of shelves. A large box of summer clothing, presumably on its way to the attic, had somehow been left on the floor. The vacuum cleaner and a rack of TV trays were hiding behind a chest she'd hoped to refinish . . . someday.

"Miss Clare, you're running around like a chicken with its head cut off. You get upstairs and change clothes while I take care of this."

Clare looked down at her cut-off jeans that she normally painted in. "You're right. And I've *got* to do something with my hair!"

She ran from the room and climbed the stairs two at a time. A gallery owner had searched *her* out! Where had he heard of her? Had he come to town specifically to see her? Thoughts jumbled in her mind as she showered. What should she wear? The burgundy blazer? No, she looked like an accountant in that one. The red dress? No, it was at the cleaner's.

She blew her hair dry and thanked heaven for the natural waves that made it unnecessary for her to fuss over it. What did a real professional artist wear at home? It had to be casual enough not to look as if she'd dressed as frantically as she indeed was doing, yet be striking enough for him to remember her easily. With trembling fingers, Clare applied eyeshadow and lip gloss. Over her shoulder, she could see the open closet door and mentally considered and discarded every garment in there.

"This is silly!" she chided herself. "He isn't interested in me, only my paintings." But she knew this wasn't entirely true. An artist, like an actor, sold his charisma as much as his craft. How she presented herself could make a difference in whether or not her canvases hung in the Anderson Gallery.

Clare tried on one dress after another as the hands of the clock moved inescapably toward the hour. In exasperation, she pulled on a tunic top made of red silk and a pair of cream pants. Leaving the blouse unbuttoned lower than she'd normally wear it, she placed a thin gold belt around her waist. Not bad, Clare decided, glancing critically in the floor-length mirror. She put on gold earrings and two delicate gold chains of slightly different lengths at her throat. The hands of the clock stood at the hour. Quickly, she stepped into beige sandals and ran from the room. As Clare raced down the hall, she heard the doorbell sound. He was certainly prompt!

Skidding to a halt, she slowly walked down the stairs, feeling ridiculously like Gloria Swanson in *Sunset Boulevard*.

Betty had already opened the door, and a tall, silver-haired man was appreciatively watching her descent. Clare smiled dazzlingly.

"Hello, I'm Clare Marshall." She held out her hand.

He took it and smiled. "I'm Cliff Anderson. I never expected you to be so young. Most of the artists I deal with are middle-aged, and few are as attractive as you. You're a very welcome change." His expression told her he meant every word.

The man was a natty dresser. The charcoal-gray, three-piece suit he wore was well-tailored, and his light blue tie was perfectly coordinated with his oyster-white shirt.

Wondering if Betty had had time to turn the erstwhile storeroom back into a studio, Clare murmured her thanks.

"Won't you come in, Mr. Anderson? I have several canvases in the den and living room. Perhaps you'd like to see them first?"

He followed her into first one room, then the other, silently perusing the paintings. Clare tried to hide her nervousness, but her hands were trembling. Why didn't he say anything? Were they *that* bad? From the corner of her eye, Clare saw Betty in the hall. The maid nodded her head, winked and made a mysterious gesture that Clare assumed meant that the studio was presentable.

"The majority of my work is in my studio," Clare said confidently. "Will you follow me, please?"

Still silent, Cliff Anderson went with her. The studio adjoined the portico on the end opposite the morning room and had large windows facing both north and east. The pervading smell of linseed oil and turpentine lingered in the air, but the leafy odors and musty smell of the plants had gone away with the excess pots of foliage. Clare was relieved to find nothing remained in the room except her art equipment and paintings. Unfortunately, Betty preferred the tourist-priced New Orleans oils to the more classic ones, and several of these were prominently displayed. Clare quickly whisked away the small canvases with a mumbled comment about them being experiments and replaced them with her gallery pieces.

Anderson wandered around the studio, silently fingering his strong, square chin and occasionally making a low humming sound under his breath.

He hates them all, Clare thought. He's trying to find a way to exit gracefully.

"They're good," he said abruptly. "Very good. I'd like to have these two, and the field scene over there, and the one of the pond as soon as possible. If you don't have any exhibits lined up for early February, I'd also like for us to set up a private showing. Do you have the first week free?"

Clare's knees felt as if they'd buckle at any moment. "Yes, I believe I'm free then. I'll have to consult my calendar, of course, but I don't recall a commitment at that time." She went to a small desk calendar and held it so he couldn't see the conspicuously blank squares. "The first week in February? Yes, I'm available then. How many canvases would you like?"

"My gallery can handle about a dozen paintings. Bring some extra ones, of course, to replace the ones that sell."

"Of course," Clare said coolly. Why hadn't *she* thought of that?

He glanced at his watch. "It's getting near dinner time. Why don't we discuss the details over a steak?"

"I'd love to, Mr. Anderson."

"Please, call me Cliff. I prefer to maintain a less formal and more sociable relationship with my artists. I find it's more conducive to their creative flow."

"All right, Cliff," Clare smiled. "Just let me get my coat."

The roads had cleared of ice, but the trees, still heavily laden with a silver sheath, groaned stiffly in the slightest wind. The grass blades had become tiny, frozen spears that crunched brittley underfoot, and the air was bitter cold.

Clare huddled into her coat as her breath made a cloud about her. "It feels as if there's nothing between us and the North Pole but one strand of barbed wire fence," she said as she slid into his car.

Cliff Anderson laughed, and she noticed for the first time that he was a handsome man. His well-tailored coat set off his snowy hair and blue eyes in a way that would be enticing to almost any woman. Clare wondered why it had taken her so long to notice.

The meal was pleasant enough, although Cliff lacked Ryan's endearing humor. He was very interested in her art and, Clare suspected, in her as a woman. But she found no answering interest toward him as a man.

Strange, she thought. He's really quite nice. Just not terribly exciting. She tried to pick up the thread of the story he was telling.

"Where did you happen to see my work?" she finally asked out of curiosity. "Was it in New Orleans?"

"No. Actually, I never saw anything you had done before today."

Clare looked at him in confusion. "Then why are you here?"

"We have friends in common, Marla and Tom Gentry. She

called me a few days ago and, in the course of the conversation, she mentioned your work. I was coming through Kilgore on my way to Shreveport and I told her I'd take a look at it."

"Oh." Clare felt deflated.

He caught her tone and added, "Of course, if I hadn't liked what I saw, I would never have made you an offer. The Gentrys and I aren't that close. I'm in the art business as a monetary profession, not a charity. You really are very good."

Clare brightened. "Marla is really dear to help me make connections this way. I do appreciate it. But I needed to hear that you aren't doing it only because she called you."

"Absolutely not. Usually I ignore such calls, but I know Marla has a good eye for talent."

"Why don't we drop by there on the way home?" Clare suggested.

"Excellent idea. I haven't seen them in months." Cliff signaled the waiter for the check.

As they walked out of the restaurant, a black Trans-Am passed by. Its driver did a double take and almost ran into a parked car.

"Who's that with Clare!" Ryan exploded as he steered back into the correct lane. The man wasn't familiar to him, but he certainly seemed to be familiar to Clare. In the rearview mirror, he saw the man take Clare's arm in an overly possessive manner and then he helped her over an icy puddle to a waiting Cadillac.

"Damn," Ryan muttered.

He peered again in his rearview mirror, but Clare and her escort were already out of his field of vision. He turned at the next corner and circled the block, but by the time Ryan had driven back to the restaurant, the Cadillac was gone and another car was pulling in. His frown deepened and he circled two more blocks in hopes of catching sight of the elusive couple. Was Clare seeing someone else? He could think of no other explanation for what he had seen.

Giving up his search, Ryan drove home to his apartment. There was a perfectly logical explanation, he told himself as he took his coffee thermos and lunch box out of the backseat and grabbed his hard hat from the seat beside him. He went up the concrete steps to his room. Of course she had a reason, he repeated to himself. She must have one.

Still frowning, he hung his jacket and hat in the closet beside the door, pulled off his stained khaki work clothes and heavy boots and tossed his shirt and pants into the basket of washing that was waiting for his attention. He showered quickly, then toweled himself dry. Still he couldn't think of a single reason for Clare to be seen at a restaurant with the stranger . . . except for the most obvious one. His scowl deepened as he put on jeans and a velour sweater.

Ryan gave Clare ample time to reach home as he paced in his apartment, then he dialed her number. Betty told him she was out.

As he hung up, Ryan reasoned with himself. After all, Clare had told him she was not interested in any other man. He felt ridiculous at his unprecedented outburst of jealousy and was glad Clare hadn't been a witness to it.

He cooked a hamburger for supper and washed it down with a Dr. Pepper. Nonchalantly, he dialed her number again. Again Betty assured him Clare wasn't home.

Ryan frowned. Most of the ice was gone from the streets, though the bridges outside of town were still hazardous. But Clare didn't have to cross a bridge between the restaurant and her house. Not if she went straight home.

He turned on the television to a station that specialized in old movies and pretended to watch *Desk Set,* but not even Spencer Tracy and Katharine Hepburn could get his attention off Clare. Who was that man? he wondered. Clare had said she had no family. That ruled out uncles and cousins.

Again Ryan rang her number. This time, no one at all answered, and he realized Betty had gone to her own home. He flipped off the television and paced from the windows to the kitchen to the bedroom on a dozen useless errands. With nightfall, the temperature had dropped, and the streets were becoming slicker. He gazed out at the crawling traffic below his second-floor window.

Once more he called; again no one answered.

Had Clare somehow been abducted? She was a rich woman and kidnappings were not unheard of. His frown deepened and he paced faster.

And if she *wasn't* being kidnapped—which seemed unlikely as he doubted such people took their victims out to dinner first— who *was* that man? Jealousy again flared within him.

In the next three hours, Ryan called Clare five times.

When, at last, she answered, he had progressed from concern to open anger.

"Where the hell have you been?"

"Ryan?" she asked in surprise.

"I've been worried half to death over you. You could've been in a car wreck a dozen times over."

"Well, I wasn't," she said, miffed at his tone of voice. "Calm down."

"I am calm!" he roared. "And who was that old man I saw you out with at that restaurant?"

"He's not old and he's the owner of an art gallery in Dallas," she said frostily. "It's none of your business what I was doing with him."

"What do you mean, 'it's none of my business!'" he thundered. "Doesn't what we have between us matter at all to you?"

"Certainly it matters!" Clare's voice was also rising. "But this has nothing to do with us! Don't you trust me?"

"You're a fine one to talk about trust!"

"Don't you dare talk to me like that, Ryan Hastings! You don't own me and you never will!"

"Does that mean you're going to see him again!"

"That means it's none of your business whether I do or not!" Her voice trembled with rage. "Why are you being so unreasonable? Are you drunk?"

"Not yet!" Ryan snarled, and slammed down the receiver.

Chapter Fourteen

Ryan sat in the smoky bar and motioned for the barmaid to bring him another bourbon. The music didn't seem to be as loud as it had been when he'd arrived, and the people all seemed to be moving more slowly, as if they were underwater. He correctly assumed the alcohol was working; but the aching pain of Clare's apparent unfaithfulness was undiminished. He paid the girl for the drink and tossed half of it down in one gulp.

"Hello there," a sultry voice said quite near him. "Care if I join you?"

He looked up at the tall blonde and shrugged. "It's okay with me."

"I'm Regina Wharton," she purred.

"Ryan Hastings." He wished he hadn't let her join him. Her perfume reminded him of Clare.

"I haven't seen you around here before."

"I haven't been in Kilgore long."

She took out a cigarette and gave him an opportunity to light it, but he appeared not to notice. She lit it herself and blew a stream of smoke upward. "This place is usually quite crowded, but tonight it's dragging. Must be the weather."

"I hadn't noticed." Why didn't she go away? Her knee brushed his beneath the small table and he shifted to give her more room.

"Have you been to the piano lounge at Nathan's? It's much nicer."

"I know." He tried to resign himself to her company.

"You don't talk much, do you?" she observed with a smile. Breathing smoke, she French exhaled. Ryan glanced at her and looked away quickly, as if he had caught her doing something not quite proper.

Once more she nudged her knee to touch his and he looked at her sharply, though his vision was somewhat blurred.

"I'm so glad I came here tonight. Otherwise, we might never have met. What brings you to Kilgore?"

"I'm a geologist. I'm drilling a well outside of town." He felt her foot rubbing against his ankle in an unmistakable signal. Although he started to pull away, he didn't move. There seemed to be no reason to resist. The woman was not unattractive, though she looked too hard and calculating for his taste. At least she seemed to want him and not some gray-haired man that was old enough to be her father, as Clare apparently preferred. Ryan gazed at his glass.

"How fascinating! I've been in Mexico and have gotten *so* out of touch with what's going on around here." Regina leaned forward slightly so that the neck of her blouse parted to reveal her breasts. "Are you going to strike oil?" Her narrowed eyes gave the words a deeper meaning.

"That's the general idea," he said, tossing down the last of his drink.

She laughed delightedly. "That's marvelous!" she exclaimed theatrically. "That calls for a celebration."

"We haven't hit it yet. In fact, we've only begun drilling." In spite of himself, Ryan felt himself responding to the woman's advances. After all, he reasoned, Clare doesn't own me, either!

"Why wait until the last minute?" Regina murmured. "We could have our own celebration. Tonight."

Ryan regarded her through the warm haze of his bourbon-clouded reason. Why not? he asked himself. Why the hell not? "Let's go."

He followed in his car as she drove slowly through the nearly deserted streets so as not to lose him at a stop light.

She pulled up in front of her ostentatiously large French provincial home and waited for him to open her car door.

By this time, the bourbon had dulled Ryan's senses to the point of not noticing the piercing cold, and he had become somewhat maudlin—even to the point that the creaking of the icy trees sounded remarkably like a heart breaking. He supposed, philosophically, that meant he was drunk. As he followed her into the house, he wished heartily that he was with Clare. Perhaps he could still leave.

"What can I fix you to drink?" Regina asked. "Brandy?"

"Bourbon. On the rocks." One more drink couldn't hurt. *Then* he would leave.

Regina handed him a glass of amber liquid and sat down on the silver couch. The room was done in neutrals and seemed to Ryan to be as frigid and stiff as the night outside. She patted the cushion beside her and he sat down.

"Are you always this quiet?" she queried.

"Sorry. I have a lot on my mind tonight." Without the smoky stench in the bar, he was even more aware of her perfume, and the dull ache in his chest deepened.

Regina sipped her brandy and studied him. He was easily the most handsome man she had ever seen—not in a pretty way, but rugged. Like the men on the beer commercials who rescued the floundering calves from the snow or plunged on horseback through flooded streams. She smiled. Lately, she had felt Neal Thorndyke's interest was waning, which had prompted her visit to the bar. What better way to make him attentive than through jealousy, and who would do better for the job than the gorgeous man beside her?

"I don't mind if you don't feel talkative. Sometimes words aren't necessary." She lifted her finger and tickled the hair at the nape of his neck.

Ryan wished he hadn't come, but he could see no way to leave gracefully now. And why should I? he asked himself. Clare doesn't love me. Maybe she never will. I wonder if she let that man kiss her.

"Do you mind if I slip into a robe? This dress isn't very comfortable," Regina was saying seductively.

Ryan felt as if he had somehow stumbled onto a bad movie set. "It's okay with me," he said obligingly as the bourbon traced a trial of forgetfulness down his throat.

I can't leave now, he thought as she left the room. But as

soon as she comes back, I'll tell her I have to go. Then he thought, I wonder just how far Clare *did* let him go! The idea made Ryan shake with frustration.

Regina appeared in the doorway and, like an actress from an old, old movie, struck a seductive pose. "Miss me?" she breathed.

"Yeah, well, maybe I'd better be going," Ryan said, after glancing at the transparent robe and the nakedness beneath. "It's getting late and—"

"Silly," Regina purred. "It's not all *that* late." Sensuously, she began to trace a design on his chest with her fingers.

A maddening vision of Clare doing exactly that with the stranger made Ryan wince. What if she let that bastard make love to her! Ryan's intentions of leaving melted, and he let his desire for Regina build. Why should he let Clare get to him? She wasn't the only woman in the world, nor even the only one who found him appealing! He could get by without her, if that was the way she wanted it, though it would take some effort. Regina's red-tipped fingers were unbuttoning his shirt. As she slipped her hand inside his shirt and caressed his skin, Ryan gave in. He put down his glass, took her in his arms and kissed her. She wasn't the woman he loved, but she was there. And maybe in her arms he could forget Clare and ease the pain that tore at his heart.

Regina held her lips more firmly than he liked and she jabbed at him with her tongue in a way he found almost repelling. The cigarette smoke on her breath was distasteful after the sweetness of Clare, but Clare had given herself to another man. The thought made him groan with pain and he kissed Regina roughly.

Her features were too knowing to be pretty, he reflected, and she was overly thin, with skin that had seen too much sun. But many of the men he knew would have found her desirable. Even if her eyes were blue rather than smoky gray and her hair unnaturally blond rather than rich brown. Ryan fumbled at her small breasts and tried to forget Clare's supple body.

Feeling his passion rising as Regina expertly unfastened his zipper, Ryan untied the belt of her robe and kissed her thin shoulder. As he touched her hard breasts, Regina squealed playfully.

"Not *here*," she protested coyly. "Not in the living room!" She caught his hand and led him into the hallway.

Ryan followed her upstairs to the pale, monotone bedroom. As she pulled down the silver satin bedspread, he silently removed his clothes.

"Oh, my!" she actually giggled. "You *are* fine!" She grasped his erect manhood firmly and stroked the shaft admiringly.

Ryan wished that he had left but felt unable to act upon the wish. Instead, he willed the bourbon to keep his brain foggy as Regina giggled again. Quickly, he pulled the robe away from her shoulders and kissed her.

"Not like that. You'll rip it." She stepped back and wriggled out of the robe like a snake shedding its skin. "There!" she said with a triumphant flourish.

Ryan appraised the length of her naked body noncommittally. It was no better or worse than others he'd seen. It would serve the purpose of making him forget Clare . . . if only momentarily.

Regina sidled up to him and pretended to pout as she ran her bony fingers over the hard ridges of his muscles. "Don't you think I'm pretty?" she coaxed.

"Of course," he said gallantly, hoping she wouldn't sense his insincerity, as he fondled her breast.

"Well, then *say* so," she teased, pulling his hand away.

Ryan sighed. He was in no mood for games. "You're pretty." Before she could demand more, he clamped his mouth to hers and eased her back onto the bed.

She arched her body beneath him and spread her legs invitingly. As Ryan entered her, she locked her legs around his waist.

Ryan was aware of her yelps of delight, but they were as a thing apart. He sought only the blinding oblivion of mounting passion and quick climax.

Soon they lay spent, their skins slick with sweat from exertion. Regina made a mewling sound, and he rolled over to let her breathe more easily.

"Oooh," she sighed. "You don't talk much, but you don't need to. You're great!"

Ryan grunted in what he hoped was a tone that implied the same about her performance. The last of the alcohol had left his brain; and her chatter, as she recounted every detail of their physical encounter, prevented the escape of sleep. When at last she finished recapping their individual climaxes, he slid away.

"Thanks," he said, trying not to notice the black smudges of mascara beneath her eyes and the lipstick-smeared sheet.

"You don't have to thank me," she smiled, running her hands provocatively over his hips.

Quickly, Ryan swung his legs over the side of the bed and stood up. The brief interlude had not helped, and he felt only guilt at having used the woman.

"Wait a minute," Regina protested as he pulled on his pants. "Where are you going?"

"Home. I have the early shift tomorrow." He was lying, but she would never know.

"Oh." Disappointment was written clearly on her face. "You're welcome to stay the night, you know."

"Thanks, but I really have to go."

Regina yawned and stretched. "Well, we'll have to do this again sometime."

"Yeah, sure." Ryan pulled on his shirt, stepped into his shoes.

"Okay if I don't walk you to the door?" she asked. "I'm really tired."

"That's fine. No problem. I'm sure I can find my way out." He strode with determination down the hall.

"Be a darling and lock up as you leave," Regina called sleepily after him.

Ryan didn't answer, but pulled the front door closed harder than was necessary to insure the house was secure. He felt such a disloyalty to Clare that he would have gladly turned back time to undo the last several hours if he could.

When he reached home and went to bed, sleep eluded him. All his thoughts were on Clare and his ridiculous jealousy. He thought uneasily about his tryst with Regina, but put it from his mind. He had no intention of ever seeing her again.

Regina knocked on the door of Neal Thorndyke's office and went in without pausing. He greeted her with a smile and a kiss that was meant for her lips, though she turned her head to receive it on her cheek.

"How are you today?" he asked. "You look as if cold

weather agrees with you." He sat back down behind his desk and moved a pile of papers over so Regina could sit on the corner nearest him.

"Why, thank you, Neal," she replied as she eased one hip onto the desk and swung her silken leg back and forth teasingly. "As a matter of fact, I feel especially good today."

"I suppose our date is still on for Friday night," he said confidently.

She hesitated for a fraction of a second. "I suppose so."

"What? You 'suppose so?' What does that mean?"

"Oh, nothing, Neal," she soothed. "Just . . . nothing."

He looked at her closely, and she averted her eyes and pretended to be very interested in the ring she wore on her right hand. "I know you too well, Regina Wharton."

As if caught in a web of intrigue, she sighed. "I said it's nothing."

"Are you seeing someone else?" he asked, choosing the most unlikely suggestion that occurred to him.

Regina let her eyes grow big. "Who on earth told you?"

Neal stared at her in stunned disbelief. "What?"

She tried to blush but settled for looking flustered. "I haven't known him long. He's a geologist." She checked Neal's reaction out of the corner of her eye. "Ryan Hastings."

"Hastings! *Ryan* Hastings?"

"You know him?" Regina asked in genuine surprise.

"I've heard of him. Everyone in oil has. He's the top geologist in the business. I knew he was in town, but I had no idea you'd met him."

She shrugged. "I don't know. We . . . well, we never got around to talking about that." She reached across the desk and picked up the paperweight she'd brought Neal from Mexico and examined it as if she had never seen it before.

"What's *that* supposed to mean?" He was turning a deep red and stood up abruptly.

"Really, Neal, I don't think I should tell one man about another. It's so tasteless." She put down the paperweight and slid off the desk as if she were about to leave.

"Blast 'tasteless.' Tell me. Did he kiss you?"

Regina smiled reminiscently. "Maybe." She turned to walk toward the door.

Neal pulled her around to face him. "Regina! You didn't go to bed with him! Did you?"

Again she hesitated a second longer than she should have. "I don't want to talk about it."

"You did!" he thundered. He'd been so positive Regina would wait until he got around to marrying her!

"You needn't take that attitude with me, Neal," Regina pouted. "After all, we don't have an agreement between us." She gazed up at him from under her lowered eyelashes—a trick she had learned that was supposed to make her seem demure. "Do you still want me to go out with you Friday?"

"Yes," he answered absently. Hastings was a dangerous rival and Neal wanted him out of town—quick. "I've had the tickets to the play at the college for a month. It's the one you said you wanted to see."

"Marvelous." Regina smiled.

"Then you'll go with me?"

"Of course. After all, you asked me first." She patted his cheek and brushed against him as if by accident. "I have to run now. I have a *million* things to do. Oh, by the way, Dyna Carrington's party is Saturday. You haven't forgotten, have you?"

"No, no, of course not."

"Good. 'Bye now." She swept grandly from his office.

Thorndyke pursed his lips thoughtfully. He had no intention of giving Regina up without a fight. Purposefully, he sat back in his chair and punched the button on his intercom. "Miss Parson, send in Pete Hammly."

When the young man entered, Thorndyke said, "Good morning, Pete. I have something I want you to do. Could mean a Christmas bonus for you." He chuckled condescendingly. "We can all use a little extra money at Christmas, can't we?"

"Yes, sir," his employee admitted.

"There's a geologist in town. A man named Ryan Hastings. He's drilling a well for Clare Marshall. I want you to find out all you can about him. Where he lives, who's on his crew— that sort of thing. You can do that for me, can't you, Pete?" Neal tapped on his desk with a yellow pencil.

"Yes, sir." This was better than serving foreclosure notices, which Hammly was usually sent to do. "I'll get right on it."

"Oh, Pete. All this is just between the two of us. No need for anyone else to know what you're doing, especially Hastings. Understand?"

"Yes, sir."

Thorndyke watched the man leave, then snapped the pencil in half.

Ryan awoke that morning and was immediately sorry that he had. His head roared as if a freight train were racing through it and his mouth tasted foul and furry. With a groan, he recalled the evening before in vivid detail. What was her name? Oh yes . . . Regina. Damn! What could have possessed him to do such a stupid thing? Kilgore was not a large town and from the looks of Regina's house and clothes, she had to be one of the more prominent citizens. The possibility that she and Clare didn't know each other was too remote to be considered.

Against his better judgment, Ryan tried to sit up. It was his second mistake of the day. He felt as if he were inside out and surrounded by a yellow-green cloud of vague nausea. Knowing all too well nothing was going to help much, he stumbled to the medicine cabinet and took some aspirin. The image in the mirror was not encouraging, and he realized with a leaden certainty that he would have to die to feel better.

Doggedly, he went to the kitchen to make coffee. While it was loudly perking, he made two pieces of dry toast and wondered if the clock had *always* made that annoying buzzing sound.

By noon, he felt half-human again and lifted the receiver to call Clare. Realizing she'd probably hang up on him, Ryan replaced the phone and drove over to see her.

With the blue norther much further south, the sun had returned, turning each sliver of ice into a magnificent prism. Several tree limbs had broken off during the night and lay like masses of shimmering lace on the frozen ground. The world hovered in the wondrous moment between raging ice storm and melting slush, and all of it hurt Ryan's bloodshot eyes.

He rang Clare's bell, and in a few minutes she answered the door. Her long hair was pulled back from her face and tied with a narrow velvet ribbon the same shade of orange as the bittersweet bulky knit sweater that she wore. Her jeans hugged her rounded hips and molded smoothly over her long, graceful legs. Ryan had only an instant to think how lovely and feminine she looked in comparison to Regina's brittle sophistication, because when Clare saw who was standing on her porch, she tried to slam the door. Ryan caught it before it closed and wedged his foot inside.

"I've got to talk to you," he said.

"I don't have anything to say to you. Move your foot!"

Seeing that she was in no mood to be philosophical about their argument, Ryan firmly pushed the door open and stepped into the entryway. "I came to apologize."

"I accept," she ground out. "Now leave."

"It's not fair to lie about accepting an apology. Especially to a dying man."

"You *do* look terrible," she said with some satisfaction. "You must have let all the stops out last night."

"I did. Can I get myself a cup of coffee, or should I just lie down in a corner and quiver?"

"I'll get you some coffee. Otherwise, you'll be in the way when Betty does the floors. It's this way."

He followed her toward the kitchen, already feeling more cheerful. "Do you realize this is the first time I've been in your house?"

"You came here to pick me up every time we've had a date."

"I only saw the entryway and the living room. Those don't count. When a woman shows you her kitchen, then you know you belong."

Clare smiled in spite of herself. "If I had known it meant so much to you, I could've brought a photograph of it to New Orleans that weekend. Want to take a peek at my garage?"

"Nope. Some things must be kept sacred." Ryan took off his tan suede jacket and tossed it over the back of the chair, then sat down at the table and took the coffee she offered him.

Clare couldn't help noticing how handsome he looked in the gold and brown western shirt. It was tailored to his lean body as if it had been sculpted to fit him, and accentuated his broad chest and flat stomach. "I'll ask you again," he repeated, "will you forgive me? I acted like a jealous fool last night."

"An hour ago, I was still ready to rip your heart out," she confessed, "but, yes, I really do forgive you. But don't do it again."

Ryan sipped his coffee and sat stoically silent.

"Well? Aren't you going to ask me who he was?"

"Who?" Ryan responded innocently.

"The man you saw me with."

"Nope."

"I'm going to tell you anyway. His name is Cliff Anderson and he owns a large gallery in Dallas. He's going to hang some of my paintings and is arranging for me to do a private showing in February."

Ryan smiled wryly and took Clare's hand. "Now I really *do* feel bad. You meant it when you said it was business."

"Forget it," she said. "It was a misunderstanding. I guess I'd feel the same way if I saw you out with another woman."

He moved uneasily and lifted the cup to his lips. There was no way he could tell Clare about Regina. He hoped fervently that Regina was not prone to gossiping about her conquests.

"After supper, we went to Tom and Marla's. All the details about my show are worked out, and all I have to do is to be there on time with my canvases. He took four of them back with him this morning. He stayed with the Gentrys," she added pointedly.

Ryan ignored the barb. "I'm happy for you, honey. I don't know much about art, but I can tell this is an important step."

She nodded. "It could be the turning point of my career. Marla says the Anderson Gallery is very prestigious, and Cliff is sending announcements to some of his biggest patrons."

Ryan leaned over and kissed her lightly. "That's for luck. But you have enough talent not to need much of it."

"I thought you said you didn't know much about art," she teased.

"I don't. But I know a great deal about what I like . . . and I like your pictures. So will everyone else. When the time comes, I'll form your fan club."

She laughed. "In the meantime, will you go with me to a party? It's being given by someone I know but don't especially like, and I don't want to go alone."

"What man could refuse so flattering an invitation? Of course I'll take you. When is it?"

"Saturday. Why is it I always seem to be the one asking for the date around here?"

"You're right. Will you go out with me on Friday and Sunday? It's necessary for the maintenance of our status quo."

"You're crazy," she laughed. "I'd love to."

Chapter Fifteen

Dyna Carrington's house, like Dyna herself, was spare and austere. The cavernous living area contained so little furniture that Clare had wondered after her first visit whether or not the movers had finished unloading. Highly polished hardwood floors ran uncluttered to the stark white walls that seemed to extend forever before vaulting overhead to form an arched ceiling. Three low red couches formed a plush horseshoe around an even lower table of polished black marble. On opposite walls hung enormous matching prints that only their creator and Dyna could love—they exactly matched the red couches.

Clare hated coming to Dyna's home for two reasons. First, she always felt like a naughty child who was bound to leave grimy fingerprints on something before she left. Second, Dyna made it a habit to invite ten people more than her couches could seat, so that her guests would have to mingle. But Clare rebelled against the manipulative trick. More than once, she had wondered what Dyna's reaction would be if she plopped down cross-legged on the floor or dragged a chair out from the kitchen to sit on.

To celebrate the approach of Christmas, Dyna had draped herself in silver lamé—to accentuate her recently frosted, bouffant hairstyle—and had erected an aluminum Christmas tree. The tree was hung with couch-red ornaments; four red presents, one for each member of the family, reposed beneath it.

Within five minutes after Clare and Ryan arrived, Dyna was reporting the latest scholastic achievement of her twins. They were always the smartest, the most athletic, the most mature in their class. Clare knew they were both boys, but their mother never gave a clue, as she invariably referred to them as "the twins." A matched set; indivisible. Their father was never referred to at all.

As with all Dyna's parties, the tone was one of hushed familiarity. Neither she nor her silent house encouraged gaiety, and only a low murmur ruffled the cloisterlike serenity.

"How proud you must be of the twins," Clare said smoothly, as she had on many occasions before.

"Yes, they are incredible. I was talking to their math teacher just last week, and he assured me they're capable far beyond their years. He said he wouldn't be surprised if they make their mark on the world." Dyna smiled knowingly. "Of course, that's hardly news for us, though, is it?"

"Certainly not. They have always been quite extraordinary."

"How old are they?" Ryan asked, more out of politeness than curiosity.

"Eighteen next month," the proud mother announced.

"Both of them," Clare added innocently.

Ryan hid his smile. "I suppose they'll be going away to college next year." He wondered how long he could endure such inane conversation. Yet Clare seemed to be interested in the twins' progress.

"Heavens, no. They wouldn't think of leaving. They're already enrolled at our own college. Their major is physics."

"Both of them?" he asked.

"Naturally," Dyna said with mild surprise. "I must ask you to excuse me. More guests are arriving." With polished expertise, she glided away.

"These twins aren't Siamese, are they?" Ryan asked dubiously.

170

"No, but they may as well be. She even still encourages them to dress alike." Clare rolled her eyes.

"Let's go over there and get some punch," Clare suggested as she placed her hand on his arm and led him into the crowd. "Dyna is known for her innovative punch recipes, and we really must try this one. I hear she's done something with apricot nectar and rum." She grimaced playfully at Ryan as the subdued murmur of conversation surrounded and enfolded them into its midst.

For an hour or so, Clare and Ryan mingled with the other guests. Often their conversation involved people and events Ryan was neither familiar with or interested in, but it gave him an opportunity to view Clare from another perspective. He was not fond of what he saw.

In this crowd of plastic, posing socialites, Clare was fitting in perfectly. He could find no trace of the effervescent woman he had so recently fallen in love with; all he saw was proper responses to polite conversation. Suddenly, he realized he was seeing the mask Elliot had forged for his wife. How Ryan knew this, he wasn't sure, but he knew it was true. Or had her parents built this socially acceptable mold for her? Somehow he sensed the mask she presented was more recently acquired. There wasn't a slip of etiquette or turn of phrase, for Clare knew her role perfectly. He had stumbled onto a new piece to the puzzle that was Clare, but he didn't yet know where it fit in.

Clare steered him toward a gangly brunette who had just entered with a dark-haired man an inch shorter than herself. "Marla," Clare said. "I'd like you to meet Ryan Hastings. Ryan, Marla and Tom Gentry."

He was surprised to find that Marla's handshake was almost as firm as her husband's. Her eyes met Ryan's as a friend and equal.

"I've heard Clare mention you," Marla said. "You're the geologist from New Orleans."

"That's right. I've heard her talk about you, too. It's nice to meet you."

"Clare says you think there's oil down there," Tom said, gesturing toward the floor.

"We hope so. Only time will tell. Drilling for oil is always a gamble, especially on a deep well like this. But I'll be amazed if we don't find it. Everything looks good."

Tom and Marla launched into a reminiscence of their parents' tales of Kilgore's Great Oil Boom. It occurred in 1930, before either had been born, but to hear them talk, the memories were personal ones. Ryan listened with interest, but his attention was suddenly focused sharply on a blonde who had just entered the room.

Regina.

Ryan wondered how long it would be before Regina noticed him and came over to speak to him. He wondered what excuse he could possibly give for sneaking Clare out the back door. In his lifetime, he had made love to many women and he had no regrets; but he'd never been in love before, and he knew instinctively that a single word from Regina could wither the love before it could ever take root. He tried to force his attention back to the conversation.

In the same carefully modulated tones she had used since entering Dyna's house, Clare was telling one of her garden club friends about her art classes. Marla had turned to another woman, who was saying, "I hear the twins are still at it. This time it's the math teacher who's prophesying their mastery of the world."

Marla nodded. "She told me. Also, that they only want a few of Mummy's friends at their next birthday party."

"Do you suppose they could be possibly be robots?" the woman asked lightly, but with obvious sarcasm.

"I suspect as much. If they weren't boys, I'd start a rumor that Dyna had had herself cloned."

Clare caught the end of the last statement and asked, "Dyna had herself what?"

"Cloned. You know, the twins," Marla repeated, delighting in the joke.

"Marla!" Clare cautiously exclaimed. "Dyna might hear you."

"I was only kidding, you know that." Marla's expression became serious for a moment, then impish again. "I dare you to do a tap dance on the coffee table."

With a smile, Clare said, "It's tempting. However, I seem to have misplaced my tap shoes. I'll have to do a toe dance. I brought all my toes," she said as she fought back the laugh which threatened to burst out.

The maid who had approached with a tray of champagne tried to pretend she had not overheard, but the crinkle at the corners of her lips gave away her amusement. Clare was pleased. With the rigidity of the party, the maid probably needed a laugh.

Ryan was glad to finally see Clare drop the facade. Out of all the room, only Marla had fit in with the woman he loved. Why did she continue to associate with the others, who so obviously bored her? Against his will, Ryan glanced back at the woman by the door.

Tom followed his gaze. "That's Neal Thorndyke coming in. He's the president of the bank. Have you met him?"

"No," said Ryan, hoping Tom wouldn't suggest an introduction as Thorndyke was obviously with Regina.

"If you're a betting man, watch him," Tom warned jovially. "Neal Thorndyke is a card player and a half. I've seen him win several thousand dollars in one game and never bat an eye."

Clare had stopped talking and was listening intently to Tom, who wasn't aware she heard him.

"I recall one night he took Howard Wharton for every cent he had on him. Suckered him right in. It was a shame, but nobody could get Howard to leave the table."

Her face pale, Clare said, "I didn't know Neal was a gambler. What's his game?"

Tom shifted uneasily. He was all too aware of where this would lead. "Poker. Five-card draw."

"That was Elliot's game, too. Kilgore's not a very big town. There aren't many games around. Would you say he and Elliot got together?" Her voice sounded almost too casual, but her eyes were filled with hurt.

"Yeah," Tom said with unhappy certainty. "Yeah, they played together a lot. I didn't want you to know . . . nothing can be done about it now. Neal and Elliot were regulars, only Neal rarely lost."

Clare stared fixedly at Tom as the full realization hammered in on her. "But Elliot lost? To Neal Thorndyke?"

Tom nodded miserably.

Now it was all clear! Thorndyke had won Elliot's money; then, when Elliot couldn't pay, he had talked him into mortgaging her land! Then Neal had won that money, too!

Red anger misted Clare's mind and she turned to Ryan. "Take me home, please. Now."

"Clare, I'm sorry," Tom said. "I really am."

"It's okay," she said. "I'm glad I know. That explains a lot that didn't make sense before." She even managed a weak smile, but she felt close to tears. "Ryan?"

"Of course. I'll get your coat."

With perfection, Clare made her goodby speech to Dyna, then they left.

Across the room, Regina saw Ryan, did a double take, then noticed he was with Clare. Clare Marshall, of all people. Elliot's wife. Regina allowed no frown to trouble her face, but she seethed inside. Clare was one of the few single women in town who was rich enough to be a rival. She had somehow trapped Elliot into marriage, now she was after Ryan. And after the night Regina had spent in Ryan's arms, she was reconsidering her decision to marry Neal. Seeing Clare with Ryan confirmed it.

"Who's that with Clare Marshall?" Neal asked. "I haven't seen him around."

"*That,* darling, is Ryan Hastings," Regina replied with a knowing look and a lifted eyebrow.

Neal felt the fun leave his day. If that was his rival, he was in trouble. He had been concerned lately that Hastings might be able to strike oil before Clare's lease was up . . . It was a slim chance, but the man was good enough. The best way to get him out of town was to ruin the well, or at least stall the drilling until foreclosure could be brought on Clare's mineral rights. Thorndyke's expressionless eyes blinked and his calculator-like brain ran through all the possibilities. Killing Ryan would be difficult but not impossible. He mentally went over the list of crew members Pete Hammly had brought him. One name seemed perfect, Neal Thorndyke's lips smiled, but not his eyes.

The owner of the Cowboy Lounge had conceded to winter by nailing a sheet of plywood over the large fan mounted on the back wall, and by turning on several gas heaters along each wall. The room was not warm, but that prompted more drinking among his clientele.

Thorndyke motioned for the owner to bring two more whiskeys. He hated the place, but he was there on business. Waiting patiently for the drinks, he watched the man beside him. Sebe Youngblood had been born and raised in Kilgore just as he had. They had gone to the same school until the eighth grade, when Sebe quit school books for farm work. Thorndyke had known Sebe all his life. . . . He had spoken to him for the first time only three weeks before.

"How's the drilling coming along, Sebe?"

The man was staring hypnotically at the glass the bartender was filling and trying to keep his hands from shaking. "I'm doing my best," he whined. "That Mr. Hastings, he's all over the rig. Him and Mr. Talmidge. I've loosened bolts, hid tools, everything I can think of. They always come along and set things straight. They ain't caught me, though."

Thorndyke frowned. This wasn't what he wanted to hear. "You're going to have to do better than that. I'm not paying you to do this penny ante stuff. I want that well slowed down or ruined!"

"Yes, sir, I know." Youngblood grabbed the glass when it was placed in front of him and downed it in one gulp. As the fire spread through his body, calming his frazzled nerves, he closed his eyes and sighed. "I'm doing the best I can."

"Tomorrow I want you to put the boiler out of commission."

Sebe Youngblood's red-rimmed eyes widened and his mouth gaped open in his loosely wrinkled face. "The boiler! How'm I supposed to do that?"

"Hell, man, do I have to tell you everything? You know that equipment better than I do. Plug up the vent valve and overpressure it until it blows. I don't care how you do it, so long as it looks like an accident. And wear work gloves so you don't show up with scalded hands."

Sebe grinned slowly, showing the yellowed stumps of his teeth. "That'd put them off for sure. A thing like that could happen easy. It's an old boiler. Don't know why Mr. Hastings didn't put in a new one, anyway. It ought to set them back at least a week."

"Good," Thorndyke said with relief. "I'm buying you one more drink, then you're leaving. I want you sober enough tomorrow to do the job."

"Yep. Without no boiler, they can't make the machinery work or nothing." He nodded with respect for Thorndyke's wisdom. "That's real sharp."

"Thanks," Neal said wryly. He detested having to deal with a drunk like Sebe Youngblood.

The bushy pine tree spread its aroma as well as its limbs into the paneled den. Clear glass ornaments, as fragile as soap bubbles, floated among the dark green needles. Tiny sleighs pulled by miniscule reindeer flew between the branches, small angels perched beside little drums and minute stockings stuffed with peppermints and chocolates adorned the large tree.

"Are you sure that thing isn't alive?" Ryan asked as he edged beside a sweeping branch.

"Nonsense. It's a *beautiful* tree. I cut it down myself. It's a family tradition that I intend to carry on."

"But, Clare, shouldn't you have measured the room first? I mean, it's so big!"

"You're just used to buying a horrid tree from one of those lots. They're all painted green to cover the dead needles and look as if they're made from plastic. All the same shape, all the same height. Prickly little bottle-brush limbs and lots of bare trunk showing. Now *this* tree, on the other hand, has style. Personality. A tree to be proud of." She stroked the long, shiny needles admiringly. The angel sleeves of her silvery silk hostess gown flowed softly about her graceful arms with the movement, and her cloud of umber hair tumbled over her shoulder and onto her breast. She had no idea what a beautiful picture she made to Ryan's eyes.

"You've convinced me. From now on, I'll have only big, round Christmas trees," Ryan teased. "I guess that means you aren't fond of *my* tree."

She sniffed disdainfully. "A rubber plant decorated with a chain made from beer can pull-tabs and three pretzels tied on with string is *not* a Christmas tree."

"Maybe, maybe not," he said, reaching into the pocket of his navy blue slacks. "But look what grew under it." He handed her a small box wrapped in silver paper.

She took it from him and smiled. "Thank you, Ryan."

"You don't know yet whether to thank me or not. It might be peanut hulls. Open it up."

"Maybe I'd better. It *is* pretty light," she said, shaking it experimentally. She reached under the tree and pulled out a large package for him.

"For *me?*" he gasped in a parody of surprise. "You shouldn't have!"

"I'm beginning to think you may be right," she said with a grimace. "Open it up before I take it back."

Ryan sat on the carpet and pulled her down beside him. "You have to sit on the floor to open your gift on Christmas. Otherwise, the Christmas fairy will be offended and blow up your tree."

She laughed. "That must be a custom I'm not familiar with."

"You mean you've lived with exploding Christmas trees all these years and never asked why? Foolhardy youth." He carefully began to unwrap his present. "The secret is to take the paper off slowly, make it last."

"If you don't hurry, Christmas Day will be over."

Soon the paper fell away, and he saw the painting she had done for him. It was of the pine forest where they had made love. She had captured the slanting sunlight, the golden pine needles, the incredible majesty of the trees. In the clearing, she had depicted Ryan leaning against a tree trunk. One thumb was casually hooked through the belt loop of his jeans and his other arm rested on the tree. He was smiling as if he'd only that instant caught sight of someone he welcomed. Although his pose was relaxed and comfortable, Clare had lost none of his male magnetism. He looked real enough to move at any moment. It was one of the best portraits Clare had ever done.

"When did you do this?" he asked. "I had no idea."

"I carry a picture of you in my mind, too," she said, looking at him rather than at the painting. "I was only going to paint the woods, but it seemed empty without you, so I changed it into a portrait." She paused self-consciously.

"You did a magnificent job! I can almost feel the wind through the pines. But why aren't *you* in the picture?"

"I didn't feel as if I should be. Not in your painting. I don't belong."

He gazed down at her and let his eyes rove caressingly over her face, her hair, her throat. "Yes, you do," he said tenderly. "You belong there very much." He lifted his hand and gently stroked the curve of her cheek, letting his fingers trace the clean line of her jaw and travel down her slender throat to the warm hollow where her pulse had begun to beat rapidly.

Clare knew they were discussing more than a composition, and she felt a blush steal across her face. To cover her nervousness, she began to open her own gift.

Inside the shiny paper was a dark blue velvet box. Slowly, she opened it, and sighed with wonder. An incredibly delicate opal pendant on the tiniest of gold chains lay in the velvet. Subtle fires of blue, green and gold flashed in the milky depths that shaded to pale pink and mauve. Awed, she lifted it from the box and held it up to the light. The stone seemed to pulsate with a life of its own and the chain shimmered as it laced through her fingers.

"It's beautiful!" she gasped.

"When I saw it, I knew it was yours. You're as delicate and feminine as it is. And, when we make love, I see the same fires burning deep in your eyes."

She looked at him in astonishment. "That's the most romantic thing I've ever heard," she said softly. Tears of happiness welled in her eyes. "You're so good to me."

"I'm only getting started." He reached out and took the necklace and fastened it around her neck. "It's not as beautiful as you are, but then, nothing is."

"Oh, Ryan," she sighed, putting her arms around his neck. "I'm so glad I know you."

"I'm glad I know you, too," he whispered.

The emotional warmth they both felt was accentuated by the flames that blazed cozily in the hearth. As they flickered onto the honey-gold oak paneling, it gleamed like satin. Ryan rose from the rust-colored plush carpeting, pulled some huge floor pillows from the corner and piled them in front of the fire.

"What are you doing? Making a nest?" she teased.

He caught her hand and drew her down beside him. "This is the only way to enjoy a fire," he said as he guided her head onto his shoulder. Protectively, he put his arm around her and stroked her arm as she rubbed her cheek happily on his midnight-blue sweater. The collar of the white shirt he wore beneath it contrasted sharply with the tan of the strong column of his neck, and his gold-brown hair fell easily across his brow. She sighed happily.

"You're right," she agreed as she snuggled closer. "I'm

glad you didn't have to work today. Everyone should be allowed to take Christmas Day off."

"It's not that simple," he said as he caressed the top of her shining hair. "We can't shut down the machinery. Most of the men are off today, though."

"How are things coming along? I mean, do you think we'll have any more problems?"

He gazed into the fire for a long while before he answered. "I think we have everything back under control. All these slowdowns have held us back, but some rigs are like that. They seem to have personalities of their own after a while. . . . Some never give any trouble and others seem to go wrong every time you turn around." He stared silently at the flames as he continued in his thoughts. The kind of problems he was having with the well were not the sort that happened consistently by accident. Could one of his crew be responsible? Nonsense, he chided himself. What would anyone possibly stand to gain by sabotaging Clare's well? He kissed her forehead and smiled. "Let's not talk shop tonight. I just want to think about you."

Clare smiled up at him and kissed him lightly. "All right. The well is forgotten."

The hypnotic flames leaped and sank to leap again on the logs. Beneath the andirons, a red, orange and yellow landscape glowed in the embers. Now and then, a bead of sap exploded into sparks like miniature fireworks.

"This has been a good Christmas," he mused. "The best one I can remember."

She nodded. "Almost perfect."

"Almost?"

Clare had been thinking that she wanted this day to go on forever. Just the two of them. But she was afraid to tell him that. "I'm too full," she said instead. "Betty's too good a cook."

"Tell me about it," he groaned. "One more slice of pie would have done me in."

The fire crackled and sputtered; and neither Ryan nor Clare voiced the true thoughts that each longed to share.

If only I could freeze time, he was thinking, I could hang on to this—keep her here beside me from now on. Aloud, he said, "The reason this Christmas is so good is because of you."

"It's lonely not having a family," she told him. "Sometimes it's worse if you *do* have one, though," she added, thinking of the times she had spent wondering whom Elliot was with. "That can be lonely, too."

"I wasn't thinking of my family. I meant it's good to be here with you." He rubbed his cheek against her fragrant hair.

Clare's heart beat faster. "I'm glad you're here, too. There's no one else in the world I'd rather have spent Christmas with."

"Do you mean that?" He gazed down at her as he gently stroked the rose-petal softness of her skin.

"Yes." She felt her eyes melt into his and had the sensation of feeling their souls touch, and merge.

Slowly, he bent his head and lifted her chin to meet his lips. He kissed her wonderingly, lovingly. Then more thoroughly as her warm lips parted beneath his. He held her close, his heart pounding.

"Clare, I've never known anyone like you. The more I see you, the more I want to be around you. I can't get enough of you."

She held to him tightly and wished she knew more about men. Did he mean those words? Were they only said lightly? She had no yardstick of experience with which to measure. Except Elliot. "Please, Ryan. Don't."

"Why not? Why are you so afraid to hear how I feel about you?"

"I'm afraid I'll get hurt again."

"Are you going to let one bad experience ruin the rest of your life?"

"It wasn't just an experience, it was a marriage," she defended herself. "And I haven't known you that long."

"What if I assure you my intentions are honorable?" he asked wryly.

Clare took a deep breath and plunged on. "What if I ask you who Doré is?"

The crackling of the fire emphasized the sudden silence in the room. Ryan wondered if he could possibly have heard right. "Doré?" he asked incredulously.

"Yes, Doré. I saw her photograph in New Orleans beside your bed. From the way she signed it, she must think there's something between you." She held her breath.

"I forgot the picture was there," he said absently.

"I don't want to play games. I don't want to share. That sounds childish, I know, but that's the way I feel."

"Doré Armound is dead, Clare. She died last summer in a car accident."

A wave of embarrassment washed over her. "Oh. I'm sorry. It must be very painful for you. I shouldn't have asked."

"How could you know? It was bad at the time. We had had an argument and she left angry. I followed her and saw the accident. She died instantly."

Clare tightened her arms around him as if she could protect him from the memories.

"I wasn't in love with her. I doubt that she was really in love with me, though she said she was. At any rate, she's gone. She has no place in our lives."

"I feel terrible about bringing it up. I thought . . . I thought she was in New Orleans waiting for you."

"I'm not like that, Clare."

"My husband had an affair. It started a few months after our wedding and lasted until he died. I knew about it from the beginning, although I tried to pretend I must be mistaken. I even know the woman quite well. You haven't met her," she added. "At any rate, I was afraid you wanted me to accept that there was someone else. I can't. Not ever again." Not with someone I may be falling in love with, she thought.

Ryan was silent. Now, more than ever, he knew he had to keep Clare from learning about his night with Regina. Clare would never understand that it had been triggered by seeing her with the gallery owner from Dallas. That it would never happen again.

"I understand," he said. "Clare, I'm telling you something important, so listen. I'm not seeing anyone but you. I have no one hidden in the wings, nor do I want to have, nor will I have. Understand?"

"Yes," she said with a smile. "I understand."

He kissed her tenderly and marveled at the way her body fit into the curve of his own, as if it belonged there. In time, he thought. In time, she will be ready to hear of my love.

The fire cast shadows of bronze on their gold reflected skin. The warm scent of wood smoke lightly touched the room. They lay together comfortably, watching the dancing flames.

"This is perfect," he said. "Let's do this again next year."

"All right. We can form a pact."

"Right."

"Should we throw salt over our left shoulders or something?"

"Nope, too messy. Let's kiss instead." He brushed her lips with his. "That seals it. A year from now. Right here. Together."

Clare smiled and nodded as she cuddled against his shoulder. But she wondered fleetingly if she would still own her home by the next Christmas. She wouldn't unless the oil well came in. "Next year," she said. "If not here, at least together."

Two days later, Joe Talmidge, wearing a new set of khaki work clothes that were already smeared with grime and grease, shoved the heavy iron lever into place. The chain screwed the upper section of pipe onto the length being held securely at the platform level. The bit had been changed and the many lengths of pipe had to be reattached and put back down the hole . . . one at a time. The job was tedious and very time-consuming, but it had to be done, and done right. Although he couldn't take his mind too far away from his work, Joe Talmidge was vaguely aware of someone almost out of sight beneath the platform, near the boiler. Like all the roughnecks, this person was dressed in a khaki shirt and pants, and from that angle Talmidge couldn't identify him.

Oh, well, he thought, what difference does it make? It's almost time for the next shift. It's probably one of them come early. He watched the newest section of pipe slide down into the earth. When it was flush with the platform, the giant clamp slammed around the pipe so that it and all the pipe below would not fall to the bottom of the hole. High above them, on the derrick's monkey board, a man pulled another pipe away from the steel forest leaning on the rig, fastened the hoist collar and let it swing over in a controlled arc to the roughnecks below. Skillfully, Talmidge joined this length to the others, and on went the process of "making a trip."

Ryan climbed the steps and stood beside him. "The last logging we did looked good. The mud we pulled through to four thousand feet proves part of my theory. The Woodbine sand stops east of here about two miles, that's why this land never produced any oil in the 1930's," he yelled over the roar of the machinery and the clang of the pipes.

"That's good news," Joe yelled back. "Do you think we'll have to go much deeper than twenty thousand?"

Ryan shrugged. "I can't tell yet. The other two wells south of here haven't hit anything, but they haven't gone that far down yet, of if they have, they're not telling. Come on over to the trailer when you're relieved and I'll show you the charts."

But before Ryan could reach the wooden steps, there was an asthmatic cough of the machinery, and then the drive belt quit turning, leaving a length of pipe swinging like a hanged man in the air. The rig was suddenly quiet except for a screaming hiss.

"What happened?" Joe asked.

"I don't know, but from the looks of all that steam, I'll bet we blew the boiler." Ryan went down the steps and under the platform. "Yeah. That's what it was," he said as he squatted down on his heels away from the hot cloud of vapor.

"How did that happen? It was doing fine when I came on this morning."

Ryan shook his head. "I guess it was older than I figured. That's what I get for trying to cut corners. Think you can fix it?"

Joe studied the boiler as well as he could through the steam. "I doubt it. That's a good-sized hole. I reckon we'd better get another one. This'll set us back at least a week, that is, if you can find a replacement."

Ryan hesitated. "Don't say anything to Clare, all right? I'll take care of it. I'll get a new one this time."

Joe looked at his friend questioningly. "*You're* buying the boiler? It'll run you ten to twelve grand. What's up?"

" 'What's up' is that we need a new boiler and the time delay alone is going to cut heavily into our budget. Besides, I think I can get one in Shreveport instead of having to go all the way to Houston."

On the platform above them, Sebe Youngblood loosened a bolt that worked one of the levers. His nerves were frayed, but he smiled. His task had been accomplished and he felt good about it.

Chapter Sixteen

Clare got in the elevator of Dallas' Hyatt-Regency hotel and pressed the button for the fourth floor. She still felt chilled from the cold February wind outside, but of necessity she'd left her coat locked in her car. Had she been staying at the Hyatt-Regency, which she was not, she would have had no reason to wear her coat to the hotel's dining room. The elevator glided to a stop and she got off. Good. The halls were lined with rooms and would serve her needs.

As she had in New Orleans, Clare had taken a room in an unpretentious motel at the edge of town. From there she'd gone to her show at the Anderson Gallery. The exhibit had gone much better than she had dared to hope, even to the extent that one of the clients, a handsome Venezuelan, had insisted she and Cliff Anderson join him for dinner afterward. For her convenience, they'd suggested they dine at her hotel. This time, Clare had been prepared. She had predetermined that if anyone asked, she would tell them that she was staying at the posh Hyatt-Regency. Having no reason to doubt her word, they had agreed to meet her for dinner and cocktails at eight.

Clare had found the hotel, but not without some difficulty and several wrong turns. She had left her car in the garage, and was now doing what she and Marla referred to as "casing the joint." Because Anderson was a friend of the Gentrys, Clare had been afraid Marla might mention the name of the hotel where she'd actually reserved a room. So she had taken Marla into her confidence. Marla had agreed the plan was a good one and even offered to call and have her paged if Clare thought this would help carry off the deception. Clare had declined, feeling anonymity was best in this instance.

Slowly, the chill was leaving her body, and she pressed the elevator button to return to the lobby. Nervously, she checked her hair and makeup, both of which were flawless. She wore a tangerine chiffon dress with a flowing scarf-pointed skirt and with cutaway sleeves that revealed her nicely shaped arms. The neck plunged to a deep V, exposing the curve of her breasts. Her small waist was encircled with a tie belt of the same fabric. Her hair was piled on top of her head in a seemingly innocent tumble of glistening brown waves that accented her large eyes and delicately pointed chin. She felt very daring and free.

After only a short wait in the lobby, Clare saw Cliff and the Venezuelan gentleman, Raoul Gutierrez, coming in the main entrance. With a charming smile, Clare went to meet them. Their spontaneous looks of appreciation told Clare her choice of dress was the right one. Together they went up Reunion Tower to the Top of the Dome for cocktails.

The lights of Dallas stretched out in all directions below them as the dome slowly revolved in the night sky. She ordered a gin and tonic and relaxed into the pampering atmosphere.

Raoul Gutierrez was a small man, more intriguing than handsome, with thinning brown hair and dark eyes which had the intenseness of a predatory bird. When he moved, it was with quick, jerky movements; and his voice was more reso-nant than Clare would have expected from the looks of him. He quickly made it obvious he was an art collector, though on a small scale, and that it would be a plume in Clare's bonnet if her work interested him.

Clare couldn't see how placing her pictures in his secluded summer house on an obscure mountain top in Venezuela would benefit her much in the long run, but she saw a great short term benefit in the thousand dollars he was willing to pay. Although she didn't like him personally, she was more than willing to flatter him along into a sale. So she pretended not to notice that his jokes were rather blue and that he persisted in referring to her as a "girl," though he seemed to recognize Cliff's status as an adult.

"Ready for dinner?" Gutierrez asked as he got to his feet.

"Certainly," Clare said, though her glass was only half empty. Put up with it, she told herself. This can't last forever.

They went down to the Antares Room, where Anderson had made reservations. As in the lounge above, a panorama of Dallas shimmered below them. Gutierrez asked for a table away from the window and she sighed with resigned disappointment.

The menu was varied and tempting, and Clare felt instantly hungry as she tried to decide between shrimp and the flounder dishes.

"Garlic steak for us all," Gutierrez told the waiter. "And a bottle of your finest Moet et Chandon Dom Perignon champagne."

"What?" Clare said, startled out of the Garbo-like façade that she and Marla had decided would make her seem more artistically eccentric and less likely to disclose her amateur status. "What did you say?"

"Garlic steak. You will love it. It is the most expensive item on the menu."

"But I prefer something less spicy," she protested as the waiter reached for her menu.

Gutierrez flicked the waiter away with his fingers. "Nonsense. I know what ladies prefer. Trust to me. You will love it."

Clare decided that enough was enough. Fixing the waiter firmly with her eyes, she said, "I'll have the broiled flounder. And sour cream on my baked potato."

Gutierrez rolled his eyes at Cliff and looked slightly irritated at the headstrong folly of American women.

"Tell me about your new yacht," Cliff said smoothly, as if he sensed no conflict. "Is she entered in the races this year?"

Clare again put an aloofness between herself and her companions and wondered if Cliff, too, were wearing a mask. Gutierrez accepted the offered wine from the waiter, sipped it and reluctantly pronounced it good. He was watching Clare for more signs of rebelliousness, but she merely looked enigmatic and smiled.

The meal was well-prepared and delicious. Clare enjoyed her fish but noticed Cliff ate with far less gusto than his client. Evidently the garlic steak was not his choice, either. She felt a sudden pride in her newborn streak of assertiveness; certainly Elliot's wife wouldn't have done that! She pulled her attention back to the conversation.

"It was disgraceful!" Raoul Gutierrez was declaring. "I had invited him to my home—to a dinner party—believing him to be one of us! True, I had only seen his paintings, but I believed him to be an aristocrat! You can perhaps imagine my plight when I overheard him tell a guest that his fathers works in a car garage! I was filled with mortification."

Cliff tried to look understanding.

"Was his art good?" Clare couldn't resist asking.

Gutierrez looked at her as if she were changing the subject. "That truly isn't the point. In my country, the commoners know their place."

Clare clamped her mouth shut to hold back the words that threatened to bubble forth. This sale was far too important both to her career and to her pocketbook to let a personality conflict ruin it. She struggled to regain her detachment as a chill coursed through her that had nothing to do with anger. That could so easily be her own story!

She took a sip of champagne as her eyes roamed over the room. Such a thing wouldn't happen to her! There was no way Gutierrez would know of her background unless she told him, and she had no intention of making such a mistake. Her eyes fell on a waitress with frizzy red hair, passed by her, then snapped back. The woman was balancing a tray of dirty glasses on one hand and wriggling her fingertips at Clare in recognition. Instantly, Clare gasped and choked on her champagne. She needed no second look to know it was Reba Fae Mattison. They had gone from first grade through their high school graduation together, though they had never been close friends. Already Reba Fae had deposited her tray and was threading across the dining room to speak to Clare. But the Clare *she* knew was the daughter of a dirt farmer and not at all the woman Clare was trying so hard to portray.

"Are you all right?" Cliff asked with genuine concern. "Take a sip of water."

Clare tried, but it only made matters worse. People at the next table were staring and she was totally embarrassed. Reba Fae was halfway across the room.

"Excuse me," Clare croaked, pushing away from the table. Hurriedly, she walked toward the ladies room, still trying to catch her breath.

"Are you okay?" Reba Fae asked, coming into the powder room area behind her. "I thought that was you, but I wasn't sure until you looked at me."

Clare was regaining her composure now and managed to smile.

Reba Fae patted her on the back. "I guess something went down the wrong way. That happens."

Clare nodded. "Thanks, I'm better now. It's been a long time since I've seen you."

"Yeah, I left Gladewater right after we graduated. Came to the city. You're looking good. What're you doing in Dallas?"

"Trying to sell some pictures," Clare said truthfully. "My husband died last summer and I'm working as an artist."

"That's real tough. Mine just up and left me. I've got two kids now. You have any?"

"No."

"They're a handful. Have you seen anybody lately we used to know?"

"No, I don't get over that way too often."

"I wrote letters to some of 'em for a while, but I finally quit. Well, I better get back to work before the boss catches me."

"Me, too," Clare said, realizing their positions were not so different, after all. "Take care of yourself."

"Sure enough," Reba Fae grinned as she left.

Clare smoothed her hair and put on fresh lip gloss. She wasn't eager to rejoin the men. When she came back to the table, however, Gutierrez showed great concern as to her welfare, while Cliff seemed to assume she was all right.

"You must let us see you to your room," Gutierrez said. "I could never forgive myself if you were ailing and I gave you no help."

"Really," Clare protested, "I'm fine now. It's nothing."

"No, no. Women are to be cared for. I insist."

How can he make even thoughtfulness seem insulting? Clare wondered. "Please, don't concern yourself. I only choked on the wine."

Gutierrez gestured to the waiter and paid for the meal. "Please. I insist."

"She seems to be okay now," Cliff said doubtfully.

"You Americans. You don't understand women. They desire to be pampered and protected."

Clare was opening her mouth to speak and Cliff correctly read her expression. "Perhaps we *should* call it a night," he said quickly. "It's getting late and you have an early flight tomorrow."

They took the restaurant elevator down to the lobby. Clare was wishing she had the financial independence to refuse to do business with the little man, but her reason overrode her emotions.

At the other bank of elevators which gave access to the rooms, Gutierrez asked Clare for her floor number.

"Four," she said coldly as he followed her inside.

He pressed the button and the elevator glided up. When the doors opened, she stepped out, Gutierrez on her heels.

Clare halted abruptly. "I can find my way. Thank you for dinner. I hope you'll be pleased with the paintings you selected."

"I'm certain I will be," he assured her. "But I could not possibly abandon you in the hallway of a hotel. I will see you to your room."

Placing her hand firmly on her Latin rescuer's chest, Clare maneuvered him back into the elevator. "It's so good of you, but I must insist. We artists do have our eccentricities, you know. I never allow anyone to see the door of my hotel room." With a dazzling smile, Clare watched the elevator doors close between them. Instantly, her smile disappeared. That had been too close for comfort. How could she possibly have explained having no room? On the outside chance that they might still come back, Clare hurried to the nearby stairway.

Going down one flight, she went back to the elevator and pressed the button for the lobby. She had a long drive back to her motel and she hoped she could find her way in the dark.

Dallas' freeway system was not familiar to her, nor was she fond of going alone into covered parking garages at night.

As the elevator doors opened, she was searching in her purse for her car keys and almost ran into Cliff and Raoul. They stood only a few feet away but luckily, they were deeply engaged in conversation. Clare wheeled around and stepped back into the elevator, stifling a gasp. With her head averted, she punched the button for the second floor. After what seemed to be an eternity, the doors closed and she felt herself rising.

A short search revealed another stairway at the end of the hall, which led her to the end of the lobby opposite the elevators. Cliff and Gutierrez were still talking intently and showed no signs of preparing to leave. Steeling herself not to run, Clare crossed to the street exit. Getting to the garage would have meant having to walk right by the two men. As she waited for the valet to bring her car around, wondering if she had enough money for a tip, she shivered. The wind had subsided, but the air was icy cold after the warmth of the lobby.

At any moment, she expected her companions to walk out. There was no way at all to explain leaving the hotel without even a wrap. Nervously, she wrapped her arms about herself and tried not to let her teeth chatter.

The Mercedes came to a smooth stop and the attendant held the door for her. The heater was already warming the interior. Clare tipped him as generously as she felt she could and got inside just as the front door of the hotel opened.

There was no need to turn her head to identify the men's voices, and she drove away without looking back. Slowly, she let out her pent-up breath. This had been too narrow an escape.

Sebe Youngblood labored feverishly in the shadow of the derrick. From time to time, he glanced up and around but didn't dare pause in his work. Beneath his busy fingers, bright silver filings began to litter the ground and a shiny line appeared in the upper grove of the pipe's threads beneath his small hacksaw.

Sweat beaded his grimy forehead despite the coldness of the early morning. There would not be much time before someone noticed his absence from his post. Slowly, the metallic shavings peeled back and fell to the ground. The pipe was harder to cut than he had expected. But Neal Thorndyke had been very insistent.

"Sebe?" a man called out. "Come give me a hand here."

"Coming!" he answered quickly, grinding the bright shavings into the ground with the heel of his scuffed work boot. "I'll be right there!"

He hurriedly smeared axle grease onto the line that scored the end of the pipe, obscuring the telltale brightness. Nervously, he flicked the shiny flecks off the cuffs of his khaki work trousers and kicked dirt over them. Sebe tossed the saw into the murky slime of the nearby slush pit, where it sank without a ripple. Keeping to his normal rolling gait, he ambled back to his position on the rig. His shift was about to begin.

As Ryan supervised the pipe going into the opening in the center of the rough wooden platform, Sebe found himself staring anxiously at the piece he had cut. It had just been pulled from the storage rack and was being positioned upright in the derrick framework. Had he covered all the signs? Had he had time to weaken it enough? Would Hastings notice? Sebe ran his soiled handkerchief across his forehead.

Another section was lifted over, screwed into place, then lowered into the well. The worn bit had been replaced earlier in the morning, and several hundred feet of the drilling pipe had already been lowered into the hole. Ryan estimated that by the following morning the bit would be back at work, nearly six thousand feet below. The roughneck working on the monkey board halfway up the tall derrick pulled yet another section of pipe from the rack and secured the collar.

It was the length Sebe had cut.

New beads of sweat trickled down his face. He'd never done this before and he had no idea how deep the cut should have been made. Would it break off above ground, where no harm would be done?

The pipe swung up and over. Ryan whipped the chain around it, positioned it and threw the lever which tightened it to the segment below. Then he released the brake, lowered the pipe and readied it for another length to be fastened to its upper end. As the pipe disappeared below the platform, Sebe sighed raggedly. At least it was in the ground.

For what seemed to be endless hours, Sebe worked in a state of high anxiety. How would he face Thorndyke if the section didn't break?

Clare walked past the old house and gazed at the derrick at the edge of the pasture. She reminded herself that it was her interest in how much progress had been made in the well during her absence that brought her here, but she knew the real reason. She had driven out to see Ryan. Although she didn't relish the truth about her feelings, she'd missed him far more than she'd expected. He was becoming all too important in her life.

"I can still walk away from him," she told herself. "I can do it any time I want to." But she no longer thought so convincingly, and she even found her fear of commitments was dissolving.

Ryan's shift was ending and he waved as he came off the platform. Without hesitation, she waved back and hurried to meet him.

"You're back!" he said as soon as he was beside her. "God, I've missed you! If I wasn't such a greasy mess, I'd hug you." He gestured at his stained clothes.

Clare reached up and kissed his cheek. "There's a clean spot. How's the well coming along?"

"Everything is going fine for a change. Maybe our luck's improving. How would you like to go out for a steak tonight?"

"Great! I'd love it."

"Does Nathan's sound good to you? I'll make reservations and pick you up at seven-thirty. We have nearly a whole week to make up."

"I missed you, too, Ryan," she said softly. "It's good to see you again."

Ryan looked down at her tenderly. Had she realized the message her words conveyed?

"Ryan?" Joe's voice interrupted them. "We've got a problem!"

He turned and saw the driller hurrying toward them across the pasture. Joe's words had been unnecessary. Ryan could see trouble, big trouble, written on Joe's face.

"Evening, Mrs. Marshall," he said in a rush, his ingrained

manners never lapsing even under stress. "Ryan, we just lost some pipe down the hole!"

"Damn! Are you sure?" Ryan asked rhetorically.

"Yeah, broke about three hundred feet down. We've pulled out of the hole, but there must be a thousand feet of pipe at the bottom. I can't figure out how it happened. Broke clean off at the threads. If it had been some of that used pipe we bought, I could understand it, but this was a new load."

Ryan frowned and looked over at Clare. "I guess we'll have to go out another time," he said regretfully. "That pipe has to come out of the well before we can go any further. I'll have to go back to work."

"Can you get it out?" Clare asked anxiously. "This doesn't mean the well is gone, does it?"

"No, nothing that bad. But it'll delay us. Joe, you go around to the other wells and see if you can find a wall hook. I'll rig up the cable and be ready for you when you get back."

"What will you do?" Clare asked. "How much time will we lose?" Her loan could not be extended and she felt panic beginning to rise.

"It's hard to say. Sometimes you can get the broken piece out on the first try and only lose a couple of days. Then again, you may have to try for months and even spud in a new well."

"Abandon my well!" Clare felt sick.

"Don't get too upset yet. It depends on whether the pipe twisted when it hit bottom or whether it imbedded itself in the wall. If it's imbedded it'll be a lot tougher, but maybe we were lucky for a change." He tried to mask his concern, but Clare found little reassurance in his words.

"How will you get it out?"

"Unfortunately, this happens sometimes. There are quite a few tools we can use to fish it out. Some spear the hole in the pipe, some fit over the rim like a collar, some are barbed to pull the pipe to a position where the others can be used. You just have to work with it until you get it out."

Clare began to relax. The problem didn't sound so bad, after all.

"But we can only go by feel, and that pipe is about a mile underground."

Clare's frown deepened.

"At any rate, we'll do our best. It's really rough that this had to happen on top of all the other problems we've had, but if we're lucky, it may not hold us up too long."

At the edge of the cow lot, Clare stopped. Here, she was well out of the crew's way yet had a view of everything going on. A tear of frustration formed up at the corner of her eye, but she refused to cry. Leaning on the cracked concrete cylinder that had once held water for the livestock, she watched the men working.

After a while, Joe returned with two large, heavy tools. As he helped Joe unload, Ryan told her these were called a center rope spear and a bulldog spear. His face looked grim, however, and Clare felt the knot in her stomach tighten.

The laborious chore of trying to pull the lost pipe out of the ground began. Now the men's camaraderie sounded strained, and she could sense tension in them all. As the rows of electric lights came on to dispel the growing darkness, Clare went home, leaving the drama that was being enacted far, far below her feet.

For the next week, the men probed and teased inside the hole. Joe's daily log entry simply read, "Fishing." Ryan's face was drawn with fatigue, but he spent every possible minute coaxing with first one tool, then the other, trying to snag the recalcitrant pipe.

Then, at last, it caught.

Slowly, so as not to lose it again, the crew pulled out the broken length. Everyone, including Clare, breathed easier once again. The end of the pipe was examined and it was agreed that the threads must have been flawed. But Ryan and Joe exchanged a long, meaningful look. There had been far too many "unfortunate coincidences" on this project.

Ryan said nothing to Clare, but he and Joe began watching the men more carefully as the drilling process began again.

Ryan sat in his apartment, going over the charts of the logging data. The findings tallied with his geological theories, but there was still no sign of any oil. Tiredly, he rubbed his eyes.

Unexpectedly, the doorbell rang, and before he could reach it, someone knocked. With a frown, he glanced at his watch. It was nearly ten o'clock at night. Could something else have gone wrong with the well?

He opened the door, and Regina, carrying a bottle of wine and two glasses, stepped in.

"Hello, there," she said sultrily.

"Regina." Ryan couldn't have been more surprised.

She closed the door behind her and walked past him, looking around his living room as if she were considering buying it. "Nice place. Did I get you out of bed?' She glanced hopefully at him and shrugged. "I guess not."

"How did you know I live here?"

"Kilgore's not all that big," she responded as she slipped off her coat. She wore tight knit pants, a see-through blouse, and nothing else. "I phoned apartment house managers until I found you. It wasn't difficult." She draped herself on the couch seductively.

"Listen, it's pretty late," he said uncomfortably, "and I have a lot of work to do. You'd better leave."

Regina pouted. "Aren't you even a little glad to see me?" She stood up and put her arms around his neck. "I'll go as soon as we've had some wine."

As she rubbed against his chest, Ryan felt her hard nipples beneath the scanty fabric of her blouse. "No, I'm too busy. Besides, I'm dating Clare Marshall, and I'm not interested in seeing anyone else."

Regina looked as if she had been slapped. No man had ever turned her down before. "I see. Would it matter if I told you I don't care if you're seeing Clare?"

"No." He held her coat for her, but she ignored him.

"Keep the wine . . . and the glasses. You may change your mind." Grabbing her coat, she stalked out.

And you *will* come to me, she vowed silently. One way or another, *I'll* have you; not Clare.

Clare sat opposite Regina and wondered what had prompted the visit. They rarely spoke any more, even at social gatherings, and Clare sensed Regina was up to no good.

"I saw Dyna the other day and she was looking marvelous. Too thin, but that's just the way she is. The twins are running neck and neck for valedictorian of their class."

"Naturally," Clare murmured over her coffee cup. Why was Regina here?

"There's a sale at that little dress shop in Longview. What's the name of it? You know, the one you like. I never can

remember the name of it, since I never shop there myself."
The disdain in Regina's voice was unmistakable. "Anyway, it
started today. And the college drama department is present-
ing *Blithe Spirit* again. As I was telling Ryan, it's an *ancient*
play, but it might be amusing. Spring will be here before you
know it, and I *must* find another pool-cleaning service."

"What?"

"The pool service I have simply isn't satisfactory. Can you
recommend one?"

"No. Who did you say you're going to the play with?"
Clare's heart was pounding and her mouth felt dry.

"Ryan, Ryan Hastings. I understand he's drilling your well.
He's such a marvelous person."

"I didn't realize you'd met." Clare carefully put down her
cup.

"Oh, goodness, yes. We met several months ago. We're old
friends by now." She smiled and gave a deeper meaning to
the term. "*So* romantic. He's certainly a step up the ladder
from the others I've dated around here—in every way." She
put down her coffee and stood up. "I have to run now. The
sale will be picked over if you don't hurry, and I know you'll
want to get there before that happens. They carry so few
really smart styles as it is. Are you coming to garden club next
week?"

Clare followed her to the door, answering in monosylla-
bles. Ryan and Regina! The pain inside Clare's chest threatened to rip her apart. She'd trusted him and this was how he
treated her! Reason told her to believe Ryan's actions more
than Regina's words, but the seeds of doubt hit fertile
ground.

Regina left, smiling.

Chapter Seventeen

Doggedly, Clare patted the rich brown dirt around the small bean plant. A long row of tender green lay behind her and a long line of tilled soil lay in front of her. Eldon had grumbled heatedly when she'd insisted he plow up the carefully clipped and cultured yew hedges that had formed a French Provencial garden.

Now the ornate copper sundial stood incongruously in the center of a large vegetable garden-to-be. She had planted several rows of corn as a backdrop to the beans she was now putting in. Squash, tomatoes and potatoes would go between where she now worked and the house. This spot had been chosen for several reasons. Clare had never cared for the sterility of the maze of low hedges and they were too time-consuming for Eldon, since he no longer had a yard boy to help him. But, primarily, the shrubbery had given way to vegetables because the entire garden was hidden from view by a tall hedge row. No one would ever suspect the erstwhile formal garden would now supplement the dining table fare.

Clare crawled along the row, being careful not to crush the small plants. She hadn't had the heart to ask Eldon to help her after having him tear out the hedges he had trimmed for nearly forty-five years. Perhaps once the plants took hold and began to grow, Eldon would find it in his gardener's heart to accept them, but in the meantime, Clare was stubborn enough to take on the responsibility of caring for them.

"Old family retainers are not all they're said to be," Clare grumbled as she squatted on her heels and examined a broken fingernail. Her back ached from the unaccustomed labor and the March sun was growing unexpectedly hot. For some unaccountable reason, she found it was much harder to plant necessary vegetables than it seemed to be to plant decorative flowers. She wiped the perspiration from her brow and left a streak of dirt in its place.

She recalled how often she'd helped her mother plant spring gardens. And how often she'd promised herself that when she grew up she would never do it again. She placed another plant in the ground. A garden the size of this one would provide almost all the food she, Betty and Eldon would require for months.

"Miss Clare?" Betty called out, coming around the opening in the hedge. "Miss Marla's come to see you. I told her she had to wait on the portico because I wasn't sure where you were." She lowered her voice even further and said in a stage whisper, "I didn't know if you wanted her to know about the garden patch and all."

"You did right, Betty," Clare said as she dusted her hands on her old jeans. "I don't care if Marla knows, but I sure don't want anyone else to."

"Eldon ought to be doing that, not you!" Betty complained. "I'm going to go find him and straighten him out!"

"No, Betty. I told him I'd plant the seedlings," Clare told the older woman. "It's not his fault."

"You go on up to the house now and see your company. I'll be up directly and serve the coffee." Betty turned away in the direction she had last seen Eldon take, grumbling about her husband as she went.

Clare went through the arched opening in the hedge and tried to wipe the dirt from her hands onto her stained jeans. The paving stone path was littered with golden pine needles from the tall trees to either side of her, and she noticed the jonquils and narcissus beds were already showing buds. A smell of spring was decidedly in the air, and Clare found herself smiling as she walked by the lagoon-shaped pool.

In an irregular pond beside it, water lillies grew in a mass along one side. Bright orange and white goldfish of an immense size swam lazily, like beams of light in the murky depths. Lacy green ferns grew in profusion beside the border, along with violets that were already showing early purple blooms.

The path became the edge of the still pool, one flat rock jutting out over the water to form a diving platform. Clare reminded herself to see that the pool got an intensive spring cleaning.

Continuing along the graceful curved path, Clare stared up the slight incline to the back of the house. Marla saw her and came running down the slope.

"What's the hurry?" Clare asked. "Nothing's wrong, is it?"

"Lord, no!" Marla gasped, catching Clare's hands in hers. "Clare, they struck oil!"

"Oil? On my land?"

"No, no. The other two! The well below town came in last night. We heard about it on television. This morning the one between here and Tyler came in, too. They say it's a boom! We're sitting on a lake of oil!"

Clare's heart raced. "You're sure? Where did you hear this?"

"It's all over town. Tom says it sounds as if it may be even bigger than the field that was found here back in 1930! He said something about a theory of underground caverns collecting the oil from the field above. I didn't understand it, but he says it's big!" She pulled Clare toward the house.

"Come turn on the radio. The local stations haven't talked about anything else all morning."

Clare kicked off her dirty shoes at the door and hurried through the house to the morning room, with Marla right behind her. She turned on the stereo and sat down on the wicker chair as the KGRI announcer's voice filled the room.

". . . biggest oil find in history," he was saying. "Due to the distance between the wells and the rate at which the oil is flowing, experts say this one field could be the answer to energy independence for this country. The weather today—"

"See?" Marla said. "Your land is just north of there. So is mine! God, I'm glad I didn't sell out to that land developer last year!"

Clare's mind was racing. "Both wells are south of here and

they're almost even with each other. If the field runs north to south, it could be very large. But, if it's a narrow field, running east and west? It could miss us altogether!"

"I know, but it may not. This could solve all your problems! Besides, Ryan figures it must be this far north or he wouldn't be drilling where he is."

Clare nodded. "I have to go talk to Ryan about it." She touched her tousled hair without realizing she had done so. "When I get back, I'll come tell you what he said. Keep your fingers crossed," she added.

"You'd better change clothes first," Marla suggested. "What have you been doing? Playing in the mud?"

Clare noticed her jeans and jumped out of the chair. "I was putting in a new garden out back. Do you think this dirt will wipe off the chair?" She applied her shirttail to the rattan seat.

"Probably. But when that well comes in, you can get a new one," Marla observed happily. "I'll let myself out. See you later."

Clare ran up the stairs two at a time and quickly washed her face and hands as she kicked off her clothes. Two wells had come in! And both within hours of each other! Oil fever gripped her. She grabbed the first pants and blouse she saw, and while still buttoning the top, Clare hurried down the stairs to her car. An oil boom was more than even *she* had hoped for!

Ryan was coming out of the geologist's trailer as she drove up, and came to meet her. "I see you've already heard the news." The expression on her face was unmistakable.

"Yes! Isn't it marvelous?"

"You bet it is! I went down this morning to get the information first hand. It sounds like the biggest strike I ever heard of."

"When will we hit oil here?" she demanded, her eyes sparkling eagerly.

"Whoa, slow down," Ryan said. "Those wells make things look good, but oil deposits are funny. The farmers between those two sites are most likely sitting on a gold mine, but we don't know for sure that it runs up this far. If my theory is right, we're on the northern edge. We'll have to wait and see."

This was uncomfortably close to the words Clare had said to Marla, and she frowned. "You mean we may miss the oil?"

"All I'm saying is that we don't know for sure. One of the men I talked to this morning told me that his company had drilled to eighteen thousand feet a couple of miles north of here and found nothing. I wasn't even aware of that well."

Keen disappointment knifed through Clare. "We may be too far north?" All the sparkle had left her eyes. "When will we know?"

Ryan put his arm around her shoulder. "It won't be much longer. A month, maybe two." Anyone would want to strike oil, he told himself. But if we don't, she'll have a great tax write off. He tried to ignore the avariciousness in her voice and the hanuted look on her face.

"Please hurry, Ryan," she said simply. "Find my oil for me. It *has* to be there."

"Why, Clare?" he asked. "What's all the hurry? If the oil is there, we'll find it. Those two wells can't possibly suck it dry before we get to it."

"Just hurry," Clare said, more sharply than she had intended. "It's terribly important to me." She turned and walked away to avoid having to confide her very real need to the man she was beginning to love. Unbidden, Regina's words came back to her, and she hurried to her car, leaving Ryan staring after her.

"I *won't* love him!" she told herself. "I won't!" But she watched with longing as he strode across the pasture to the rig.

News of the oil strike spread over the country and the world; and oil companies, both great and small, flocked to the area. Soon all the available housing in the five-town area was gone, and the roughnecks began moving trailer homes, campers and even tents into what once had been open grazing land.

Due to the stringent restrictions on well spacing, the derricks could not be erected with their legs overlapping as had been done in the earlier boom; but a steel forest was growing as densely as the law allowed. Fast food drive-ins and liquor stores seemed to blossom overnight. Enterprising citizens put out signs of rooms for rent in the morning and were able to bring them down again before dark. Old movie theaters were resurrected and businesses of all kinds expanded. A new, more boldly dressed breed of woman could be seen on the streets both by day and night. Preachers railed against these "moralless" women, but their businesses also flourished.

Struggling in the midst of such frenzied plenty, Clare considered taking in boarders but rejected the idea. The roughnecks were known for their rowdy behavior and rarely had their familes in tow. She had no intention of turning her home into a low class hotel or of giving over her privacy to the whims of the changing shifts.

So she watched Kilgore and the surrounding towns prosper, and wished the boom would increase the sale of her paintings. For her sales went down as the economy went up; and her major income, other than her art classes, which were thriving, was the small tourists pictures from New Orleans.

Armed with sketch pad and charcoal pencils, Clare went to the oil fields. Her sketches formed the basis of a new line of work, some pen and ink, and some watercolor, of the active lives of the drillers and roughnecks at work. She took slides of the best of these and mailed them to various cities to increase her lower to middle sales outlets. While the elite of the art world moved like turgid oil toward her work. Clare took her paintings to the average person.

Soon letters of acceptance began coming in from various dealers, shopping centers and art clubs around the state. Clare packaged up her less expensive works and shipped them out to all the stores that were interested.

Chapter Eighteen

The day was cool and clear with the excitement of spring in the March air. People were tempted to put aside their coats and venture outside in only shirt sleeves despite the continued crispness of the nights. Tentative buds appeared on the trees and bushes, then burst open in a symphony of greens. As the leaves unfolded, the flowers joined the race to express life, and thousands of early blossoms spangled yards and fields.

Joe Talmidge had worked the day shift and was about to leave and go home. His wife, Eula, was tired of their temporary quarters and lately had been complaining that she wanted to return to their real home. The Clare Marshall Number One *was* taking much longer than anyone had foreseen, but he felt Eula was being testy. The big companies could and did bring in wells much faster than Ryan's shoestring outfit could, but that was neither here nor there, he felt. In order to preserve his peace of mind, Joe often tended to prolong his ride home.

Joe was leaving at the same time as Sebe Youngblood. Of all the crew, Joe knew and trusted Sebe the least. Joe had had reservations about hiring an alcoholic, but at the time, Sebe had been all he could find. True, he'd only had to be dragged out of bars only three times in order to sober him up for work, but for a teetotaler like Joe, that was three times too many.

With these thoughts on his mind, Joe followed Sebe, not so much as a conscious effort but as a thing to do. He was curious as to where the loner went after work; Sebe had no family or friends. Eula had said that was a sad thing, even as she'd sniffed at the tales of his drunkenness.

Yet there was a quality about Sebe that Joe distrusted. He was always going around with a hang-dog expression on his face, very seldom showing any real emotion. But on a few occasions, Joe had seen him watching Ryan with a look of contempt, maybe even of hate. And the pipe had been lost in the hole on Sebe's shift. Things always tended to break or be misplaced when he was around.

Sebe was driving down the main street of town, his rusted truck jerking spasmodically. Beginning to feel a bit foolish about his suspicions, Joe was about to go home, when Sebe slowed almost to a stop as if he were looking for something. Then, he turned into the alleyway which led to the back of the Farmers' Bank and Trust.

Joe knit his brows in puzzlement. Only the people who worked in the bank parked back there. The alley wasn't a shortcut to another street. Joe pulled over to the side of the road and waited.

Fifteen minutes went by, then twenty. Still Sebe didn't return. More perplexed than ever, Joe started his car engine and went home.

Throughout supper, Joe was quieter than usual, and Eula finally gave up trying to carry on a conversation. He was still wondering why Youngblood had gone down a blind alley and not come back out. It didn't make any sense.

Joe had worked in the oil field since he was fourteen; it was in his blood. The rig he was working on became his mistress and he knew her every mood. The crew became his family and he made it his business to learn each man's strengths and weaknesses. Something was wrong. It was only a hunch; he had nothing to prove it by, but there were too many mistakes being made on the Marshall well. Too many unfortunate coincidences. Too many problems.

Joe stood up and put his jacket on.

"Where are you going?" Eula asked in surprise. "You just got home." She looked at him steadily while her knitting needles flew through the stiches as if they were thinking creatures.

"I know, but something's wrong at the site. I can feel it." He zipped up the jacket and kissed his wife on the cheek. "I'm going back out there. I won't be late."

Eula tightened her lips in disapproval but nodded.

The night was clear and a full moon hung like a beacon in the depthless sky, a mist of stars softening the blackness further. Joe appreciated the sight. Pollution and city lights made the Milky Way invisible far too often. He drove along the dark country road that led to the Marshall farm. Even the air was still, as if it were listening to spring unfold. As he pulled up to the drilling site, the quietness was broken by the drone of human activity.

The strings of electric lights defining the sides of the derrick splashed brightness on the wooden platform where the night shift was working. Joe could see one of the men who made up part of his permanent crew giving directions to a local roughneck. Everything looked normal. Joe parked outside the ring of light and thought as he watched the activity going on.

"Maybe I'm getting old," he muttered. "Maybe I'm like the old maid that checks under the bed for burglars every night." He was about to start the car to leave, when a battered truck drove up and also parked in the dark.

A man got out and, picking his way carefully in the blackness, circled outside the ring of light. With a frown, Joe eased silently out of his car and followed. If it were only a crewman who was coming in late, why didn't he merely walk over to the others?

The shadowy figure avoided the far end of the slush pit drain off and slunk toward the patch of trees beyond. More intrigued than alarmed, Joe did the same.

In the gloom, Joe saw the vague outlines of the shack that had been erected by the crew. It was made of cast off lumber and tin and was kept locked at all times. Inside were the drilling explosives. Because of the potential danger, the shed was always built far beyond the well. Few people even knew it existed. Joe walked faster. Even with a locked door, he didn't want anyone prowling around it.

Before he could decide whether or not to call out, the other man stopped at the shed, looked around and took a key from his pocket. He had only glanced briefly in Joe's direction, but Joe had had time to recognize the features of Sebe Youngblood.

The door swung open and Sebe disappeared inside for a matter of seconds. Then he was back outside and relocking the door with one hand. In the other he held two small bottles of nitroglycerin.

"Hey!" Joe shouted, at last aware of the man's intentions. "Hey, you! Sebe!"

Startled, Youngblood halted for an instant, then turned and ran toward the well site.

Joe could hear him ahead, thrashing through the dry branches of the post oak trees. "Stop, you fool! That's *nitro!*" he yelled.

Sebe broke out of the brush and ran into the pasture. The well was only a hundred feet away. Joe knew he could never reach the man in time, and no one at the rig could hear him above the clamor of the machinery.

"Stop!" Joe yelled again, his voice straining desperately.

For a moment, Sebe looked over his shoulder to see who was chasing him. Then his toe caught in an armadillo hole. Sebe Youngblood was silhouetted against the glare of the lights as in seeming slow motion, he half turned, tried to regain his balance and failed. The light glinted off the bottles as he hugged them to his chest. Then he hit the ground.

The blast was enormous, the shock waves knocking Joe off his feet. The ground trembled under him as he scrambled to stand up.

On the rig, everyone froze, then began racing in separate directions. No one knew what had happened or where the explosion had come from.

The driller Joe had seen earlier ran toward the shed, carrying a lantern. By the time he reached the shallow gouge in the earth, Joe was already there.

"Who was it?' he asked, fighting back nausea at the sight of what had once been a human form.

"Youngblood," Joe managed to reply through his chattering teeth. "Sebe Youngblood." He stumbled away and was violently ill.

The next day, Clare and Ryan met Joe in the geologist's trailer at the site.

"At least he didn't ruin the well," Joe said. "If he'd been much closer, the whole thing could've been destroyed. We might have lost more lives than one and we would've had to start over again from scratch."

Ryan shook his head. "What I can't understand is why! Clare, did Sebe Youngblood have anything against you?"

"No, I didn't even know him." She tiredly rubbed her forehead. There had been no sleep for any of them all night.

"What gets me is that I knew something was wrong and couldn't stop it!" Joe said.

"You did all you could," Ryan comforted him. "By the way, why were you here last night?"

"I had a funny feeling. You know. Like you just get sometimes. After work yesterday, I followed Sebe and saw him turn into that little alley behind the bank. Now that struck me as being a funny thing to do, but I still can't make heads nor tails of it. Then, after supper, I got to feeling restless, like something was going to happen." He put his empty coffee mug into the stainless-steel sink. "I sure wish I could have stopped him. What a godawful way to die." He felt bile rising again in his throat and tried to calm his stomach.

"You say Sebe went to the *back* of the bank?" Clare asked. "That's odd. They keep that door locked." A terrifying idea suddenly began to dawn on her.

"Clare? Are you all right?" Ryan asked. "You look pale."

She wrapped a cloak of composure around her. "Of course. I'm only tired, that's all."

Ryan looked unconvinced but turned back to Joe. "I'm going to go talk to the sheriff. Maybe he can tell me why Sebe would do this." He held the door open for Clare. "I'll drop you off at your house on the way. You get some rest."

"No, I'm coming with you," she said stubbornly.

"Why?"

"It's my well. I want to hear what the sheriff has to say."

As they drove toward town, Ryan was unusually silent.

Before they reached the highway, he pulled off the road and stopped under a large tree.

"Why are you stopping here?"

"We're going to talk. First of all, I want you to tell me what you know about this that I don't."

"I don't know what you're talking about." Clare gazed obstinately ahead.

"Yes, you do. I can wait here all day if it's necessary."

Clare sighed and grimaced. Obviously, Ryan was prepared to do just that. She selected a portion of the truth and replied, "Neal Thorndyke's the president of that bank. A few months ago—the night before I met you, in fact—he came to my house. He knew I was alone and he . . . tried to force himself on me." Even the memory of that dreadful night made her tremble.

Ryan was silent, but his knuckles were white in his effort to control himself.

"You said he tried to . . . to rape you. Did he succeed?"

"No," she said softly.

Ryan's muscles were taut under the fabric of his shirt, and his voice was low and measured. "If he hurt you, I'm going to kill him," he said quietly.

Clare looked at him in amazement. He clearly meant every word. "He didn't . . . that is, he didn't hurt me. I had a gun and I drove him away. That's why I had that .38 in my hand the day we met. I was afraid he'd come back."

Silently, Ryan pulled her to him and buried his face in the fragrance of her hair. She could feel his body trembling and knew he was torn between anger at Thorndyke and fear for her safety in her large, lonely house.

"Why did he do that, Clare?" he asked at last. "Had you been seeing him?"

"No. Never. Only on business at the bank." Careful, she cautioned herself. Don't slip up.

"Has he bothered you since then?"

She shook her head. "No, but I have reason to think he holds it against me."

"Holds it against *you?* For not letting him rape you?" Ryan ground the words out angrily.

"For not giving in. Not many people have ever told him 'no.'"

"If he ever even looks at you again, I'll break him in half."
Ryan hugged her protectively and kissed her forehead.

"No one has ever treated me the way you do," she said,
after a short silence. "You make me feel so safe. Yet, at the
same time, I feel like a whole person when you're around. I
don't think anyone has ever . . . cared about me before."

"Not even your husband?" he asked glumly.

"Especially not him," she said as a shadow of sadness
darkened the gray depths of her eyes.

"He must have been a damned fool. If you were my
wife—"

"Hush," she whispered quickly. "We'd better find the
sheriff. And Ryan, please don't say anything about Neal
Thorndyke. I'd be too embarrassed if that got around town."

"All right," he agreed grudgingly. "But if Thorndyke
makes another move toward you, you're to tell me."

"I will," she promised. "And Ryan, thank you."

When he bent his head and kissed her, Clare thought of
Regina and what she had said about Ryan taking her out to
the play. At the garden club, Regina had said she had seen
him several times since. Although Clare couldn't prevent
herself from returning Ryan's kiss, nor from the surge of
excitement she felt, she tried to keep herself in check.
Whether he cared for her as well as Regina wasn't important.
Clare wanted no part of a man she would have to share.
Especially with Regina. Clare pulled away from the embrace
first.

Clare crossed the lobby of the Farmers' Bank and Trust and
rapped firmly on the president's door. At his growled summons, she stalked in and walked up to his massive desk.
Leaning on it, she glared into his startled eyes.

"I came to tell you my well is still in good condition . . .
despite an *accident* there last night." She reached into her
purse and slapped a sheaf of bills onto the desk in front of
him. "Here's my monthly payment."

"As I've told you before, Clare," Thorndyke said, his
green eyes turning cold, "you can give this to one of the
tellers."

"No, this is between you and me. Besides, I knew you'd
want to know that the well wasn't damaged and the work is

still going on. In a month, I'll have enough money to pay you off in full."

Neal Thorndyke smiled thinly. "We'll see. We'll see. Dry holes have been drilled before. All the wells that have been brought in have been to the south of your land." He steepled his white fingertips. "Why do you think I'd be interested in the accident at your well? I heard about it, of course, but accidents happen every day."

Clare lowered her voice dangerously. "I know Sebe Young-blood didn't act on his own. Somebody put him up to it."

"Are you accusing me of something?" Thorndyke's voice was icy.

"No, you'd only deny it. And I have no proof . . . yet. But I know he came here a few hours before he tried to blow up the well. You don't do business in the parking lot. Or do you? I'm warning you. I won't stand for anybody tampering with my well or endangering my crew!"

"That sounds like a threat!"

"Let's call it a promise."

Neal Thorndyke calmly picked up a pencil and tapped it maddeningly on the desk. "Can you afford the publicity?"

"What do you mean by that?"

"Only that the police will find no connection between me and this Youngblood person. But I would be forced to tell what I know about *you*. For instance, your financial problems. How you stand to lose everything if the well is dry. Do you really want that?"

"That's blackmail!"

"That's good business. The door is over there. Leave."

"Be careful," she said in a tight voice. "If you make one mistake, I'll be on you. My well is worth risking my reputation for." Clare glared at him for a few seconds longer, then turned on her heel and left, slamming his door behind her.

Thorndyke shoved aside the papers he'd been working on. The business was already overdue, but he didn't care. All he was interested in lately was chasing Ryan Hastings away from Regina and taking over the Marshall land before the well could come in. Gulf Oil was literally drilling in his own backyard, but he owned only one small lot. He hungered for Clare's farm. With all the wealth it could bring him, he could have Regina at his beck and call.

With a scowl, Thorndyke stood and looked out his window.

A building across the street had been torn down for the construction of a derrick. The sites of most of the derricks from the early boom again sprouted steel towers. Neal wanted that wealth for himself. And Regina Wharton. She was the epitome of all he desired in a woman. Before Hastings had come to town, she had been totally his.

It would be an easy matter to have Hastings killed now that the boom had brought in hordes of unsavory characters. Because he and Ryan Hastings had no dealings with each other, it would be doubtful anyone would suspect the bank's president had arranged the geologist's death. Especially if the killer were paid in cash and met with a fatal car crash. Doubtful, but not positive. Thorndyke had no intention of gaining Regina and the oil-rich land, only to have to spend the rest of his life in Huntsville State Prison.

As he watched, a truckload of drilling pipe rolled down the street. With the sudden need for supplies, pipe was in great demand and not easily obtainable. Thorndyke smiled without mirth. Hastings would have a hard time proceeding without equipment . . . and deep wells required a great deal of pipe.

Chapter Nineteen

Neal Thorndyke shouldered his way past some half-drunk roughnecks and into the dusky air of the Cowboy Lounge. Carefully, he scanned the room, his expressionless eyes narrowing to slits to peer through the smoke. He saw the man he was searching for and made his way through the crowd, threading his way between the sweaty bodies and the drink-begrimed tables. He sat down beside the man and ordered a beer. "Your note is due on that boiler, Harvey," he said conversationally.

The grease-stained man merely glared at him. Finally, he replied, "Since when do you do the bank's collecting, Thorndyke? I figured you never left that slick office of yours."

"Now, Harvey, that's no way to talk. I thought maybe we could work this out, man to man." Thorndyke showed no outward sign of trepidation, but his stomach was knotted tightly. Harvey Petrie was an enormous man and was known to have a temper like a buzz saw. He was one of the many independent drillers who had flocked like carrion crows to plunder the new pool of wealth below Kilgore. It was also known that he had few scruples about how he came by either money or his drilling supplies.

Harvey Petrie took a swallow of beer from his bottle and let the air hiss out between his yellow teeth. "What do you have in mind?"

Neal gave him his most comradely grin. This would require delicate handling. "I hear there's a big demand for pipe with all this drilling going on—that folks can't get enough of it."

"That's right. Same's true of all the equipment. So?"

"So if a man was to come onto, say, a truckload, he could pay off his debt and still have some to put in his pocket, couldn't he?"

"Sure. I don't reckon you happen to know where pipe is growing wild around here, do you?" Harvey Petrie guffawed.

"No, but I know where you can get a load for nothing."

Petrie elavuated the banker. "Ain't nothing free these days."

Thorndyke took another drink before he answered. "If a truck driver were coming out of Houston, he'd be likely to come along the Henderson Highway, wouldn't he?"

"Probably."

"That's a lonely stretch. Lots of road. Not too many people in through there. Most of the truckers stop at that café in Seven Oaks for a cup of coffee, don't they?"

"Maybe."

"If a person just happened to be waiting around, he might just drive away with a truckload of pipe and nobody would know the truth of it."

Petrie looked at Thorndyke as if he were out of his mind. "Now why on earth would any driver be stupid enough to let his truck get away from him like that?"

Neal smiled. "Money." He reached into his pocket and pulled out a roll of green bills. "There's enough there to more than pay for a load of pipe. You use it to pay off the trucker. Tell him you have a buyer and that the two of you can make a handsome profit. Then take the pipe to Tyler or Henderson and sell it . . . but not here in Kilgore and not to Ryan Hastings or Joe Talmidge. You and the trucker split the cash. He goes his way and you go yours."

"What about you? Where do you come in?"

"Think of it as an extended loan. When your well comes in, you can pay off the bank and everybody will be happy."

Petrie stared from the banker to the money. "Any truck?"

"No, no, there's one catch."

"I thought there might be."

"I want you to stop the load meant for the Marshall well, just north of town. I don't want that shipment delivered. I'll find out which outfit is doing the supplying and when the next delivery is expected."

Petrie again took the banker's measure. A slow grin split his face. "You got it."

"And of course you never talked to me about it," Thorndyke cautioned him. "You never even saw me."

"I never laid eyes on you before in my life," Harvey Petrie grinned, the money buried in his huge hand.

Neal nodded and left the Cowboy Lounge. The money he left behind had come from the bank's vault and not his own pocket. He hoped he had chosen his tool well, but he felt Harvey Petrie could be trusted. Greed spoke a universal language and made unlikely brothers of its victims. The money would be back in the vault long before it was missed.

Clare hung up the telephone and turned triumphantly to Marla. "It's all settled. The oil transport company will advance me the money to pay off the bank as soon as the well comes in."

"Great. I thought they would."

"I had much rather owe them than Neal Thorndyke," Clare added. "I just hope it doesn't take much longer."

"Surely it won't! Wells are coming in all around you. Gulf has even started one on my place and it's further north than yours."

"We've had so many problems. Several of the crew quit last week for no reason. Ryan replaced them, but it caused a slowdown."

"When is your note due?"

"The last of June."

"This is only April. You have plenty of time. By the way, what ever happened to that good-looking geologist of yours?"

"Ryan? He's been working pretty hard, especially while they were short handed." Clare tried to sound causal, but she found it difficult.

"I think he's handsome. And the way he was looking at you when you were over at our house for dinner. Lord, if Tom ever looked at *me* like that, I'd melt on the spot!"

"Ryan is very special," Clare said. "Sometimes I'm afraid I care too much about him."

"Nonsense. Turn loose all those old mind tapes and let yourself get close to him."

Clare smiled. "You sound like you've been reading psychology journals again."

"It shows, huh? But they may be right. You look like the perfect couple to me."

"Not to change the subject or anything, but do you think it'll rain?"

"I can take a hint. Let's go see if Betty remembered to buy Cokes this time."

As Clare followed Marla to the kitchen, she told herself she could trust Ryan. He wouldn't be taken in by Regina's flashiness as Elliot had been. But she wondered if the well were really the reason she had seen so little of him lately.

Clare stood among her oil paintings in the sunken lobby of Houston's Hyatt-Regency Hotel and smiled. Thanks to Cliff Anderson's contacts, she had been invited to present a one-woman show in one of the city's most prestigious locations. Yet, while she was very grateful to Cliff, she knew she'd never have been asked if she hadn't had the talent. This made her feel very good.

On the theory that an exotic artist gets more attention than a mousey artist—a theory that had proved itself to be true time and again—Clare had let her hair grow until it now hung in luxurious dark waves well past her shoulders. She wore a Grecian style gown of lemon silk that perfectly set off her mysterious gray eyes and gave her a slightly foreign look. Earlier in the day, she had been interviewed and photographed by reporters from both *The Houston Chronicle* and *The Houston Post*. Publicity for artists was hard to achieve and she hoped her flamboyant appearance would earn her a place in one or both papers.

Graciously, Clare explained to an overstuffed woman that yes, these were original paintings, done from live sketches; and no, she did not work from photographs. The questions of the people who wandered in off the street amused Clare, and she understood more and more why most artists refused to attend their own showings. As the woman moved away, Clare heard a thin man explaining to his companion that the symbolism of Clare's paintings was quite evident to the metaphysical eye and that her metaphorical message was poignant. Clare wondered what he meant but felt it would not be politic, as the creator, to ask.

Behind and above Clare, the glass elevators soared to dizzying heights in the ceilingless lobby. Row upon row of rooms stacked up, one on top of the other, to the floor of Spindletop, Houston's high revolving restaurant and club. Thoroughly bored, she was watching the ascending elevator and trying to guess at which floor it would stop.

"If you're a good girl, I'll take you for a ride in it later," a deep voice whispered in her ear.

"Ryan!" she gasped. "What are you doing here? I thought you were in Kilgore!" Clare couldn't keep the note of welcome from her voice, but she glanced over his shoulder to see if he was alone. No matter how she might philosophize, she couldn't bear it if Regina were with him.

"We can talk about it later. Are you staying here?"

"No," she said before thinking. "That is, I thought I might go home tonight."

"Drive all that way by yourself after a full day's work? I have a better idea. Stay with me and I'll drive you home in a few days." He had lowered his voice to a very intimate level that made her tremble.

"And your car? Shall we tow it behind us?" she bantered to cover her traitorous emotions.

"I flew down."

"Oh." Seeing Ryan for even one day was a heavenly prospect to her. And he had not brought Regina. "In that case, I'd love to."

"You're a sucker for air travelers, aren't you, kid?" he said in his worst Bogart imitation.

She laughed. "Actually, I only want a strong back to help me load my paintings into the car. The show closes in half an hour."

He lifted a glass she had put down near one of the easels. "I'll get you another . . ." he sniffed the clear liquid that remained. "What *is* that?"

"Ginger ale, with a mint leaf, but don't spread it around. I'm being exotic."

"You can take the girl out of the country," he intoned, "but ginger ale is forever."

"Is that supposed to make sense?"

"Only after you've had a gin and tonic. I'll prove it to you. Be right back."

Clare watched him walk toward the cocktail lounge that was in a portion of the sunken and carpeted lobby. His broad shoulders and narrow hips moved with a catlike grace and his hair gleamed like a cap of gold. Clare wondered why even the sound of his voice thrilled her. Surely she had more control over her emotions than this!

Only then did she realize he hadn't told her why he'd come to Houston. Was there more trouble at the well? Had he come to tell her that he was involved with Regina? Both possibilities seemed equally catastrophic. But if he wanted Regina, why had he suggested that Clare stay with him? A topsy-turvy dread filled Clare that this time *Regina* would be the wife and *Clare* would be the mistress. Her palms grew moist.

They ate dinner at the Brownstone, an elegant restaurant which had once been a stately home. Clare had been concerned that her elaborate dress would be out of place, but she blended perfectly with the elegance of Oriental carpets, tapestries and antiques that filled the old house. They were served in the room that overlooked the grotto-blue pool and fountain behind the building. To their right was the brick arched room which was separated for private dining parties by black, wrought-iron gates. Their silverware and china was unique to their own table and not like the services on any other table in sight.

"This is marvelous," Clare exclaimed. "How did you ever discover this place?"

"It was recommended to me by a friend. The food is actually as good as the surroundings."

A tall woman with black hair began playing softly on a concert grand at the other end of the room. Candlelight glinted in the mirrors and crystal; the deep wine-reds and blues of the chairs, couches and wall hangings deepened to velvety richness. Clare sipped her wine and felt a similar glow spread through her body. Ryan was so thoroughly a romantic, she mused. Candlelight and soft music was his element. For the first time, she wished she could tell him who she really was and why this meant so much to her. But, of course, that was impossible.

"What are you thinking?" he asked, taking her hand in his.

"I was only enjoying myself. Most especially I was being glad you came down."

"I'm glad I got to the Hyatt-Regency in time to catch you before you left. Incidently, I liked your paintings. Did you get a good reception?"

Clare nodded. "I'm half afraid to see the reviews in the paper, but the people generally liked what they saw. I sold several."

Ryan let Clare order for herself—a detail she appreciated after the disastrous dinner with Cliff Anderson and Raoul Gutierrez in Dallas. As they ate, Ryan seemed unusually quiet, and again Clare felt a twinge of fear.

As before, he had taken a room at the Warwick. Clare experienced a feeling of homecoming as they entered their suite. This room, like their former one, was done in delft blue and cream, in French Provencial style, but this one had a sitting room as well as a bedroom.

"We're moving up in the world," she commented. "Two rooms. One for each of us." She was nervous and afraid to let Ryan begin to talk. He looked so serious. "A hotel with a telephone in the bathroom can't be all bad."

"Clare, I have to talk to you." He led her over to the couch and pulled her down beside him.

"You look so serious. What's wrong?"

"I got a phone call this morning. The man we had dinner with when we were here before? The one that agreed to back the well? He was killed two days ago. His lawyer called me. The police say it was set up to look like a robbery, but they have reason to suspect it was premeditated murder."

"How terrible," Clare gasped, not yet aware of the implications. "That poor man!"

"He'd only partially transferred his share of the backing money to the syndicate. Now all his assets are frozen."

Clare began to feel cold all over. "What does that mean?"

"It means we have to either find another investor very quickly, or suffer a costly delay. Our payroll is large and we've had a lot of costly problems. We won't be able to continue long without more money."

Clare stared at him.

"Would one of your friends back us?" he asked. "I've called everyone I know of here and in New Orleans, and no one is able to make a commitment on such short notice."

"All my friends," Clare said slowly. "Marla is the only one I'd feel comfortable to ask, and she's drilling her own well. She can't help us."

"Well, what about you? I know you've already invested quite a bit, but we could lose it all unless something is done fast."

"Me?"

"Of course. After all, it *is* your well. I've put all I can into it myself. Will you take up the share we've lost?"

"I . . . I can't," Clare stammered. "It's out of the question." Now, more than ever, she wanted to tell him the truth about herself. To blurt out that she had barely enough money to live on and that the strain of just making ends meet was almost more than she could manage. But she couldn't. So many small deceits lay between them. If she confessed that she was destitute, Ryan would know she'd lied to him, and often. Worse still, he might think she was trying to marry him for his money! Clare snapped her mouth shut.

Ryan glared at her. "What the hell is it with you and money? Don't you realize we may have to abandon your precious well for lack of funds?"

Large tears formed in Clare's eyes and overflowed onto her cheeks. "I *can't*. Don't you know I would if I could?"

Gently, Ryan reached up and brushed the tears from her face. "I don't understand," he said in a softer voice. "Explain it to me."

Clare was unprepared for the rush of emotion she felt, and she burst into tears. Instinctively, Ryan took her into his arms. He had no idea why she was sobbing so brokenheartedly, but he held her tenderly and stroked her until she calmed. He hadn't touched her for weeks—Clare had unaccountably become very distant and aloof toward him—and he longed to hold her forever.

Without loosening his protective embrace, Ryan fished a handkerchief from his pocket and dried her eyes, then gave it to her. Clare dabbed at her nose and wondered how she could possibly explain her unprecedented outburst. "Ryan, I—"

"Hush. I don't understand what it is about money that

makes you so . . . strange, but whatever it is, you don't owe me an explanation. We'll find another backer somehow."

Overwhelmed with relief at this reprieve, Clare felt new tears forming.

"There's one more possibility. A man named Maxwell Tucker. He's a bit of a recluse, though, and won't do business by phone. We'll go see him tomorrow."

Clare dried her eyes. "He lives here?"

"No, in Colorado. We'll fly up in the morning."

"Oh!" Clare looked up at him in astonishment.

"I've already made the reservations. We leave from Intercontinental at ten. We can leave your car in one of the rental lots and pick it up when we return. Now what's wrong?"

"I'm embarrassed," she confessed, feeling a blush spread over her face. "I didn't bring any extra money."

Ryan shrugged. "I'll pay for it."

"But you're paying for the room!" she protested. "I can't possibly let you buy my ticket, too!"

"There you go with the money phobia again!"

"I am not!"

"Yes, you are!"

"No, I'm not!"

Ryan grabbed her to him and silenced her with a kiss. "Yes, you are," he whispered when he released her.

"I heard that!"

He kissed her again. This time it mellowed and became tender and she slipped her arms around his neck. All the hard-headed business woman and the eccentric millionaire melted away and he held only Clare—vulnerable and passionate. Ryan felt his world become the circle of her arms.

Wordlessly, he pulled her to her feet and led her into the bedroom. Clare started to loosen her dress, but Ryan caught her hand. "Let me."

Expertly, he freed the fastenings of her dress and let it drop to lie like a cloud of sunrise about her feet. One by one, her silken undergarments followed and he held her close. "Your hair has grown so long," he said huskily as he knotted his fingers in it. "Soon it'll reach your waist."

"Is it too long?" she whispered.

"It's perfect."

The scratchy texture of his clothing made her bare flesh tingle, and Clare reached up on tiptoe to kiss his smoothly shaven jawline. Her fingers were not as adept as his, but she removed his clothes hastily. Now that she was here, with him, alone, she could hardly wait to feel his muscular body's warmth against her own. All her reservations fled and she ran the tip of her tongue across the smooth skin of his broad chest.

Ryan's arms were like ropes of iron about her, and his large hand traced fire along the swell of her breast. Clare moaned as he caressed the curve of her waist where it flowed into her hip. His other arm encircled her slender body and held her to him as close as a breath.

"You fascinate me," he said with awe. "Every time we make love, I'm amazed at your perfection. I think I must have imagined how satiny your skin is, how small you feel in my arms, how lovely your eyes are. Yet, when I hold you like this, I find my memory hasn't done you justice."

"Ryan," she murmured, "how can you be so wonderful? Nobody has ever treated me the way you do."

"Nobody has ever loved you as much as I do," he said softly.

Clare's body tensed and she caught her breath at his words.

"I do love you, Clare, with all my heart. I've wanted to tell you for so long." He held her tightly as if he could keep back the words she was trying to say.

"Don't, Ryan. Please."

He grew still. "You don't love me, then? Is that it?"

She buried her face against his chest. "No, that's not it. I don't know. I'm all confused!" She felt herself trembling at his words of love, but she could not echo them. All too clearly, she could hear Regina's voice describing the details of her most recent date with Ryan. She had implied that he was about to propose. Clare steeled herself. "I'm not ready to make any commitments."

"I don't recall having asked you to," Ryan said in a carefully controlled voice. "I merely said that I love you."

So that was it, Clare thought. The proposal would go to Regina; the proposition to herself. Angrily, she tried to pull away.

Ryan held her easily. "What goes on in that beautiful head of yours?" he demanded, his hands clamped onto her arms. "Why do you try to run from me every time I show you that I care for you? Well, you're going to have to get used to the idea, Clare Marshall! Because I *do* love you and I intend to tell you . . . and show you . . . at every opportunity!"

"Let me go!" Clare snapped.

Instead, Ryan crushed her to him. He knotted his fingers in her hair and tilted her head until her lips were offered to his. Kissing her deeply, passionately, he felt her struggles growing weaker and weaker. At last, she put her arms around him and eagerly returned his kisses. With a chuckle, he lifted her in his arms as easily as if she were a child.

"Put me down," she murmured in token resistance.

"Gladly." He lowered her to the bed and lay half-covering her, his arms supporting his weight. Again he cupped her face in his large hand and kissed her, long and persuasively, until he felt her surrender.

Tracing his fingers along her cheek and down the slender column of her neck where her pulse raced wildly, he wondered about her. Was his love so unwelcome? Why, then, did she melt so easily in his embrace? He pulled back and looked for the answer in her eyes.

Clare's eyes were misty and tender, as dark as wood smoke in her passionate mood. He could swear they mirrored his love; every inch of her lovely body seemed to be crying for him. Could it be only physical passion that so rocked her? He doubted it; though from the first time he'd held her, their bodies had been marvelously in tune.

"Why are you so afraid of love?" he whispered tenderly. "Have you been hurt so very badly?"

Unable to speak, Clare nodded, and her luminous eyes filled with tears.

Ryan felt an almost overwhelming impulse to destroy Elliot, who had so badly scarred his darling's soul. Instead, Ryan said, "Clare, let me love you. Don't be afraid of me. I promise that I won't hurt you."

She studied his earnest face and found only truth and love there.

"I don't ask you to say you love me," he continued. "But let me love you. Let me show you what it can be like between a man and a woman."

"I'm afraid," she whispered so softly that he had to strain to hear the words. "So afraid."

Damn him! Ryan thought. What did the bastard do to her? Not trusting his voice, he rolled to one side and cradled her head on his shoulder. Gently, he smoothed her long hair and kissed her protectively.

"Trust me, Clare," he said at last. "Just don't shut me out."

She shook her head. "I can't shut you out. I can't even be objective when you're near. I'm afraid to let myself love you, but I can't seem to stop. Please, Ryan, be patient with me. I *am* trying."

"That's all I ask, love," he said huskily. This time when he kissed her, it was as if something new had been added. A depth had opened up between them and he felt his love filling it. She had, in effect, said she loved him!

As tenderly as if she were made of spun glass, Ryan tilted her chin for his kiss. The love he felt made him all but groan, and he longed to engulf her and protect her, all at the same time.

Clare felt his warm lips open beneath hers and she met the caressing tip of his tongue with her own, as tingles of delight raced along her spine. Everywhere her body touched his she felt more alive than ever before, and she moved against him eagerly.

How easy it would be to love him, she thought, not realizing that she already did. And how fortunate a woman would be who had the whole love of a man such as this.

She ran her fingers through his thick hair and planted small kisses around his ear and down the curve of his jaw. His skin was a dark gold from exposure to the sun and had a clean, natural smell like fresh air and sunshine. His eyes were the color of a woodland pond with autumn leaves below the surface, and she saw a love there that she could not doubt. If only it were all for her!

With a moan of near-pain, she clasped him to her. Beneath his skin she could feel the ripple of his iron muscles. The hardness of his ribs blended into the swelling muscles of his back, and she felt the leashed strength beneath her fingertips. He was like a stallion she had once seen; all silken coat and sinewy muscles, perfectly proportioned and giving the impression of incredible strength held in check. Although she had had little experience with men, she knew Ryan was a thoroughbred.

Coaxingly, he stroked her back and side and ran his hand along her hip and thigh, massaging her warm, pliant skin.

Then he moved his hand up to cup the softness of her breast. Between his thumb and forefinger, he rolled her taut, rosy nipple. Clare pressed her body against him. His fingers and then his lips urged her to greater surrender, and she felt as if she'd burst from the teasing motion of his tongue across her tender nipple.

Easing her legs apart, Ryan touched the softness of her most intimate parts. Clare moaned in pleasure. Suddenly, she found herself exploding into the heights of ecstasy, and she lifted her body, seeking his.

Ryan stroked her until her delight began to slacken, then he entered her, pulling her hips to meet his in pleasure. At once Clare felt herself quicken again, and she moved with him in a golden cloud of love. Never had she felt so much a part of him. It was as if his mind and hers had merged as had their bodies. Together they shared the ecstasy that before each had known only in themselves. When Ryan reached the peak of his passion, Clare felt as if she were of him; and he knew her pleasure when she reached hers.

Satisfied and deeply content, Clare curled in the warm circle of Ryan's arms, one of her legs looped across his. Half awake and half asleep, she stroked his chest, now and then kissing the warm skin nearest her lips. As sleep claimed her, she heard him say, "I love you, Clare, with all my heart."

Clare awoke with a feeling of wholeness and snuggled closer to the warm body beside her. A sweet smile of remembrance tilted the corners of her lips, and she slipped her arm over his chest. Feeling the steady rise and fall of his breath gave her a sense of peace, and she sighed happily. When she opened her eyes, she found Ryan watching her.

"What were you dreaming?" he asked. "You looked so happy."

"I wasn't asleep. I was thinking about you."

He grinned. "That's even better." After a short pause, he said, "I love you, Clare."

A small frown puckered her forehead.

Smoothing away the lines, he added, "I'm not asking you to say you love me. Not until you're ready. So don't look so distressed."

"How can you be so patient?" she asked. "I don't deserve it."

He silenced her with a kiss. "Don't you ever say that again. You're talking about the woman I love." He patted her on her bare bottom. "And I don't take that from anyone. Now get up and let's go eat breakfast. Our plane leaves in two hours."

Clare rolled out of bed and put on wine-red slacks and a white blouse with a froth of ruffles down the front. She pulled her hair back into a smooth chignon and watched Ryan dress. He was whistling softly and looked as contented as anyone she had ever seen. Could he be in love with both her and Regina? What was this fascination men seemed to have toward the blonde woman? Clare wondered sickly if she'd have to share her lover with the same woman who had shared her husband. Feeling almost incestuous, Clare went in the bathroom and brushed her teeth.

Chapter Twenty

The Braniff jet landed smoothly at Denver's Stapleton Airport, and they had no trouble getting a rental car. At that time of the day, traffic was light as Ryan drove toward Boulder.

Clare's parents had never had enough money for a vacation, and during her short marriage, Elliot had never taken her anywhere, although he'd insinuated that Regina had often accompanied him. Consequently, Clare was spellbound at her first sight of the Rocky Mountains.

"Look, Ryan!" she exclaimed as they left Denver behind and the mountains loomed before them. "There's snow on the tops of them!"

He smiled but was studying her curiously. One would think she'd never seen mountains before. Yet how could that be, when almost everyone with any money at all went to the mountains at least every other year?

"They look so craggy and awesome!" she marveled. "I never dreamed they'd really look blue-purple in the distance!"

So she hadn't seen mountains before! Ryan took her hand and kissed her fingers one by one as he drove. She was a puzzle he couldn't solve. In so many ways, it was as if Clare had just begun her life—so many things that he took for granted, she saw as new experiences.

"Would you like to drive up one?" he asked.

"Can we? I mean, they look so . . . steep." She heard her words and blushed. "You must think I'm acting like a fool. It's just that I've never been here before."

"No, love. Never a fool. The Rockies are always awesome the first time you see them. I'm still impressed by them, and I come here often."

Their motel had a view of the foothills, and Clare stood on the small balcony gazing at them. They looked like brown rocks piled in random heaps by some Titan child. Over the jagged crests, fleecy white clouds passed in the windy blue sky. She understood now why the mountains were named Rocky.

"We're going to have dinner on top of that one," Ryan said as he came out beside her. "I called Mr. Tucker and then I made reservations at the restaurant there."

"Do you think he'll invest in the well?' Clare asked, looking at the mountain.

"I hope so. He's the last lead I have."

Without answering, Clare shivered and went back inside. She unpacked the dress she planned to wear that night and rummaged through the suitcase until she found both shoes.

"It's a good thing I don't pack efficiently," she commented. "I put this dress in as a backup for the art show. Otherwise, I'd have to wear jeans or my artist costume."

He smiled. "You look great no matter what you're wearing. Tucker will be charmed."

"I hope he's charmed enough to invest." She wriggled out of her sweater. "I'm going to take a shower."

"I'll wash your back," Ryan volunteered. "We can conserve water that way." He grinned when she looked surprised.

Clare had never showered with a man before, and she felt unaccountably shy. But as Ryan soaped her body, she felt herself learning to love it.

Mist from the water made a cap of jewels in his hair, and his skin was as slick as satin. Clare ran her hands over him, leaving a foamy coat of lather. Always before she had bathed for cleanliness, but now she was discovering new dimensions.

"I never knew this could be so much fun," she said over the noise of the water.

Water clung to her long eyelashes and trickled down her creamy skin. Her rosy lips were slightly parted, and Ryan could see her snowy teeth. The spray had dampened her hair, and it was curling over her shoulder and onto her breast. He brushed the tendril aside and ran his soapy hand over her slippery skin. At once her nipples firmed and she involuntarily swayed toward him.

"Your hair is getting wet," he said reluctantly. "Do you want to pull it back or something?"

"No. I have my hair dryer."

"That's what I like about you," he said. "You don't get upset over your hair getting messed up or not having your makeup in perfect order. You're just not fussy. Maybe that's why you always look so beautiful."

"I look beautiful because my hair is messy and my makeup is smeared? You certainly have a flair for words."

"You know what I mean. Some women's hair looks like a helmet and you can't see their skin under all the cream and powder. You look . . . accessible."

"Thanks?" Clare said. "I think."

"What I'm trying to say is that I like you just the way you are—uncontrived and natural."

"I like you just the way you are, too," she teased. "Naked."

He laughed. Pulling her to him, he kissed her tenderly. The water pounding on them was exciting, and Clare felt her pulse begin to race. She ran her hands over the expanse of his back, feeling the new texture of his wet skin. All thoughts of oil were far from her mind and she was aware only of Ryan. His hand caressed her breast and slid down over her hips, pulling her closer to his firm, male hardness. Clare gave a sigh of pleasure and moved sensuously against him.

"Is it possible to make love in a shower?" Clare murmured against the curve of his neck. "And do we have time?"

"Yes and yes."

He sat down and pulled her onto his lap, facing him. As she lowered herself over him and felt him slide into her, she cried out. The rain of water stung her skin and stimulated her further as she moved, bringing them both to a quick, ecstatic climax.

Ryan shuddered as the fire burst in his loins and he held her close. "You're marvelous," he said in her ear. "And so damn fine to make love with."

"So are you," she whispered. "I'm so glad I found you."

They were a little late reaching the restaurant, but neither cared. Maxwell Tucker, a big blond bear of a man, was waiting for them. Over prime rib and chicken Diane, he and Ryan discussed the well. Clare sipped her wine and tried to follow the conversation. But she found her attention wandering to the way Ryan's hands were shaped and the way his hair fell across his forehead and the resonance of his voice that had been so tender an hour before but was now so business-like.

Mentally, Clare shook herself. This was important! She couldn't merely sit there daydreaming about Ryan. Next she'd be falling in love with him! Uncomfortably, Clare forced herself to listen to Ryan's geological findings.

Tucker, though bluff and hearty socially, was in dead earnest when faced with finances. The questions he fired at Ryan were knowledgeable and searching.

"Well," he said after a prolonged silence, "I'd rather have a piece of an oil well than a sharp stick in my eye, but I'm going to have to think about this."

Ryan nodded. "I expected you would. We need to know as soon as possible, however."

"Sure thing. I'll mull it over and let you know tomorrow night."

"All right. Our flight leaves Denver at three tomorrow afternoon."

"You can call and leave a message at my house," Clare said. "My maid will take it if I haven't reached home yet."

"Will do. I have your number right here," he said as he patted his coat pocket. "You'll hear from me before ten tomorrow night. If I do buy in, I'll want to come down there and take a look at things afterward."

"Sure thing, Max. You'd be welcome any time," Ryan assured him.

True to his word, Ryan woke Clare up at dawn and enticed her out of bed with the promise of driving up a mountain. As the sky became white, then deepened into blue, they topped a rise and gazed down at a jewel of a town in the valley below.

"Estes Park," Ryan said.

To the right of the road sprawled a lake as blue as the dome of sky it reflected. Broad grasslands cloaked in new spring grass nestled the small town in rich fertility. Behind and on either side were immense mountains capped in snow and skirted in trees, with huge outcroppings of rock jutting from the surfaces.

Ryan drove through the town, sleepy now after the winter skiers and not yet swollen with summer tourists. He took a road that soon became dirt and was wide enough for only one car.

The ascent was steep as the road meandered up and across the mountain. Ryan obligingly turned off at every overlook and let Clare gasp and marvel at the panorama spread beneath them. Although he looked where she pointed, his attention was completely on her.

At a roaring mountain stream, he parked the car and they walked along the smooth boulders that had tumbled down the mountainside ages ago. Clare put her hand in the icy water and laughed delightedly as her fingers went numb from the cold. As carefree as two children, they climbed onto the largest rock and sat on its sun-warmed surface.

"This is perfect," Clare said happily. "This is exactly what I hoped mountains would be like."

"You've never seen mountains before," Ryan stated, rather than asked. "Where did you go on vacation? The seashore?"

Clare ached to tell him the truth, yet she again knew she was caught in the intricate web of lies and half-truths she had woven. She felt her heart would break if she saw the love die in his gold-green eyes. "We didn't take vacations when I was a child. And, as I've told you before, Elliot never took me anywhere."

"Why not?"

For a painful moment, Clare considered blurting out the truth about her husband and Regina, but she couldn't do that. Not to Ryan. "We didn't love each other. We were happier when we were apart. So he traveled and I stayed home."

"Why didn't you go places with your own family?" He knew he was on treacherous ground and chose his words carefully.

"I don't want to talk about it."

"You stayed in Kilgore all your life?"

"I *won't* talk about it," Clare amended. "Please, Ryan, don't ask me so many questions. Just let me be real and accept me as I am."

A strange choice of words, he thought, but he said, "I love you, Clare . . . exactly as you are. Whether you've ever seen mountains or not."

Clare leaned over and kissed him, but she was filled with confused thoughts. *Did* he love her? Or did he love only the woman he thought she was? Uncomfortably, she tossed a twig into the rushing water and watched it float out of sight behind a mass of root-entwined rocks.

"Do you think there are any deer here?" she asked, peering into the dense woods across the stream.

"Undoubtedly. Also elk, bear, woodchucks, chipmunks—you name it and it's here."

She nodded with satisfaction. "I thought so. And fish?"

"By the thousands. As well as all kinds of birds. Are you thinking of opening a zoo?"

"No, I just wondered. In case I never get here again, I wanted to know everything that's around me."

"You'll be here again."

"How do you know?"

"Because I'll bring you. I want you to see the mountains in the fall when the aspen are gold. The least little breeze makes them shimmer. It's an incredible sight. This road is closed in the winter, but I want to show you the mountains in the snow. I know another place we can go and get a cabin. Each season has a different personality here."

"I'd love that," Clare sighed. "There's so much I want to see and do!"

"We will. We have lots of time."

She glanced at him, but he gave no sign of awareness of the permanence his words implied. For a heady moment, Clare dared to wonder what it would be like to be Ryan's wife. To have him to love forever. Tears stung her eyes. She had no reason to believe marriage wouldn't destroy the peaceful compatibility they shared as surely as it had in her first marriage. And there was always Regina.

"Are you cold?" Ryan asked when she shuddered.

"A little." She accepted his hand and he helped her stand.

He jumped to the ground, then put his hands on her waist and swung her down to join him. Carefully, they picked their way over the spongy moss and leaves strewn between the gray-black fallen trees and brown rocks.

When Clare reached the car, she was breathless. "You'd never believe this," she said between gulps of air, "but I'm really in good shape."

"It's the altitude," he explained, breathing deeply himself. "We're well above ten thousand feet now. The top is about thirteen thousand."

The summit of the mountain was rounded like a huge cypress knob. Rills and ridges made the surface appear to undulate, and a coarse tundra plant covered the smooth ground. The treeline was far below. Across the horizon and even with their eyes lay piled a mass of mountain tops as far as the eye could see.

"It's even better than I expected," Clare gasped out against the steady gale that blew cold. "Is it always this windy?"

"Yes, there's nothing to break it. Look over there. See that path? It was made by Indians, hundreds of years ago. Nothing changes up here."

Clare snuggled closer to his warm body. "I think I would have found a warmer route."

He laughed. "Let's get back in the car before you freeze. There's something else I want to show you."

The road snaked downhill steeply. Soon, the scrub pines began to reappear, then taller hemlock and cedar as they reached a lower altitude. Ryan turned the car off onto an even smaller dirt road that wound through an outcropping of rocks and into a high valley that was still filled with snow.

Clare caught her breath at the unexpected beauty. Wordlessly, she pointed at a large buck and two doe which were moving into the heavy green shadows of the forest.

"See? I told you there are elk here."

"I never saw one before. They're so big!"

"Come on," he said as he opened the door. "We have to build a snowman."

Because of the cold, they compromised on a small one. As Ryan packed the head onto the body, Clare went into the woods to find suitable eyes, nose, and mouth.

"There!" she said with satisfaction. "Our first snowman."

Ryan noticed her wording and smiled. Taking a stick, he began writing in the virgin snow. "I love Clare."

"What are you doing?" she asked.

"There now," he said, signing his name. "Our love is part of this mountain. When the snow melts, it'll run into the streams and soak into the ground and be here forever."

Clare forgot the cold wind and put her arms around him. "You have the soul of a poet," she said softly, "but you're so strong."

"Weakness and gentleness aren't synonyms, Clare," he said. "Love isn't painful."

"No," she said in wonder, "it's not."

He lowered his head and kissed her.

The flight to Houston was bumpy and Clare was exhausted by the time the plane landed. They retrieved her car from the parking lot and began the three-hour drive to Kilgore. When they finally saw the lights of town, Clare felt relieved. She lay her head against Ryan's shoulder and yawned. "I thought we'd *never* get here," she sighed. "It's taken us longer to drive to Kilgore than it did to fly back from Colorado."

Ryan glanced at his watch. "I'm going to take you home and put you to bed."

Clare snuggled closer to him. "Yours or mine?"

"Either." Now that she was back in her familiar surroundings, Ryan was afraid she'd again withdraw from him.

"Mine. With you."

He relaxed and smiled. "I was hoping you'd say that."

"Tucker has probably called by now. You can help me find Betty's note. But, believe me, it won't be easy. Once I found a phone message underneath the flour cannister, without even a corner sticking out. She said she hadn't wanted it to blow away." Clare paused and said hesitantly, "You *do* think he will back the well, don't you?"

"I hope so. Tucker is known for gambling on high risk investments."

"It wouldn't be too risky," Clare commented as she gestured toward a rig that was being erected on the hospital green. "Oil is being found all over town."

"Yes, but your land is three miles north. None of the wells around yours has hit oil. And we've had an uncommonly bad run of luck from the very beginning. Tucker is very superstitious. He may take that as an omen."

"Are you serious?"

Ryan pulled up in front of her house and stopped. "I've heard that he is. He might even be spooked at the fact that you have that old relic derrick in your front yard. Gamblers are odd."

Clare recalled a certain silver dollar key ring that Elliot had always carried, and she nodded. "That's true."

Ryan took their bags from the backseat and opened the trunk. "I'll help you carry these inside."

Clare shook her head. "Don't bother. Those paintings have been in the trunk for two days without any problem. They can go one more night. Besides, it doesn't look like rain. We can unload them in the morning."

She unlocked the door and flipped on the entryway light. "I'll look for Tucker's message. Would you like a drink?"

"No, thanks. I'll help you look."

They found the note under the refrigerator magnet along with the grocery list and two recipes clipped from the newspaper. Clare handed it to Ryan. "You read it," she said nervously.

He read it through silently and his frown told her the answer. "He's turned us down. He says the risk is too great and he's sorry but wishes us luck." Ryan crumbled the note and tossed it into the wastebasket. "I'm ready for that drink now."

Slowly, Clare poured him a bourbon on the rocks and made a gin and tonic for herself. "Does this mean what I think it does?"

"I *know* there's oil down there! I can *feel* it!" he said as they sat in the darkened morning room. "All I need is time!"

"But I haven't *got* time!" Clare blurted out heedlessly.

"What do you mean by that?" Ryan demanded. "Damn it, Clare, you've got to level with me!"

She gazed out the picture window toward the pool that was so subtly lighted it might have been real moonlight shimmering on the glossy black surface of the water and the silvered fern leaves. "Nothing," she said dully. "There are some things that can't be said. Not now. Maybe not ever."

"I don't understand," Ryan said, pulling her head onto his shoulder and rubbing his cheek against her hair. "At one time, I thought you were a greedy, grasping socialite. Now I know that's not true, but I can't figure out why you're so insistent on this well being finished in such a hurry. Why is it so important to you?"

"I can't tell you. Please don't ask me. And *please* don't think I'm greedy. I'm not like that."

"I know," he said tenderly. "If you were, I wouldn't love you so much." He kissed her and held her tightly. "I want to protect you, Clare, whether you need it or not. When I see you so worried, it makes me want to go out and fight your dragons."

She smiled and sighed. "My sweet knight, Sir Ryan of Hastings, out to do battle on his snow-white charger. Unfortunately, my dragons are too large and fierce to name. I'll have to fight them myself."

"Someday you'll trust me enough to let me help you," he said hopefully. "Or love me enough."

Clare's heart swelled with love for him and she felt tears dimming her sight. "It's the same thing, Ryan."

He stood and pulled her to her feet. Silently, they left the morning room and went upstairs, hand in hand. Clare felt a twinge of ingrained modesty as she led him into her bedroom, and wondered what Betty would think when she discovered Ryan at the breakfast table in the morning. Then Clare put her arms around Ryan's neck and forgot everything in his embrace.

Chapter Twenty-one

Ryan unpacked his suitcase by dumping it upside down on his bed. Whistling cheerfully, he sorted through the clothing, tossing the soiled items into a pile to be washed and hanging up the others. Snapping the suitcase together, he put it on the floor and kicked it under his bed in one fluid motion.

The ringing of the telephone made him smile. It was sure to be Clare. The night before, she'd been even more loving toward him, and he no longer believed she would put the aloofness between them.

"Hello," he answered cheerfully.

"Hello, Ryan," a sultry voice purred. "Did I catch you at a bad time?"

"No, not really. Who is this?" His smile had faded.

"Regina Wharton. I thought I'd call and ask you over for dinner tonight. It'll be very informal—just the two of us."

"No, I'm afraid I can't do that," he said with a frown. "Clare and I already have plans."

There was a short silence. "I thought Clare was still in Houston. I assumed you'd be lonely, so I called you up to console you. Are you sure you wouldn't like to come over?"

"Regina, I told you that Clare and I are seeing only each other."

"Are you so sure of that?" Regina asked in surprise. "I hear Clare has been dating Cliff Anderson. You know, the art dealer from Dallas? I thought you knew."

Angrily, Ryan fought to steady his voice. "I don't know where you got that idea, but it's a lie. Goodby." Without waiting to hear if she had more to say, Ryan hung up.

"That's ridiculous," he said to himself. "Clare wouldn't do that to me." But it would explain her avoidance of him in the past few weeks. He snatched up the laundry basket and strode out to the laundromat.

Clare led Ryan through the lane of willow trees that grew along the bank of the creek. The air was fragrant with the scents of spring and a warm breeze ran through the newly green leaves. Beneath their feet, last fall's leaves made a soft carpet, and beside them, the water swelled against the cocoa-brown banks and made a whispery noise as it tumbled over the red-black river rocks.

"This is my favorite place," Clare said as she leaned against a mossy oak that stretched out over the water. "No one ever comes here but me, and I know I can be alone here." She pointed to a place where the creek made a natural pool. "That's the swimming hole. The bottom slopes down gradually and the water is always calm. I learned to swim there."

"All by yourself?"

"Yes, I don't have any brothers or sisters. It's not that deep, really. Just enough to paddle around in."

Ryan wondered at Clare having learned to swim in a muddy pool; he'd learned in the indoor pool at his parents' house. And why was she allowed to wander in the woods so far from town? There was no sign of a house on the farm except for the ramshackle cabin in the pasture. Slowly, a new solution to the puzzle of Clare began to dawn on him, but he put it aside. It was simply too far-fetched to imagine the elegant Clare living in such a place. Yet that would explain so many things. Ryan watched her silently.

"It's warm enough for picnics now," she was saying. "There's no chance of another blue norther spoiling one. Wasn't that a sight, though? I never saw one move in so fast."

She chattered happily, not noticing his quietness. "I could pack us a lunch. Would you like that?"

Ryan smiled away his fanciful imaginings. "Sounds good. I'll bring the wine."

"It can't be on Thursday, because of my art classes. Friday Marla has asked me to come to a brunch with her. I suppose I ought to go, but I'm not looking forward to it." She took a cautious breath and proceeded casually. "It's to organize a fund raising campaign for the new hospital wing. Regina Wharton is giving the party. Do you remember her?" Clare held her breath. She had to find out it there was any truth to Regina's claims on Ryan. No matter how much it hurt.

Startled, Ryan said, "Yes. I know Regina." Should he tell Clare? he wondered. If he didn't, would Regina? After all, he'd only been with the woman once, and that was after he'd seen Clare with Cliff Anderson. Ryan knew now that had been business. Was it still?

"Clare, I have to tell you something." What if she *is* seeing Anderson, Ryan thought. And even if she wasn't, could she ever learn to trust him if she knew he'd been to bed with a friend of hers? No, he couldn't take the chance. "It's about the well on the land just north of here. They've had to abandon it as a dry hole."

Only the music of the river and the call of mockingbirds broke the silence.

"That's only a mile away," she said at last. "Are they sure it's dry? There's no mistake?"

"No, there's no mistake. The crew was pulling out this morning." Seeing the look on her face, Ryan wondered if this had hurt her as badly as hearing about his indiscretion with Regina.

"Then my well may be dry, too," she said numbly. This was a possibility that she had never dared voice before.

"I've drilled a lot of wells, honey," Ryan said. "You get to the point where you can sense whether or not one will pan out, and yours feels good. I'd stake everything on it being a good producer."

"But what if it isn't!" Clare looked about her at the land she loved so well. How could she bear to lose it?

"I have no reason to believe your well is dry. The last core samples looked promising. We just aren't deep enough yet. I'm placing an order for more pipe tomorrow. That'll be enough to take us to the depth of the other producers. The dry hole north of here may not mean a thing. We aren't about to give your well up."

"I can't give it up," she whispered as she fought back tears. "I can't."

Again Ryan wondered if he was right about Clare. Through the trees, he could glimpse the weather-beaten gray house. Quietly, he took her into his arms. He couldn't care less if she had money or a prestigious family tree; he had enough of both to satisfy her.

"I love you, Clare," he said softly.

Suddenly, unexpectedly, a gentle rain began to fall.

"Look," Clare exclaimed, struggling to hide her worry, "the sun is shining as it rains. Maybe it's a sign."

The crystal drops of rain clung to the leaves, surrounding them in a magic bower of tiny rainbows. A shaft of weak sunlight made the falling rain look like a shower of diamonds and the soft hiss was like a fairy song.

Clare looked up at Ryan, raindrops and tears glistening on her long dark eyelashes. Her soft lips were slightly parted to reveal her white teeth and her cheeks were as rosy as if she had been running.

"Clare," he said softly.

He bent his lips to touch hers and kissed her long and slowly, with a depth of feeling that shook them both. The gentle rain touched them, caressed them and seemed to enclose them in a place of their own.

Clare ran her fingers through his hair, now damp from the rain. A sigh escaped her.

"I'm tired of games, Clare," he said as he held her close. "I don't know why you're so afraid to trust me, but you should know by now that you can. I need to know where I stand with you. If you don't love me, say so, but don't keep me wondering." He waited for her answer.

As suddenly as it had started, the rain stopped and a bird flew into the tree above their heads.

"I want you, Ryan," she answered at last. "I'm terribly afraid of it, but I do. I can't say what you want to hear. Not yet. It's not that I don't feel it, but the words are hard for me."

Only then did he realize he had been holding his breath. "Do you, love? Are you sure?"

She nodded. "I've tried not to, but I do. I told myself I'd never let myself be so vulnerable again, but I can't seem to help it."

"You made it sound like a sentence," he said disappointedly.

"Oh, no. Never that. I was afraid. I still am. I don't want to be one of several. I've never been very good at sharing."

"I don't want to share you, either. There's no one else."

Could she believe him? she wondered. Regina had been so convincing.

Ryan kissed her and held her as if he'd never let her go. She felt the strong, steady throb of his heart against her cheek and the security of his arms. Slowly, Clare tired to release her last inhibitions. Yet her fear was too strong. To tell Ryan she loved him would be a commitment, and she didn't want that. Not as long as the shadow of Regina hovered near. "Please give me a little more time," she said.

She felt so small and defenseless in his arms. Ryan was newly amazed at the protectiveness she aroused in him, as well as the passion. He felt he would never be able to touch her enough or hear her voice too often. He was willing to wait for her love, no matter how long it might take.

Clare felt her heart race in time with his and she pressed closer to him, moving her cheek against the smooth texture of his pullover shirt. Marveling at the way her mind seemed to entwine and mingle with his, Clare lifted her head for his kiss.

His lips were warm and sensuous and Clare felt a mellowing fire envelop her. "Let's go home," she whispered, when she could bring herself to speak. "I want you."

A tiny muscle moved in his jaw as he gazed down at her. "Let's go, love," he said, taking her hand in his.

Once more she looked around the green glade. "This will always be our special place," she sighed. "It was the magic rain, I think." She fell into step beside him.

The pasture was green with new grass, and buttercups had recently sprung up and blossomed beside the crimson Indian paintbrushes. Queen Anne's lace softened the riot of spring colors with its delicate snow, and several lemon-yellow butterflies fluttered above the flowers.

"It's a perfect day," Clare sighed happily, avoiding a clump of wild violets that still sparkled with raindrops.

"In spite of the rain?" Ryan asked. "I thought women

complained if their feet got wet," he teased. Small droplets of water glistened in her hair.

"Not me. I love rain. Besides, I'm with the most wonderful man in the world, and he's in love with me."

Ryan caught her hand and pulled her to a stop. "Does that mean you're no longer afraid of loving me?"

"I don't know if what we have will last," she said seriously. "Maybe what we feel is too strong and will burn itself out. Maybe when you get to know me. . . ." she paused. "For however long it lasts, I want to be with you. I've never felt like this before and it's a little scary."

Clare glanced back at the dark path they had left in the wet grass and smiled. "I'm going to want to be with you for as long as you let me. Probably even longer. Besides," she said mischievously, "I think I can beat you to the house." Without warning, she sprinted away, running with the sheer joy of living.

Ryan laughed and ran after her, close on her heels but allowing her the lead. At the porch, she ran up the steps two at a time, but Ryan stretched his long legs and leaped straight onto the porch and reached the covered dog-run a split second before she did.

"That's no fair!" she gasped, happily out of breath. "You didn't go up the steps!"

"We never mentioned that," he teased. "We were racing to the house, not the steps."

She collapsed against the door and giggled like a school girl as she fought to catch her breath. "I must be getting out of shape," she wheezed.

"No, you're just getting old," he comforted her. "Your shape is just fine."

"Oh!" she laughed, swatting at him playfully. "I'll get you for that!"

Ryan bent over her and kissed her into silence. Suddenly, they were both serious; he kissed her again, more deliberately. "I love you, Clare."

"Hush, Ryan," she begged. "I can't—"

"Then don't say anything," he interrupted. "But I'm going to keep telling you until you get used to the idea. Until you can admit that you love me, too."

"Ryan—"

"Be quiet."

He drew her into his arms and she felt his tongue tease her lips, urging her to respond. She returned his kiss with growing passion, letting her tongue meet his and explore.

"You make me feel shameless and abandoned," she murmured when he released her. "Also, a little bawdy."

"Only a little? I'll have to work on that."

Holding hands, they walked across the covered alleyway and gazed up into the thick, bottle-green umbrella of the old chinaberry tree. A breeze ruffled the leaves and was captured in the cool porch.

How strange life is, Clare thought. If things had worked out differently, I would have brought Ryan home to meet my parents there in that very living room. They would have loved him, she mused. Reality again inserted itself and she sighed. No, things could never have worked out *that* differently. He was in love with the heiress to the Marshall fortune, not the girl she had been.

"How long has it been since this house was lived in?" Ryan asked. "It seems to be in good condition."

"About four years. The structure is better than it looks. It needs paint and a new roof."

Ryan lifted a small cross made of horseshoe nails from the wall. Clare felt a tug of memory. Her mother had hung it there and said it would protect and bless their home. That had been the year before Clare had gone to college.

Carefully, Ryan replaced the homemade cross. "Who lived here?"

Clare swallowed and said, "A family named O'Brian. He died four years ago and she only lived three months longer. They were very close." She hoped she wouldn't cry. Not now.

"Did you know them well?" Ryan asked without looking at her.

"Quite well." Clare walked purposefully down the front steps and into the yard. "Let's go, Ryan. I feel too cold with these damp clothes on."

Clare was silent on the way to town and during dinner, and Ryan wondered if he had gone too far with his questions. Yet he still couldn't see Clare Marshall living in the small cottage. He wondered if he were mistaken, but somehow knew he wasn't. All evening he tried to think of some tactful way to tell her that her background was not important to him.

When they drove back to her house, Clare took his hand and they went upstairs.

"Should I move my car?" he asked as she turned on a lamp. "I don't want you to feel compromised."

She shrugged. "I don't care about that. The neighbors can't see the house from the street, and even if they could, it doesn't matter." She paused in flicking back the bedcovers. "Unless, of course, *you* would rather not take the chance. Someone could always drive up." Like Regina, she thought sickly.

"In that case, woman, come here and be compromised," he grinned.

He removed Clare's clothing slowly, kissing each new part he exposed. Clare moaned with excitement and helped him out of his clothes until they stood naked in the dim light.

"You get more beautiful every day," he assured her.

Clare raised her arms and loosened her hair, then shook her head to tumble it down her slender back. "I never knew making love could be so much fun!" She stretched like a cat in warm sunshine, rubbing her body against his.

Ryan watched her with amusement. "You're shameless." he confirmed, "and more than a little bawdy."

"Yes," she whispered, teasing the curve of his neck with the tip of her tongue. "I think I may be just that."

Unable to wait any longer, Ryan led her to the bed and pulled her down onto the silken sheets. Kissing her hungrily, he caressed her breast and gently rolled the already erect nipple between his fingers. Her low moan of ecstasy fired him to the depths of his being, and he lowered his face to her breast.

His tongue teased her nipple, licking faster and faster, flicking the tautness into flame. Gently, he took it into his mouth, and she arched her back to meet him.

She felt him stroke her side, her stomach, her thighs, then push her legs apart. As his fingers played in the dark curls and moved even deeper into her most secret place, Clare moaned. Ryan left her breast and moved his face downward, leaving a trail of kisses across her flat stomach, while his other hand toyed with her breast.

Suddenly, Clare felt his tongue between her legs, arousing her in a way she had never experienced. He chuckled at her exclamation of surprise and she felt the growing need begin to skyrocket deep inside her. The sensation she had learned only in his arms began to claim her, possess her. With a cry, she felt herself swept up to the highest peak and plunged into the space of delight as wave after wave of pleasure thundered through her.

Then, and only then, did he come into her. She gasped at the hard warmth of his manhood as he possessed her with tender passion. Again and again, he played her body like a fine musical instrument, bringing her to one soaring crescendo after another. At last, he could wait no longer for his own fulfullment, and with a shuddering moan he gave himself totally to her.

They lay locked in each other's arms, lightly dozing, only to wake, murmur words of contentment, touch a cheek with wonder, brush back a lock of hair. Then to drift again into sleep.

At last, Ryan reached across her and turned off the small lamp. "You're beautiful in the moonlight, too," he whispered as he nuzzled in her soft hair. "In the daylight, your skin is silver. In the sunset, it was golden. Now it's silver again. I'm looking forward to seeing it in the dawn light."

Clare ran her hand over the hardness of his muscled arm. "You'll stay with me all night?"

"If you want me to. I don't want to leave you."

"Stay. Never leave me, Ryan. Never." She cuddled sleepily into the curve of his arm and pillowed her head on his shoulder.

Ryan lay his head back onto the pillow, his cheek against her forehead. "I love you," he said.

Clare heard him as she drifted into sleep, and she smiled.

Chapter Twenty-two

Dawn turned the room to a pale pink, less flamboyant than a sunset, as if it were reluctant to awake those who slept.

Clare opened her eyes and blinked sleepily. Languorous memories of the night's loving made her smile. When she looked over at Ryan, she found he was propped up on one elbow, watching her.

"Good morning," he said. "In the dawn, your skin turns rosy."

"How long have you been awake?" she asked, touching his face lovingly.

"Only a little while. I've been watching you sleep. Did you know you are also beautiful then?"

Clare laughed. "Oh, Ryan. You're incurably romantic." She ruffled his hair playfully.

"Complaining?"

"No," she answered softly. "Just being thankful."

When they made love this time, it was slowly and tenderly. The new familiarity of their bodies did nothing to dispel the wonder they felt. Each time was like the first to them.

"I love you," he said gently. "I think you love me, too."

"Please, Ryan, don't try to pin me down." She turned aside.

"Clare, why are you like this? I thought women always wanted to know a man is in love with them."

Had he learned that from previous experience? Clare wondered. Had Regina been telling the truth about his infatuation with her? Clare moved away from him.

"Don't turn away like that. Look at me." He made her face him. "Do you love me?"

"I care a great deal about you," she hedged. "When I don't see you, I'm miserable. And, when I do, I'm happy. Last night was wonderful, as are all the times we make love. I feel closer to you than I've ever felt to anyone."

"But do you love me?"

"I don't know," Clare had to admit. "Please try to understand and be patient. I don't know if this is love or not. I only know I don't want to lose you and I'm afraid."

Ryan drew her close to comfort her. "I don't understand you, Clare."

"I don't understand myself," she agreed. How very easy it would be to allow herself to return his love! If only she knew if he were telling her the truth.

"Ryan, just hold me," she sighed. "Don't let me think or doubt you. Just hold me."

When Ryan left Clare later that morning, he didn't notice the dark blue Cadillac that drove in front of him.

Regina watched him in her rearview mirror and tried to calm her anger. So Clare had let him spend the night, had she? And he had stayed! He hadn't left afterward as he had the night *they* had been together. Regina sped up and raced through the yellow light that turned red for Ryan. Jealousy blazed over her, making her face hard and calculating.

"We'll see about that, Clare," she muttered. "We'll see who gets him in the end."

She altered her route to drive by Neal Thorndyke's house. He was a source of information that had proved invaluable to her. If there was anything derogatory about Clare's past or anything unsavory about her present, Neal was likely to know.

His car was in the drive and Regina pulled in behind it.

Clare was amazed at the fire of passion Ryan stirred in her. He just had to look at her to cause her pulse to quicken, and the mere sound of his voice could drive all previous thoughts from her head. She'd never seen anyone who could affect her in such an alarming—yet very pleasurable—way.

The one block to Clare loving him totally and unequivocably was Regina. Not only were they thrown together at Kilgore's many social functions, Regina had developed an annoying habit of stopping by to see Clare at odd times of the day. Whenever possible, Clare told Betty to say she wasn't home, but often Regina simply drove up when Clare happened to be out in the yard or on the broad porch, and then escape was impossible.

Always, Regina brought Ryan's name into the conversation, and always Clare felt a knife twist in her stomach. Sometimes Regina merely dropped his name as if she were accustomed to saying it; sometimes she mentioned a play or movie they had seen and what he had later told her about this or that scene.

Since these reports always tallied exactly with the times he was not with her, Clare didn't know what to think. If Regina was lying, how did she know when he was there and when he was not? Because Clare wasn't of a suspicious nature ordinarily, she never noticed how often a certain Cadillac was parked just down the street from her driveway. Or the blonde woman that watched from inside.

Consequently, Clare didn't allow herself to admit her love for Ryan, nor did she let him know that Regina so often spoke of him.

As she pondered these things, Clare packed a picnic lunch. The day was unseasonably warm and spring would soon give way to summer. She put in some of the crisp Granny apples that she knew Ryan preferred.

"Regina must be making it all up," Clare assured herself. "She's never liked me and would do anything to make me uncomfortable. Ryan is here as often as he can get away from the rig. When would he have *time* to see anyone else?" But she frowned as she put the tuna sandwiches in the sack with the apples.

Ryan knocked on the kitchen door and Clare called out for him to come in. The sight of his well-loved frame and his tawny hair put Regina from her mind.

"Are you ready?" he asked.

"Yes. Let's go down to the creek. It's warm enough to wade."

They drove to the farm and, like playful children, they crossed the pasture, laughing and bumping into each other, holding hands, and then running off in odd directions.

The willows closed over their heads in an arch like a green cathedral, and the blue sky could only be seen in patches behind the lace of the emerald leaves. As always, the glade's hush was broken only by the murmur of the flowing water and an occasional bird song.

Clare led Ryan upstream a few yards to the large tree that jutted out over the water. It was as broad as a bench and the angle of one of the limbs formed a perfect backrest.

Impulsively, she loosened her hair and let it blow about her. In her bower of leaves, seated on the tree with its thick carpet of green moss and tiny ferns, she looked like a dryad.

Ryan climbed out over the water to join her. Beneath them, the water gurgled toward a small waterfall they had passed. Tiny leaves and shiny black water bugs floated on its amber surface.

"Look," Clare whispered, and pointed to the water nearest the bank.

In a small pool formed by a tangle of the tree's roots, a large catfish swam lazily. "He's a magical fish," she said in a mysterious voice. "He'll grant us one wish for having discovered him."

Ryan smiled at her. "I wish this could go on forever."

"That was *my* wish!" she exclaimed. "But you shouldn't have told. Now it may not come true."

"Some wishes don't come true unless you do tell them," he said. "For instance, my next wish is that I had a sandwich, right here!" He closed his eyes and held out his hand.

Clare gave him one and laughed. "I hope you wished for tuna."

"Right. Now I wish for a Coke."

She passed one to him. "I said the magic fish would grant you one wish, not an even dozen."

"What? No potato chips?" Ryan pretended to be dismayed. "I'll tell you what, you wish for potato chips and I'll eat them for you."

She dug into the sack again and handed him a bag of chips. "You sure are a lot of trouble," she teased. "Anything else, or can I eat, too?"

"Sure, go ahead. If I think of anything else, I'll let you know." He grinned and leaned back on the mossy limb. "This is the life. No rush, no hassle, no people around but you . . . and you look like a wood nymph. Let's run away from it all and become hermits. Right here."

Clare laughed. "You might change your mind when the food is gone."

"That's the best part about this place. Your house is only ten minutes from here. When we run low on food, we can go make some more."

"You have a point there," she said, joining in his game. "This is a perfect parlor, the kitchen is just down the road, but knowing us, we'll need a bedroom."

Ryan thought for a minute. "There it is, over there." He pointed upstream.

"Where?"

"There. On that sandbar by the swimming hole. Come on, I'll show you."

They stuffed the leftover food, paper and Coke cans back into the sack and climbed down from the tree.

Clare followed Ryan along the narrow cow path that paralleled the creek. A tall dogwood tree spread above them and the blossoms were like thousands of snowy butterflies frozen in mid-flight. Sprays of blackberry flowers made pale drifts below. The entire woods smelled fresh and fragrant. Lifting above the water's surface was a cocoa-brown knoll of fine sand. Beneath the clear water, Clare could see the reddish-black pebbles like garnets in the golden depths, but the knoll itself was made only of soft sand.

Ryan pulled off his shoes and socks and rolled up his jeans. "Come on," he said, picking his way with tenderfooted caution to the water.

Clare needed no urging. She kicked off her shoes and followed.

The ground sloped gently down to the water and up again on the other side. Further upstream, the banks reared sharply out of the water in cliffs above her head. This made the swimming hole seem sheltered and private, and was one reason Clare had chosen it as her special place when she was a child.

Stubble and small vines pricked Clare's bare feet and she hurriedly stepped into the water.

"This isn't nearly as cold as I thought it would be," she exclaimed. "In fact, it's pretty warm." She wriggled her toes on the pebbly bottom and splashed at a school of minnows that were swimming by. A fog of red-brown sand clouded the water, then was swept away by the current.

"Come over here," Ryan said. "The bottom's not nearly so rough here."

Clare felt the stream bed become less gravelly as she went toward him, and soon she stood on the sandbar, her feet on the soft sand. "It's so clear," she marveled. "The swimming hole must be four or five feet deep, and yet I can see all the way to the bottom."

"Let's go skinny dipping!" Ryan suggested.

"Now? Here?" she gasped. Clare hadn't gone swimming without a suit since she was a little girl.

"Sure. Who's going to see us? Hermits can do anything!" Ryan shucked off his clothes and tossed them onto the bank with his shoes.

Clare hesitated, then followed his example. In all the years she'd been coming to this place, she had never seen anyone else. Her pullover and jeans landed near Ryan's clothes.

The breeze blew across her skin in a way she'd almost forgotten about, and the water splashed in silver ripples against her skin as she waded deeper.

She gasped at the unexpected coolness as the water covered first her hips, then her waist, and she buried her feet in the combination of silky ooze and pebbles of the creek bed.

Ryan jumped up and grabbed the thick rope of muscadine grapevine that grew wild along the bank and looped over the water. Pulling himself up, he swung several feet over the water, then fell back into the stream.

Laughing, Clare plunged after him. The water was too shallow and the swimming hole too small to swim properly, but they splashed happily, each trying to outdo the other.

Clare ducked under and pushed against the back of Ryan's knees. With a yell, he went under. Her victory was short-lived, however, for he grabbed her around the waist and pulled her under, too.

Coming up gasping, Clare splashed him and ran for shallower water, with Ryan in hot pursuit.

At the sandbar, he caught up with her and they collapsed, laughing, onto the sand, their bodies still in the shallow stream.

Ryan pushed a wet strand of hair from Clare's face and kissed her. "You taste like creek water," he teased.

"So do you. Your lips are cold on the outside and warm on the inside." She kissed him again, locking her arms behind his neck.

She ran her hands over his wet back, feeling the skin cool and slick beneath her fingers. Again her lips found his and her tongue enticed his mouth to open.

His hands traced her body beneath the water and she rolled her head on the pillow of dry sand. The lapping of the water aroused them even more and he rolled onto his back, pulling her on top of him.

He gazed up at her, silhouetted against the sun-spangled leaves that shimmered in a green veil. Beads of water on her creamy skin made miniature prisms in the sunlight and dripped onto him in a small shower. He pulled her down to him. Clare lay on the warmth of his body, the cool stream surging around them, a butterfly flitting nearby.

With a soft moan, she positioned herself so that his erect manhood entered her. The sensation was one of both cold and warmth and she giggled. "That feels funny."

"'Funny,' is it? I'll make you think 'funny,'" he grinned back, and began rotating his muscular hips to thrust against her.

Clare put her hands on his shoulders and pushed herself to a sitting position across him. Teasingly, she moved her own hips in rhythm with his, urging him to even greater pleasure.

The golden glow of passion began rising in her at once, and she moaned as she felt him move faster inside her. Ryan reached up and fondled her breasts, squeezing, soothing, pinching her nipples gently. Clare felt the familiar but ever new sensation course through her and she cried out.

Ryan raised his head and licked the drops of water from her

breasts, then sucked gently on her throbbing nipples. As he did, she felt another wave of pure pleasure rise in her and burst into a firework display throughout her body.

She rolled over, locking her legs around Ryan, and pulled him on top of her. As she licked the cool hollow of his neck, her fingernails gently, ever so gently, scraped along his hard ribcage. Her hair, seemingly black in the water, swirled around them like a fan of seaweed or mermaid's hair.

With a groan of pleasure, Ryan brought her to ecstasy again as he gave himself over to his own passion.

Little by little, they again became aware of the leafy dome above them, the wind's rustle in the muscadine vine and the sensuous movement of the water they lay in. Ryan kissed her and stood up, pulling her up beside him.

"Are you cold?" he asked tenderly as he held her close.

"No," she breathed contentedly. "Are you?"

He laughed. "I can't tell. I don't have my nerve endings back yet." Again he kissed her, then led her up the bank. Gently, he helped her dress.

"Not like that," she protested as he tried to put her sweater on her backward. "It goes the other way."

"Who can tell with women's clothes?" he pointed out. "Half the time the front and the back look just alike. Besides, it's a lot easier to take them off than to put them on."

Unbidden, the thought rose in her mind: How many women *had* he undressed? She tried to put the jealousy away from her. After all, Ryan had certainly had other women before her. Was Regina one of them?

"I'm getting cold," she said quickly, and tried to smile naturally. "Let's go home."

Ryan knew something had disturbed her, though he didn't know what, so he tried to put her at ease again with plans for the evening. He'd heard of a new place in Tyler to go dancing and they decided to go. As they crossed the pasture, he bent down and picked a spray of Queen Anne's lace and handed it to Clare.

She placed it behind her ear and picked a wild violet to put in his buttonhole.

"How is it coming along?" Clare asked, her eyes following the distant movements of the drilling crew and the machinery through the pines that edged the drilling site.

"Pretty well. I haven't received that new shipment of pipe yet, but sometimes it takes a while for the plant to fill an order. It'll be here soon."

Clare put her hand into his. "Sometimes it seems like forever since the well was started. There have been so many delays." She walked in deep thought for several steps, then burst out, "Ryan, when the well is finished, are you going to leave?"

"I have to someday, honey. You know that. If you want me to stay and drill more wells, I will, but I can't stay here forever."

"Of course not," she mumbled. "It's just that I'll miss you."

He pulled her to a stop. "You don't have to, Clare. You can go with me," he said quietly.

The warm breeze ruffled his hair and the sun made his skin golden and set strange flecks of amber in his hazel eyes. Clare felt her heart begin to pound.

"Go with you?" she repeated. "But I can't go with you." Never once had she thought in terms of leaving the only place she had ever considered home. Even those of her friends who traveled extensively never really moved away.

Ryan's face grew hard and pain filled his eyes. "How long are you going to play games with me, Clare? What do you want from me? I say I love you and you tell me to hush. I ask you to be with me and you say no." He glared at her. "I don't think I even know who you are at times. How can you make love with me the way you do and *not* care for me?"

"I *do* care for you, Ryan. It's not fair to say I don't!" she exclaimed. How could he be so unreasonable? she wondered. Surely he must know she couldn't give up her home and the social position she had sacrificed so much to retain and just follow after him like a . . . a camp follower!

"Then say it! Say, 'Ryan, I love you!'" he demanded.

"Ryan, stop it! You're being unreasonable!" Clare said with growing anger.

"*I'm* being unreasonable!" he thundered. "Your heart is made of ice and *I'm* unreasonable? Listen, Clare, when you decide to trust me and let yourself feel, then let me know! Until then, I quit!"

"What do you mean, you quit?" she demanded.

"I mean I don't like dangling on a string. Not even for you! When you feel you're ready to make some commitment, let me know!" He turned and strode off angrily.

"But where are you going?" Clare hurried to catch up with him. "Where will you be?"

"If you want me, you can find me," he snapped back over his shoulder. "It's about time *you* felt some uncertainty!"

The ride back to town was heavy with stony silence, and Clare never noticed when Ryan's flower slipped from her hair.

Ryan sat in the smoky bar and tried to ignore the crowd as he drank. This was his third whiskey and he was slowly beginning to pacify his temper.

How had she been able so easily to reject his marriage proposal if she cared for him at all? He fumed. At least she could have been more tactful. Ryan had never proposed to a woman in his life, but he felt he had not done badly—not the way he had staged it in his mind—but not badly.

And she had flatly refused!

The pain knotted his middle and he tossed the amber liquid down in one gulp. He'd never thought she would say no. He had been in the bar for an hour or more, he reflected. Obviously, if Clare were interested in finding him, she was in no hurry. He ordered another drink.

As the alcohol numbed his senses, Ryan relaxed. Maybe he could learn to live without her . . . someday. The only trouble was that he didn't even want to try.

"Ryan?" an all too familiar voice said. "I didn't expect to see you here today. Mind if I join you?" It was Regina.

He groaned and tried to think of some reason to send her on her way, but his mind was dulled by the alcohol.

Regina saw the pain in his eyes and sat down. "What's wrong? Are you sick?"

"No. Clare and I had a fight."

"Oh, poor baby," Regina said with sticky compassion to cover her rush of elation. This was the chance she had been waiting for. "Tell me all about it," she murmured as she covered his hand with hers and leaned forward eagerly.

At that moment, Clare walked through the door.

Her eyes met Ryan's over Regina's head and she had to

force herself not to turn and run. "Am I interrupting something?" she asked coldly.

Regina jumped and turned quickly to face her.

Ryan belatedly jerked his hand away from Regina. "Clare! Let me explain—"

"I've looked for you for over an hour!" Clare stormed as rage burned away her shock. "I see it took me too long!"

"It's not what you think!" Ryan protested desperately as he stood up to detain her.

"Ryan," Regina spoke at last, "don't. She had to see us together sooner or later." Her voice was oozing contriteness and she rose to stand beside him, facing Clare.

"What?" Ryan asked. What was Regina talking about? Surely she wouldn't tell Clare now about the night they had spent together!

Before Regina could continue, Clare gave a strangled cry and ran from the room.

"Clare! Wait!" Ryan called out.

"Let her go," Regina said. "It's best to give her time to cool off. She's always been rather hot-headed."

"Let go of me!" he growled, shaking her hand from his sleeve.

Clare had already driven away when he reached the parking lot. Ryan drove to her house, but her car wasn't there. He waited for thirty minutes, then an hour. Frustrated and angry, he finally gave up and went home.

Clare had gone to Marla's, two doors down. There she spent the rest of the afternoon and a good part of the night crying out her pain over losing Ryan to Regina. Marla was sympathetic and let her cry, knowing this was more healing than logic at the moment. At length, Clare's misery dulled into numbness and she stemmed her flow of tears.

"You can't trust them, Marla" she said despondently. "Elliot, Ryan. They're all alike."

By the next day, Clare had managed to wall up her bruised emotions enough to face Ryan, and she sought him out at the rig. When he came to her car, she stayed inside with the window rolled down.

"I don't want to hear your explanations, if there are any. What I saw was clear enough, and I'm not here to discuss you and Regina Wharton. I want you to continue work on my well—at this point I can't afford to let you go. But, in the future, I want our relationship to be as it should have been—business only. Do you have any questions?"

Ryan glared through the red haze of a staggering hangover at the woman who had shunned his love. "None! I agreed to drill you a well and I don't break contracts. And, incidentally, since I'm a major investor in the well, you can't fire me, anyway!" He turned before she could see the moistness in his eyes and walked away. "I have to get back to work."

Clare blinked back the tears he had not seen, either, and didn't trust herself to answer.

Chapter Twenty-three

After a week of smarting over Clare's rejection and being unable to get her to speak to him by phone or in person, Ryan turned to Regina. She opened her ivory-colored front door to see him standing there.

"Why, Ryan! I had no idea you were coming by. Goodness, I must look like a fright!" Regina patted her perfectly coiffed hair and stepped back from the doorway. "Won't you come in?"

She summoned the maid and asked for cocktails to be brought to the sitting room. When they were served, she dismissed her servant with a flick of her manicured nails. "How nice of you to drop by. Are you able to stay for dinner?"

Ryan, who was there only because he hated to get the blame without the offense, shrugged and tried to smile naturally. "Sure. I'd like that, if it's no trouble."

"Of course not, silly." Regina again rang for the maid and gave orders for another place to be set for dinner.

"Your house is very . . . elegant," Ryan said to break the silence. He hated the austerity of her colorless walls and neutral furniture, but they did have a look of unbridled expense.

"Thank you. I decorated it myself. I had a decorator in, but he had the most outrageous ideas I ever heard, and I simply sent him packing and did it myself. It's not difficult, really. Not if you have a flair for that sort of thing."

"I see." Ryan was sorry he'd come and regretted saying he would stay for dinner. Before he had met Clare, a sophisticated woman like Regina would have certainly attracted him. Yet now she seemed artificial and plastic; her conversation inane and boring.

"Have you seen dear Clare lately?" Regina asked sympathetically.

"No. 'Dear' Clare is avoiding me."

"Oh, surely not. Perhaps she's merely out of town. Marla tells me she's going to shows in Dallas quite frequently. In fact, it's become a grapevine news item."

"Her art is doing that well?"

"Goodness no," Regina laughed. "I'm talking about her and Cliff Anderson. I hear they're becoming a regular couple."

"I don't believe it," Ryan said bluntly. "What would she ever see in him?" Clare *had* mentioned going to Dallas often, he recalled.

"Surely you're joking! Cliff is *wickedly* handsome. All the girls think so. And he's quite well off financially." She paused to see if Ryan were aware of the most interesting bit of news she had uncovered about Clare. And about Clare's bankbook.

Ryan shrugged, but a thunderous look darkened his eyes. "That's Clare's business. I have no claim on her, nor she on me."

Regina smiled. So he didn't know. "How is the well coming along? I think it's just *fascinating* that you can dig way down in the earth and find oil."

"We're having a lot of problems. We lost one of our most important backers and haven't been able to replace him yet. It's slowing us up."

"How interesting." Regina leaned forward so that her blouse gaped open. "I've always wanted to invest in some madcap scheme like drilling for oil. Tell me more."

Unable to believe his ears, Ryan explained the investment to Regina. She listened carefully, her eyes like blue slits. Then she smiled.

"So, essentially, I'd have a large percentage of the oil money?"

"Yes, you and the other backers. Clare, of course, put up the largest investment and has the controlling interest."

"I see. What would you say if I wrote you out a check for, oh, say, three hundred thousand? Would that get *me* the controlling interest?"

Ryan looked at her a long time before answering. "Yes, it would. But it's more than we need."

"So? It's a good investment." She lifted her martini glass and studied him over the rim.

"I can hardly turn it down," Ryan confessed. "That will be enough to bring the well in."

"It's not totally free, however," Regina said offhandedly. "There's one little provision I insist upon."

"What's that?" Ryan was mentally ordering new pipe and hiring at least half a dozen additional roughnecks.

"I want you to marry me."

"I beg your pardon?" Ryan said, after a brief pause. "I must have misunderstood you."

"I doubt it. I said I want to marry you. That's my stipulation to providing the funds you need."

"What?"

"Why not? I doubt you can afford to lose what you've invested. As for myself, I'm bored with the single life. It was fun for a while, but I'm ready for new adventures. I know you don't love me, but we can't have everything."

"Why in the hell would you want to marry a man who is in love with another woman!" he exclaimed.

"Are you in love with Clare?" she said innocently. "She certainly isn't in love with you. I can tell by the way she talks about you at our ladies' clubs. She has her cap set for Cliff Anderson."

Ryan stood up abruptly. "It's out of the question! I'm not for sale! I'll find another backer!"

She smiled smugly. "Go ahead and try. When you give up, I'll be waiting. But, Ryan," she said as he strode toward the door, "don't be too long. I might grow impatient."

He slammed the door so hard the mirror on the wall rattled. Regina smiled. She had not played her ace yet.

Clare was trying to paint and was having little success. Her inspiration was down to zero, though she needed more of the better canvases for a new outlet in one of the Houston galleries. She felt sore all over as if a cold were coming on, but she'd felt this way ever since she and Ryan had had their argument. Although she missed him terribly, she refused to make the first move and call him. Of course, she had been in Dallas the week after, but there had been no calls since she'd returned. If Ryan had wanted her, he could have left word with Betty or called until he found her.

Doubtless, he was forgetting her in Regina's skinny arms. Clare slashed violent red paint into the café scene she was laboring over. Damn Regina! Damn them both! She blinked the moistness from her eyes.

The doorbell rang and Clare tossed down her brushes. There was no use trying to create when she felt so rotten. Swinging open the door, she found herself facing Regina, and immediately, Clare felt worse than ever.

Regina wrinkled her nose at the odor of turpentine that clung to Clare's painting clothes and said, "May I come in? I won't keep you long, but I feel we must talk." Before Clare could react, she came into the house. "Please, Clare, dear. Hear me out. It's as painful for me as it is for you." Regina preceded Clare into the living room and sat on a velvet chair.

Clare stood, her clothing too paint-smeared to dare sit on one of the chairs. "What do you want, Regina?"

"Ryan and I . . . that is, we seem to have fallen in love."

Clare slowly sank down onto a chair and all the color drained from her face.

"We tried to fight it. God knows we did! I told him it wouldn't be fair to you. But love is like that—unpredictable. All those times I told you about us, I was only trying to let you down easy. I never dreamed you'd discover us together." Regina extracted a lacy handkerchief from her clutch purse and dabbed at her eyes. "I'm afraid we've been . . . intimate, and—"

"Why are you telling me this?" The words were barely audible from Clare's frozen lips.

"We . . . well, marriage has been mentioned. No date has

been set. I wanted you to know before it becomes general knowledge. I feel so . . . *concerned* for you!"

"Get out," Clare said very quietly. "Get out now and don't ever come back into my house again."

"But, Clare!" Regina gushed. "We couldn't help it! Please don't be angry with us."

All the years of concealed hurt and pent-up anger welled up in Clare, and she trembled with the impact of her emotions. "*Angry* at you!" she exploded. "After all you've done, what else could you expect? Now you tell me that you and Ryan. . . ." The words choked in Clare's throat and she stood up abruptly, her arms hugging her aching chest. "You've done a lot, Regina, but this is too much!"

"Why, Clare, I don't know what you're talking about." Regina stared at her with feignèd innocence. "Surely you can't think that I—"

"I *know* what you did! There's no need to put on that act with me!" Clare fought for control, but her face was pale and rigid and her eyes were an icy gray. "Do you really think I'm so stupid as to have missed all the barbed insinuations you've thrown at me for years? All the sly innuendos? Not just with reference to Ryan, but to Elliot as well!"

"I never—"

"Be quiet and let me finish! I knew all about your affair with my husband, but I let it go because I no longer cared about him. But I'm not going to let you get away with lies like this about Ryan! I know you've deliberately set out to get him, but he's not the fool Elliot was! You can't make me believe that he is! Now, get out of my house and don't ever come back again!"

Affecting a sob, Regina got up and ran out of the house. Clare remained stock still in the center of the room and fought against the tearing pain that said she had lost, despite her brave words.

As Regina drove to Ryan's apartment, she hummed a tune. Everything was working exactly as she had hoped it would. She hadn't realized Clare had known about Elliot and herself, she mused as she turned left onto Henderson Boulevard. Perhaps Clare is smarter than I gave her credit for, Regina thought. Well, that hardly matters anymore. She could see no way for her plan to fail now.

She parked in the apartment lot, angling her car over two spaces so some careless driver wouldn't scratch her car in passing. Taking her handbag and smoothing the non-existent wrinkles from her camel-tan suit, Regina went up the steps to Ryan's apartment and imperiously rang the bell.

Ryan opened the door and scowled. "Haven't I told you plainly enough that I don't want to have anything to do with you?" he demanded before she spoke.

"I think we really should talk," Regina said. "I believe I know something that you don't, something that will matter to you a great deal." She brushed past him and sat down on his couch.

"So tell me," he snapped. "But it had better be damned important!"

"It is. If the well folds, Clare will be ruined."

"What are you talking about?"

"It's true. I got it from a very reliable source. Her husband left her penniless. She has mortgaged everything to drill this well. The note is due at the end of next month. Without my backing, your precious Clare will be out on the street with only the clothes on her back." Regina smiled triumphantly.

"I don't believe it." Ryan stared at her. But he knew she was telling the truth. This was the final missing piece of Clare's puzzle. Suddenly, he knew why she was so intent on striking oil as if her livelihood depended on it. It did!

"I think you do. Therefore, I believe you will change your mind about my proposal."

"Does Clare know you learned this?" he demanded.

"Certainly not. Her pride couldn't handle it."

Ryan walked slowly across the room and leaned on the window sill. Lovely Clare, with her mountain of pride and her great capacity for stubbornness. Why hadn't she told him the truth?

"If you agree to my terms," Regina was saying, "no one need ever know of her destitution. If not, well, what can I do?"

"It's blackmail."

"Probably. But I want you. And if you don't marry me,

Clare will not only be homeless, but she will never be able to look her friends in the eye again."

The silence grew longer and strained, and Regina wondered if he intended to reply at all.

"I'll do it," he said dully. "But only for Clare. Have the money available in the morning."

Chapter Twenty-four

For two weeks, Clare had avoided everyone she knew. The possibility of running into Ryan, Regina, or worse, both, kept her at home. With morbid fascination, she dwelt on the compliments he had paid her, the things he had said that had made her smile, the times they had made love. Incredible as it seemed, she had to conclude that he'd merely been playing with her. There was no other explanation.

At last, she reached the point where her pain dulled to an ache and she knew she had to join the living once more. Hoping to bolster her confidence, Clare selected a pale green wraparound dress with delicate embroidery at the neck and sleeves. She'd always felt a little perkier wearing that dress until today. Checking the mirror again to see if she could still conjure up a smile, she left for Marla's May Day party.

The yard was garlanded with satin ribbons of pink, green and yellow. Huge pots of flowers from Marla's carefully tended greenhouse bloomed in strategic places on the patio. Colored Ping-Pong balls floated in an ever-changing mosaic on the surface of her grotto-blue pool, and the cupid fountain sported a wreath of daisies. The flagpole, *sans* flag, was transformed into an enormous maypole with streamers of pastel colors that fluttered in the breeze. Marla, who always looked most comfortable in faded jeans, wore a pink crepe dress and a flower in her dark hair.

Clare tried to join in the social chatter but found it impossible. Always her eyes roamed the crowd, dreading but unable to stop searching for Ryan. Marla's parties were the events of the season, and it was unthinkable that Regina wouldn't be there.

Trying to look attentive, if not interested, Clare listened to Dyna explain how a coin-toss decided which of her twins was to be valedictorian and which salutatorian.

The day was warm and an endless blue sky spread above the arch of the sycamore trees. In the sunlight, their scaly bark was as white as birch and the leaves as large as plates. An occasional butterfly or a bumble bee hovered over the flowers. Clare gradually felt herself relaxing. There was no sign of either Ryan or Regina. Perhaps the day would pass without a conflict. She smiled and nodded at the appropriate times to show she was listening.

After a while, Dyna moved away to talk to another friend, and Clare took a glass of lemonade from the maid's tray. Perhaps, she thought, she had worried for no reason. Sipping the cool liquid, she wandered down by the pool.

Tom was arguing politics. The topic was oil deregulation, so Clare moved hastily away. Oil was a subject she had no intention of dwelling upon today.

A light breeze shifted the floating balls on the pool, and they formed a swirl of pink, green and yellow. Clare smiled as she recalled how long it had taken Marla and herself to paint them. She wondered if anyone really appreciated their efforts.

Marla was making her way over to Clare and she looked disturbed. "I've been looking for you," she said. "Come help me for a minute?"

"Sure." Clare nodded toward the pool. "It looks great. You're a genius."

"Thanks. Let's go in the kitchen. I have to talk to you."

Clare looked closely at her friend. "All right. Marla, is something wrong? What do you want to talk about?"

Marla's expression was meant to be inscrutable but she had a face that could be read by anyone. Marla was obviously upset.

"I know something's wrong," Clare said as they made their way through the guests. "Did the dip curdle? Did the maid run away with the gardener? Slow down, you're losing me!"

Suddenly, the crowd parted and Clare found herself face to face with Regina, who was clad in an expensive white knit dress trimmed in beige. She was clinging possessively to Ryan's arm. On Regina's left hand was an enormous diamond.

"Clare!" she gushed. "How *marvelous* to see you!"

Dumbfounded, Clare stared at the ostentatious engagement ring.

"Oh, I see you've noticed," Regina said coyly. "Isn't it *gorgeous?* Ryan and I bought it last week. He's *such* a darling!" She reached up and kissed Ryan's cheek.

Tearing her eyes from the ring, Clare looked at Ryan.

He kept his eyes veiled and distant, his face deliberately expressionless. In no way could he allow himself to give Clare even a hint of the inner turmoil he was feeling. The pain on her face tore through him, however, and he mentally cursed Regina for her deliberate cruelty.

"Congratulations," Clare said frostily to Ryan.

He opened his mouth to reply, but Regina hugged herself against his arm and interrupted. "Why, thank you, Clare. We haven't set the wedding date yet, but I do hope you'll come. As a single girl, you might catch the bouquet." Her eyes flashed triumphantly.

"Sorry. I'm busy that day." Turning, she walked away. Tears blurred her vision and she almost ran into Marla.

"Damn!" Marla snarled, "I was trying to get you off to one side and tell you before Regina did. The bitch!"

"You knew?"

"Not until she walked in the door. What a rotten way for you to find out!"

"I already expected it," Clare lied. "It was just a shock. Do you have anything stronger than lemonade?"

"Sure, honey. Come on. This calls for a stiff one."

Clare took the glass Marla gave her and sank into a chair in the den. "I know you can't stay while you have a party to manage, but I can't go back out there. Not yet."

"I understand. You stay here. When everyone leaves, we'll talk. You know where the bar is. Just make yourself at home."

"Thanks," Clare whispered. "You're a good friend."

She leaned her head back on the leather cushion and tried to erase all thoughts from her mind. Later, she thought, later I'll think about this. Right now I can't handle it.

She'd just started to regain her composure when the den door opened. Clare turned her head, expecting Marla.

Ryan's large body filled the door frame, and in spite of herself, Clare felt the familiar quickening of her pulse. His masculinity was overwhelming, especially dressed the way he was. His light beige pullover fit closely across his broad, muscular chest and was carefully tucked in at the waist of his chocolate-brown slacks. Clare remembered when she had last seen him wear that shirt—it had been so soft against her cheek when he had held her in the moonlight. Even though she knew he was lost to her forever, she couldn't stem the surging emotion he always ignited in her. She wanted to leave, but there was no other door to escape through. Ryan shut it behind him and came and sat down beside her.

"*Why?*" Clare ground out. "Why!"

"I didn't want you to find out about it like this. Regina told me you wouldn't be here."

"Why didn't you call me?"

"I tried. You didn't answer the phone. Every time I came by, Betty said you couldn't be disturbed."

Clare couldn't deny that. Instead, she took another drink. "Then it's true? You're really marrying her?"

Ryan hesitated. There was no way to explain his reasons to Clare. "Yes. It's true."

"Why did you tell me you loved me, when you really wanted her? Why, in God's name, did you do that to me?"

"I can't explain. I meant everything I ever said to you, Clare. I never once lied to you."

"I see. I'm good enough to be your mistress, but not your wife!"

"What the hell are you talking about? I asked you to marry me and you turned me down!"

"When? I did no such thing!" Clare gasped.

"Yes, you did! In the field the day we had that big argument!"

"That was a *marriage* proposal? I thought you just wanted me to follow you about the oil fields!"

He stared at her in shock. "Clare—"

267

"So *there* you are!" Regina exclaimed as she swept into the room. "I declare, you're hard to keep up with." She came over and perched on his lap and kissed him in spite of his thunderous scowl. "You're going to have to be careful of that after we're married."

"Get off me," he said warningly.

Regina looked at him calculatingly, and moved to the arm of the chair. "Have you told Clare about my little investment, darling?" She turned her mirthless eyes toward the other woman. "I'm putting my money into your well. Ryan told me you lost your biggest backer, and, well, I saw no sense in not going ahead. After all, Ryan says it's a good investment and he certainly has my best interests in mind."

Ryan glared at her, but she only smiled.

"He also has *his* best interests in mind as well. Don't you darling?"

Clare stood and put her glass down. "If you'll excuse me, I have to leave now."

"So soon? I wanted to ask your opinion about having new linens monogrammed. As an artist, I thought you'd have some really unique idea, perhaps using the fact that Ryan and I have the same initials . . . or will have."

Anger flashed in Clare's eyes. "I have a very unique suggestion about your linens, Regina, but it doesn't involve a monogram."

Regina gasped and pressed her hand to the area where she presumed her heart lay.

When Clare reached the door, Regina called after her, "By the way, you really shouldn't closet yourself away with my fiancé. It doesn't help your reputation any. A *single* girl can't be too careful in a small town."

Clare turned and said smoothly, "Don't worry, Regina. I won't try to move in on what you've clearly defined as your territory. I never share. Not when it's something worthwhile." With a frigid smile, Clare left.

"What was she talking about?" Ryan demanded. "What have you told her?"

"Nothing, really. She wasn't talking about you at all."

"What do you mean?" Ryan grabbed her and his fingers bruised her arm.

"Her husband had a crush on me! Could I help that?"

He pushed her from him. "You're despicable!"

"Careful, *darling,*" she warned, "or I'll take my money out of that well so fast you won't know which way it went! And your precious Clare will be disgraced!"

He shoved her into a chair and placed his large hands on the arms, cornering her. Not two inches from her face, he growled, "Careful, Regina. I won't be pushed or bullied or frightened. I'm doing this for Clare's sake, but don't overplay your hand. I can ruin your reputation as easily as you can ruin hers, so don't expect me to dance to your tune. We have an agreement, but it doesn't include hurting Clare. Understand?" His voice was low and steady, and frighteningly dangerous.

Regina shrank back but snarled, "The same goes for you. I can crush her like a peanut shell, so don't break our bargain. You're mine!"

Sounds of the distant party wafted into the silence-filled room.

"Go tell your friends goodby," he said, straightening up. "I'm driving away in three minutes. With or without you."

"But we just arrived! What can I tell Marla?"

"You'll think of something," he said as he left the room.

Regina had no doubts as to whether he meant it, and she hurried to find her hostess. She paid no attention to the burly man who was talking to Tom, but he followed her movements with his expressionless green eyes, and he saw the brilliant flash of her new diamond ring. Neal Thorndyke had had no inkling that Regina had become engaged to Ryan.

Chapter Twenty-five

Clare sat the large tin wash tub down on her outside patio and straightened her back painfully. Eldon had said he'd do it, but he had other chores to see to. She went back to her car for the bags of ice.

For months she'd put off having a party because of the expense involved. She made just enough money to live from month to month, but not nearly enough to buy wine and bourbon for the sort of evening out her friends had come to expect. Although she knew she was earning the name of miser for herself, she could do nothing about it.

Then, the week before, she had received a substantial check from the New Orleans gallery: Her two paintings had sold! The windfall allowed her to bring her electricity bill up to date, with some left over.

The surplus, however, was still not enough to hire a bartender and extra maids, and supply drinks for the people she wanted to invite. Despondently, Clare had sat in front of her television and tried to figure a way to hold her own place in the demanding social structure. A commercial had come to her rescue.

As two stereotyped patrolmen worried over the latest Lone

Star beer theft by the dread "giant armadillo," Clare had sat up and watched more closely. The mythical "giant armadillo" had become a familiar byword every place Lone Star beer was sold, and had probably prompted Texas' unofficial adoption of the small animal as its state mammal. The seed of an inspiration took root in her mind.

Now, as Clare emptied the ice into the tub, she smiled. Next she added bottle after bottle of Lone Star beer. Her party's theme was a Giant Armadillo Entrapment. The beer was "bait" and the dress was boots and jeans. Eldon had put bales of hay around the patio for seating, and Clare had persuaded three boys from the college to supply the western music—cheap. They had agreed to play for beer, fifteen dollars each and her written recommendation as a boost for other gigs.

She wrapped a quilt around and over the top of the tub to hold in the cold and, after a long deliberation, went back to her car. As she drove along the road to her farm, she tried to sort out her thoughts. Now that it was too late, she was all too aware that she loved Ryan. At least, Clare comforted herself, she'd never let him know. He had played her false, but she still had her love as a secret. Somehow this held little comfort.

She reached the rig just as the shift was changing. Across the clearing, Ryan watched her park beside the old barn, then he walked over to her car. Clare got out and waited for him to come closer.

"Ryan, this isn't easy for me to say. Please understand. As you know, my party is tonight."

He nodded, not trusting himself to speak. She looked so beautiful and so vulnerable. So determined to make the best of the situation, even though her pain and loneliness were so obvious.

"I . . . I'd rather you and Regina didn't come. I know I invited you, but, well, I just can't go through with it. You and I—Seeing you with her bothers me too much."

"I understand."

"It's not that I don't want you to be happy . . . I do! . . . but Regina—we've never liked each other. Today it dawned on me that I don't have to see her if I don't want to. Not at my own party, at least!" She paused for breath. "I've never taken back an invitation before, and I'm terribly embarrassed."

"Don't be. As a matter of fact, we can't come anyway."
Ryan spoke the lie smoothly though the "we" still felt bitter
in his mouth.

Clare's dark eyes held so much hurt that he longed to take
her in his arms. But, of course, that was impossible. Instead,
he said gruffly, "The well is coming along nicely now. The
truckload of pipe will be here any day now. We should hit oil
depth in another month."

She tried to smile. How meaningless it all was now that she
had lost her love. "Good. I have to go or I won't be on time
for my own party. Thanks for understanding."

"Sure." He reached out his hand but dropped it again
before he touched her.

Quickly, Clare got in her car and drove away.

She showered and dressed in her best jeans, buttoning a
madras plaid shirt that emphasized her slender waist and
perfectly molded her full breasts. Instead of putting her hair
up, she braided it in a thick rope over one shoulder and
fastened it with a leather thong. As she pulled on her
hand-stitched boots, she heard the doorbell ring.

Betty opened the door for Cliff Anderson, who looked
determinedly western and very uncomfortable in his new
jeans. Clare forced herself to smile; she had forgotten she'd
invited him.

"Cliff! I'm so glad you could come. Let's go into the back.
You're the first to arrive." She linked her arm with his and led
him onto the porch.

The sun was hanging low over the pines, tinting the sky. In
the shrubbery, a cricket sang and a lightning bug flashed
intermittently in the lengthening shadows. The white porch
and balcony took on a purple hue in the fading light.

"You look lovely," he said as he patted her small hand that
lay in the crook of his elbow.

"Thank you. You look nice, too. And very different from
your usual attire."

He smiled. "I like to go casual from time to time. It gives
me a chance to relax." He walked stiffly, his movements
belying his words.

Clare suppressed a smile. "Look, there're Tom and
Marla."

"*I* know about the giant armadillo. *I* know about the giant
armadillo," Marla chimed, mimicking the beer commercial as

they came across the back lawn. Only when she wore the most formal of dresses and the highest of heels did Marla forsake the grass for the sidewalk. "This is a darling idea! I wish I'd thought of it first!"

Clare pulled the quilt off the tub. "Help yourself. The beer's cold and the boys are ready to play." The plaintive strains of "San Antonio Rose" sweetened the night as the backyard lights came on.

"It's good seeing you, stranger," Marla said as she hugged Cliff. "I didn't know you had come to town."

Clare glanced at Cliff. She had assumed he was staying at their house as he usually did when he was in Kilgore.

"I'm going back to Dallas tomorrow. You ought to get that lazy husband of yours to bring you to a real city sometimes."

"Yeah, Tom, how about it?" Marla teased.

Clare shrugged. Cliff probably had an early appointment and didn't want to disrupt the Gentrys with a pre-dawn departure. He must have taken a room at the Community Inn.

As the guests trickled in and the small band toned its music to a volume more suited to an intimate gathering than to an acid rock festival, Clare began to relax. The novel idea of a Giant Armadillo Entrapment party was unique enough that even the most dedicated drinkers never thought to ask for anything stronger . . . and far more expensive. Now and then there was a "sighting" of the armadillo lurking in the azalea hedge or beyond the fern-encompassed lagoon.

Dyna, in a pair of denims as new and as uncomfortable as Cliff's, expounded on Clare's originality in glowing terms. Clare had no doubt that her party would be written up in the Sunday edition of the paper as the *fête champêtre* of the season.

While Dyna cooed over the "authentic" hay bales and sipped from her bottle of beer as if it were champagne, Clare smiled smugly. Her social status had taken a giant stride upward. She was so engrossed in Dyna's praises that she jumped when she felt a man's arm slip around her shoulder.

"I agree with everything she says," Cliff said, hugging her. "Your party is a roaring success." He left his arm proprietarily around her.

Clare moved away slightly. "Cliff, this is Dyna. She has the most marvelous stories about her twins. Dyna, do tell Cliff about the time they accidentally locked their chemistry teacher in the storage closet."

This was all the encouragement Dyna needed, and Clare managed to escape Cliff. It wasn't that she found him unattractive, far from it. But his touch had made her feel edgy. She didn't want him to take that liberty again.

Effortlessly, Clare turned a small band of armadillo hunters back toward the party and away from the path that led to her prospering vegetable garden. Soon the first of her produce would be ripe, and she had no intention of explaining to anyone why she'd plowed up a formal yew maze that was the envy of several of her friends. No one in the garden club would ever believe she might have done it in a moment of back-to-basics passion. Vegetables were planted by farmers' wives; roses and yew hedges by society ladies with gardeners. There were virtually no exceptions. Clare felt it would be easier to hide the garden than to explain her improbable actions.

When Clare was mingling with her guests, she was surprised to overhear Cliff coupling her name with his in an anecdote. True, she had been in the scene he was describing, but his words implied a bond between them that didn't exist. Frowning slightly, she moved away.

The party progressed well. No one got drunk and jumped in the pool, no one discovered her secret vegetable garden, no one trounced her marigolds into the ground. All in all, it was better than she had expected. When the bulk of guests began to leave, Clare was exhausted but happy. Even without Elliot to dominate her and to countermand her orders, Clare's party had been a success.

Only three people remained, and Clare joined them around the emptied wash tub.

"This has been so much fun!" Marla exclaimed. "God, I thought I'd die when Mildred told that joke about the man who found the mermaid!"

Tom chuckled appreciatively. "I've got to remember that one to tell at the club."

"That may be where she heard it," Cliff grinned. "I doubt that one came from the church sewing circle."

There was nothing in his tone to give offense, but Clare felt as if her sex had somehow been put down. "You might be surprised, Cliff," she said. "You don't know how raunchy we are when men aren't around."

He pulled her to him. "I'll bet you are," he said intimately. "Come sit down and tell Tom about the time we sold those paintings to that client from Venezuela." He turned to his friend. "Clare was staying in the Hyatt-Regency and, tell him, honey. You do it so well."

"Honey" stared at him as if he had lost his mind. "We sold some paintings to a man from Venezuela," she parroted.

Marla caught Clare's coolness and nudged her husband. "We'd better go, sweets. I'm asleep on my feet all of a sudden."

"In a minute," Tom responded. "What happened?"

"Nothing. He's going to hang them in some house on top of a mountain. I don't know what Cliff's referring to."

This time, even Tom heard the remoteness in Clare's voice. "Yeah. Well, I'm beat, too. It's been a long day. How about it, Cliff? Need a bunk for the night? " Marla dug her elbow into Tom's ribs.

"No," Cliff said as he snaked his arm around Clare's shoulder. "I have a place to stay."

Marla exchanged a quick look with Clare, saw her friends's startled anger, and swung Tom around and propelled him toward the gap in the back hedge. "See you tomorrow, Clare," she called over her shoulder.

Clare shrugged off Cliff's arm and demanded, "What's gotten into you?"

"Nothing, baby. I just thought they'd never get around to leaving." He tried to pull her to him. "Let's go inside. The night is getting damp."

Clare put her hands on his chest and pushed him firmly away. "Somehow I get the feeling that you're taking an awful lot for granted. Where do you think you're staying tonight?"

"Here, of course. With you."

"Here! Where did you get an idea like that?"

"From you! After all, you invited me."

"I asked you to the party, Cliff. I never suggested that we have a slumber party afterward!"

He stared down at her in genuine surprise. "I'm sorry. I thought . . . God, I feel like a fool."

With a sigh, Clare put her hands on his shoulders, "No,

Cliff. It was just a misunderstanding. I can see now where I must have left the wrong impression. I'm sorry."

He put his arms around her waist. "You can still change your mind," he said hopefully as he bent his head and kissed her.

Clare was at first shocked, but then thought wryly, why not? Maybe I can learn to respond to him if I try. If she could teach herself to love him, even a little, she could ease the aching void that Ryan had left in her life. Clare kissed Cliff back and he darted his tongue into her warm mouth. His lips crushed hers and she felt smothered by his rough desire. After a minute, she pulled away.

"No, Cliff. I'm sorry, but I just don't feel that way about you. You're my friend and you've done wonders for my career, but I don't love you." Her basic honesty prevented her from playing games with anyone's feelings, especially those of a man like Cliff, whom she liked and respected as a friend.

"You don't have to love me to go to bed with me," he protested. "If it helps any, I don't love you, either."

Clare smiled sadly and said with her newly discovered truth, "It's necessary for me. I'm sorry, Cliff, but I think you'd better go."

He gazed down at her and finally shrugged, releasing her. "Okay. If that's the way you feel."

"Thanks, Cliff. I'm really very flattered." She stood on tiptoe to kiss his cheek.

When he drove away, she felt no more lonely than she had while he held her. She went inside and turned out the yard lights.

Regina drove down the dirt road, following Ryan not so much by seeing his car, as by watching the cloud of red dust that enveloped it. This was not the first time she'd done this, nor did she intend for it to be the last.

During the weeks of their engagement, Regina had become suspicious of Ryan's long work hours. Before their "agreement," he had worked fairly normal hours. She knew this because she'd used the information to foster the doubts and jealousy in Clare. Now he worked twelve hours a day, sometimes even longer. A few times, she'd actually driven out to the rig at midnight to see if he was really working. He had been, and the arguments that had followed made her cautious of being so overtly suspicious of him.

Through trial and error, she had learned that she could accuse him of almost anything and not get him to pay her the slightest attention. Or she could make the smallest reference about Clare and he'd leap to defend his former love. When enraged, Ryan was fearsome, and Regina seldom resorted to that method of goading him. It was, however, the reason she followed him. If he was seeing Clare, she wanted to know.

That night she went to his apartment, unannounced as usual, to see if he was really alone. As always, he was.

"What's taking you so long on that well?" she demanded as she made herself a drink. "Any other driller could have hit oil twice over by now."

He frowned. "It's rather hard to drill without pipe. And Joe's the driller, not me."

"So what? I'm getting bored with Kilgore. Leave the well to Joe and let's go somewhere. I want to see California."

"That's out of the question. I have a job to finish here. Besides, we aren't married yet. Don't you think a honeymoon would be rather premature at this stage?" He pointedly put one TV dinner in the oven.

"You weren't so squeamish about that with Clare," she said acidly. "You can drill a well out there just as easily as you can here, and I can see Hollywood."

"It's not quite that simple," he said, as if he were talking to an obnoxious but simpleminded child. "It doesn't do any good to drill wells unless you plan to hit oil, and Hollywood isn't in an oil field."

"How do you know unless you try?" Regina demanded unreasonably.

"I know. Just take my word for it." He flopped down on the couch and propped his feet on the coffee table.

"Get your feet off the furniture," she ordered automatically.

He didn't move. "I wouldn't leave town before I brought in this well."

"You mean you won't leave Clare!" Regina sneered, her face contorted with hate.

"Haven't you ever heard of a contract? I have a job to do. Besides, one field looks pretty much like another. Don't be too eager to trade your fine house for a trailer."

Regina looked aghast. "Me! In a trailer? That's preposterous! Out of the question!"

Ryan smiled. "Not all fields are in towns like this one. I spend most of my time living in the trailer you've seen at the rig. The one with the green trim," he added.

She tossed her head and lit a cigarette. "Well, *I* certainly won't. I think I'll go to California without you."

"No, you won't," Ryan said quietly.

"Why not?" she demanded.

"Because you're the one that's so intent on getting married, and once you're my wife, you'll go wherever I go."

"So that's it! I ruined your chances with that mealy-mouthed Clare, and now you think you're going to lord it over me!"

Ryan smiled. "Now you've got it."

Regina glared at him. "You're despicable! Nobody tells me what to do! If I didn't let *Elliot* run over me—" she stopped short.

"Elliot? Your husband was named "oward." Memory tugged at him. "Who's Elliot?"

"None of your business," she snapped.

Silence grew long between them as Ryan tried to recall where he had heard the name. Regina slid nearer and kissed his cheek.

"Let's not fight."

Ryan endured her caresses for as long as he could, then he stood up and went to check his supper unnecessarily.

Regina frowned. "Why are you so frigid toward me? If I didn't know better, I'd say you're a sexless eunuch."

"I'm tired, Regina. Go home."

"Damn you! Why won't you go to bed with me!"

"I agreed to marry you. I don't believe I ever agreed to consummate the marriage."

Shock made Regina's jaw drop. "You . . . you mean . . .!"

"Want to back out? There's still time."

"No!" she snarled. "You'll come around. You need my money too badly!" She got to her feet and stalked toward the door. "You'd better reconsider! You can't afford to be that independent!" The door slammed behind her.

Ryan let rage flood over him. The bitch was right! He

wondered for the hundredth time how he could raise enough money to rid himself of her.

Clare replaced the receiver on the hook and glared at her newest watercolors of the French Quarter. Then she stomped out of the house and drove to the drilling site without even a thought about the speed limit.

"Ryan, I've got to talk to you!" she fumed as she stormed into the geologist's trailer.

"What's wrong?" he asked, looking up from a chart. "You look mad."

"I am mad! I just got a call from the state police!"

"And?"

"They said they found the body of the truck driver that was bringing our pipe from Houston. He'd been killed and his truck was stolen. They don't know yet who did it, but the patrolman said they had some leads."

"Damn!" Ryan muttered.

"You never told me the pipe was stolen!"

"I saw no reason to worry you. I was sure I could get another shipment here before we run out. I still think I can."

"You should have told me! All my life, people have tried to treat me like a child. I'm a grown woman! I have a right to make decisions!" The long weeks of tension had frazzled her nerves until she trembled with anger.

"I was trying to protect you from more worries. There's nothing you can do about the pipe!"

"Protect me!" she shouted. "I don't need protecting! I need honesty for a change! I'm no china doll that has to be carried on a pillow so I won't break! It's *my* well!"

"As long as I'm in charge here, it's *my* well, and I'll see to the supplies!" Ryan was now as furious as she was.

Almost nose to nose, they glared at each other. Suddenly, she became aware for the first time that they were alone in the trailer. They hadn't been alone since Marla's party. Clare's eyes faltered and she felt the urge to put distance between them. Fast.

"You see that you do, Ryan. I want this well to come in," she said between clenched teeth.

"I'll get that damned pipe if I have to steal it, piece by

piece!" he growled. Then he, too, became aware of her closeness and a tremor ran through him. "Don't worry, Clare," he said far more gently than he had intended.

The air between them felt charged with a more dangerous emotion than anger. With a cry that resembled a sob, Clare turned and ran.

Chapter Twenty-six

Ryan parked at the rig and sat looking at, but not seeing the derrick. How would he ever be able to live with Regina? Since childhood he had detested quarrels and he found nothing about his fiancée that he could even like, much less love. Certainly not as he loved Clare. He tried to put the dark-haired woman from his mind. He'd made a bargain with Regina and he felt honor-bound to at least try to make a go of it. Workable marriages were not necessarily only the ones based on love. He was willing to give up a great deal for Clare's sake.

Ryan let his eyes focus on the towering lines of the derrick. Drilling was a dirty business and it took a real oil man to see the beauty in a rig as Ryan did. To him, there was a kind of savage loveliness in seeing men working as one, drawing the bounty from the depths of the earth. The clang of the heavy machinery and drone of engines mingled with his crew's shouts to form a crude melody that stirred him. The cocoa-brown earth below his feet was his adversary; a miser hoarding gold from those who needed it. Even though Ryan cursed the time this well was taking, he had to admire his opponent.

Ryan got out of his car and walked through the field. Most of the earliest spring flowers were gone and he was glad. They had reminded him far too much of the last day he had spent loving Clare. Above him, threatening clouds were gathering and a fitful wind tousled his hair. There was a heavy smell of rain in the air. Ryan thrust his fists into his pockets and turned back toward the oil well.

Across the pasture, Clare watched him from behind a thicket of wild plum trees. The sprays of pink-white flowers foretold a good fruit crop that she could jelly for the coming year. She had driven out—telling herself that she was interested only in seeing the potential fruit, and parked behind the barn so her car would be less obvious to Ryan . . . if he should be there. Now that she saw him, she was glad for the blossoms' concealment.

She knew from his posture and the movements he made that Ryan was unhappy, and this made her sad. Although it tore at her to think of him with Regina, laughing with her, talking to her, doing all the small things he had once done with herself—she never let her mind go up the ivory-beige staircase to Regina's bedroom—she wanted him to be happy.

The damp wind tossed the blossoms, and a shower of petals fell around her. She knew a storm was building, and at this time of year, one could gather fast. Yet she couldn't cross the pasture while Ryan was there. Her temptation toward him was far too strong and she didn't trust herself.

As she watched, he began to move away, his shoulders hunched against the building wind. She waited until he crossed the dry gully where a creek had once run before she stepped out into the open. The chances of his turning and seeing her were less likely after he passed the ditch.

Clare's loose blouse whipped about her and molded itself against her full breasts. As she left the shelter of the plum thicket, the wind jerked loose a tendril of brown hair. Uneasily, she looked up at the sky.

It was taking on an alien, yellowish tinge, rather like an old an old bruise, and a coppery smell hung in the air. In the woods behind her, the birds had grown eerily silent and huddled nervously toward the thick trunks of the trees. Clare began to walk toward the barn and the shelter of her car.

In the distance, she could hear thunder rolling, and at times lemony-pink lightning flashed. Gigantic thunderheads were towering above and behind her and she saw a jagged scar of lightning spear the earth between the trees that bordered her land and the town. The accompanying clap of thunder seemed to shake her, and she quickened her pace.

Suddenly, the air, sky and clouds turned a sickly green, and a darkness heavier than twilight covered her. Clare knew all too well what that meant, and she began to race for her car.

All at once, Ryan was beside her, his strong arms around her waist. "To the ditch!" he yelled over the wind. "Run to the ditch!"

Clare did as he said, knowing they could not reach shelter in time. From the corner of her eye, she saw a movement and turned her head to gape at the twister that was snaking out of the black lid of boiling clouds.

"Run!" Ryan shouted, half-dragging her with him.

Her heart was pounding and she was more frightened than she had ever been in her life. The tornado didn't seem to be moving at all. But she saw it growing larger.

"It's headed straight for us!" he yelled.

Clare threw herself into the dry creek bed and felt Ryan's body cover her protectively. Now she could hear it—a noise that sounded exactly like a freight train. She closed her eyes and tried to burrow deeper in the dirt.

Then, as quickly as it had begun, the sound moved away and huge, fat drops of rain splattered the earth.

"Ryan!" she cried. "Are you all right?"

He rolled her over and held her close, both of them trembling. "Yes, honey, yes. I'm all right. Did I hurt you?" His arms tightened possessively, as if he could never bear to let her go.

"Yes, yes, I'm okay." She wrapped her arms tighter about him and tried to blot out her terror of moments before.

The rain fell in heavy sheets, plastering her clothing to her body and his hair to his head like a cap of gold. Neither of them noticed.

"Clare, Clare," he murmured hoarsely. "When I saw that twister form up right behind you, I was scared to death that I wouldn't get to you in time!" He buried his face in the curve of her neck to reassure himself of her safety. "Are you sure you're all right?"

"Yes."

He pulled back to look at her and their eyes met and held.

"Ryan," moaned Clare. "No. Let me go." But she couldn't force herself to take her arms from around him.

"Clare," he whispered as if her name meant love.

"It can't be," she murmured. "You're engaged to Regina. There can't be anything between us."

Reluctantly, his entire being warring with his reason, he rolled off her. "I know," he said dully.

Slowly, Clare moved from him. The rain washed her tears from her face as quickly as they fell, and she wondered from the expression on his face if he, too, had tears mixed with the rain. She had never seen such agonized longing on a person's face, yet she knew it matched her own. Numbly, she started to struggle to her feet.

"Clare," he said catching her arm and stopping her flight. "I never lied to you. I want you to know that."

She gazed deep into his eyes. There was no answer she could make. Finally, she nodded. "I was such a fool not to have . . . trusted you," she said so softly that he could hardly hear her words over the sound of the rain.

She climbed up the bank of the ditch and ran toward her car. Ryan followed her out of the gulley and slowly returned to the rig which the capricious tornado had spared.

Beneath the partial shelter of the drilling platform, Joe watched them and shook his head. "Damn fools, both of 'em," he said dismally to the boiler.

Regina reclined on her rattan chaise longue beside her pool and filed vigorously at her daggerlike nails; she knew the sound irritated Ryan like chalk on a blackboard. "I don't see why you don't give up on that silly well," she complained. "You can't get any more pipe before Clare's note is due. The company told you so. Why bother?" She wore a scant bikini of a day-glo green hue and her leathery skin was oiled to a high gleam. She smelled like a piña colada.

Ryan pretended to be engrossed in the newspaper. "We still have some pipe in the rack. Joe's going to Shreveport today to see if he can find us a load."

Regina tossed her file onto the small glassed-top table beside her. "Why couldn't we do that? We never go any-where."

"I don't think you'd go in for visiting pipe companies. They don't sell it in downtown boutiques, you know."

With a loud sigh, Regina closed her eyes. The silence stretched out heavily between them. Ryan turned the page and the paper crackled noisily.

"Don't you ever look at me?" she asked peevishly.

"Sure."

"Well? How do you like my new bikini?" She arched her back and her ribs protruded even more.

He glanced at her. "Fine."

"*I* think it's adorable. This color makes me look more tan, don't you think?"

Ryan turned back to his paper. There was no point in arguing with her, and he doubted that his opinion would be very important to her, anyway. "I saw your car at Conjunction Junction last night. Did you see anybody I know?"

"No. And it's no concern of yours where I go. After all, we aren't married. Even then I expect to have my freedom. You'll never own me, Ryan." She frowned. He wouldn't be nearly as easy to control as Howard had been.

He shrugged. "I don't want to 'own' you."

He wondered if he'd be able to keep her convinced of his intentions to marry her until the well could be brought in. It was as if they were playing a grotesque game: She was the predatory hunter out to trap him; he was the prey, willing to send out all the false signals necessary to win his freedom. After seeing Clare, holding her, even for a short time, he knew he could never go through with a marriage to Regina. Regina was no fool, he mused, how long could he keep her at bay?

As if she read his thoughts, Regina said, "I think we should set the date for our wedding. Early June would be nice. Perhaps the first weekend."

"No. That's too soon. I can't marry you in two weeks."

She frowned. "All right. The second week in June."

He tossed the paper onto the Astroturf-covered cement. "I'll marry you in late July."

"I'm afraid not," she countered. "By then the note will have fallen due on Clare's land. You'll have no reason to marry me."

Getting up, he walked over to the pool and looked in. The water was clear and looked brilliantly blue. At the far end, the drain hole wavered in the depths and looked like a black navel. He turned back to her.

"Why are you doing this?" he said, almost conversationally. "I know you don't love me. You know I don't love you. We don't even *like* each other. So why do you want to marry me?"

"Because I want you. I've had a taste of what it would be like with you. And because I don't want Clare to have you."

"Why not?" he demanded. "What do you have against her?"

"Everything! She managed to wile her way in with Elliot. and made him marry her. God knows how! He was *my* boyfriend! I won't let her have you, too!"

Ryan moved toward her with catlike grace, his anger barely controlled. "You set this up out of jealousy over a dead man? That's crazy!"

"Don't you dare call me that!" Regina sprang up and faced him furiously. "She made him miserable and she'd do the same to you! You're better off with me! And I'll tell you something else, Ryan Hastings! I took Elliot back in all but name. I'm the one he loved! But I'll never share you with her! Never!"

Speechlessly, Ryan glared at her. Finally, he said, "Are you trying to tell me you and Elliot had an affair? That Clare knew about it?"

"Of course! We went everywhere together! He would have left her for me, if he hadn't died in that accident!"

"I'm not Elliot!" Ryan thundered.

"You're going to marry me!" she yelled. "Otherwise, I'm going to ruin Clare! She won't have two pennies to rub together! She won't even have that shack on her farm to go back to! Either way, I win and she loses!" Her face was contorted and her blue eyes protruded with vehemence.

"It's off! If I had known about all this, I would never have let you blackmail me into agreeing to marry you." He wheeled and was striding away when she screamed after him. "Don't you leave me! If you don't marry me, I'll *kill* myself!" The words slipped out in a flood of hysterical tears.

Ryan stopped as if he had run into a wall. In a strained voice, he said, "Don't say that!"

Startled at his reaction, Regina seized her advantage. "I mean it! I will kill myself, if you break off the engagement!"

Against his will, Ryan saw Dofe as he had seen her on that last, fatal night. Screaming that she'd die if he didn't marry her. Again, as if in a nightmare, he watched her car careen into the inky bayou. Again he felt the lung-bursting dives into the solid blackness as he struggled to find her and save her. And how she had looked when the rescue squad had at last pulled her out of the water. Regina was at least as hysterical as Dofe had been.

"I have pills," Regina shrieked, sure now of her weapon. "I know how to do it!"

He wheeled and came back to her. Grabbing her roughly, he pulled her to her feet. "You'd do that?" he demanded.

"Yes!" she hissed. "I'd do anything to destroy Clare Marshall!" His fingers bit into her arms and she felt an odd surge of excitement at the pain. "If you don't want me to kill myself, marry me! The second week in June!"

Ryan glared at her, but he felt a wave of near-nausea sweep over him. He hadn't believed Dofe's threat and now Dofe was dead. "All right!" he snapped. "The *last* weekend in June!" Shoving her from him, he left abruptly, hating himself already for giving in.

Chapter Twenty-seven

Clare sat nervously at the table in the morning room. Ryan sat across from her, the chart from the latest core sample between them. She was trying to follow his explanation about the depth of the oil-bearing limestone caverns, but her mind refused to concentrate. Although she looked at the chart, she was only aware of the way his strong hand looked as he pointed out the various phases. How often she had held that hand, kissed it, felt it caress her body. And his voice, now so business-like, not too long ago had gentled her and spoken words of love. Now the very tone of it made her ache. How could I have been so foolish, she wondered.

What would he do, she thought, if I reached out and touched him. Would he draw back? Be angry? She sighed. His reaction would always remain a mystery, because she could never allow herself to try. She wrestled her mind back to the chart.

Ryan pointed out the depth they hoped to drill before the pipe was gone. The chart required little of his attention. He'd gone over it again and again in hopes of discovering some clue to the elusive oil. Instead, his attention was focused solely on

Clare. A beam of sunlight touched her face and made her skin seem translucent and her eyes jewellike. Now that he knew her secret, he no longer found her interest in the well compulsive. He doubted he could have been any more detached had it been his own finances that were at stake. If the well had to be abandoned, he'd lose some, but certainly not everything as Clare would.

What would happen, he wondered, if he swept the chart aside and took her in his arms? But, of course, that would never do. Clare didn't love him . . . She never had. And he certainly couldn't tell her that he was marrying Regina to save her. If only Clare cared for him—even a little—he could marry her and her problems would be solved. In time, he could regain his money, and in the meantime he'd have the woman he loved. Mentally, Ryan shook himself. It was only a daydream. Clare didn't love him; she never would.

"What about the pipe?" Clare asked. "Did Joe find any?"

"No. With the new boom, it's being sold before it's made. I didn't have much hope that he could get any, but it was worth a try. I've placed a order with several companies in the hope that we can get some before . . . we run out," he finished lamely.

"Good." Clare knew her next question would be as painful as probing a sore tooth, but she had to know. "Have you set a date for your wedding?" She hoped she sounded casual, but her heart was pounding.

"Yes. It's at the end of next month."

"Oh."

Silence hung like a curtain between them. Slowly, Ryan began to roll up the chart.

Clare sought wildly for something to break the tension, but her mind was blank. She had never considered that the wedding would be so soon. Yet why should it be delayed? They were free of ties and in love. A long engagement would be senseless.

The telephone at her elbow rang and Clare jumped. Quickly, she picked it up. "Hello?"

Cliff Anderson's voice came over the wire. "Hello, Clare. I have some good news for you. A collector in California wants two of your canvases. He's offering even more than we expected to get."

"That's marvelous," she said, wishing she could sound more enthusiastic.

"How about if I fly down and we go out to celebrate? I can be there by eight."

"Eight?" she glanced at Ryan, but he appeared to be engrossed in putting the charts back in the cylindrical containers. "All right, Cliff. I'd love to."

"Great. See you then. Goodby."

"Goodby." Clare replaced the receiver. "Some of my paintings just sold."

"Congratulations," he said coldly. That hadn't sounded like a business call to him. Again he reminded himself that he had no claim on Clare. Quite probably that pompous art dealer would be just the kind of man she wanted. Ryan slammed the lid on the cannister and screwed it tightly shut.

Clare looked at him. Why did he seem so angry? Surely she must be mistaken. Or perhaps he was upset at her question about his wedding. It had really been none of her business.

Ryan was profiled against the sunlight and she had a rare opportunity to study him. His hair fell boyishly over his forehead and his straight nose was as classic as any Greek statue. His lips were sensitive, almost in contrast to his rugged masculinity. His firm chin evoked no sign of weakness and the strong column of his throat rounded into his open-collared shirt. Clare allowed her eyes to go no further. She still yearned far too much for his muscular body and the arms that had held her so tenderly yet with such passion.

"Thank you for coming by," she said.

"Sure. Anytime."

Without speaking, they walked to the door. As Clare reached for the handle, Ryan's fingers accidentally brushed hers. A shock of fire raced up her arm and she jerked back her hand.

"Goodby," she said.

"Goodby," he answered.

When she closed the door, she resisted the impluse to kick it, and instead leaned her head against the wooden frame. Gently, she touched the metal where his hand had been. Then, feeling silly, she went to her studio.

Canvases ranged the walls, all in various stages of completion. After Ryan had left her for Regina, Clare had been unable to paint for days. Then, enexpectedly, she found herself unable to stop. Ideas flowed from her brush to the canvas in a seemingly unending stream. Nights were long now, and often she slept for a couple of hours, came back down to the studio for feverish bouts of painting, then staggered upstairs for another hour of sleep before dawn. The result was a loss of weight, tired circles under her eyes and an array of paintings such as she would not have believed herself capable of producing.

A new depth had come into her paintings. A wistful sadness, a poignant longing, a bittersweet truth that had never appeared before. And her increased sales and asking prices reflected it.

With the movements of a sleepwalker, Clare picked up her brush and began to paint. Beneath her skillful fingers, a smudge of white on a sky of blue-gray became a lone seagull. Beneath his wings spread a panorama of beach sand, salt grass and foaming waves. It was the first in a series she planned for a famous Galveston gallery.

All afternoon she painted, and finally, exhausted and drained, she cleaned her brushes, put aside her paints and went upstairs to dress for her date with Cliff. As she showered and went through the automatic motions of washing her hair, Clare thought of her future. The prospects of hitting oil in the next few weeks with their limited supplies seemed slim. Her art was already developing a following, and in time would earn her a nice living, but not soon enough to pay off her debts. As for her personal life, the outlook was bleak. Someday, she reasoned, she'd get over her longing for Ryan, or at least it would dull to a bearable degree. But she knew she would never fall in love with anyone else as deeply as she had with him. He was the great love of her life, and she'd been too foolish to recognize it until it was too late.

With her hair wrapped in a fluffy towel, Clare pulled her robe about her and lay across her bed. She had to find another place to live. Preferably away from Kilgore. Once she had to declare bankruptcy, she didn't want to have to face her friends. Only Marla would remain steadfast. The prospect of going to another town and finding a small house that she could afford was draining, and she closed her eyes.

"I wonder if I'm catching something," she mused. All her

normal energy had left her, and she ached as if she had held her muscles tense for hours. "Too much painting," she diagnosed.

She lay still for a few more minutes, then glanced at the bedside clock. She'd be late if she didn't get dressed. Forcing herself off the bed, Clare dried her hair, put on makeup and dressed in an apple-green silk dress that she hoped would enliven her mood. In the distance, she heard the doorbell and left her room. She sighed and checked her appearance in the mirror. Except for the hurt expression that always lurked in her wide-set eyes these days, she looked quite presentable. At the head of the stairs, she smoothed her hair, straightened her collar and put on a smile as she descended to the entryway.

"You look magnificent," Cliff said when she opened the door. "As lovely as your paintings."

Clare laughed. " 'Lovely' is rarely a word artists prefer to hear in reference to their work, Cliff. You should know better than that."

"In that case, may I say you look meaningful and poignant?"

"No. Let's go back to 'lovely.'" Her smile was real by this time, and she was beginning to be glad she'd agreed to go out with him. At least it would get her out of the house, and she really did enjoy his company.

He escorted her to his rental car and opened the door for her. When they were driving away he said, "I made reservations at Nathan's. I've heard the food there is excellent."

"Nathan's?" she whispered. It had been a special place for Ryan and herself.

"That's all right, isn't it?"

"Yes," she made herself reply. "Nathan's is fine." Ryan was no longer a part of her life, she told herself. The sooner she laid aside the memories, the better off she would be.

Night had fallen by the time they reached the restaurant, and pewter clouds hid the crescent moon. Clare was glad that she had at least been spared the sight of sunset on the glassy lake. They were shown to a table in the center of the room, away from the huge glass windows that overlooked the water.

"Your work is moving very well," Cliff said after he ordered their meal. "I want to have another private exhibit for you this fall. Also, you may want to do a few lectures for some of the area art guilds. Word of mouth is so important in this field."

"All right," Clare said, although she wondered where she'd be in the fall. Certainly not in the Marshall mansion. Would Cliff be as attentive to a truly struggling artist? "I'm free for the second week in October. Does that fit your schedule?"

"Probably. I'll have to look on my calendar and get back to you."

Dinner progressed smoothly. Cliff was an amiable companion, though a somewhat boring one, and Clare felt herself relaxing. They could never be more than friends, but she felt at ease with Cliff. If only she could learn to love *him*, she thought, life would be so simple.

After dinner, they went upstairs to the lounge and danced on the tiny dance floor. Cliff was an unimaginative dancer and Clare had no trouble following him, but they didn't merge into the music as had she and Ryan. Nor did the pressure of his arms send chills through her, even when he pulled her close and kissed her forehead.

"Clare, I have to level with you," he said beneath the flow of sensuous music. "I think I'm falling in love with you."

Clare was silent for a moment. She had guessed as much already but hadn't expected him to tell her yet. "Cliff, I. . . ."

"I know you aren't head over heels in love with me," he said quickly, "but you may learn to love me. We enjoy being together and our career goals match. Clare, I'm asking you to marry me."

Surprised, Clare lost the rhythm of the music and faltered. Catching herself, she replied, "I can't marry you, Cliff. You know nothing about me."

"I know all I need to know."

"But I don't love you," she protested. "I can't marry you if I don't love you. It would never work out."

"You may grow to love me. It's happened in marriages before."

She took a deep breath and said the words she had never expected to say. "I love someone else, Cliff. A man I met last summer."

"Oh. Then why are you here with me?" he asked stiffly. Competition had never occurred to him.

"He's . . . he's engaged to marry someone else. I know I'll

never have him, but I can't find room for anyone else. At least not yet. I'm sorry Cliff. I really am."

The music ended and he took her back to their table. In a remote tone, he said, "It's getting late. I'd better take you home."

Clare nodded miserably.

The drive back was strained, and when he walked her to the door, he bent and kissed her chastely on her cheek. "Goodby, Clare. I'll get back to you about the October show." Without waiting to see if she got safely in the house, Cliff went back to his car and drove away.

"He's like Elliot!" Clare exclaimed as she let herself inside. "Totally self-centered and uninterested in anything that doesn't relate to himself." She slammed the door behind her. "Ryan would never have reacted that way!" Realizing what she had said, Clare's anger dissolved into depression, and she slowly went upstairs to her room.

Ryan had suffered through a formal dinner party given by Regina for twenty of her "closest" friends. He had always hated formal occasions, and was not in the best of moods. Inane conversation bored him, and he saw no reason to pretend otherwise. At every opportunity, Regina touched him or made a sly innuendo of a sexual nature —usually striving to look embarrassed at her "slip" or glancing at him in a seductive manner. Ryan compensated by drinking more than he liked and ignoring her whenever he could.

As the last guests took their leave by kissing the air close to Regina's cheek, she escorted them out the door and called cheerful injunctions after them to drive carefully. When the door was closed and she and Ryan were alone, the change in her was startling. Her mask of smiles dropped and an angry sulk spread over her features.

"Well, you certainly managed to make a fool of me tonight!" she snapped. "You talked far more to Dyna than to me!"

He shrugged. "She was a guest. You wanted me to be polite to them, remember? You said so half a dozen times before they arrived."

Regina grabbed a cigarette from the silver container on the coffee table and let it dangle from her lips as she flicked the lighter. Blowing a stream of smoke above her, she said, "You also drank too much."

"I'm a long way from drunk, Regina. Unfortunately. I don't like parties where everyone says only what's expected of them."

"Get used to it! After we're married, I expect to do this often. You're only a geologist. If you're going to fit into my social set, it's going take some effort."

"Quit pushing me!" he growled. "I'm willing to try to work this out with you because we have an agreement, but nobody is going to treat me the way you are now! Got that, Regina? Nobody! Especially not you!"

"Don't you dare use that tone with me!"

Ryan crossed the room and towered over her. "I've tried. I've been reasonable and I've tried to understand you, but you're impossible! Nothing suits you. Nothing is good enough for you!"

Regina glared at him. "I suppose I am rather different from that slut you knew, but that's the way it is! You might as well get used to it!"

He grabbed her and shook her roughly. "Don't you ever call Clare that again! She's worth ten of you!" Suddenly, he seemed to hear his words. "My, God!!" he said hoarsely. "Is this all we'll ever be? Is this what it will always be like?"

"Yes!" she hissed. "Unless you learn to give me what I want! Better men than you would give anything to be in your place! Neal Thorndyke, for instance!"

Ryan's eyes narrowed. What did the banker have to do with this? "Thorndyke?"

"Yes! He's been in love with me for years!"

Gradually, the final pieces of the puzzle formed and slid into place. "You two planned it all, didn't you?" he said incredulously. "The slowdown on the well, the lost pipe shipment, everything! Without the well, Thorndyke gets the land, you get a husband and Clare is left holding nothing! Good Lord! What kind of monster are you?" He stared at Regina, reading the truth in her contorted face.

"My plan can't fail now! It's taken me years to get even with her, but at last I have!" Triumph blazed malignantly in her eyes.

Ryan dropped his hands from her arms. After looking at her another long moment, he turned and strode to the door.

295

"Don't you leave me!" she shrieked.

"The wedding is off," he said quietly. "I wouldn't marry you if you held a loaded gun to my head."

"Don't you walk out on me! I'll *kill* myself!" she threatened.

Ryan turned and looked at her. "No, you won't. I know that now. You are all that's precious to you."

"You're wrong!" She ran to a side cabinet and grabbed a small handgun. Placing it dramatically to her temple, she cried, "Look! I'll pull the trigger! I *will!*"

Almost sympathetically, Ryan shook his head. "Go ahead."

Regina's hand trembled and her eyes bulged wide. He made no move to stop her. With a scream of rage, she threw the gun at him.

Ryan caught it and tossed it onto the couch. "Next time you threaten suicide, be sure not to use this gun. The clip is missing." He turned and walked out into the night.

Chapter Twenty-eight

After Ryan left, Regina cried for a while, but without an audience, she soon dried her tears. He had left her and he would not be back. The house was uncannily quiet.

Blotting at her puffy eyes, Regina went upstairs to her room and sat on the edge of her bed. She hadn't expected him to call her bluff.

"Damned son-of-a-bitch," she muttered to comfort herself. "I'll make him sorry he left me!" Again her tears started, and she lay back and let them flow onto her satin bedspread.

Nothing about her engagement to Ryan had been the way she had expected. Especially their sex life . . . which had been nonexistent. Another tear rolled down her cheek. He had never appreciated her. Never!

She told herself she was lucky to be rid of him. Living with him would have been miserable. He'd never done the things she had wanted him to do, and he had done many things she had not wanted him to do. Howard had been so easy to manage; where had she failed with Ryan? Regina pulled a tissue from a gilt box by her bed and blew her nose.

For a while, she contemplated suicide—not a successful

one, but an attempt that would bring Ryan to his knees. She pictured herself in bed, propped on fluffy pillows, a pale hand trailing from silken sheets and the sleeve of a lace bed jacket—perhaps her pink one would do. She could smile wanly and offer to forgive him for everything as he knelt by her bed. With scores of nurses and doctors in attendance to see that he didn't tire her too much. Regina smiled.

But what if he *didn't* come? What if she staged a suicide attempt and he didn't care? Her smile disappeared. Even in her fantasy, it was hard to picture Ryan Hastings kneeling beside her bed and pleading for forgiveness. She'd never seen him show any sign of tenderness, and she doubted he was capable of it.

Regina wadded up the tissue and threw it in the general direction of the filigreed wastebasket that stood by her dressing table. She was better off without him.

She got up and crossed the room to her full-length mirror. "He's crazy," she told her reflection. "He doesn't realize what he's throwing away." Again a tear rose in her eyes. She admired the way the moisture made her blue eyes look dewy and tragic. She thought it gave her a rather poignant look that was quite pleasing to her. She leaned closer and studied her reflection. Was she getting old? Was that a new wrinkle there at the corner of her eye? She examined her face closely. No, it was only a trick of the light.

Ryan had never appreciated her, she thought dismally. He had never seen her sterling qualities of management, her well-pampered beauty, her resourcefulness. Why, she was welcomed in any house in town! She looked lovingly around her room, which was an exact duplicate of one she'd seen in a decorator magazine.

"He'll never be anything but a geologist. A working man. I can do better than that without even trying!"

His profession was not one that would enable her to give cocktail parties, formal brunches or elegant buffets. He would never fit into the higher social strata. His performance that night had proved it! If she married him, she'd come down in the world. Even Ryan's incredible body wasn't worth it, especially since he refused to let her anywhere near him.

Regina frowned. Neal had never treated her like that!

Slowly, Regina realized her mistake. Neal wasn't as handsome or as young as Ryan, but he had everything else she wanted—social position, prestige, money. And he couldn't keep his hands off her.

Regina made a lightning decision and sat down at her dressing table. As she smoothed rouge onto her pale cheeks, her mind raced.

Neal carefully laid his monogrammed shirts with the French cuffs in his leather suitcase. Then he put in his silk pajamas and his smoking jacket. He had gone into the bathroom to pack his electric razor and toothbrush when his doorbell chimed, followed by a loud knock.

He blanched. Were they here already? How could they be? The knock sounded again.

That morning, he had heard that the police had arrested Harvey Petrie for the murder of a truck driver who had been delivering pipe to Kilgore from Houston. At the moment, he was in an Arkansas jail, but he'd soon be testifying before a judge. Had Petrie already implicated him in what Neal had intended as a simple theft?

Or could someone at the bank have already noticed the absence of the money he had taken from the vault?

A cold sweat beaded Neal's brow as the doorbell rang again.

Perhaps if he didn't open the door, they'd go away. Perhaps he could get to his garage and drive away before they came back.

Then he heard a familiar voice. "Regina?" he called out. "Is that you?"

"Yes. Let me in."

Color flooded back to his face and his hand was nearly steady as he opened the door. "Regina! What are you doing here?" He glanced over her shoulder at the empty street illumined by street lights. "Come in, come in."

"Oh, Neal, I've made the most *horrible* mistake!" she wailed as he closed the door behind her. "Whatever shall I do?"

"Why, what's wrong?" he exclaimed as she threw herself sobbing into his arms.

"It's Ryan," she cried. "He's . . . he's left me for Clare Marshall!"

"No! How could he do that?" Neal said, holding her trembling body close. "You must be mistaken!"

"No, no! I'm not mistaken at all! He told me so. She's been after him for months! Even now, they may be . . . may be. . . ." She broke off and sobbed brokenly.

"There, there now," he soothed, trying to forget the fast ticking of the clock. "It will be all right."

"Never! I'll never take him back!"

"He left *you* for *Clare?* The man must be out of his mind. You're twice the woman she is!" In Neal's viewpoint, this was true.

Regina looked up at him artfully, tears glistening on her mascaraed eyelashes. "Do you really mean that, Neal?"

Suddenly, he had never meant anything more sincerely in his life. "Come away with me, Regina!" he said impulsively. "Let's leave all this and run away together!"

Regina stared at him. This was far more than she had expected and her mouth dropped open.

"We could leave tonight! Right now! Will you come?" He gripped her arms and waited impatiently for her answer.

"Where?" she stammered. "Where could we go?"

"Mexico, for openers. We can fly down tonight and be married before anyone knows where we've gone! Think of it, Regina! A honeymoon in South America! We can live there the rest of our lives!"

"Mexico? South America?"

"Yes!" The clock seemed to be ticking louder and faster.

Regina laughed nervously. "You want me to elope with you? Now?" The timing couldn't be more perfect! Everyone would think she left Ryan for Neal, and she could think of no better method of revenge. "Yes!" she said happily. "I can be ready in an hour!"

"So can I," Neal said, thinking of his bags that were already packed. "But make that half an hour. If you don't get everything packed, I'll buy you whatever you need in Mexico. Hurry!"

"Right!" Regina actually giggled. "I'll be ready when you drive up!" She kissed him on the lips and ran back to her car.

Neal smiled at his perfect *fait accompli.* Not only would he escape the charges Harvey Petrie could level against him, and

300

abscond with most of the bank's liquid assets, he would have Regina. He had bested Ryan Hastings! True, Neal would have to give up his feud with Clare over her land, but the bank would still foreclose in two weeks. And Regina had money of her own! Chuckling, Neal locked his apartment.

Chapter Twenty-nine

Ryan rolled his long legs over the side of his bed and sat up. Rubbing the sleep from his eyes, he looked at his clock. Five-thirty. The sun would be up soon. For the past week, he'd gone to his apartment only when it had become necessary to sleep. With so little time left, he couldn't afford to leave the well site. The lengths of pipe were dwindling and he had only a few days of drilling material left, but in a week it wouldn't matter, anyway.

He had had no word from Regina, but he was glad of that. Perhaps she had decided to be reasonable about the well and leave her money in the syndicate as an investment. It seemed too much to hope for, but he had no other explanation for her silence. After their turbulent engagement, the peace was welcome. He assumed she was still pouting and would try another ploy to win him over. It wouldn't work. He had no intention of even talking to her.

Switching on the lights, he staggered into the kitchen and put water on to boil for instant coffee. While he waited, he happened to glance at the counter top and saw a small ceramic frog that Clare had given him. Their conversation drifted through his mind.

"Kiss me," he had teased her. "I'm a prince in disguise."

She had thrown her arms around his neck and embraced him spontaneously. "You'll always be a frog to me," she had confided endearingly.

The next day, a small parcel had been delivered to his door. Inside was the ceramic frog with a note tied around its neck. "A prince, disguised."

Gently, he picked up the frog and held it. How badly he missed her! Strangely enough, it wasn't the large things he missed, but the small ones. Being able to hear her voice or her laughter or her slightly off-key singing. The way sunlight looked on her skin, or the wind caught in her hair. The sweet scent of her skin. A longing so strong he could hardly bear it seized him. He could call her, he thought. If he called now, he'd wake her up and her voice would be fuzzy with sleep. Or he could call later and her voice would be clear and verging on laughter. Though she rarely laughed these days . . . or at least not in the few times he'd seen her.

Could it be that she missed him as much as he missed her? No. Clare had never cared for him. She and Cliff Anderson were frequently seen together, and it was general knowledge that they were unofficially engaged. As painful as it was to be away from her, Ryan knew it would be even worse if she rejected him again. No, there was no point in going through that again.

He put the frog down and poured water over the instant coffee in his cup. Dawn was pearling the sky into a leaden gray. Soon the new shift would begin. Perhaps if he worked even harder, he could make himself too tired to dream. Then he wouldn't wake each morning to find the Clare he held in his arms was only a phantom.

He went back into the bedroom and pulled on his khaki work clothes and ran a comb through his hair. As he shaved, he ran over the day's agenda in his mind. If only he could get more pipe! If Regina left her money in, he could manage to forestall the bank.

A voice called out to him as he laced his steel-toed work boots. "Mr. Hastings? Are you home?"

Ryan opened the door. "What is it?"

"A letter for you. Sent special delivery. Hope I didn't wake you up."

"You didn't." Ryan drew a bill from his pocket and gave it to the mailman. "Thanks."

The stamp was from Mexico; there was no return address. He tore it open.

Ryan,

I know you must be wondering where I've gone, but you needn't.

"What is this?" he muttered, then continued.

I've withdrawn all my financial support from the well. Nothing you can say or do will change my mind. There- fore, I've put no return address on this letter. I have no intention of allowing you to come after me and cause an unpleasant scene. Don't try to find me. Incidentally, by the time you recieve this, Neal and I will be married and on our honeymoon. You seem to have lost out all the way around.

Regina

Ryan reread the letter twice, then a third time. Regina had taken away her financial support. Clare was ruined.

"Clare," he said hoarsely. "I've got to find Clare before she hears it from someone else!"

He pulled off his work clothes and put on jeans and a pullover. Knowing Regina, Clare most likely would receive a letter, too. One gloating Regina's triumph.

He drove to Clare's house and ran up the steps. After pounding on the front door and getting no answer, he ran down the porch and around the corner to the side door and knocked again.

Betty, who had reached the front door just as he was rounding the corner, jerked the side door open. "What you want, banging on doors this time of the morning?" she demanded. "Don't you have a watch?"

"Sorry. Where's Clare? I have to see her."

"Well, she's not here. I don't know where she's gone to. She left half an hour ago."

Ryan took the porch steps two at a time and dashed

for his car. A new possibility had occurred to him. With no place else to go, Clare might turn to him! In time, she might even learn to love him!

But where could she have gone to so early in the morning? Ryan's car wheels sent spurts of gravel into the air as he tore out of the driveway.

Clare sat on the tree that grew out across the water and gazed at the shoal of sand that protruded like the back of a whale from the creek. In her mind's eye, she saw them as they had been—lovers splashing happily in the water, not a care between them. How long ago it seemed! She sighed. How very differently it might have turned out.

Because of the pain these memories brought her, Clare seldom came to the river any more. Its magical peace was broken and dead. But sometimes her longing for Ryan was so strong that she crept back to the last place they had loved, hoping to capture a glimpse of the happiness she had lost.

And then, suddenly, she looked up and saw him across the creek. For an instant, the world stopped.

He stood there, framed in the leafy vines of the ripening muscadines, his dark gold hair ruffling in the slight breeze, his skin bronze against the greenness of the leaves. At first, she thought she only imagined him, as he stood so still. Then he took a step forward and she drew her breath in sharply.

"Clare, I have to talk to you," he said softly.

"No," she whispered. "Not here!" Quickly, she scrambled out of the tree and would have run away, but he leaped across the stream and caught her.

"Clare, wait! Please!"

His touch burned her arm and she looked up into his hazel eyes and saw none of the carefully erected barriers there.

"No," she whispered again. This was too close; she was too vulnerable. She tried to pull free, to run from the great temptation to fall into his arms.

"Listen to me," he said again. "I have to talk to you. I couldn't have found you in a better spot."

Clare stared at him. How could he be so unfeeling? Surely

he must know this place was the very symbol of their love to her!

"If I say I'll stay, will you turn my arm loose?"

"No, I know you better than that. If I turn you loose, you'll run away."

She sighed. "You know me too well," she admitted. "That's exactly what I'd do."

"Clare, she's gone," he said simply.

For a moment, she merely looked at him. "What are you talking about? Who's gone?" she asked in confusion.

"Regina. I broke our engagement and she has eloped with Neal Thorndyke. She's out of our lives forever."

"What?" The news was so unexpected Clare couldn't comprehend the import of his words.

"Unfortunately, she took her money out of the well. I'm afraid it's finished."

Clare stared at him, then looked away. "I . . . I can talk to the bank, put more of my assets into it." Her mind fluttered against the inevitable like a frightened bird. "I just need more time. We can get another backer."

"Clare," he said gently. "I know."

Her torrent of words faltered. "What?"

"I know about your mortgages. I know all of it. That's why I agreed to marry Regina. She said she'd supply the necessary money if I did. Otherwise, you'd be turned out of your house and off your land."

"You . . . *agreed* . . . to marry Regina?"

He nodded. "It was the only way I could help you. I never wanted to go through with it and she knew it. That's why she forced me to set the date before the well would be finished."

"But," Clare said in confusion, "you love her."

"No. I never loved her. She knew that, too. I've never loved anyone but you."

Clare felt her knees go weak, and she would have sunk down to the log if he had not put his arms around her. "What are you saying?"

"Clare, I've made a lot of mistakes, and one of them was that I didn't make myself clear. I plan to do it right this time, so pay attention. Clare Marshall, I want you to be my wife. I love you and I want to live with you and love you for the rest of our lives." He paused, fearful of her possible rejection. Would she have him? "Will you marry me?"

"I . . . Ryan, you don't know about me. Not really. That shack across the pasture? That's where I grew up. My father worked in a cotton gin until he got his arm crushed in the press. After that, he couldn't work at all. My mother took in washing and ironing to feed and clothe us. At Thanksgiving and Christmas, we were the ones the church sent charity baskets to! I never owned a new dress or coat until I was almost grown. I'm not who you think I am!" Tears sparkled in her eyes and her voice broke.

Ryan pulled her close and held her against his broad chest. "I already know, love. I've known for weeks. It wasn't easy, but I figured it out from the other things I learned about you. But you haven't answered my question. Will you marry me?"

Tears spilled down her cheeks, but now they were tears of happiness. "Yes!" she cried out, burrowing deeper into his arms. "Yes, Ryan. I'll marry you! Today, tomorrow, as soon as we can!"

They held each other close as if they were afraid of being torn apart. The sounds of the woods enveloped them and a breeze rustled the leafy dome high over their heads. The small waterfall sounded silvery beside them.

"I was so stupid," Clare murmured as her hands clasped behind his muscular back and his familiar clean scent intoxicated her. "For so long I thought it was just the oil well I wanted. I know now that I wanted your love so much more. I didn't realize it until I had lost you! Oh, Ryan, Ryan, are you sure you love me?"

"Yes. I love you more than anyone I've ever known. These weeks without you were hell. You're everything to me. You're my life." He rubbed his cheek against her sun-warmed hair and the delicious curves of her body molded against his. Gently, he put his hand beneath her chin and raised her face to his.

Hesitantly, almost shyly, his lips caressed hers. He felt her breath on his cheek and tasted the sweetness of her kiss. Passionately, possessively he kissed her until she swayed weakly against him.

"God, I've wanted you," he said huskily, devouring her face with his eyes, then pulling her close. "I want to look at you and hold you, all at the same time."

Happily, she nodded her head against his chest. The feel of

his body beneath her hands was like a feast to her starving soul. "I had no hope of ever holding you again. Never kissing you!" She pulled his head down to hers.

"We almost let the most precious thing in life escape us," he said. "But no more. Nothing will ever come between us again." He pulled back to gaze wonderingly down at her face. "I love you, Clare."

Without hesitation, she said the words he had longed to hear. "I love you, Ryan. More than I ever dreamed it is possible to love. Never leave me again."

"Never," he whispered. "My darling Clare. I'll never leave you."

Clare drew the brush through the dark cloud of her hair and smiled. Basking in Ryan's love for the last few days had erased the tight lines around her mouth and at the corners of her eyes. Her skin glowed and her eyes were dreamily radiant. A secret smile lifted her lips most of the time now, and her movements were carefree. Loving and being loved had swept away the sad woman her mirror had reflected a week earlier.

Brilliant sunlight streamed through the bedroom window and made the curtains gleam snowy white before dappling her carpet with a pattern of leaves from the trees outside. It was a beautiful day, and the sky outside the window arched high and blue.

No less sunny was the yellow chiffon dress that she wore. The soft folds of the skirt flowed gently about her silken legs, and the scarf sleeves floated caressingly on her smooth arms. Clare had brushed her hair until it flowed in shining waves down to the middle of her back, accentuating her narrow waist. As a finishing touch, she combed one side back and tucked in a rose that was as bright a yellow as her dress.

"Are you nearly ready?" Ryan asked, coming around the corner of the dressing room as he adjusted his tie. On seeing her, he gave a low whistle. "Hi there, beautiful," he said appreciatively. "Want to marry me?"

Clare laughed. "Don't you know it's supposed to be bad luck to see your bride before the wedding?"

"I've already seen you," he grinned. "Remember?"

She blushed happily as she recalled waking in his arms that

morning and the tender loving that had followed. "I love you."

"I love you, too." Ryan slipped on his suit jacket and gave himself a quick glance in the mirror. "I even wore a tie for you."

"You look marvelous," she assured him. "Did you know you're the most handsome man I've ever seen? With or without a tie."

He put his arms around her and kissed her lovingly. "It's possible you're prejudiced. But if we're going to get to the church on time, you'd better not tempt me. Otherwise, the preacher will have to wait."

Clare laughed and slipped out of his arms. "Come on."

The church they had chosen for their wedding was the small one just beyond Clare's farm. Her parents had been married there and she had been baptized there as a child. Neither wanted a large ceremony, and its size fit their needs perfectly. As a bonus, it was cradled beneath enormous oak trees whose massive branches swept the ground.

As they drove by the farm, Ryan nodded toward Joe Talmidge's car driving up the lane toward the well site. "I wonder if something's wrong. I told Joe how to find the church. Maybe we should go see."

"All right. We're a few minutes early, anyway, and besides, he's our best man. He really should be there," she smiled.

Ryan turned in, driving far enough behind Joe to avoid most of the red dust that clouded behind the car. "I'm really sorry about the well. If we could have gotten more pipe and had more time, I still say it would have paid off. We just couldn't go deep enough."

Clare reached out and took his hand. "I'm sorry too. It would be a lie to say I'm not. I'll miss my house and furniture, not to mention my land. I think I regret that most of all. But we might have decided not to stay here, anyway, and I like your apartment in New Orleans."

"I think I would have liked to stay here. It's quiet, but I enjoy that. Someday I want to settle down in one place. When we have our family, I don't want to move them all over the country. I had too much of that when I was growing up." He stopped the car and they got out.

Hand in hand, they walked down the well-worn path to the rig. Clare said, "I agree. Maybe we can find another place like this one and settle down there. Just think, Ryan, we can really have a home of our own and children. I feel like Cinderella whenever I think about it. I hope they all look like you."

"I want half of them to look like their mother," he replied. "You're so beautiful, Clare."

"All brides are beautiful," she said smugly. But she glowed from his compliment.

"Joe?" Ryan called out to the driller. "Are you lost? The church is down that way." He pointed back toward the road.

"I know it. Eula told me ten times already. But I forgot to write something in the ledger when I finished my shift last night. Won't take me but a minute." Joe looked miserably uncomfortable in his black suit and tight dress shoes. He hurried toward the trailer.

Ryan and Clare stopped at the base of the drilling rig. Only three lengths of pipe remained on the platform. The steady chugging sound of heavy machinery broke the country's silence.

"Why are they still drilling?" Clare asked. "I expected them to close down."

"I guess it's just stubbornness," he answered. "I'm too bullheaded to quit before I absolutely have to. Maybe I just never quit believing in miracles."

"I'm glad you're like that," Clare said quietly. "I'm like that, too."

Joe came out of the trailer and went up the steps to the platform where the men were working. He carried on a short conversation with the man in charge of the shift, nodded and started down the steps. As he came, he took out his handkerchief and began to wipe the grit from the handrail off his palm.

Unexpectedly, there was a low rumble. It was so soft at first that Clare could only feel it through the soles of her feet, then it grew louder, like the roar of a tornado. Yet the sky above them was clear. Suddenly, loud alarms began clanging, splitting the air with urgent shrieks.

Joe froze at the base of the ladder, as did the workers on the platform. Ryan's jaw dropped in amazement. Clare formed a question, but she had no time to ask it.

"Run!" Ryan yelled. He grabbed her arm and put his arm